"I'm Dangerous Tonight" by Cornell Woolrich—A dress cut from Lucifer's cloak ignites a deadly power in each woman who wears it—and the one man who can't escape it!

"That Hell-Bound Train" by Robert Bloch—The son of a railroad man, he knew all about the legendary fire and brimstone train, but he'd never expected the devil to try selling him a ticket for it!

"The Making of Revelation, Part I" by Philip José Farmer—When God wanted to produce the end of the world, he chose the best in the business, Cecil B. DeMille, but getting Satan to play a starring role required a contract that was out of this world!

These are just a few of the sinfully intriguing tales to revel in—

Isaac Asimov's
Magical Worlds of Fantasy #8
DEVILS

DEVILS

ISAAC ASIMOV'S MAGICAL WORLDS OF FANTASY #8

Edited by

Isaac Asimov,
Martin H. Greenberg,
and Charles G. Waugh

A SIGNET BOOK

NEW AMERICAN LIBRARY

PUBLISHED BY
THE NEW AMERICAN LIBRARY
OF CANADA LIMITED

Acknowledgments

"I'm Dangerous Tonight" by Cornell Woolrich. Copyright © 1937 by Cornell
Woolrich. Reprinted by permission of the agents for the agent's Estate,
the Scott Meredith Literary Agency, Inc., 845 Third Avenue, New York,
NY 10022.

"The Devil In Exile" by Brian Cleeve. Copyright © 1968 by Brian Cleeve.
Reprinted by permission of the author.

"The Cage" by Ray Russell. Copyright © 1959 by Ray Russell. Renewed
© 1987 by Ray Russell. Reprinted by permission of the author.

"The Shepherds" from *The Long Christmas* by Ruth Sawyer. Copyright ©
1941, renewed copyright © 1969 by Ruth Sawyer. Reprinted by permission
of Viking Penguin Inc.

"He Stepped on the Devil's Tail" by Winston Marks. Copyright © by King-
Size Publications, Inc. Reprinted by permission of the Scott Meredith
Literary Agency, Inc., 845 Third Avenue, New York, NY 10022.

"Rustle of Wings" by Fredric Brown. Copyright © 1958 by the Estate of
Elizabeth C. Brown. Reprinted by permission of Roberta Pryor Inc.

"The Hell-Bound Train" by Robert Bloch. Copyright © 1958 by Mercury
Press, Inc. First printed in *The Magazine of Fantasy and Science Fiction*.
Reprinted by permission of Kirby McCauley, Ltd.

"Added Inducement" by Robert F. Young. Copyright © 1957 by Mercury
Press, Inc. First printed in *The Magazine of Fantasy and Science Fiction*.
Reprinted by permission of the Scott Meredith Literary Agency, Inc., 845
Third Avenue, New York, NY 10022.

"The Devil and Daniel Webster" by Stephen Vincent Benét. Copyright ©
1936 by the Curtis Publishing Company. First printed in *The Selected Works
of Stephen Vincent Benét*. Copyright renewed © 1964 by Thomas C. Benét,
Stephanie B. Mahin, and Rachel B. Lewis. Reprinted by permission of
Brandt & Brandt Literary Agents, Inc.

"Colt .24" by Richard Hautala. Copyright © 1987 by Rick Hautala. Used
by permission of the author.

"The Making of Revelation, Part I" by Philip José Farmer. Copyright ©
1980 by Philip José Farmer. Reprinted by permission of the Scott Meredith
Literary Agency, Inc. 845 Third Avenue, New York, NY 10022.

(The following page constitutes an extension of the copyright page.)

CONTENTS

THE DEVIL

by Isaac Asimov

Nature is indifferent to human concerns, and it is erratic, too. Storms may come, floods, droughts, blizzards, searing heat, pestilence, and so on. And in between these natural disasters, there can equally well be periods of salubrious weather, peace, and happiness.

You might say that there are so many complex factors that must be understood in order to be able to predict these events and put them in orderly perspective, and the human ability to do so, in ancient times, was so limited, that it might be better simply to dismiss natural events as the randomness of an impersonal Universe.

That is a hard thing to think, however. It seemed much easier to suppose that all the manifestations of nature were in the charge of invisible superhuman entities (let us call them "gods") who just happened to be childishly erratic and unpredictable in their behavior.

A good deal of primitive effort, therefore, was put into determining ways of cajoling gods into being kind. No one ever showed that this cajolery ever did any good in the sense that disasters grew fewer or less intense, but it continued anyway.

Even the logical and rational Greeks, who set up a group of extremely attractive gods, and who viewed them as essentially beneficent, nevertheless imagined that any one of them might suddenly devastate a region if he or she was slighted in some trivial way.

It is, however, wearisome to live with childish gods. It is much more heartwarming to think of them as loving, caring entities who will protect and foster humanity. In that case, though, how explain evil and misfortune? The search was out for a scapegoat. Perhaps there was one malignant god who disliked humanity and who was responsible for evil. In the Norse pantheon, there was Loki, the god of fire. Fire itself was a great boon to humanity—but it could also do great harm, and the fire god partook of this double character. Loki was by far the cleverest of the Norse gods (a pretty dumb lot, particularly as described by Wagner), but was also a mischief-maker and destroyer.

It was the ancient Persians, however, who developed a particularly dramatic view of the problem of good and evil. In their Zoroastrian religion they pictured the existence of a principle of good, Ahura Mazda, and one of evil, Ahriman. These two were engaged in a cosmic battle, and so evenly balanced were the forces that the addition of the minuscule power of humanity committed to either side would assure the victory of that side. Consequently, humanity participated in this battle, willy-nilly, and was constantly being drawn to one side or the other.

Judea was under the Persian Empire from the sixth to the fourth century B.C., and during that period, Judaism picked up this dualistic notion of good and evil. In those portions of the Bible that date back to the pre-Persian period, God is supreme and is the author of both good and evil—the evil being either a punishment of sin or a clever device (beyond human understanding) to bring about good for humanity.

In the later portions of the Bible, a principle of evil is introduced. The Jews called him Satan, meaning "adversary," since when human beings are judged by God, Satan testified against them as their adversary (or, as we might say, a prosecuting attorney calling for damnation). To the Greeks, Satan became *diabolos*, meaning "slanderer," since he spoke evil even of good men when these stood before the Judgement Seat. And *diabolos* has become our "devil."

Of course, the Jews insisted on the supremacy of God. They could not allow Satan to be equal to God in power, Persian-fashion, and to have the outcome of the battle uncertain. Satan had to be subordinate to God, to have been created by Him, and to be controlled by Him.

In the Book of Job, for instance, Satan speaks ill of the saintly Job, and God grants him permission to afflict Job, as a way of testing Job's love of God. In the process, Satan not only destroys Job's property but even his family (killing his numerous sons and daughters) and his health. (I have always thought God is made to look bad in this book. Satan is merely following orders and fulfilling his God-given function, but it is God who allows the destruction of innocent children merely in order to show how loyal a devoted follower is. This behavior would never be praised in an ordinary sinful human being and I don't see how it can be praised in a supposedly all-perfect, beneficent God.)

Nevertheless, even though God and Satan are fighting an unequal battle in the Judeo-Christian view, and God's victory is certain and inevitable, the human involvement of the Persian view is kept. Satan is pictured as constantly trying to win over human beings and possess their souls, even though such dubious conquests are surely meaningless and won't help him in the least, in the long run.

So eager is Satan for human souls that he stoops to bribe people, offering them all sorts of worldly advantages in return for those souls. The classic tale of this sort is that of Dr. Faust, which reaches its most sublime form in Goethe's great epic drama.

And yet this has always struck me as silly. It is generally agreed in the Christian view that all men are sinners and that salvation is hard to attain. In the end, it is usually suggested there will be a mere handful of saints going to heaven, while everyone else howls in hell. Why, then, is Satan so eager? He's getting almost everyone anyway. And those few whom

God has determined to withhold from him are surely beyond his reach.

Then, too, why give these people any bribe at all? The minute a human being consents to deal with Satan and to barter his soul for worldly benefit, he has surely committed a mortal sin. There is no need to actually sign any document with blood or anything else; Satan *has* him (or her) and its all over.

However, when I argue in this way, I am merely bringing logic to bear on something that is thoroughly emotional.

Human beings *want* the worldly benefits that are traditionally associated with evil. (After all, to grow wealthy—judging from the wealthy of the world—it is necessary to cheat, and scheme, and steal, and slay, and, in short, be thoroughly evil.) However, human beings are also reluctant to pay the penalty that religion calls for in such a case. They don't want to be the beggar Lazarus, and dine in heaven. They would rather be the rich man, Dives, but *not* burn in hell.

Therefore, writers never tire of describing how human beings can outwit the devil—get benefits out of him and then refuse payment—and readers never tire of reading about such cases. Even Marty, Charles, and I never tire of it, so we have prepared a whole book of stories about the devil. Some, but not all, deal with the devilish documents that human beings are talked into signing (as in Benét's classic "The Devil and Daniel Webster"), for instance.

Still, I'm sorry for the devil. Cheating is wrong, even when the devil is the victim.

I'M DANGEROUS TONIGHT

by Cornell Woolrich

Prelude

The thing, whatever it was—and no one was ever sure afterwards whether it was a dream or a fit or what—happened at that peculiar hour before dawn when human vitality is at its lowest ebb. The Blue Hour they sometimes call it, *l'heure bleu*—the ribbon of darkness between the false dawn and the true, always blacker than all the rest of the night has been before it. Criminals break down and confess at that hour; suicides nerve themselves for their attempts; mists swirl in the sky; and—according to the old books of the monks and the hermits—strange, unholy shapes brood over the sleeping rooftops.

At any rate, it was at this hour that her screams shattered the stillness of that top-floor apartment overloooking the Parc Monceau. Curdling, razor-edged screams that slashed through the thick bedroom door. The three others who shared the apartment with Maldonado—her maid, her secretary, her cook—sat bolt upright in their beds. They came out into the hall one by one. The peasant cook crossed herself again and again. The maid whimpered and seemed ready to add her own screams to those that were sounding in that bedroom at the end of the hall. The secretary, brisk, businesslike, modern, and just a little metallic, wasted no time; she cried out,

"Somebody's murdering *madame!*" and rushed for the bedroom door.

She pounded, pushed at it; it wouldn't open. But then they all knew that Maldonado habitually slept with her door locked. Still, the only way to reach her was through this door. The screams continued, a little less violently now than at first.

"Madame Maldonado!" the secretary cried frantically. "Open! Let us in! What is the matter?"

The only answer was a continuation of those long, shuddering moans of terror. "Come here and help me!" the secretary ordered the cringing cook. "You're strong. Throw your weight against the door. See if you can break it down!"

The husky Breton woman, strong as an ox, threw her shoulder against it again and again. The perpendicular bolt that held it was forced out of its groove in the sill, the two halves shot apart. Something streaked by between the legs of the three frightened women—Maldonado's Persian cat, a projectile of psychic terror, its fur standing like a porcupine's quills, its green eyes lambent, its ears flat—hissing, spitting.

The secretary was the first to enter. She was an intelligent young woman of the modern breed, remember. She believed only what her eyes saw, what her ears heard, what her nostrils smelled. She reached out quickly, snapped the light switch. The screams died with the darkness, and became instead a hoarse panting for breath. Eve Maldonado, greatest of all Paris designers, lay crouched across the bed like a terrified animal. There was no sign of a struggle anywhere in the big room. It held no intruder in it, no weapon, no trace of blood or violence. Maldonado was very much alive, unbruised and unhurt, but her face was the color of clay, and her whole body trembled uncontrollably. She couldn't speak for a long time.

Her overtaxed vocal cords refused to respond.

But there were things in the room that should not have been there—a thin diaphanous haze of smoke, as from a cigarette, suspended motionless halfway between floor and ceiling. The bowl beside the bed was crammed with cigarette ends, but none of those butts in it were smoldering any

14

longer, and both windows overlooking the Parc were wide open. The fresh before-dawn breeze blowing through them should have dissipated that haze long ago. Yet it was plainly visible in the electric light, as though it had been caused by something heavier than burnt paper and tobacco. There was a faintly noticeable odor also, an unpleasant one. A little like burnt feathers, a little like chemicals, a little like—sulphur or coal gas. Hard to identify, vague, distinctly out of place there in that dainty bedroom.

"*Madame!* What was it? What has happened?" the secretary asked anxiously. The other two were peering in from the doorway.

A steel gleam on the nightstand beside the bed caught her eye. She put out her hand and quickly hid the needle before the other two had seen it. "Madame," she whispered reproachfully, "you promised me—!" Maldonado had been in a severe automobile accident a year before. To relieve the pain she had suffered as an aftereffect it had been necessary for a while to—

The young woman went over and hid the needle swiftly in a drawer. Coming back, something on the floor touched her foot. She stooped to pick up some kind of triangular cape or cloak. It was black on one side, a bright flame-red on the other. At first glance it seemed to be brocaded satin, but it wasn't. It glistened. It was almost like the skin of a snake. An odor of musk arose from it.

Maldonado affected exotic negligees like this one; she must have dropped it in the throes of her nightmare just now. But then as the secretary prepared to fling it back across the foot of the bed, she saw that there was already one there, an embroidered Chinese thing. At the same instant the designer caught sight of what she was holding; it seemed to renew all her terror. She screamed once more, shrank away from it. Her voice returned for the first time.

"That's it! That's *it!*" She shuddered, pointing. "Don't bring it near me! Take it away. Take it away, I'm afraid of it."

"But it's yours, *madame*, isn't it?"

"No!" the woman groaned, warding it off with both hands and averting her head. "Oh, don't—*please* take it away."

"But it must be yours. How else did it get here? You must have brought it home with you from the atelier. You've forgotten, that's all."

Maldonado, beside herself, was holding her head between her two hands. "We have nothing like that at the shop," she panted. "I *saw* how it got in here! I *saw* how it came into this room!"

The secretary, holding the thing up by one hand, felt a sudden inexplicable surge of hatred well up in her. A hatred that was almost murderous. She thought, "I'd like to kill her!" And the craving was literal, not just a momentary resentment expressed by a commonplace catch-phrase. She could feel herself being *drawn* to commit some overt act against the whimpering woman on the bed. Crushing her skull with something, grasping her throat between her hands and throttling her. . . .

It must have shown in her face. Maldonado, staring at her, suddenly showed a new kind of fear, a lesser fear than before—the fear of one human for another. She drew back beyond the secretary's reach.

The secretary let the thing she was holding fall to the floor. The impulse died with it. She passed the back of her hand dazedly before her eyes. What had made her feel that way just now? Was Maldonado's hysteria catching—one of those mass psychoses to which women, in particular, are sometimes susceptible? This woman before her was her employer, her benefactress, had always treated her well. She admired her, respected her—and yet suddenly she had found herself contemplating killing her. Not only contemplating it, but contemplating it with delight, almost with an insatiable longing. Perhaps, she thought, it was the reaction from the severe nervous shock Maldonado's screams had caused them all just now. But even so, to take so horrible a form—

Something was affecting the other two, too; she could see that. Some sort of tension. The maid, who was a frivolous little soul, kept edging toward the door, as if she didn't like it in here, without knowing why. The Breton cook had her underlip thrust out belligerently and the flesh around her eyes had hardened in hostility, but against whom, or what was causing it, there was no way of telling.

Maldonado said, "Get them out of here. I've got to talk to you." The secretary motioned and they went.

The maid returned for a moment, dropped the fugitive cat just over the threshold, then closed the door on it. The animal, perfectly docile in her arms until then, instantly began to act strangely. Its fur went up and its ears back, it crouched in wary retreat from the inanimate piece of goods on the floor, then finding that its escape was cut off, sidled around it in a wide circle and slunk under the bed. No amount of coaxing could get it out again. Two frightened green eyes in the shadows and a recurrent hissing were all that marked its presence.

Maldonado's face was ghastly. "That," she said, pointing below the bed where the cat lurked, "and that," pointing to what lay on the floor, "prove it was no dream. Do dreams leave marks behind them?"

"What was no dream?" The secretary was cool, patient. She had humored Maldonado before.

"What I saw—in here." She caught at her throat, as though still unable to breathe properly. "Get me some cognac. I can speak to *you* about it. I couldn't in front of them. They'd only say I was crazy—" She drank, put the thimble glass down. A trace of color returned to her face. "There was someone in this room with me!" she said. "I was lying here wide awake. I distinctly remember looking at my watch, on the stand here next to me, just before it happened. I can even recall the time. It was four thirty-five. Does one look at the time in one's sleep?"

"One could dream one had," the secretary suggested.

"That was no dream! A second later, as I put the watch down, there was a soft step on the balcony there outside my window, and someone came through it into the room—"

"But it's seven floors above the street, there's no possible way for anyone to get on it! It's completely cut off!'' The secretary moved her hands.

"It didn't occur to me to scream at first, for that very reason. It seemed impossible that anyone *could* come in from there—''

"It is," said the secretary levelly. "You've been working too hard."

"It was no burglar. It seemed to be someone in an opera cloak. It made no hostile move toward me, kept its back toward me until it had gone all the way around here, to the foot of the bed, where you found that—thing. Then it turned to look at me—'' She shuddered spasmodically again, and quickly poured out a few more drops of cognac.

"And?" the secretary prompted.

Maldonado shaded her eyes with her hand, as though unable to bear the thought even now. "I saw its face—the conventional face that we all have seen in pictures and at plays. Illuminated from below with the most awful red light. Unspeakably evil. Little goat horns coming out of here, at the side of the skull—''

The secretary flicked her thumb toward the bureau drawer where she'd hidden the needle. "You'd used—that, just before this?"

The secretary's glance was piercing.

"Well, yes. But the cat didn't. And how do you explain what—you picked up from the floor? Whatever it was, it was all wrapped in that thing. It took it off, kept swirling it around there in the middle of the room—a little bit like matadors do in a bullfight. I distinctly felt the *breeze* from it in my face, coming from that way, toward the windows, not away from them! And then he, it—whatever the thing was—spoke. I heard it very clearly. There were no sounds from the street at all. He said, 'Why don't you create a dress like this, Maldonado, and dedicate it to me? Something that will turn whoever wears it into my servant. Here, I'll leave it with you.' That was when I at last found my voice and began to scream. I thought I'd go insane. And even through all my screaming I could hear Rajah over there in the corner with his back up, spitting madly—''

The secretary was getting a little impatient with this preposterous rigmarole. Maldonado was supposed to be one of the brainiest women in Paris, and here she was driveling the most appalling nonsense about seeing a demon in her room. Either the sedatives she was using were breaking down her mind, or she was overworked, subject to hallucinations. "And did this visitor leave the same way, through the window?" the secretary asked ironically.

"I don't know. I was too frightened to look."

The secretary tapped her teeth with her thumbnail. "I think we'd better tell Dr. Renard that that"—she indicated the drawer—"is beginning to get a hold on you. He'd better discontinue it. Suppose you take another swallow of cognac and try to get some sleep—"

She brushed the fallen cloak aside with the point of her toe, then stopped, holding it that way. Again that sudden urge, that blind hatred, swept her. She wanted to swing the cognac decanter high over her head, to brain Maldonado with it, to watch the blood pour out of her shattered head.

She withdrew her foot, staggered a little. Her mind cleared.

Maldonado said: "Take that thing out of here! Don't leave it in here with me! How do we know what it is?"

"No," the secretary said weakly. "Don't ask me to touch it anymore. I'm almost frightened myself now. I'm going back to my room. I feel—strange." She pulled the door open, went out without looking back.

The cat, seeing an avenue of escape, made a belated dash from under the bed, but the door was already closed when the animal reached it again. The cat stood up on its hind paws, scratching and mewing pathetically. Maldonado slipped off the bed and went to get it. "Come here, come here," she coaxed. "You seem very anxious to leave me—" She picked it up and started back with it in her arms, stroking it. As she did so she trod unwittingly on the cloak, lying there coiled on the floor like a snake waiting to strike.

Her face altered; her eyebrows went up saturninely, the

19

edges of her fine white teeth showed through her parted lips; in an instant all tenderness was gone, she was like a different person altogether.

"Well, leave me then, if you want to so badly!" she said, as the cat began to struggle in her arms. Her eyes dilated, gazing down at it. "Leave me for good!" She threw the animal brutally on the bed, then with a feline swiftness that more than matched its own, she thrust one of the heavy pillows over it, bore down with her whole weight, hands turned inward so that the fingers pointed toward one another. Her elbows slowly flexed, stiffened, flexed, stiffened, transmitting the weight of her suspended body to the pillow—and to what lay trapped below it.

The little plumed tail that was all that protruded, spiraled madly, almost like the spoke of a wheel, then abruptly stopped. Maldonado's foot, unnoticed, was still caught in a fold of the cloak, had dragged it across the floor after her.

Hours later, the secretary returned to tell her she was giving up her job. She was putting on her gloves and her packed valise stood outside in the hall. The little maid had fled already, without the formality of giving notice. The pious cook was at Mass, trying to find an answer to her problem: whether to turn her back on the perfectly good wages she was earning, or to risk remaining in a place where inexplicable things took place in the dead of the night. As for the secretary herself, all she knew was that twice she had been tempted to murder within the space of moments. There was some unclean mystery here that she could not fathom. She was modern and sensible enough to realize that the only thing to do, for her own sake, was remove herself beyond its reach. Before temptation became commission.

What had precipitated her decision was a phone call she had made to the workshop in an effort to trace the cape that was the only tangible evidence of the mystery. Their answer, after an exhaustive check had been made, only bore out Maldonado's words: there had never been anything answering its description in the stockroom, not even a two-by-four sample. An account was kept of every button, every ribbon.

So whatever it was, however it had got into Maldonado's room, it hadn't come from the shop.

The secretary saw at a glance that a change had come over Maldonado, since she had left her several hours before. A shrewd, exultant look had replaced the abysmal terror on her face. Whatever unseen struggle had taken place in here in the interval had been won by the forces of evil. Maldonado was sitting at her desk, busy with pencil and sketchpad doing a rough draft. She had the cape draped around one shoulder.

"Three times I took this thing to the window, to throw it out into the street," she admitted, "and I couldn't let go of it. It seemed to cling magnetically to my hands. The idea wouldn't let me alone, it kept me hypnotized, until finally I had to get it down on paper—"

A cry of alarm broke from the secretary. "What happened to Rajah?" She had just seen the lifeless bedraggled tail hanging down below the pillow. "Take that off him, he'll suffocate!"

Maldonado paid no attention. "He has already suffocated." She held up the sketch. "Look, that's just the way—what I saw last night—carried it. Call the car. I'm going to get to work on it at once. There's money in it, it'll be worth a fortune—" But her eyes, over the top of the sketch, had come to rest on the secretary's slim young throat. There was a sharp-pointed ivory paper cutter lying on the desk. As she held the drawing up with one hand, the other started to inch uncontrollably toward it, like a crawling five-legged white beetle.

Inching, crawling—

The secretary, warned by some sixth sense, gave a muffled cry, turned and bolted down the long hallway. The street door of the apartment slammed after her.

Maldonado smiled a little, readjusted the cape over her shoulder, went on talking to herself as though nothing had happened while she studied the finished sketch. "I'll advertise it as—let's see—*'I'm Dangerous Tonight—a dress to bring out the devil in you!'* "

And so a deadly thing was born.

Chapter 1
American in Paris

She was standing on a small raised turntable, about two feet off the floor, which could be revolved in either direction by means of a small lever, on the same general principle as a mobile barber's chair. She had been standing on it since early afternoon, with short rest periods every half-hour or so; it was eleven at night now.

They were all around her, working away like ants, some on their knees, some standing up. The floor was littered with red and black scraps, like confetti. She had eyes for only one thing in the whole workroom: a pair of sharp shears lying on a table across the way from her. She kept looking at them longingly, moistening her lips from time to time. When they were closed, as they were now, they came to a sharp point, like a poniard. And when they were open, the inner edge of each blade was like a razor. She was digging her fingernails into her own sides, to keep from jumping down to the floor, picking them up, and cutting and slashing everyone within reach with them. She'd been doing that, in her brain, for hours; she was all black-and-blue from the pinch and bite of her own nails. Once, the seamstress kneeling at her feet had saved her. She'd already had one foot off the stand, on her way over to them, and the latter had stuck a pin in her to make her hold still. The pain had counteracted the desperate urge she kept feeling. It did no good to try to look at anything else; her eyes returned to the shears each time.

The funny part of it was, when she was at rest, off the stand in just her underthings, and had every opportunity of seizing them and doing what she wanted to, she didn't seem to want to. It was only when she was up there with the dress on her that the urge swept over her. She couldn't understand why her thoughts should take this homicidal turn. She supposed it was because she was due to meet Belden at the Bal au Diable at midnight, and just tonight they'd picked to work overtime, to finish the thing, keeping her here long after she should have been out of the place.

Meeting him wasn't like meeting anyone else; he was living on borrowed time; he couldn't stick around any one place too long waiting for anyone. He was wanted for murder in the States, and there was an American detective over here now, looking for him; he had to lie low, keep moving around fast, with this Government man always just a step behind him, creeping up slowly but surely. Twice now, in the past two weeks, he'd just missed Belden by the skin of his teeth. And Belden couldn't get out of town until the fake passports his friend Battista was making for him were ready. He'd have them by the end of this week, and then he was going to head for the Balkans—and take her with him, of course. Until then, he was caught in a squirrel cage.

He was a swell guy; suppose he did run dope from France into the States? *She* was for him. She'd rather part with her right arm than see him arrested and taken back to die.

He'd killed one of their Department of Justice agents, and they'd never rest until they'd evened things up. They sat you in a chair over there, he'd told her, and shocked you to death with electricity. It sounded awful, a million times worse than the swift and merciful guillotine.

She was crazy about him, steadfast with that utter loyalty only a woman in love can know. She'd have gone through fire and water to be with him, anytime, anywhere. She was ready to be a fugitive with him for the rest of her life— "Whither thou goest, I will go; thy people shall be my people"—and when a Parisienne is ready to leave Paris behind forever, that's something. She hadn't seen him in five days now; he had to keep moving—but last night he'd got word to her along the underworld grapevine: "The Bal au Diable, Wednesday at twelve." And here it was after eleven, and she wasn't even out of the shop yet! Wouldn't that look great, to keep him waiting, endanger him like that?

She couldn't hold out any longer. Pinching herself didn't do any good, her sides were numb now. Her eyes fastened on the shears; she started to edge toward the edge of the stand, her hand slowly stroking her side. One good jump, a grab, a

23

quick turn—and she'd have them. "I'll take Maldonado first," she decided, as she reached the edge of the platform. "The sewing woman's so fat, she can't get out of the room as fast—" Her knees started to dip under her, bracing for the flying jump.

The designer spoke. "All right, Mimi, take it off. It's finished."

The sewing woman pulled; the dress fell to the floor at the mannequin's feet, and she suddenly stopped eyeing the scissors, wavered there off-balance, got limply to the floor. Now she could get at them easily—and she didn't try, seemed to have forgotten.

She staggered into the little curtained alcove to put on her street clothes.

"It's been a hard job," Maldonado said. "You all get a bonus." She went downstairs to her car. They started putting the lights out. The rest of the staff, the pieceworkers, had gone home hours ago. The sewing woman stayed behind a moment to stitch in the little silk label: *I'm Dangerous Tonight, by Maldonado*. Without that label it was just a dress. With it, it was a dress worth twenty thousand francs (and if the buyer was an American, twenty-five thousand).

Mimi Brissard looked at the junk she wore to work. Stockings full of holes, sloppy old coat. And it was too late now to go back to her own place and dress decently for him. She'd never make it; she lived way out at Bilancourt. She'd look fine, showing up in these rags to meet a swell guy like Belden! Even if he was a fugitive, even if the Bal au Diable was an underworld hangout, he'd be ashamed to be seen with her. He might even change his mind about taking her.

The sewing woman had finished the label, hung the dress up. "Coming, Mimi?"

"Go ahead," the girl called through the curtain. "I'll lock up." She'd been with them for five years, they trusted her. There was no money or anything kept up here anyway, just clothes and designs.

"Don't forget the lights." The old woman trudged wearily down the curved stone staircase to the street.

The girl stuck her head out around the curtain, eyed the dress. "I bet he'd be proud of me if I dared wear that! I could bring it back before we open up tomorrow, and they'd never even know." She went over to it, took the hanger down. The dress swept against her. Her eyes narrowed to slits. Her indecision evaporated. "Let anyone try to stop me and see what they get!" she whispered half audibly. A minute later she had slipped the red dress over her lithe young body and was strutting—there is no other word for it—before the mirror. She hadn't heard the step on the stairs, maybe because the watchman wore felt-soled shoes to make his rounds. He must have come up to see what was taking her so long.

"Eh? Wait, where do you think you're going in that? That's the firm's property." The old man was standing there in the doorway, looking in at her.

She whirled, and the tiny arrow-headed train, that was like a devil's tail, spun around after her. The shears were still lying there on the table, midway between them.

"Where do you think I'm going? I'll tell you where *you're* going—right now! To the devil, and you're not coming back!"

There was no excuse for it. The rebuke had been paternal, half humorous. He was a good-natured, inoffensive old man, half crippled with rheumatism. He was certainly no match for her young and furious strength. And the lust to kill—this dynamic murder-voltage charging her—that gave her the force and determination of two able-bodied men.

Her hand gave a catlike pounce, and the shears clashed; the blades opened, then closed spasmodically, like a hungry mouth, as her fingers gripped the handle. They came up off the table point-foremost.

He saw in her eyes what was coming. "Wait, *mademoiselle!* Don't! Why—?"

She couldn't have told him even if she wanted to. There was a murderous frenzy in her heart. She closed in on him as he tried to retreat, facing her because he was too horrified to turn his back. There was a spasm of motion from her hand, too quick for the eye to follow, and the point of the shears suddenly sank into his chest.

25

He gave a cough, found the wall with his back, leaned against it. His head went down and his old black alpaca cap fell off. He could still talk. "Have pity! I've never harmed you! I'm an old man! My Solange needs me—"

The shears found his throat this time. He fell down on top of them and was silent.

Something dark like mucilage glistened where he lay.

She had jumped back—not in remorse, but to keep the bottom of her skirt clear of his blood.

Tensed, curved forward from the waist up, peering narrowly at him like something out of a jungle that kills not for food but for love of killing, she executed strange gestures, as though her arms were those of a puppet worked by strings by some master puppeteer. Stretched them full-length up over her head, palm to palm, as if in some unholy incantation. Then let them fall again and caressed her own sides, as though inordinately pleased.

At last she moved around him, retrieved the ring of keys that he carried beneath his blouse. She would need them to come back into the building later on. She found the light switch, plunged the room—and what it contained—into darkness. She closed the door, and moved down the circular stone stairs with a rustling sound, such as a snake might make on a bed of dry leaves.

Chapter 2
First Night of a Gown

The *bal* was not on the list of synthetic Apache dens that guides show visitors to Paris. It was too genuine for that; sightseers would have been disappointed, as the real thing always makes a poorer show than the fake. It did not pay those who frequented it to advertise themselves or be conspicuous. Nothing ever seemed to be going on there. People would come in, slump down in a chair; no one would pay any attention to them; they would sometimes sit for hours, seemingly lost in dreams; then as suddenly be gone again, as unnoticed as they had come.

There was an accordion fastened to the wall, and a man who had lost an arm in the trenches would occasionally come in, sit down by it, and play softly sentimental ballads with his one hand only, pulling it in and out of the wall.

The *bal* consisted of simply a long, dingy, dimly lighted, smoke-filled semi-basement room; no one ever spoke above a low murmur. If the police never bothered anyone, possibly it was because that was the smartest thing to do. The *bal* often came in handy as a convenient starting point for a search for any wanted criminal at any given time; it was a focal point for the Paris underworld.

When Mimi, in her red-and-black dress, came down the short flight of stone steps from the street level, Belden wasn't there. At one table was a soiled glass in a china saucer stamped: *1Fr50*. As she passed by she glanced into it; in the dregs of vermouth-and-cassis floated a cigarette end. That was Belden's unmistakable trademark; that was where he'd been sitting. He never drank anything without leaving a cigarette in the glass or cup.

She sat down one table away. She knew all the faces by sight, but she gave no sign of recognition, nor was any given to her. No . . . there *was* one face there she didn't know. Out in the middle of the room, only its lower half visible under a snapdown hat brim. It didn't have the characteristic French pallor. The chin was squarer than Gallic chins are apt to be. There was a broadness of shoulder there, also, unknown on the Continent.

The man had a stale beer before him. But that was all right; no one came in here to eat or drink. He was staring at the red-and-white checks of the tablecloth, playing checkers on the squares with little *sou*-pieces. He looked at nothing, but he saw everything; it was written all over him. The atmosphere was tense, too. Without seeming to, all the others were watching him cautiously; they scented danger. His presence was a threat. . . .

Petion, the proprietor, found something to do that brought

him past her table. Carefully he removed the neglected glass and saucer from the one ahead.

"Where's Belden?"

Petion didn't seem to hear. The corner of his mouth moved in Apache argot. "Get out of here fast, you little fool. That bird over there is the one that's after him. The American *flic*. Luckily Belden saw him arrive. We got him out the back way. He's up at your place, waiting for you. His own room is too hot." Petion couldn't seem to get the grimy cloth at Belden's table straight enough to please him.

The man in the middle of the room jumped a five-sou piece with a ten-sou piece. You could almost *feel* the eyes peering through the felt of the shadowing brim.

"Now, watch out how you move—you may draw him after you without knowing it and put him onto Belden."

There was a fruit knife on the table. She glanced at it, then her eyes strayed to Petion's fat neck, creased above his collar. He caught the pantomime, gave her a surprised look, as much as to say, "What's got into *you?* He been feeding you some of his product?"

He straightened the empty chair and said aloud: "Well, what are you hanging around for? I tell you the dog is a United States Government agent."

"All right, clear away," she breathed impatiently. "I can handle this."

She got up and started slowly toward the stairs to the street. Death by electrocution, the thing she'd always dreaded so, ever since Belden had first told her what he had coming to him. Death by electricity—much worse than death at the point of a pair of shears or a table knife. She veered suddenly, as uncontrollably as though pulled by a magnet, turned off toward that table in the middle of the room, went directly over to it. She was smiling and her eyes were shining.

There was a small, nervous stir that rustled all over the room. One man shifted his chair. Another set his glass of *vin blanc* into a saucer, too noisily. A woman laughed, low in her throat.

He didn't seem to see her, not even when her fingertips were resting on the edge of the table.

"Soir, m'sieu."

He said: "Wrong table, *petite. Pas libre ce soir.*"

She'd learned some English from Belden. So now she pulled a second chair out, sat down, helped herself to one of his cigarettes. Her hand trembled a little, but not from nervousness. In the dim recesses of the room whispers were coursing along the walls: "She's giving him the come-on, trying to get him somewhere where Belden can finish him. That's the kind of girl to have!"

"She'll trip herself up. Those fish are no fools."

She began to speak quietly, her eyelids lowered. "I am Mimi Brissard, and I live at Bilancourt, number 5 rue Poteaux top floor front."

The line of his mouth hardened a little. "Move on. I told you I'm not int—"

"I am Belden's girl," she continued as though she hadn't heard him, "and he is up there right now, waiting for me. Now, are you interested?"

He pushed his hat back with a thumb and looked at her for the first time. There was no admiration in his eyes, not any gratitude, only the half-concealed contempt the police always have for an informer. "Why are you welshing on him?" he said warily.

She couldn't answer, any more than she could have answered the old watchman when he had asked her why she was stabbing him to death. She fingered the dress idly, as though she sensed something, but it eluded her.

"You better go back and tell him it won't work," he said dryly. "He's not getting me like he got Jimmy Fisher in New York, he's not dealing with a green kid now. I'm getting him—and without the help of any chippy either!"

"Then I have to prove that this is no decoy? Did you see that vermouth glass with the cigarette in it over there? That was he. This goes with it." She palmed a scrap of paper at him: *Bal au Diable 24h.* "I was to meet him here. You spoiled it. He's up there now. He's armed and he'll shoot to kill, rather than go back—''

"What did you think I expected him to do, scatter petals at my feet?''

"Without me you haven't got one chance in ten of taking him alive. But through me, you can do it. And you want him alive, don't you?''

"Yep," he said curtly. "The man he killed—Jimmy Fisher—was my brother. . . .''

She squirmed eagerly inside the glistening cocoon that sheathed her. But a change had come over him meanwhile. Her nearness, her presence at the table, seemed to be affecting him on some way. He had come alive, menacingly, hostilely, and he was . . . dangerous, too. His jaw line set pugnaciously, a baleful light flickered in his gray eyes, his upper lip curled back from his teeth. His hand roamed down his coat toward the flap of his back pocket. "I never wanted to kill anyone so much in my life," he growled throatily, "as I do you right now!" He started tugging at something, at the small of his back.

She looked down, saw that a flounce of her dress was brushing against his knee. She moved her chair slightly back, and the contact broke.

His hand came up on the table again, empty. His face slowly slipped back into its mask of impassivity. He was breathing a little heavily, that was all, and there was a line of moisture along the crease in his forehead.

"So he's at Bilancourt, 5 rue Poteaux," he said finally. "Thanks. You're a fine sweetheart. Some other dame, I suppose.''

"No," she said simply. "I loved him very much only an hour ago, at eleven o'clock. I must have changed since then, that's all. I don't know why. Now I'd like to think of him being electrocuted and cursing my name as he dies. . . . Follow me there and watch which window lights up. Keep watching. My window shade's out of order. Tonight it will be especially so. I'll have trouble with it. When you see it go up, then come down again, you'll know he's ready for the taking.''

"Okay, Delilah," he murmured. "When I first hit Paris I thought there was no one lower than Belden. He shot an unarmed kid of twenty-five—in the back, without giving him a chance. But now I see there's someone lower still—and that's his woman. He, at least, wouldn't turn you in; I'll give him that much. But let me warn you. If you think you're leading me into a trap, if I have to do any shooting, you get the first slug out of this gun! That's how you stand with me, little lady.''

She smiled derisively, stood up. She didn't bother to reply to his contempt. "Don't leave right after me, they're all watching you here. I'll wait for you under the first streetlight around the corner.'' She added dreamily: "I couldn't think of anything I wanted to do more than this. That's why I'm doing it.''

She went slowly up the stone steps to the street door, her pointed train wriggling after her from side to side. She turned her head and flashed a smile over her shoulder. Then she went out and the darkness swallowed her.

Frank Fisher rinsed his mouth with beer and emptied it out on the floor.

Chapter 3
Mademoiselle Judas

The room was dark and empty when she stepped into it from the hall outside. The dim light shining behind her outlined her; her silhouette was diabolic, long and sinuous and wavering. Two ridges of hair above her ears looked almost like horns. Something clicked warningly somewhere in the room, but that was all. She closed the door.

''*Chéri?*'' she whispered. "I'm going to put up the light. It's all right. *C'est Mimi.*''

A bulb went on, and its rays, striking out like yellow rain, touched off a gleam between two curtains pulled tightly together across a doorless closet. The gleam was black in the middle, holed through. It elongated into a stubby automatic; and a hand, an arm, a shoulder, a man, came slowly out after it toward her.

Steve Belden was misleadingly unogre-like, for a man who had poisoned thousands of human lives with heroin. In repose his face was almost pleasant-looking, and his eyes had that directness of gaze that usually betokens honesty.

The girl glanced quizzically at the gun as he continued to point it at her. "Well, put it away, *chéri,*" she protested ironically. "Haven't you seen me someplace before?"

He sheathed it under his arm, scowled. "What took you so long? D'you know he nearly jumped me, waiting for you at the *bal* just now? Petion got me out the back way by pretending to shake out a tablecloth, holding it up at arm's length for a screen. For a minute we were both in the same room, he and I! I hope you haven't steered him over here after you without knowing it."

"He wasn't there anymore. Must have looked in merely, then gone away again."

"What's the idea of that dress? I nearly took a shot at you when you opened the door just now."

"It's what they kept me overtime working on tonight. I left it on to save time. I'll sneak it back first thing in the morning—"

"You'll have to have some reach, if you do. Battista finally came through with the passports. We're taking the Athens Express at daybreak. Matter of fact, I could have made the night train to the Balkans, if it hadn't been for you. I waited over so I could take you with me—"

"So four hours more in Paris does the trick?" she said, looking at him shrewdly.

He frowned.

"Yeah, and then we're all set. Fisher's extradition writ's no good in Greece, and Panyiotis pulls enough weight there to fix it so we both disappear for good. If I've outsmarted him for three weeks now, I can outlast him the few hours there are left. What'd you say?"

She's said, "If—" in a low voice. "When did you get any sleep?"

"Night before last."

"Well, take off your coat, lie down here, rest up awhile. I'll keep watch. I'll wake you in time for the train. Here, let me have that, I'll keep it trained on the door."

"What do *you* know about these things?" he grinned, but he passed the gun over to her, stretched himself out. "Put out the light," he said sleepily. He began to relax, the long-sustained tension started to go out of his nerves; he could trust her. She was the only one. . . .

The gun was not pointed at the door, but at him—at the top of his head from behind, through the bars of the bed. Her face was a grimace of delight. Then slowly she brought the gun down again. A bullet in the brain—you didn't feel anything, didn't know anything. But electrocution—what anguish, what terror preceded it! Electrocution was a much better way.

A sharp click from the gun roused him, after he had already begun to doze off. He stiffened, looked at her over his shoulder. "What was that?"

"Just making sure it's loaded." She kicked something along the floor with the tip of her foot, something metallically round. It rolled under the bed.

His eyes closed again. He turned his head toward the wall. His breathing thickened.

A warning *whirr* of the shade roller roused him a second time. He raised half upright on his elbow. His free hand clawed instinctively at his empty shoulder holster.

She was reaching for the cord, pulling the shade all the way down again to the bottom.

"What're you doing?" he rasped. "Get away from that window! I told you to put the light out, didn't I?"

"It slipped. It needs fixing," she murmured. "It's all right, there's no one down there. Here goes the light—"

The last thing he said, as he lay back again, was: "And take that damn dress off too, while you're about it. Every time I lamp it on you, it throws a shock into me all over again. I think I'm seeing things—''

She said nothing.

He drowsed off again. Then in the dark, only seconds later, she was leaning over him, shaking him awake. Her breath was a sob that threatened to become a scream. The whiteness of her form was dimly visible. She must have discarded the dress while he slept.

"Steve. *Mon* Steve!" she was moaning. "Get up!" She pulled him frenziedly erect with both arms. "*Sauves-toi!* Out! File—*vite!* Maybe you can still make it by way of the roof—''

He was on his feet, clear of the bed, in an instant. "What's up? What's up?"

"I've sold you out!" The groan seemed to come from way down at the floor, as though she was all hollow inside. "I tipped him off at the *bal*. I signaled him with the shade just now—''

The light flashed on.

"Oh, don't stand there looking at me. Quick, get out this door, he has four flights to climb—''

He was usually very quick, but not this time. He stood there eyeing her as though he couldn't believe what he heard. Then at last, he grasped what she had told him. He pulled the gun from her unresisting hand, turned it the other way around, jabbed it at her heart. It clicked repeatedly, almost like a typewriter.

"I—the bullets—" she shuddered. "Under the bed— Oh, get, Steve—save yourself now—''

A warped floorboard groaned somewhere outside the room. "Too late!"

Belden had dropped down on one knee, was reaching out desperately toward the bullets. There was no pounding at the door; a shot exploded into it, and splinters of wood flew out on the inside. The china knob fell off and lay there like an egg. The door itself ricocheted back off the flat of someone's shoe.

"All right, don't move, Belden. You're through."

Fisher came in slowly, changed gun hands with a sort of acrobatic twist, and brought out handcuffs.

"Pull your finger joint out of that trigger hole," he added.

The automatic turned over, fell upside down on the floor.

Fisher didn't speak again until the manacles had closed. Then he said, "Got a hat or something you want to take with you?" He seemed to see Mimi for the first time. He nodded, said curtly: "Nice work, *Mademoiselle Judas.*"

She stood shivering. The dress lay on the floor behind her, but she made no move to reach out for it.

Belden took his capture calmly enough. He didn't say a word to Mimi Brissard; didn't even look at her. "It's a pleasure," he said bitterly, as Fisher motioned him forward, "if only because it means getting out of a town where there are—things like this." He spat on the floor at her feet as he went by.

Fisher hung back a minute to look her almost detachedly, up and down. He pocketed his gun, took out a wallet with his free hand, removed some lettucelike franc notes. "What was it—money?" he said. "You haven't asked for any, but I suppose that's it. Here, go out and buy yourself a heart."

The wadded bills struck her lightly in the center of the forehead, and fluttered down her to the floor. One caught upon her breast, just over her heart, and remained poised there, like a sort of badge.

She stood there with her eyes closed, perfectly motionless, as though she were asleep standing up, while the man she'd loved and his captor began their long descent side by side down the four flights of stairs that led to the street.

When they came out of the house a moment later, they had to force their way through the crowd of people standing there blocking the entrance.

Fisher thought for a moment that it was his own shot at the lock upstairs in the house that had attracted them. But they were all turned the other way, with their backs to the building. Out in the middle of the narrow cobbled street two or three of them were bending anxiously over something. Some broken white thing lying perfectly still at their feet. One of the men was hurriedly opening and separating the leaves of a newspaper—but not to read it.

Mimi Brissard had atoned, in the only way she had left.

Chapter 4
The Lady from Dubuque

"Do I dare?" Mrs. Hiram Travis said aloud, to no one in particular, in her stateroom on the *Gascony* the night before it reached New York. Or if to anyone at all, to the slim, slinky red-and-black garment that the stewardess had laid out for her across the bed under the mistaken impression that she would wish to wear it. A stewardess who, although she had assured Mrs. Travis she was not susceptible in the least to seasickness, had come out of the cabin looking very pale and shaken after having taken the dress down from its hanger. Mrs. Travis had noticed the woman glaring daggers at her, as if in some way *she* were to blame. But this being Mrs. Travis' first trip abroad, or anywhere at all except Sioux City, she was not well versed in the ways of stewardesses, any more than in those of French couturières.

In fact she hadn't really known what that Maldonado woman was talking about at all; they had had to make signs to each other. *She* had wanted just a plain simple little dress to wear to the meetings of her Thursday Club back home in Dubuque, and then the next morning *this* had shown up at the hotel all wrapped up in crinkly paper. She hadn't wanted Hiram to think she was a fool, so she'd pretended it was the one she'd ordered, and good-natured as always, he'd paid for it without a word. Now here she was stuck with it! And the worst part of it was, if she didn't wear it tonight, then she'd never have another chance to. Because she really didn't have the nerve to wear it in Dubuque. Folks would be scandalized. And all the francs it had cost!

"Do I dare?" she said again, and edged a little closer.

One only had to look at Mrs. Hiram Travis to understand the reason for her qualms. She and the dress didn't match up at all. They came from different worlds. She was a youngish forty, but she made not the least attempt to look any younger than that. She was very plain, with her chin jutting a little too much, her eyes undistinguished, and her mouth too flat. Her hair was a brown-red. She had never used rouge and she had never used powder. The last time she'd smoked a cigarette was behind her grandmother's barn at the age of fourteen. She'd never drunk anything stronger than elderberry wine in her life, until a week ago in Paris, just for the look of things, she'd tried a little white wine with her meals. She made swell pies, but now that Hi had made so much money in the lawnmower business, he wouldn't let her do her own cooking any more. He'd even retired, taken out a half-million-dollar life-insurance policy, and they'd made this trip to Paris to see the sights. Even there the latest they'd stayed up was one night when they had a lot of postcards to write and didn't get to bed until nearly eleven-thirty. About the most daring thing she'd done in her whole life was to swipe a fancy salad fork from a hotel for a souvenir. It was also the closest she'd ever come to a criminal act. That ought to give you the picture.

She was mortally afraid of about eight million things, including firearms, strange men, and the water they were traveling on right now.

"Golly," she clucked, "I bet I'll feel like a fool in it. It's so—kind of vampish. What'll Hi say?" She reached out and rested her hand on the dress, which lay there like a coiled snake ready to strike. . . .

She drew her hand back suddenly. But she couldn't help reaching out again to touch the dress with a movement that was almost a caress.

Instantly her mind filled with the strangest thoughts—odd recollections of instants in her past that she would have said she had completely forgotten. The first time she'd ever seen her father wring a chicken's neck. The day that Hiram—way back in high school—cut his arm on a broken window. A vein he'd cut. He'd bled . . . a lot; and she'd felt weak and sick and terrified. The automobile smash-up they'd seen that time on the state highway on the way back from the fair . . .

that woman lying all twisted and crumpled on the road, with her head skewed way around as it shouldn't be—couldn't be if the woman lived.

It was funny. . . . When those things had taken place, she'd felt terrible. Now—remembering them—she found herself going over every detail in her mind, almost—lovingly.

In a magazine she had once seen a picture of Salomé kneeling on the ground holding on a great tray the head of Baptist John. The woman's body was arched forward; there was a look of utter, half-delirious absorption on her face as her lips quested for the dead, partly open mouth. And quite suddenly, with a little shock of revelation, Sarah Travis knew what Salomé had felt.

The dress slipped from her fingers. She hurried to put it on. . . .

Georges, the *Gascony*'s chief bartender, said: "Perhaps *monsieur* would desire another. That's a bad col' you catch."

The watery-eyed red-nosed little man perched before him had a strip of flannel wound around his throat neatly pinned in back with two small safety pins. He glanced furtively around over his shoulder, the length of the glittering cocktail lounge. "Mebbe you're right," he said. "But the missus is due up in a minute. I don't want her to catch me at it—she'll lace it into me, sure enough!"

Sarah, of course, wouldn't dream of approaching the bar; when she came they'd sit decorously at a little table over in the corner, he with a beer, she with a cup of Oolong tea, just to act stylish.

Hiram Travis blew his long-suffering nose into a handkerchief the size of a young tablecloth. Then he turned his attention to the live canary dangling over the bar in a bamboo cage, as part of the decorations. He coaxed a few notes out by whistling softly. Then he happened to look in the mirror before him—and he recoiled a little, his eyes bugged; and part of his drink spilled out of his glass.

She was standing next to him, right there at the bar itself, before he'd even had time to turn. An odor of musk enveloped him. The canary over their heads executed a few pin-wheel flurries.

His jaw just hung open. "Well, fer—!" was all he could say. It wasn't so much the dress she was wearing, it was that her whole personality seemed to have subtly changed. Her face had a hard, set look about it. Her manner was almost poised. She wasn't fluttering with her hands the way she usually did in a room full of people, and he missed the nervous, hesitant smile on her lips. He couldn't begin to say what it was, but there was something about her that made him a little afraid of her. He even edged an inch or two away from her. Even Georges looked at her with a new professional respect not unmixed with fear.

"*Madame?*" he said.

She said, "I feel like a drink tonight," she said, and laughed a little, huskily. "What are those things—cocktails—? Like that woman over there has."

The bartender winced a little. "That, *madame*, is a double Martini. Perhaps something less—"

"No. That's what I want. And a cigarette, too. I want to try one."

Beside her, her husband could only splutter, and he stopped even that when she half turned to flash him a smile—the instinctive, brilliant smile of a woman who knows what feeble creatures men can be. You couldn't learn to smile like that. It was something a woman either knew the minute she was born, or never knew at all.

Georges recognized that smile.

"I can't believe it's you," Hiram Travis said, stupefied.

Again that smile. "It must be this dress," she said. "It does something to me. You have to live up to a gown like this, you know. . . ." There was a brief warning in her eyes. She picked up her cocktail, sipped at it, coughed a little, and then went on drinking it slowly. "About the dress," she said, "I put my hand on it and for a moment I couldn't take it away again, it seemed to *stick* to it like glue! Next thing I knew I was in it."

As the bartender struck a match to light her cigarette, she

put her hand on his wrist to steady it. Travis saw him jump, draw back. He held his wrist, blew on it, looked at her reproachfully. Travis said; "Why, you scratched him, Sarah."

"Did I? And as she turned and looked at him, he saw her hand twitch a little, and drew still further away from her. "What—what's got into you?" he faltered.

There was some kind of tension spreading all around the horseshoe-shaped bar, emanating from her. All the cordiality, the sociability, was leaving it. Cheery conversations even at the far ends of it faltered and died, and the speakers looked around them as though wondering what was putting them so on edge. A heavy leaden pall of restless silence descended, as when a cloud goes over the sun. One or two people even turned and moved away reluctantly, as though they hadn't intended to but didn't like it at the bar anymore. The gaunt-faced woman in red and black was the center of all eyes, but the looks sent her were not the admiring looks of men for a well-dressed woman; they were the blinking petrified looks a blacksnake would get in a poultry yard. Even the barman felt it. He dropped and smashed a glass, a thing he hadn't done since he'd been working on the ship. Even the canary felt it, and stood shivering pitifully on its perch, emitting an occasional cheep as though for help.

Sarah Travis looked up, and saw it. She took a loop of her dress, draped it around her finger, thrust it between the bars. There was a spasm of frantic movement inside, too quick for the eye to follow, a blurred pinwheel of yellow. Then the canary lay lifeless at the bottom of the cage, claws stiffly upthrust. Its heart had stopped from fright.

It wasn't what she had done—they could all see that contact hadn't killed it—it was the look on her face that was so shocking. No pity, no regret, but an expression of savage satisfaction, a sense of power to deal out life and death just now discovered. Some sort of unholy excitement seemed to be crackling inside her; they could all but see phosphorescent flashes of it in her eyes.

This time they began to move away in numbers, with outthrust lower lips of repugnance and dislike turned her way.

Drinks were left half-finished, or were taken with them to be imbibed elsewhere. She became the focal point for a red wave of converged hate that, had she been a man, would surely have resulted in some overt act. There were sulky whispers of "Who is that?" as they moved away. The bartender, as he detached and lowered the cage, looked daggers at her, cursed between his teeth in French.

There was only one solitary drinker left now at the bar, out of all the amiable crowd that had ringed it when she first arrived. He kept studying her inscrutably with an expressionless face, seemingly unallergic to the tension that had driven everyone else away.

"There's that detective again," she remarked with cold hostility. "Wonder he doesn't catch cold without that poor devil being chained to him. Wonder where he's left him?"

"Locked up below, probably, while he's up getting a bracer," Travis answered mechanically. His chief interest was still his own problem: what had happened to his wife in the ten brief minutes from the time he'd left her preparing to dress in their stateroom until the time she'd joined him up here? "I suppose they asked him not to bring him up with him manacled like that, for the sake of appearances. Why are you so sorry for his prisoner all of a sudden, and so set against him? Only last night you were saying what an awful-type man the other fellow was and how glad you were he'd been caught."

"Last night isn't tonight," she said shortly. "People change, Hiram." She still had the edge of her dress wrapped around her hand, as when she'd destroyed the canary. "I don't suppose you ever will, though." Her voice was low, thoughtful. She looked at her husband curiously, then deliberately reached out toward him with that hand and rested it against him.

Travis didn't go into a spasm and fall lifeless as the bird had. He displayed a sudden causeless resentment toward her, snapped, "Take your hand away, don't be pawing me!" and moved farther away.

She glanced disappointedly down at her hand as though it

had played a dirty trick on her, slowly unwound the strip of material, let it fall. She stared broodingly into the mirror for a while, tendrils of smoke coming up out of her parted lips.

She said, "Hi, is that half-million-dollar insurance policy you took out before we left in effect yet or still pending?" and narrowed her eyes at her image in the glass.

"It's in effect," he assured her. "I paid the first premium on it the day before we left Dubuque. I'm carrying the biggest insurance of any individual in Ioway—"

She didn't seem particularly interested in hearing the rest. She changed the subject abruptly—or seemed to. "Which one of the bags have you got that gun in that you brought with you for protection? You know, in case we got robbed in Europe."

The sequence of questions was so glaringly, so unmistakably meaningful, that he did what almost anyone else would have done under the circumstances, ascribed it to mere coincidence and ignored it. Two separate disconnected chains of thought, crowding upon one another, had made her ask first one, then the other, that was all. It just would have *sounded* bad to a stranger, to that professional crime detector over there for instance, but of course *he* knew better. After all, he'd been married to her for eighteen years.

"In the cowhide bag under the bed in the stateroom," he answered calmly. "Why? Every time you got a peek at it until now you squeaked, 'Throw it away, Hi! I can't stand to look at them things!' "

She touched her hand to her throat briefly and moistened her lips.

Travis noticed something, and said: "What's the matter, you seasick? Your face is all livid, kind of, and you're breathing so fast—I coulda told you not to monkey 'round with liquor when you're not used to it."

"It isn't either, Hiram. I'm all right. Leave me be." Then, with a peculiar ghastly smile lighting up her face, she said, "I'm going down below a minute to get something I need. I'll be back."

"Want me to come with you?"

"No," she said, still smiling, "I'd rather have you wait for me here, and then come out on the deck with me for a little stroll when I come back. That upper boat deck. . . ."

The little undulating serpentine train of her dress followed her across the cocktail lounge and out. Hiram Travis watched her go, wondering what had happened to change her so. Georges watched her go, wondering what had gone wrong at his bar tonight. Frank Fisher watched her go, wondering who it was she kept reminding him of. He had thought of Belden's sweetheart in Paris at once, but discarded her, because the two women didn't resemble one another in the least.

Fifteen was the number of her stateroom, and she knew that well, yet she had stopped one door short of it, opposite seventeen, and stood listening. The sound was so faint as to be almost indistinguishable, a faint rasping, little more than the buzz of an angry fly caught in the stateroom and trying to find a way out. Certainly it was nothing to attract the attention of anyone going by, as it had hers. It was as though her heart and senses were turned in to evil tonight, and the faintest whisper of evil could reach her.

She edged closer, into the little open foyer at right angles to the passageway, in which the door was set. None of the stateroom doors on the *Gascony* opened directly out into the public corridors. There was a food tray lying outside the door, covered with a napkin, ready to be taken away. She edged it silently aside with the point of her foot, stood up closer to the door. The intermittently buzzing fly on the other side of it was more audible now. *Zing-zing, zing-zing, zing-zing.* It would break off short every so often, then resume.

Mrs. Hiram Travis, who had been afraid of strange men and who had shuddered at the mere thought of criminals until twenty minutes ago, smiled knowingly, reached out and began to turn the glass doorknob. It made no sound in her grasp, but the motion must have been visible on the other side. The grating sound stopped dead, something clinked metallically, and then there was a breathless, waiting silence.

The faceted knob had turned as far as it would go in her hand, but the door wouldn't give. A man's voice called out: "Come on, jailer, quit playing hide-and-seek! Whaddya think you're going to catch me doing, hog-tied like I am?"

She tried the knob again, more forcefully. The voice said: "Who's there?" a little fearfully this time.

"Where's the key?" she whispered.

"Who are you?" was the answering whisper.

"You don't know me. I'd like to get in and talk to you—"

"What's the angle?"

"There's something you can do—for me. I want to help you."

"*He's* got the key, he took it up with him. Watch yourself, he'll be back any minute—" But there was a hopeful note in the voice now. "He's got both keys, the one to the door and the one to these bracelets. I'm cuffed to the head of the bed, and that's screwed into the floor—"

"I left him up at the bar," she said. "If I could get near enough to him maybe I could get hold of the keys."

There was a tense little silence while the man behind the door seemed to be thinking things over.

"Wait a minute," the voice said, "I've got something here that'll help you. Been carrying it around in the fake sole of my shoe. Stand close under that open transom, I'll see if I can make it from here—"

Presently a little white folded paper packet flew out, hit the wall opposite, landed at her feet.

She stooped swiftly to pick it up, scarcely conscious of the unaccustomed grace of her movement.

"Get it? Slip it into his drink. It's the only chance you've got. Now listen, the cuff key is in his watch pocket, under his belt; the door key's in his breast pocket. He turned his gun over to the purser when we came aboard, said he wasn't taking any chances of my getting hold of it while he was asleep. I don't know who you are or what the lay is, but you're my only bet. We dock tomorrow. Think you can do it?"

"I can do anything—tonight," Mrs. Hiram Travis of Dubuque answered as she moved away from the door.

Fisher looked at her a full half-minute while she stood beside him holding her cigarette poised. "Certainly," he said at last, "but you won't find the matches I carry any different from the ones your husband and the bartender both offered you just now—and which you refused." He struck one, held it for her.

"You see everything, don't you?"

"That's my business." He turned back to the bar again, as though to show the interruption was over.

She didn't move. "May I drink with you?"

He stiffened his finger at the Frenchman. "Find out what the lady is having." Then he turned to go. "If you'll excuse me— "

"*With* you, not *on* you," she protested.

"This isn't a pleasure trip," he told her briefly. "I'm on business. My business is downstairs, not up here. I've stayed away from it too long already. Sorry."

"oh, but a minute more won't matter—" She had thrust out her arm deftly, fencing him in. She was in the guise of a lady, and to be unnecessarily offensive to one went counter to a training he had received far earlier than that of the Department. It was ingrained in the blood. She had him at a disadvantage. He gave in grudgingly, but he gave in.

She signaled her husband to join them, and he came waddling up, blowing his nose and obviously beginning to feel his liquor. Tonight was one night Sarah didn't seem to give a rap how much he drank, and it was creeping up on him.

Georges set down three Martinis in a row. Mrs. Travis let a little empty crumpled white paper fall at her feet.

"Y'know," Travis was saying, "about this fella you're bringin' back with you—"

"Sorry," said Fisher, crisply but pleasantly, "I'm not at liberty to discuss that."

Mrs. Travis raised Fisher's drink to her lips with her left

45

hand, moved hers toward him with her right. Georges was busy rinsing his shaker.

"Last spring one of you fellas showed up in Dubuque, I remember. He was lookin' for some bank robber. Came around to the office one day—" Travis went into a long, boring harangue. Presently he broke off, looked at Fisher, and turned a startled face to his wife.

"Hey, he's fallen asleep!"

"I don't blame him much," she said, and brushed the lapel of Fisher's coat lightly, then the tab of his vest. "Spilled his drink all over himself," she murmured in explanation. She took her hand away clenched, metal gleaming between the finger cracks. "Take him outside on the deck with you, Hi," she said. "Sit him in a chair, see if the air'll clear his head. Don't let anyone see him like this in here. . . ."

"You're right," said Travis, with the owl-like earnestness of the partially intoxicated.

"The boat deck. No one goes up there at night. I'll join you—presently." She turned and walked away.

She dangled the handcuff key up and down in the palm of her hand, standing back just beyond his reach. He was nearly tearing his arm out of its socket, straining across the bed to get at it.

There was something oddly sinister about her, standing there grinning devilishly at him like that, something that made Steve Belden almost afraid. This ugly dame was really bad. . . .

"Well, come on, use that key! What'd you do, just lift it to come down here and rib me with it? That knockout powder ain't going to last all night. It's going to pass off in a few minutes and—"

"First listen to what I have to say. I'm not doing this because I'm sorry for you."

"All right, let's have it! Anything you say. You're holding the aces."

She began to smile and it was a terrible thing to see.

Poisonous . . . the pure distillation of evil . . . like a gargoyle mask.

"Listen," she began. "My husband—there is a half-million-dollar insurance policy on his life—and I'm the sole beneficiary. I'm sick of him—he's a hick—never will be anything but a hick. I've got to be rid of him—got to. And I want that money. I've earned it. I'll never get another chance as good as now, on this boat. I don't want that half million when I'm sixty and no good anymore. I want it now, while I'm young enough to enjoy it. But even if there wasn't any insurance at all, I'd still want to do it. I hate the way he talks and the way he walks and the way he eats his shredded wheat and the way he always is getting colds and talking like a trained seal! I hate everybody there is in the world tonight, but him most." And she gave the handcuff key one final flip, caught it again, blew her breath on it—just beyond his manacled reach.

He rubbed his strained shoulder, scowled at her. "What do you have to have me for?" he asked. "Not that it means anything to me to put the skids to a guy, even a guy that I've never set eyes on before; but for a dame that can get Fisher's stateroom and bracelet keys out of his pocket right under his eyes—why do you have to have help on a simple little stunt like that?"

"I'll tell you why," she said. "You see, mister, I had him with me when I came aboard, and so I have to have him with me when I go ashore tomorrow. That's why I need you. You're going to be Hiram, bundled up in his clothes, with your neck bandaged, and a great big handkerchief in front of your face. You won't have to speak. I'll do all the talking. If I just report that he disappeared at sea, I'll never be able to prove that he's dead, I'll never get the half million. . . ."

"But suppose I do go ashore with you, how you gonna prove it then?"

"I'll—I'll find something—I don't know just yet. Maybe a—a body from the morgue—or something." She gave him a peculiar searching look.

Steve Belden was no fool. That look made him think that maybe he was slated to play the part of the "remains" in question, when the time came. But he was in no position to bargain. The important thing was to get these cuffs open and get off the ship. And he'd need her help for that. Then later—

"And do I get a cut of the five hundred grand?"

She laughed mirthlessly. "Why, no," she said. "I don't think so. I'm saving your life, you see, and I think it's enough. Your life—for his. . . ."

"All right," he said. "No harm in asking. Now get busy with that key."

A quick twist of her wrist, a click and a manacle dangled empty from the bed-rail. The murderer of Frank Fisher's brother was free again. His words, as he chafed his wrist and stamped back and forth like a bear on a rampage, were not of gratitude—but low growls of revenge.

"A week in that filthy pig-pen of a French prison! Four days in this coop, chained up like an animal. Chained to him while I ate, chained to him while I slept, chained to him even while I shaved. *He's* never getting off this ship alive—!"

"Of course he isn't," the woman agreed. "How can we let him? The whole idea would be spoiled if he does. That'll be your job. I'm attending to—Hiram myself."

Belden waved his fists in the air. "If I only had a gun!"

"There's one in my cabin, in a cowhide suitcase under the bed—" Then as he turned toward the door: "Wait a minute. You can't do that. You'll bring the whole ship down on us, the moment you show your face, and there'll be a general alarm raised. Now if you go into my cabin next door, you can hide in the bath. I'll go up and find a way of bringing him down there with me—after I—Somehow your—Mr. Fisher—we have to get him in there before he comes back here and finds you gone. Now wait a minute, we can fix this bed in case he takes a quick look in here first."

She pushed pillows together under the covers, made a long log-like mound. "Give me your coat," she said. "You'll be wearing Hiram's clothes, anyway." She extended the empty sleeve out from the coverings, locked the open manacle around it's cuff. "You want to bed fully-dressed, waiting for him to come down and tuck you in!"

"Hurry up," he kept saying. "We ain't got all night! We must be near Ambrose Lightship already."

"No. We mustn't rush," the lady from Dubuque, who had been afraid of strangers and weapons and violence, said quietly. "Follow me, and I'll get the gun out for you and rig you up in Hiram's things." She eased the door open, advanced to the mouth of the foyer, and glanced up and down the long passageway. "Come on."

She joined him a moment later, unlocked her door for him. She crouched down, pulled out the valise, found the gun and held it up. "You'll have to use this through pillows," she said, "or you'll make a noise." She was handling the weapon almost caressingly. It pointed at his chest for a moment, and her eyes grew misty.

Belden jumped aside out of range, pulled the gun angrily away from her. "What's the matter with you anyway?" he barked. "You kill-crazy? I thought it was Fisher and your husband you were out to get!"

"Yes," she said sullenly. That was the greater treachery, so it had first claim on her. " But I told you, I hate everyone in the world tonight. Everyone—you hear?"

"Yeah? Well, we need each other, and until we're out of this squeeze, let's hang together. Now go on up there and get that dick down here. I'll be just behind the bathroom door there, waiting for him."

She grabbed up a long gauzy handkerchief and sidled out of the room. Behind her Belden wiped his beaded brow. He'd never run into a woman like her before and—hard-bitten as he was—he never wanted to again.

Chapter 5
Collision

Travis looked up from a deck-chair at the shadowy figure looming before him on the unlighted deck. "That you, Sarah? What took you so long? I don't think it's so good for my cold, staying up here in the wind so long."

"This is going to cure your cold," her voice promised him raspingly.

He motioned to the inert form in the chair beside him. "Hasn't opened his eyes since he came up here. Sure must be dead for sleep. Guess he ain't been getting much rest, chained to that fella down there—" He tittered inanely. "Wonder what they did when they wanted to turn over in bed?"

She bent over Fisher, shook him slightly, ever so slightly, one hand above his breast-pocket, the other at the tab of his vest. Then she straightened again. "I didn't know they ever slept like that—did you?"

She turned toward the rail, went and stood beside it, outlined dimly against the stars. The wind fluttered her gown about her. She held the long gauzy handkerchief in one hand like a pennant. "What a lovely night," she said. "Come here and look at the water."

There was no one on this unroofed boat deck but the two of them—and Fisher.

"I can see it from here," her husband answered. " 'Twouldn't be good for my cold to lean way out into the wind like that." He blinked fearfully into the gloom. "You look just like— some kind of a bogey-man standing there like that, with the wind making great big bat wings grow behind your back. If I didn't know it was you, I'd be scared out of ten years' growth—"

She opened her fingers, and the handkerchief fluttered downward like a ghostly streamer. A wisp of cloud passed over the new moon just then.

'Hiram," she called in a silvery voice, like the sirens on the rock to Ulysses, "I've lost my handkerchief. Come quickly, it's caught around the bottom of the railing. Hurry, before it blows loose—!"

Hiram Travis heard the voice of the woman he had been married to for eighteen years, asking him a common favor, and the obscured moon and the simulated bat wings and the chill foreboding at the base of his skull became just the playthings of an overwrought imagination. He got up awkwardly from the deck chair, waddled across to the rail beside her, peered down. His eyes were watery from his cold and blurred from unaccustomed liquor.

"You sure it's still there?" he said uncertainly. "Thought I saw it go all the way down."

"Of course it's still there, can't you see it? Bend over, you can see it from here—" Then as he prepared to squat on the inside of the guardrail and peer through it from there, she quickly forestalled him with a guiding hand at the nape of his neck. "No, lean over from above and look down on the outside, that's the only way you can see it. I'll hold you."

On the deck chair behind them the unconscious Fisher stirred a little, mumbled in his drugged sleep. He seemed to be on the point of awakening. But the stupor was too strong for him. He sighed heavily, became inert once more.

"Blamed if I can see a dratted thing!" Travis was piping. He was folded almost double over the rail, like a clothespin, with his wife's hand at his shoulder. He made vague groping motions with one hand, downward into space; the other was clasped about the rail."

"You're nearly touching it. It's just an inch away from your fingertips—"

"Get one of the stewards, Sarah, I'm liable to go over myself first thing I know, doing this—"

It was the last thing he said in this world. The last thing she said to him was: "We don't need a steward—*for this*, darling."

She crouched down suddenly beside him, took her hand away from his shoulder. She gripped his bony ankles with both hands, thrust viciously upward, broke their contact with the deck, straightening as she did so. He did a complete somersault across the guardrail; the arm that had gripped it was turned completely around in its socket, torn free. That was the last thing she saw of him—that momentary appeal of splayed white hand vanishing into the blackness. His screech was smothered in the sighing of the wind.

She thrust out her arms wide, in strange ritual of triumph, as Mimi Brissard had in Paris. She was a black, ominous death-cross against the starlight for a moment. Then she turned slowly, her eyes two green phosphorescent pools, toward where the helpless secret service man lay.

Fisher blinked and opened his eyes. He was still groggy from the dreams he had been having. Dreams in which long, skinny black imps out of hell had pushed people over the side of an immense precipice down into a bottomless abyss below. He'd been chained down, unable to help them, though they screamed to him for assistance. Over and over it had happened. It had been the worst form of torture, the most ghastly nightmare he had ever had. Then toward the end the imps had concentrated on him himself. They had tugged and pulled, trying to get him to the edge of the precipice, and he had held back, dug his heels in, but inch by inch they had been overcoming him. . . .

He saw that he was partly off the chair he had been sleeping on. One leg, one arm and shoulder, hung down over the side, as though somebody had actually been tugging at him. But the lady from Dubuque, the harmless, inoffensive, eccentric Middle Western lady from Dubuque, was the only person around, stretched out there in the chair beside his. His mouth tasted like cotton wool, and everything looked warped, like an image in a corrugated mirror. He fell down on his knees when he tried to get off the chair.

Instantly she was all solicitude, helping him get to his feet. She said, "Well, what*ever* happened to you? My husband and I have been taking turns watching over you. We didn't like to call any of the stewards, because—well, because of your position. People talk so on these ships—"

He could feel the drug-dilated pupils of his eyes slowly contract until they were normal again. The lines of the things he looked at resumed their straightness. But even then, the "kicks" wouldn't go away altogether; he had a regular hangover from them. There was cement on his eyelids and it took all the strength he could muster to keep them open. He said surlily: "Where is he? I remember vaguely coming up here with him, leaning on him the whole way—"

She said, "He went below just a few minutes ago, to fix

you up a Bromo-Seltzer. It's just what you need, it'll clear your head marvelously. Come on down with me a minute and let him give it to you.''

He could feel a sense of resentment toward her stir through him, as when you rub a cat's fur the wrong way. Yet she wasn't doing or saying anything to antagonize him. ''Why don't you stay out of my business?'' he blurted out uncontrollably. ''What is this? I never saw you before until tonight—'' And then as though the word *business* had reminded him of something, he stabbed his hand toward his watch pocket, then upward to his breast pocket.

''Did you lose something?'' she asked innocently.

''No,'' he scowled, ''and it's no thanks to myself I didn't, either! I ought to be shot!''

She bared her teeth momentarily at that, as though she found the phrase privately amusing, for some reason of her own.

He stood up abruptly, stalked toward the faintly outlined white staircase leading to the deck below. She came hurrying after him. ''Will you help me down the stairs, please? They're hard for me to manage on these high heels—''

Grudgingly, he cupped his hand to the point of her elbow, guided her down the incline after him. Yet at the contact his antagonism rose to such a pitch it was all he could do to keep from throwing her bodily down past him, to break her neck or back. He took his hand away, jumped clear, to keep from giving in to the impulse, and a moment later she had gained the safety of the lower deck.

He didn't wait. The muscular lethargy that had gripped him was slowly wearing off. Suddenly it broke altogether, and he was normal again. By that time he was hurrying along the inner passageway toward his stateroom, to see to his prisoner. Behind him, like something in a bad dream that couldn't be shaken off, came the rustle and the slither of Mrs. Travis' dress as she followed him.

He unlocked the door, threw it open, turned on the light switch. Belden lay there sound asleep, the covers up over his head, one arm stiffly held in place by the manacle. Fisher let out a deep breath of relief.

Before he could get in and close the door after him, the rustle and the slither had come to a stop directly behind him. He turned his head impatiently. This woman was worse than a burr.

She said, "We're right next door. Won't you stop in a moment and let Mr. Travis give you the Bromo-Seltzer before you retire? He came down specially to mix it for you."

"That's good of him," he said shortly, "but I could get one from the steward just as well." An odor of musk enveloped him, at her nearness. Again his early training intervened in her favor, wouldn't let him slam the door in her face and end her importunities once and for all.

She suddenly reached past him and gently closed the door. "*He's* all right," she purred. "He'll keep a moment longer. He's not running away." She took him by the hand, began to lead him gently but persistently down toward the next foyer.

The contact, as on the stalls just now, again inflamed him with nearly uncontrollable and entirely murderous anger. His hands on her throat. . . . He pulled his hand away, face whitening with the effort to overcome it. "I can walk——"

She threw open her own door, called out loudly: "Hiram, here's Mr. Fisher for that Bromo. Did you mix it yet?"

The stateroom was empty. A cowhide valise had been pulled partly out from under the bed, allowed to remain there with its lid up.

"He's in the bathroom, I guess," she said. She moved unobtrusively around behind Fisher and closed the stateroom door.

A frog-croak from the direction of the bathroom answered, "I'm mixing it now." Fisher glanced over that way. A blurred reflection created a flurry of movement across the mirror panel set in the bath door, which was turned outward into the room.

She distracted his attention by standing in front of him, turning him around toward her, smiling that same saturnine smile that had been on her lips so often tonight.

He gave her a searching look, wary, mistrustful. "There's something about you—" The back of his hand went out and flicked her shoulder. "Where'd you get that dress? All night long it's kept reminding me of—"

"Paris," she said. "It's a Maldonado. . . ." The blur on the mirror panel had become a shadow that lengthened as it crept out over the floor into the room. "See, I'll show you." She turned an edge of the shoulder over, revealed a little silk tab with lettering on it. "Can you read what it says?"

He bent his head, peered intently, off-guard.

I'm Dangerous Tonight

Her arms suddenly flashed around him like white whips, in a death-embrace, pinning his own close to his sides. "Now, Belden, *now!*" he heard her cry.

The lurking shadow in the background sprang forward, closed in. The white oblong of a pillow struck Fisher between the shoulders, as though this were no more than a friendly pillow fight. Then through it came a muffled detonation.

Fisher straightened suddenly, stood there motionless. The woman unclasped her arms, and he collapsed to the floor, lay there at her feet, eyes still open.

From over him came Belden's voice: "Go tell your brother you weren't so hot yourself!"

"Close his eyes," she said. "You've only stunned him!" as though she were talking about some insect.

The pillow fell across him again, and Travis' revolver and Belden's fist plunged into the soft middle of it. There were two more shots. Little goose feathers flew up and settled again. When Belden kicked the scorched pillow aside, Fisher's eyes were closed.

"They don't come any deader than that!" he said.

She was crouched beside the door, listening.

She straightened up finally, murmured triumphantly: "We did it! It could have been champagne corks, or punctured party balloons. Half of them are drunk tonight, anyway!" Her lip curled.

"Let's get going," Belden answered impatiently. "We must be passing the Narrows already. We dock in a couple hours; we want to clear off before they find this guy—"

"All right, get in there and put on Hi's things, while I'm changing out here. Better put on two coats one over the other; he had more of a bulge than you. Turn your collar up around your face and hold a big handkerchief under your nose; you've got a bad cold. I'll pin one of those cloths around your neck like he had. I've got the passports and everything we need."

Belden disappeared into the bath with an armful of Travis' clothing. She stood before the mirror, started to tug at the dress, bring it down off her shoulders. It looped at her waist, fell down to the floor with a slight hiss. She stepped clear of the mystic ring it had formed about her feet, and as she did so the contact between it and her body broke for the first time since ten the night before.

She staggered against the wall, as though some sort of galvanic shock had pushed her. Her mouth opened like a suffocating fish out of water, slowly closed again. She was as limp and as inert as the bullet-riddled man bleeding away on the floor.

Her hands went dazedly up to her hair, roamed distractedly through it, dragging it down about her shoulders. She was just Sarah Travis again, and the long bad dream was over. But darkness didn't give way to light, darkness gave way to perpetual twilight. Something snapped.

She had one more lucid moment. Her eyes found the opened closet door, where some of Travis' things could still be seen hanging on the rack. "Hi," she breathed soundlessly. "My husband." Then she began to shake all over. The shaking became low laughter that at first sounded like sobbing.

Belden came out, in Travis' camel-hair coat, cap pulled down over his eyes. "Are you nearly—? What's the matter, what're you giggling about?"

The laughter rose, became full-bodied, a terrible thing in continuous crescendo.

"I'm getting out of here, if I gotta swim for it!" He could

make it, he told himself; they were far enough up the bay now. And he knew just where to go to lie low, until he could get word to—

The door closed behind him, muffling her paeans of soulless mirth that throbbed there in that place of death.

When the ship's doctor was summoned, shortly after the *Gascony* had docked and lay motionless alongside one of the new piers at the foot of the West Fifties, he found her crouched on her knees like a geisha, back to the wall, one arm extended, pointing crazily to the motionless form lying outstretched on the floor. The rise and fall of her ceaseless wrenching laughter was unbearable.

The doctor shook his head. "Bring a straitjacket," he said tersely. "She's hopelessly insane."

"Is he gone?" they asked, as he examined Fisher.

"Just a matter of minutes," was the answer. "He's punctured like a sieve. Better call an ambulance. Let him do his dying ashore."

Chapter 6
The Chain Snaps

Fisher's nurse at the Mount of Olives Hospital, Miss Wellington, was a pleasant young person with sleek auburn hair and a small rosette of freckles on each polished cheekbone. She wore rimless hexagonal glasses that softened instead of hardening her eyes. She came down the gleaming, sterilized corridor in equally gleaming, sterilized white, carrying a tray containing a glass of milk, a cup of cocoa, and a geranium. Every convalescent's breakfast tray in the hospital always had one flower on it. Miss Wellington remembered, however, that it had had a queer effect on the patient in Room Ten. He had growled he was not dead yet, the last time she had brought one in, and heaved it out of the open window with so much energy that his scars had reopened and begun to bleed again.

Miss Wellington wisely removed it from the tray, hid it in

her uniform pocket, and replaced it with two smuggled cigarettes. Fisher was a favorite of hers; she disliked tractable, submissive patients, and she was something of a philosopher anyway. A hundred years from now it would be all the same whether the poor devil smoked or didn't.

She freed one hand to turn the knob and was about to enter Ten when an alarmed "Hold it! Just a minute!" was shouted at her from inside. Miss Wellington, undeterred, calmly barged right in.

"Oh, so that's it," she remarked, setting the tray down. "And where do you think you're going, young man?"

Fisher was hanging on to the foot of the bed with one hand, to keep his balance, and belting his trousers around his middle with the other. He had on one shoe, one sock, and his hat.

"Listen," he said, "I got a job to do, a report to make, and you can have my bed back. You can keep the slugs you took out of me, too; I'm generous that way."

"You get back there where you belong." She frowned with assumed severity. "D'you realize that they could put a new roof on this entire wing of the building just with the lead that was taken out of you? And there was enough left over to weatherstrip the windows, at that! You don't deserve hospitalization, any of you young huskies, the way you crowd your luck—"

He sat down shakily on the edge of the bed. His knees had gone rubbery. "I certainly don't," he agreed. "Any guy that falls down on his job—what good is he, tell me that? They should have left me where they found me, bleeding to death on the *Gascony*. That's all I had coming to me. That's all I'm worth."

"That's right, cry into your soup," she said. She struck a match, held it for him. "Here, smoke this—on an empty stomach; you've broken every other rule of the place, you may as well go the whole hog."

"You don't know what it means. The men I work with— not to be able to look any of them in the face—to have to go

58

around tagged a failure for the rest of my life. That's all anybody has, Wellington, his pride in his job—''

She sighed. "I guess we'll have to let you go. It's better than having you die on our hands. If we try to keep you here you'll probably pine away. And I'm getting worn to a shadow pushing you back in bed every morning at eight, regularly. I'll get MacKenzie in, have him look you over. Put out that cigarette.''

MacKenzie looked him over, said: "I'd strongly advise you to give it a week more—if I thought it would do any good. But if you're going to be rebellious and mentally depressed about it, it might do you more harm in the long run. There's really no reason for keeping you here any longer, only try to stay off your feet as much as you can—which I know you won't do anyway.''

"Sure, and stay out of drafts,'' Fisher smiled bitterly, "and live to be a hundred. What for?'' He put on his coat and tie. "Where's my gun?''

"You'll have to sign for that downstairs, on your way out.''

At the door he turned and looked around the room, as though he was just seeing it for the first time. "Who paid for all this?''

"Somebody named Trilling.''

Fisher nodded glumly. "He's my boss. Why did he bother?''

MacKenzie and the nurse exchanged a look.

Fisher picked up his hat and walked out, head down, staring at the floor. Along the corridor outside he had to steady himself with one arm against the wall, but he kept going until he'd stumbled into the elevator.

Miss Wellington touched the outside corner of an eye with her finger, stroked downward. "We didn't do that boy any good,'' she murmured. "The bullets were in his soul. Wonder what it'll take to get 'em out?''

At the local FBI headquarters half an hour later Fisher's face was ashen, but not entirely from the effort it had cost him to get there. He stood facing Trilling across the desk, a proffered chair rejected in the background.

"I haven't come to make excuses," he said quietly. "The facts speak for themselves. He got away. I hashed up the job. I let you down. I begged, I pleaded with you to give me the assignment. I not only put you to considerable expense with nothing to show for it; but through me Belden even got back into the country, which he never could have done by himself."

He laid it down before him on the desk. Jealously close to him, though, as if afraid to have it taken from him. "You want this—back?" he said huskily. There was almost a prayer in his eyes.

"I'm sorry," Trilling said, and drew it the rest of the way across the desk. It fell into an open drawer, dropped from sight. "I don't, but Washington does, and I take my instructions from them. They seem to want results. What damned you was not that he got away, but some story about a woman being involved—"

Fisher just stood there, his eyes on the desk where the badge had last been visible. His Adam's apple had gone up just once, and stayed high. After a while, when he could speak again, he said: "Yes, I wonder what that story is, myself. I wonder if I'll ever know."

Trilling had turned his head away from the look on Fisher's face. He was on his way to the door now, his former superior knew. The voice came from farther away. "There's no use standing here," it said. "I never did like a guy that crawled, myself. I guess you know what this means to me, though."

Trilling said, "I ought to. I'm in the same outfit. I'm you—a couple of notches higher up, that's all. Let's not consider this irrevocable, let's just call it temporary. Maybe it will be straightened out in a few months. And again I say, this isn't me. This is word from Washington." He fumbled embarrassedly with a wallet inside his coat pocket. "Fisher, come here a minute—" he said.

But the door had opened already. He heard Fisher say, to no one in particular: "That was my whole life. This is my finish now." The frosted-glass panel ebbed shut almost soundlessly, and his blurred shadow faded slowly away on the outside of it.

Trilling resignedly let the wallet drop back into his pocket. Then he caught sight of a wire wastebasket standing on the floor beside his swivel chair. He delivered a resounding kick at it that sent it into a loop, with the inexplicable remark: "Damn women!"

The honkytonk bartender, who doubled as bouncer, waiter, and cashier, was in no mood to compromise. Mercy was not in him. He came out around the open end of the long counter, waddled threatening across the floor in a sullen, red-faced fury and began to shake the inanimate figure lying across the table with its head bedded on its arms. "Hey, you! Do your sleeping in the gutter!"

If you gave these bums an inch; they took a yard. And this one was a particularly glaring example of the genus barfly. He was in here all the time like this, inhaling smoke and then doing a sunset across the table. He'd been in here since four this afternoon. The boss and he, who were partners in the joint—the bartender called it jernt—would have been the last ones to claim they were running a Rainbow Room, but at least they were trying to give the place a *little* class, keep it above the level of a Bowery smokehouse; they even paid a guy to pound the piano and a canary to warble three times a week. And then bums like this had to show up and give the place a bad look!

He shook the recumbent figure again, more roughly than the first time. Shook him so violently that the whole reedy table under him rattled and threatened to collapse. "Come on, clear out, I said! Pay me for what you had and get outa here!"

The figure raised an unshaven face from between its arms, looked at him, said something.

The bartender raised his voice to a bellow, perhaps to bolster his courage. There had been a spark of something in that look. Just a spark, no more, but it had been there. "Oh, so you haven't got any money! So you think you can come in here, do your drinking on the cuff, and get away with it! Well, I'll show you what we do to bums that try that!''

He gripped the figure by his coat collar, took a half-turn in it, brought him erect and held him that way, half-strangled. Then, treacherously, he began to pump short jabs into the man's unguarded face, the muscles of his great beefy arm tightening and pulling like knotted ropes. Blood came, but the man couldn't fall; he was held tight by the nape of the neck. Heads in a long row down the bar turned to watch in idle amusement; not a hand was lifted to help him.

Then something happened. The bartender was suddenly floundering back against the opposite wall, the line of his jaw white at first, then turning a bruised red. He held it, steadied himself against the wall, spat out pieces of tooth enamel. The figure across the way—the width of the narrow room separated them now—was holding on to an edge of the table for support, acting as though he'd fall down in another minute. He was holding not his face where the barman had pummeled him, but his chest, as if something hurt him there.

The bartender shrieked, "You will, will ya? Sock me, will ya? *Now* ya gonna get it! *Now* I'll cut ya to *pieces!*'' He reached behind the bar, caught up an empty bottle from one of the lower shelves. Liquor dispensaries are supposed to break their bottles once they're emptied. This was the kind of place that didn't.

He gripped the bottle by the neck, cracked the bottom of it against the bar so that it fell off, advanced murderously upon his victim with the jagged sharp-toothed remainder in his hand for a weapon. And even yet, no one in the place made a move to interfere. He was only a bum; what difference did it make what happened to him?

The bum made no move to try to bolt for the door and get out of the place. Perhaps he sensed an outstretched leg would trip him if he tried it. Perhaps he was unequal to the effort. Perhaps he didn't care. He even smiled a little, adding fuel to the blazing fire of the bartender's cowardly rage. "Matter, can't you use your hands?''

The bartender poised the vicious implement, to thrust it full in his face, grind it around, maim and maybe kill him.

And then sudddenly a girl stood in between them, as though she had dropped from the ceiling. No one had seen where she had come from. A beautiful girl, shabbily dressed. Cheap little blouse and threadbare skirt; golden hair like an angel's, cascading out from under a round woolen cap such as boys wear for skating. She set down the little black dressing case she'd brought out of the back room with her, caught the bartender's thick wrist in her slim fingers, pushed it back.

"Put that down, Mike!" she said in a cold, angry voice. "Let this man alone!"

The bartender, towering over her five feet four of determination, shouted wrathfully: "What do you know about it? He's a bum, and he's going to get what's coming to him! You stick to your canarying and I'll handle the front room here!"

Her voice was like a whip. "He's not a bum. You're the bum. So much of a bum that you can't tell the difference anymore! *I* still can, thank heavens, and I'm going to get out of here for good before I lose the ability to distinguish!"

The bartender retreated a step or two, put the shattered bottle shamefacedly behind his back. A sallow-complected, chunky man, with his hair all greasy ringlets, was standing at the entrance to the inner room. The girl turned her head toward him briefly. "Find someone else to do your canarying, Angelo. I'm not showing up Wednesday." She faced the bartender again. "How much does he owe you?"

The latter had had all the ground cut away around him. "Couple dollars," he mumbled indistinctly. "He's been riding along all evenin'—"

She snapped open a ridiculous little envelope-sized bag. There were five dollars in it; she'd just been paid tonight. She took two of them out. She didn't hand them to him, she dropped them disdainfully on the floor before him, with a million dollars' worth of contempt.

Somewhere in back of her, Fisher spoke. "Let him use the

bottle. You're only pushing me down a step lower, doing this.''

She said without turning her head. "You're sick. Your mind's sick. I've watched you every night. No one's pushing you down, you're pushing yourself down.''

The ringleted man in the doorway said, "Don't do this, Joan, what's matter with you? Why you quit?''

She didn't answer. She picked up the kit bag standing at her feet, put two fingers behind Fisher's seedy coat sleeve, said: "Come on, shall we? We don't belong in here—either of us.''

Behind them, as they went out into the darkness side by side, the crestfallen bartender was saying to anyone who would give him an ear: "She must be crazy, she don't even know the guy, never saw him before!" And then with a guilty look at his partner: "She was the best singer we ever had in here too.''

A block away they stopped, in the ghostly light of an arc lamp. He turned toward her. "A man doesn't thank a woman for doing a thing like that,'' he blurted out. "That was the finishing touch you gave me in there just now. Hiding behind your skirts. Letting you buy them off for me.''

She said, almost impatiently, "You're so easy to see through! Looking at you, listening to you, almost I know your whole story—without actually knowing any of it. A code is doing this to you. A code of your own that you've violated, or think you have. You'll go down under its weight, let it push you down into what that mug mistook you for. But you won't, you can't slur its weight and responsibility off you.'' She shrugged as though that was all there was to be said. "Well, aren't you worth saving—from bottle glass?''

He smiled derisively.

She went on, "You didn't see me slowly walking around that inside room with my mouth open, from table to table, three nights this past week. You didn't hear me. But I saw you. I watched you through the cheap music. You sat there at that little table just outside the door, looking my way but seeing ghosts. Your eyes were the only ones in the place turned inward. You drank until your head fell down, but you weren't drunk—you couldn't get drunk.''

She picked up the little kit that contained her costume, made to move on once more. ''My name's Joan Blaine,'' she said, ''and I like people with personal codes, because I've got one, too. But handle it right. Don't go down under it; make it push you, lift you up, instead. Come back with me awhile and I'll make you a cup of coffee. I can see that you've been ill recently, and you've probably been sleeping around on park benches lately.''

He moved weakly after her, shaking his head. ''You're a funny girl. How do you know I won't turn on you, rob you, maybe even murder you?''

''Faces don't lie,'' she answered. ''Why didn't you run out with your tail between your legs when he came at you with the bottle? A real bum would have. You faced him, hardly able to stand up. Besides, *some*thing, *some*one's, got to come out right for me.''

''Most of it didn't?'' he said, in the pitiful little threadbare room, with its single flyblown bulb, its white-painted cot with the iron showing through.

''Most of it didn't.'' She handed him a chipped cup of steaming black coffee. ''I didn't come to New York to sing in a Third Avenue honkytonk at five dollars a throw. You'll never know how many tears and busted hopes this room of mine has seen. I was letting it get me down, too. The sight of you pulled me up short. That's why I quit my job so easily just now. Don't blame yourself for that. You've helped me, and perhaps I'm going to be able to help you before I'm through. Fisher—that what you said your name was?—you're going back and tackle this thing that threw you, all over again.''

''Yeah,'' he said slowly. ''Yeah, I am.'' There was a steely glint in his eyes that hadn't been there before. ''It isn't over. Why didn't I see that before? Just round one is over. But round one's never the whole fight. Even though I'm on my own now—''

She didn't ask him what he meant. "Then the credit and the glory'll be all your own too; look at it that way."

"I'm not doing it for the credit and the glory. I'm doing it because it was my job, and I can't find rest or peace until my job is done. And even though it's been taken away from me, I'll see it through—no matter what—!" He balled a fist and swung it with terrific emphasis around him where the shadows had been. Shadows that a man could fight, even though he couldn't understand them.

She smiled as though she'd gained her secret point. "All right, then," she said. "Tonight—there's a vacant room, little more than an attic, over me. Without a stick of furniture in it, without even a lock on the door. I'm going to give you one of the blankets from my bed, and you roll yourself up in it on the floor up there. No one needs to know. Tomorrow you and I are going out. You're going to get a shave and a necktie, and you're going after this thing that threw you, whatever it is. And I'm going to find the kind of a singing job I came to New York for, and lick it to a standstill when I do! Tomorrow—the world starts over for both of us, brand-new."

He looked at her and he said once more what he'd said out on the street: "You're a funny girl. But a lovely one, too."

It didn't work itself out in no time at all, in an hour or a day or even a week; it never does. He'd slipped further down than he'd realized, and there were certain realities to be met first of all—to keep his head above water; to keep a roof over his head; to get his gun back out of hock. But he had to have money. He wasn't on the Bureau's payroll any more. So to have money he had to have a job. He knew he could have gone to Trilling or any of the other men that had worked with him, and written his own ticket. But his pride wouldn't let him. He would have worked for nothing, without salary, but—"Washington wants results," Trilling had said. He would have swept streets, waded through the filth of sewers, if only he could have had one thing back again—that little metal disk that had dropped so emphatically from the desktop into a drawer that day, pulling the sun and the moon and the stars down out of his sky after it.

So he sought Sixth Avenue and the melancholy Help Wanted cards tacked up so thickly on its doorways, that usually mean only an unproductive agency fee. There was plenty that he could do—an agent's training is nothing if not painstaking—but most of it was highly specialized and in the upper brackets; there seemed to be more demand for waiters and dishwashers along here than for dead shots or jujitsu experts.

As he moved from knot to knot of dejected employment seekers gathered before each doorway to scan the cards, he became aware of a face that seemed to keep up with his own migrations from group to group. Which was not unusual in itself, since scores of people were moving along in the same direction he was. But this particular man seemed to be studying him rather than the employment cards. Was it somebody who had recognized him from the old days, when he was with the Bureau? Fisher had a good memory for faces. He studied the man stealthily at first—he was a slimy, furtive-looking customer; but his clothes were both flashy and expensive. Fisher took care to keep his glance perfectly expressionless, to see if he could get the man to tip his hand. The man returned the look in a sort of questioning way, as though he were trying to ask him something.

Fisher took a chance, gave his head a slight nod in the affirmative. The man instantly left the group, strolled slowly on for a few yards, then halted with his back to the window of an empty store, obviously waiting for Fisher to join him.

Fisher moved as he had moved, with seeming aimlessness and unconcern, and stopped by him. The man turned his head the other way, away from him, then spoke through motionless lips even while he did so.

"Could you use any?"

Fisher understood instantly. A peddler, the lowest cog in that devil's hierarchy whose source of supply had been Belden, and whose capstone was lost somewhere in the nebulous clouds overhead. There had been a day when Fisher had hoped that pulling Belden out from under would bring the top man toppling within reach; that hope had been blasted. Fisher had to start over, single-handed now, at the lowest pier of the structure, work his way up. This slimy individual who tramped Sixth Avenue pavements probably no more knew who the ringleader was than Fisher did himself. But he was a means to an end.

Fisher understood the reason for the mistake the peddler had made, that only a short while before would have been so irretrievable. But then only a short while before, it wouldn't have been made. Now he, Fisher, still had the telltale pallor and gauntness of his wounds and hospitalization. A misleading pallor, coupled with a suit whose cut suggested that he was not altogether penniless. So the peddler had jumped to the wrong conclusion. But then if anything backfired, the could-you-use-any gag could always be switched to shoelaces, razor blades, or anything equally harmless. Fisher knew many peddlers carried just such articles around with them in their pockets, just for an out. They never had the real thing; peddlers always traveled clean, to guard against sudden seizure and search. A second appointment was always necessary, no matter how well known both parties were to each other.

He answered the surreptitious question in a manner equally covert. "I could," he said, and saw to it that his hand trembled unnecessarily as he lit a cigarette. That wasn't wasted on the peddler.

"Who's been handing it to you?" he said. "I never saw you before."

Fisher pulled a name out of his mental card index as you do a card in a card trick. Someone that he knew had been rounded up while he was in Paris, was in a federal pen now. "Revolving Larry," he said.

"He's at the Boardinghouse. So are half the others," the man told him. "What's your dish?"

Fisher knew the different underworld abbreviations for the deadly stuff—usually a single letter. "C," he said promptly.

"We're getting forty for it now. The lid went down something fierce six months ago."

Fisher whistled. "I'll never make it."

"That's what they all say. Ain't you got some gold teeth in your mouth or something?" Then he relented a little. "I'll get it for you for thirty-five, bein' you're an old buyer of Larry's."

Things must be pretty tough, Fisher knew, for it to come to that; Trilling and the rest must be doing a grand job. Only he—he alone—had fumbled.

"I'll raise it somehow," he said. Ironically enough, he wasn't any too certain of being able to. Which was just the right attitude; too ready a supply of money would have immediately raised the other's suspicions.

"Go to Zillick's down the block. It has three booths at the back. Go in the middle one and wait. When you lamp me turning the pages of the directory outside, shove your money in the return-coin slot and walk out. Take it easy. Don't let the druggist see you. Your stuff'll be there when you get back for it. If you're even a dime short don't show up, it won't do ya no good. Twelve o'clock tonight."

"Twelve o'clock," Fisher agreed.

They separated. How many a seemingly casual street-corner conversation like that on the city's streets has just such an unguessed, sinister topic. Murder, theft, revenge, narcotics. While the crowd goes by around it unaware.

He didn't have thirty-five dollars. Go to Trilling or any of the others for it he could not and would not. Not because of any possible risk attached—he'd played and looked his part too well just now for the peddler to bother keeping him under observation.

He'd looked his part *too* well—that gave him the answer. He went back to the Mount of Olives, asked for MacKenzie. "So you want to borrow a hundred dollars?" MacKenzie said. He insisted on giving him a thorough physical examination first, as part of the bargain. Probably figuring it was the only way he could have got Fisher to submit to one. The results didn't seem to please him any too much.

"What've you been doing to yourself?" he snapped. "Not

eating, and by the looks of you— See here, Fisher, if this is for liquor, you don't get it." -

Fisher wondered what he'd have said if he knew what part of it was actually to be for. He said, "If it was for that, why would I have to have a hundred? Ten would be enough. I don't go around giving my word of honor these days. All I can say is, it's not for liquor."

"That's sufficient," MacKenzie said briskly, and counted out the money. "For Pete's sake, soak a fin of it into a good thick steak. And don't be in any hurry about returning it. You working?"

Fisher smiled. "I'm starting to again—tonight at twelve." The full story of how he had been shot on the *Gascony* had of course never been divulged—either at the hospital or to the newspapers. Trilling had seen to the former, the Compagnie Transatlantique to the latter.

Wellington, who had been in the room watching him closely, said after he had gone: "He's had a close shave, but it looks like somebody's beginning to probe for those bullets in his soul I spoke about."

"I think you love the guy," MacKenzie said testily, perhaps to get the fact that he'd loaned a hundred dollars out of his system.

"Sure I do," was the defiant reply. "You just finding out? I love every slug we ever took out of him, but what good does it do? He doesn't know a woman from a fire hydrant."

But he was beginning to, even if he didn't know it himself yet. There was a difference to Joan's knock on his room door that evening, as though she too had had a break that day. It was the twenty-third day after they'd met in the honkytonk. He had his gun out, was sitting there cleaning it and going over it lovingly. It was like a part of him. He'd got it out about an hour before, with part of the hundred. He jumped nervously, thrust it out of sight under his mattress. The door of his room didn't have a lock yet, but she wasn't the kind who would walk in on him, luckily, or she might have wondered, jumped to the wrong conclusions. He hadn't told her anything about himself yet, out of old habit and training that died hard. What he'd been, nor what it was that had thrown him. He'd tell her everything when—and if—the second payoff came. And he had a long way to go yet before he reached that. Until then—

He went over and opened the door. She was standing there glowing. It always surprised him all over again, each time he looked at her, how beautiful she really was. Blond hair, blue eyes, and all the rest; somehow it all blended together into a gem. But that was for other men, not for his business. A shield in Trilling's desk drawer—that was *his* gem.

She said, "I brought in a can of spaghetti with me. Come on down. I've got news for you." And down in her room, while he pumped a can opener up and down and—of course— gashed his knuckle, she asked: "What luck?"

"I'm on my way, that all I can say."

"Great. Looks like I am too. It's been on the fire for several weeks now, but I'm superstitious; I didn't want to say anything for fear I'd jinx it. Some fellow—he's new to show business—is opening up a roadhouse tomorrow night. He has a spot for a specialty singer. Lots of backing and he doesn't care what he pays for his talent. I've already auditioned for him three separate times; I'm beginning to wonder if it's my voice he's interested in or if he just likes to have me around. He's not using a floor show, you see—just a band, and a combination singer and hostess. So by tomorrow I'll know definitely whether I've clicked or not."

"You'll click," he assured her, "unless the guy's stone blind."

She opened her mouth in pretended amazement. "The great block of ice is actually beginning to thaw!"

Chapter 8
Hot Spot

The phone booth was cramped and stuffy, so small that the pane of glass kept clouding with his breath. He cleared it off each time with the point of his elbow, holding a dead receiver to his ear for a stall. At 12:10 the peddler was suddenly standing there at the little rack outside, wetting his thumb as he busily flicked the leaves of a city directory. He didn't look up.

Fisher took out the three tens and a five he'd prepared, wedged them tightly into the return-coin slot. He came out, walked by to the front of the store, lingered there by the door. The peddler seemed to find the elusive number he was looking for just then, went into the booth, came out again a moment later, and brushed by Fisher without so much as a glance.

It wasn't really necessary for Fisher to have the little package that was back there in the booth now. This was not a decoy sale for the purpose of getting enough evidence to make an arrest. Fisher no longer had the authority to make an arrest, and even if he did have, he lacked witnesses. But he retrieved the packet nevertheless, to prevent its falling into the hands of some innocent person. He pocketed it and turned the corner in the same direction the peddler had.

Fisher walked on, then turned to glance quickly over his shoulder.

The peddler was still in full sight. Fisher plunged into the nearest doorway, lingered a moment, and came out—not exactly disguised but with a sufficiently altered silhouette to be mistaken for someone else at a great enough distance along the dimly lighted streets. His snugly buttoned coat was open now, hanging loosely from the shoulders; instead of being bareheaded he had a disreputable felt hat jammed down on his head. A pair of heavily outlined but lensless eyeglass frames were stuck around his ears. He set out after the distant figure using a purposely altered gait and body carriage.

When he returned to his room at three that morning, he knew where this minor bird of prey lived, what his name was. What remained to be found out was where and to whom he turned over the accrued profits of his transactions. That was tomorrow's job, for the peddler had made no further sales that night after leaving Fisher. Undressing, he left the little sealed packet in his coat pocket. It was probably three-quarters bicarbonate of soda, anyway.

He didn't see Joan in the morning, but he knew she had performed her usual self-imposed chore of brushing his suit before leaving, for it was neatly folded across the back of a chair just inside the door. He went back to where he had left off last night, resumed his vigil on the street corner near the peddler's room. They were ripping up car tracks on that street, and the presence of the WPA workers covered him beautifully. He dawdled on the curb, coatless, smoking and chatting with them, indistinguishable from the rest to a casual observer. Occasionally one would go out to the middle and strike a few lethargic blows with a pickax, very occasionally.

It was well past midnight again when he wearily climbed the rooming-house stairs, but the day hadn't been wasted. He knew now where the peddler forked over his intake, where he secured his stuff. He was creeping back up the ladder again, at least as high as when they'd sent him over after Belden.

There was a dim light still on behind Joan's door and he thought he heard a sound like muffled sobbing coming from inside as he went by. Her hopes of landing the job she had spoken of must have been dashed, the thing must have fallen through. He stopped and rapped lightly, thinking he might be able to cheer her up.

She didn't open for a minute or two. Then when she did, her eyes were bright and hard, like mica. She didn't smile.

"Did you land the spot?" he asked tentatively.

To his surprise she nodded, almost indifferently. "Yes," she said coldly, looking him up and down as though she'd never seen him before. "I signed the contract this afternoon."

"You don't act very happy about it," he remarked uncertainly.

It was obvious something had happened to change her. "Don't I?" she said hostilely, and prepared to close the door in his face.

He threw out his hand and held the door open. "What's the matter, Joan? What's the rub? I thought I heard you crying just now—"

She flared up at that. "Don't kid yourself, mister!" she cried bitterly. "I don't waste my time crying over—over snowbirds!"

"So that's it!" He forced his way into the room, closed the door behind him.

She kept her back turned to him. "Go ahead; lie about it! Say that what I found in your coat pocket this morning was sugar to feed the horses, or chemical to develop films! Go ahead, alibi, why don't you?"

"No, it isn't," he said grimly, "it's cocaine. Now you listen to me, you little fool!" He caught her by the shoulders and swung her around to face him, and none too gently. "If you were a man I'd part your teeth in the middle—"

There were tears in her eyes again, tears of rage. "This crazy town's got to quit playing tricks on me! I can't take it anymore! No wonder something threw you, no wonder something got you down! And I wasted my time feeling sorry for you—"

"I wasn't going to tell you," he said, "but if you're going to go around making noises like a kitten left out in the rain, then here goes. I was a Department of Justice agent. We were cracking down on the ring that imports and sells this stuff. They waylaid my kid brother, got him alone and unarmed, and shot him down like a dog. I got myself put on that job—I was in Texas going after marijuana smugglers at the time—I followed the man that did it to Paris. I got him, and I started back with him. What happened is too long a story to go into now. I made the worst hash of the assignment that anyone could make. He got away from me almost in sight of the dock, left me for dead. My badge was taken away from me. That was the thing that got me, that had me down when I first met you. I'm trying to come back now, trying to lick the thing single-handed. I bought that stuff you found in my pocket purposely, from a peddler, as a means toward an end. Through him maybe I can get to the higher-ups."

He glared at her. "Now you either take that or leave it. I'm not going to back it up with papers and documents—to try to convince you. Believe it or not as you choose."

He could tell by her face she did. It was radiant again. "I might have known you had some perfectly good reason. The mere fact that what I found hadn't been opened— Why, I remember reading about your brother. It was in all the papers the day I first came to New York; it had happened that very day. Fisher, the lady begs your pardon."

"The lady's going to make some guy a hell of a wife," he assured her grumpily, "the way she goes through pockets. Now tell me about yourself."

She had the signed contract right there with her. Six weeks at fifty a week, and, if she went over, it would be renewed for another six at seventy-five. Graham was the man's name, and the formal opening was set for tomorrow night. Luckily she wouldn't have to rehearse much; she was using most of the same numbers she had at the Third Avenue place, only one new one. She had to supply her own costumes, she rattled on, that was the only part of it she didn't like. And, oh yes, it was a little out of the way, hard to get to, but she supposed she'd get used to that. Chanticler was what they were going to call it, and they had a great big rooster set up on the grounds, outlined in electric lights, and fixed so that its head swung back and forth and it seemed to be crowing—

She broke off short, stared at him. "What are you looking at me like that for? You're all—white."

He said in a strained voice, "In Westchester? Just within sight of the Sound? A low white rambling place?"

"Yes, but how did you—?"

"I followed that peddler there and back today. On the return trip he was carrying several little parcels he hadn't had when he went in. I suppose if they'd been examined, they'd have been found to be samples of favors and noisemakers for the festivities. He poses as a toy and novelty maker. You've signed on as singer and hostess at what's really a dope-ring headquarters."

They were very still for a while. Finally she said, in a small scared voice: "What shall I do, Frank?" She'd never called him by his given name until now. "How'll I get out of it? I can't—really I can't."

"You take the job anyway," he told her. "Nothing'll happen to you, you'll be all right. They're just using you, and the electric-lighted rooster, and the white rambling road-house, as a front. If you back out now, after wanting the job as badly as you did, you may be endangering yourself. It's safer if you go through with it. Besides, I'm going to be there—tomorrow night— within call of your voice."

She went white herself this time. "But suppose they recognize you?"

"It'll be a ticklish spot," he admitted, "but it's a risk I've got to take. Trilling never exactly handed out publicity photos of any of us around town, so I'm probably safe enough. Belden would be the only one would know me, and I hope he does!"

"But you're not going to walk in there alone, are you?"

"Certainly I'm going alone. I have to. I haven't been assigned to go there, because I'm not a member of the Department anymore, and accordingly I can't ask it to back me up. I'll either bring them this Graham, and Belden and the rest of the outfit too, or I'll end up a grease spot on one of the Chanticler's tablecloths."

She said, with almost comic plaintiveness, resting her hand on his arm, "Try not to be a grease spot, Frank, I—I like you the way you are!"

At the door he said, "I'll see you there, then, tomorrow night. Don't let on you know me; try not to act nervous when you see me, or you'll give me away. Little things like that count. I know I can depend on you." He smiled, and faked a fist, and touched her lightly on the chin with it. "My life is in your hands, pretty lady."

She said, "I had my costumes sent up there ahead, to the dressing room. My agent's smart as a whip, he dug up some notice about an auction sale they were having—the wardrobe of some wealthy Iowa woman who went out of her mind and had to be committed to an asylum. I went there today and picked up just what I was looking for, for that new number I spoke of, and dirt-cheap. Wait'll you see, you won't know me in it."

* * *

Ginger ale, the little gilt-edged folder said, was a dollar a bottle. You had to pay five dollars just to sit down, anyway, whether you ordered anything or not. Fisher'd had to pay an additional ten, at the door just now, to get a table at all, because he wasn't known. Twenty dollars to rent the dinner jacket he had on, five dollars for cab fare to get out here—and oh yes, twenty-five cents for the crisp little white carnation in his buttonhole. He smiled a little when he thought of the old days and the quizzical look Trilling's face would have worn if he'd sent him in an expense account like that. When tonight was over the only coin he'd have left would be the six bullets in the gun under his arm. He hoped tonight would bring him something; he didn't see how he could come back again in a hurry.

He was up to his old tricks again—and it felt swell, like a horse must feel when it's back between the wagon shafts—staring idly down at the little silver gas beads in his ginger-ale glass, yet not missing a thing that went on all over the big overcrowded room.

They were drinking champagne, and most of them, he could sense, were just casual revelers, drawn here unwittingly to front for Graham, to aid a cause they would have shuddered at. Graham must have decided it was high time he had some enterprise to which he could safely ascribe the money he pulled out of the air—if he was suddenly pinned down. Awkward to be raking in money hand over fist and not be able to explain what it was derived from. By the looks of this place tonight, and the prices they were charging, he needn't worry; it could account for a big slice of his profits, with just a little juggling of the books. And it made a swell depot and distribution center, Fisher could see that with one eye closed.

That gigantic electrically outlined rooster outside, for instance, that towered high above the roof of the building, must be visible far up and down the Sound on the darkest night. It could come in handy as a signal and beacon for, say, small launches making shore from larger ships further out, sinister tramps and freighters from Marseilles or Istanbul, with cargoes of dream-death.

What gave the whole plan away to him, what showed that it was meant for something more than just a wayside ad to motorists going by on the Post Road, was that the sign was unnecessarily outlined in bulbs on *both* sides, the side that faced landward, and the side that faced the building—and the Sound. The people around him didn't need to be told where they were, they knew it already. He had a good view of the sign from where he was sitting, through a ceiling-tall French window. The side that faced outward toward the highway was illumined in dazzling white bulbs, the side that faced the building—and dwarfed it— was in red. Red, the color that means *Stop—Danger*. White, the color that means *All Clear—Go ahead*.

Here and there, spotted about the room, were quiet watchful individuals, whose smiles were a little strained, whose laughter rang false. . . . They sat and minded their own business, while the rest of the guests raised the roof. They kept their heads slightly lowered, making geometric arrangements with the silverware or drawing designs on the tablecloths; they were taut, waiting for something.

Ten of them in all—no more than two at the same table. And no fizz at those tables, just black coffee and dozens, scores of cigarettes, chain-lighted, one from the last.

That stocky man standing beaming just inside the main door must be Graham, for he had an air of proud ownership, and he looked everyone over that came in, and twice Fisher had seen the maître d'hôtel step up to him for unobtrusive instructions.

Suddenly the lights went down all over the place; the lighted rooster outside peered ruddily through the window outlines. People shifted expectantly in their chairs. Fisher murmured to himself: "Here she comes now. What a chance I'd be taking, if I didn't know I could count on her!"

He settled back.

There was a rolling buildup from the drums. Twin spotlights, one red, one green, leaped across the polished floor, found the door at the rear that led to the dressing room. Joan stepped out into the green spot, and a gasp of appreciation went all around the big silent place.

Chapter 8
When Satan Sings

He thought he'd never seen anything, anyone, so weirdly beautiful in his life before. But something like a galvanic shock had gone through him just now, had all but lifted him an inch above his chair for a moment. As though some forgotten chord of memory had been touched just then. Something about Joan reminded him of someone else, made him think he was seeing someone else. Before his eyes, a ghost from the past came to life and walked about in full sight.

Wait, that French mannequin, Belden's girl in Paris—that was it! No—that woman on the *Gascony*, that Mrs. Travis, that was who it was! But could it be both? And yet it seemed to be both. Stranger still, Joan didn't look in the least like either one of them, not even at this moment.

The red spot remained vacant, yet followed her around the room; the idea—and a fairly clever one at that—being that it contained the invisible tempter whom she addressed in her song, over her shoulder.

Slowly she circled the room from table to table, filling the place with her rich, lovely voice, making playful motions of warding off, equally playful ones of leading on. Then as she reached Fisher's table, suddenly she wasn't playful any more. She stiffened, seemed to glare; there was a noticeable break in her song.

The perimeter of the green spotlight fell across him too, revealed his face like a mask. He smiled up at her a little, admiringly, encouragingly. She answered—and yet there seemed to be menace, malice, in the parody of a smile that pulled her lips back clear of her teeth more like a snarl than anything else. Unaccountably he could feel the hairs at the back of his neck bristling. . . .

"Get Thee Behind Me, Satan—
Stay where you are, it's too late!"

Her bell-like voice, singing the Irving Berlin tune, throbbed down upon him; but its tone wasn't silver any more, it was bronze, harsh and clanging. He could see her bosom moving up and down, as though rage and fury were boiling in it.

She started to move backward toward the door by which she had entered, bowing to the thunderous applause that crashed out. But her eyes never once left his face as she did so. They were beady and hard and merciless. And that smile was still on her face, that grimace of derision and spite and undying hostility.

The lights flared up and as she stood there a moment by the exit door; her eyes finally left his face to travel the length of the room to the opposite doorway. He followed their direction, and saw Graham over there, pounding his pudgy hands together to show that he liked her.

Fisher looked back to her just in time to catch the beckoning toss of the head she sent Graham's away. Then she slipped through the door.

It was so obvious what that signal meant, and yet he couldn't believe it. No, not Joan. She wanted to ask Graham's advice about an encore; something like that, that was all. For more thoroughly than he realized, he had, in Nurse Wellington's words, learned the difference between a woman and a fire hydrant these past few weeks, and he couldn't unlearn it all in a flash, couldn't teach himself to mistrust something he had learned to trust—any more than Belden could have in Paris, or Travis on the boat. Men's loyalty to their women dies hard—and almost always too late.

Graham was making his way around the perimeter of the room, to follow her back to her dressing room where she had called him. The background music kept on vamping, waiting for her to return and pick up her cue. A pale pink and a faint green ghost of the spotlights hovered there by the door, ready to leap out into full strength again as soon as the house lights went down.

The quiet, sullen men he'd noticed before didn't move their palms, their heads or their eyes. One of them glanced at his wristwatch, without raising his arm. One of the gaudy women with them yawned in boredom. Outside, the rooster's red beak kept opening, closing, as its head and neck wavered back and forth, current passing from one circuit of lights to another, then back again.

Fisher kept pinching the bridge of his nose, groping, baffled. Why had Joan reminded him of two other women—one dead, one vanished into limbo—as she stood before his table a moment ago? Why had he thought he was seeing Mimi Brissard, and the Travis woman, when she didn't in the slightest resemble either one of them physically? Nor had they resembled each other either, for that matter. Why had she seemed to be evil incarnate, the spirit of all wickedness, when he knew her to be just the opposite? It was more than just clever acting to go with her song; the very pores of his skin had seemed to exude her animosity, her baleful hatred. They couldn't be mistaken; that was an instinct going far back beyond man's reasoning power to the jungle ages.

Only a very few seconds went by; how hurried her whispers to Graham out there must have been! Graham came out again, sideways, his head still turned to where she must be standing, unseen behind the door. His face was whiter than it had seemed just now. His glance, as he turned to face the room again, arched over Fisher, purposely avoiding looking at him directly. He didn't return to where he had been. He went casually to the nearest table where a group of those silent, waiting men was. He lingered a moment, then moved on to another table. The flamboyant woman who had been the tablemate of the man he had spoken to stirred, got up, moved slowly toward the entrance as though she had been told to leave. Her companion kept his eyes lowered; but as the woman neared the door she couldn't resist throwing a casual little look over at Fisher.

He didn't see it. Graham had signaled the band, and Joan had come back. The lights went down again and Graham's movements, and the mass exodus of the lady friends of the "deep thinkers," were concealed by the darkness, while she sang.

She started her routine in reverse this time, began at Fisher's table instead of going around the other way and ending up at it. Began, yet ended there too, for she didn't move on, stayed there by him while the sultry, husky song enveloped him.

He sat there motionless, while she moved in closer, came around the table to his side. Slowly her bare arm slipped caressingly around his shoulder, inched affectionately down the satin-faced lapel toying with the white carnation in his buttonhole.

And again Fisher saw Mimi Brissard writhe her snakelike way up the stone steps of the Bal au Diable, the tiny little train wriggling after her—saw her stop and look back at him after she had betrayed her man. Again the heady, musk perfume of Mrs. Travis was in his nostrils; she seemed to stand beside him in the *Gascony's* deck. . . . Was he going crazy? Had those bullets done something to his mind? Was it just the colors of the dress—red and black—the cut of it—or was it something more?

The caressing hand had traveled a little lower than the flower now, was turning insinuatingly in under his coat. And the audience chuckled, thinking she was pretending to be a gold-digger, playfully pretending to pick his pocket. There was a momentary break in the spotlight beam, as though the switch had been thrown off then on again. For an instant or so they were blacked-out, he and Joan. Then the green glare came on again. Her hand wasn't inside his jacket anymore, it was held stiffly behind her back, hidden from the room at large. A white shirtfront gleamed there in the dimness as Graham approached her from behind, then ebbed away into the dimness again.

Fisher's hand reached upward, came to rest on her shoulder. He touched the fabric of her gown. A surge of unreasoning hatred welled through him. That too seemed to be a memory out of the past. He remembered doing this, turning his hand back like this, turning the lining of a gown—

She tried to pull away, and he held her fast. The shoulder of her dressed turned over as he pulled, and on it was a little silk cachet. In the flickering green light he made out dim lettering:

I'm Dangerous Tonight—Maldonado, Paris.

The yell that came from his throat drowned out the music, silenced it. His chair reeled backward with a crash, and he was erect, facing her. "It's the same one!" they heard him shout. "*Now* I know! *Now* at last—!"

The green spot sputtered out. The lights flared up. People jumped to their feet all over the room, staring petrified at the incredible sight taking place there in full view of everyone. For the man the girl had been teasing seemed to have gone suddenly mad, was growling like a hydrophobic dog, tearing, clawing at her gown. It came off in long, brutally severed tatters, revealing strips of white skin that grew and grew before their very eyes, until suddenly she stood there all but nude, trembling, statuelike.

They were shouting: "Stop him! He's crazy. . . !" But a mad, panic-stricken rush for the door had started on the part of all the other celebrants that couldn't be stemmed, that hampered those who were trying to reach the attacker and his victim. Other women were screaming while their men pushed and jostled, trying to clear a way for them.

She alone hadn't screamed through the whole thing. She stood there facing him quietly now, given a moment's grace while Graham and all his silent men tried to force their way to them.

He took his coat off and threw it around her. The tattered remnants of the dress lay on the floor behind her. There was a look on her face impossible to describe—the stare of a sleep-walker suddenly awakened—then she let out a low, fearful cry.

"I've betrayed you, Frank! I've killed you. I told them what you were—and what you were here for—"

His hand instinctively jabbed toward his exposed shoulder holster. It swayed empty at his touch.

"I took that too," she gasped, "while I was singing—I gave it to Graham just now—"

She was suddenly thrust aside, and they were ringed about him—ten of them and Graham, their guns bared and thrusting into his body.

Outside, the enormous rooster was slowly pivoting on its base, turning its white-lighted side inward, toward the roadhouse—and the Sound. White—that meant *All Clear—go ahead.* Far across the water sounded the faint bleat of a steamer's whistle, two short ones and a long one, that seemed to end in a question mark: "*Pip? Pip? Peep?* Are you ready?" Some lone nightbound vessel, furtively prowling these inner waters of the Sound instead of sticking to the ship lane that led up through the Narrows.

"No, not in here."

Graham's crisp command stopped death, forced it back from the very muzzles of ten guns. "Take him out where he can get the right treatment," he said and grinned a little.

Through the encircling ring of his enemies Fisher had eyes for only one thing—the face of the girl who had done this to him. She was wavering there in the background, like a sick, tormented creature, his coat still around her. He saw her clasp her hands, hold them out toward him in supplication, unseen by all the others. As though trying to ask for pardon. The coat slipped off her shoulders, fell unheeded to the floor.

He stared at her without emotion. She might have been a stone or a tree stump. She was beneath his anger. To them, scathingly, he said: "Well, get it over with. Make it fast. . . ."

One of the guns reversed, chopped down butt first, caught him across the mouth. His head went back, came forward again. A drop of blood fell, formed a splashy scarlet star.

Graham said with almost comic anxiety: "Not on my floor here! What's the water for?"

"Who's so smart now?" the girl behind them shrilled vindictively. "Use me for a stepping-stone, will you! You're going to get it now, and I hope you get it good!" She had changed again. The tattered dress was nowhere near her, its remnants lay kicked far out on the deserted dance floor, and yet she had changed back again—to all she had been before, as though the very core of her being had become corroded with hate and malice.

Graham patted her commendingly on the shoulder. "You're worth your weight in gold, honey. You wait for us here, put something over you so you don't catch cold. Graham's going to get you a mink wrap for this, and a diamond bracelet, too, if you want. You're riding back to town tonight in my own private car. We won't take long. If you hear any screaming out on the Sound, don't pay no never-mind. It'll just be the wind coming over the water. All right, boys."

As they hustled him toward the entrance, in what was almost an exact replica of the old "flying wedge" at Jack's, he glanced back over his shoulder. Again she had clasped her hands, was holding them out tremblingly toward him.

They hurried down a long slope to where black water lapped whisperingly against the gray sand. "Okay, left," Graham said tersely. They broke up into Indian file, except for the pair gripping Fisher grimly each by an arm bent stiffly backward ready to be broken in its socket at the first sign of resistance. The Sound was empty of life, not a light showing anywhere. Their footsteps moiling through the soft sand were hushed to a hissing sigh.

"Flirt a little," Graham's voice came from the rear.

Somebody took out a pocket torch, clicked it on, off, on, off again. There was an answering firefly wink straight ahead, on the shore itself. "There they are. They landed a little off-center."

The white blur of a launch showed up, seemingly abandoned there at the water's edge; there was not a soul anywhere in sight. But a human voice crowed like a rooster somewhere near at hand. *Kri-kirri-kri-kree-e-e-e.*

Graham called out impatiently, "Yeah, yeah, it's us, you fools!"

Dark figures were suddenly swarming all over the lifeless launch; their trousers were rolled up to their knees. They started passing small packages, no bigger than shoe boxes, to those on shore.

"Come on, reach! Come out closer. Don't be afraid to get your feet wet."

Fisher spoke for the first time since they'd hauled him out of the clubhouse. "Pickup and deliver. Nice work."

There was a sudden stunned silence, tension in the air. "Who's that? Who you got with you?"

"Dead man," answered Graham tonelessly. "He's going out to the ship when we get through."

"Wait a minute! I know that voice!" One of the men jumped down into the water with a splash, came wading in, stood before Fisher. A torch mooned out, upward, between them, illumining both faces.

Fisher said, almost inaudibly, "Belden. So you came back, couldn't stay away. Glad you did. You came back to your death. They can kill me ten times over, but I'm still going to get you, murderer, somehow!"

Belden lunged, grabbed Fisher by the throat with both hands, sobbing crazily: "What does it take to kill you? What does it take to make you *stay* dead?"

They had to pry him away. Graham yelled: "No, no, no. Not here. On the boat. C'mon. Break it up."

Eight of those that had come with him were toiling back, Indian-file, each with a shoe box under each arm.

"Tune her up!" A motor started to bark and cough, the boat to vibrate. Graham said something about his fifteen-buck patent-leathers, went wading clumsily out, scrambled aboard. Fisher was dragged floundering backward through the shallow water, caught at the hands and feet, hauled up over the side. He watched for the moment when his legs were freed as his spine slipped up over the rim of the boat; buckled one, shot it out full-length into one of the blurred faces.

The man dropped like a log, with a long-drawn exhalation that ended in a gurgle. They floundered around in the water over him. A voice exclaimed, "Holy—! He's busted Mickey's jaw and nose with that hoof of his! Pull him up out of there!"

Vengeful blows from the butt of a gun were already chopping Fisher down to his knees; in another second he'd gone flat on his face. He went out without a sound somewhere at the bottom of the little launch. The last thing he heard from far off was Graham's repeated cry: "Wait, can't you—and do it right? I got ideas— "

Belden was saying, in the lamplit cabin of the motionless ship, "You can give the instructions, but I'm laying it on him personally. You can even take it out of my cut if you want to, I'll pay for the privilege, that's how bad I want it!" Fisher opened his eyes with a groan.

"So you're awake, stupid!"

Fisher said, trying to stem the weakness in his voice: "Just how personal do you want it, louse? 'Cause I want it personal too. You remember Jimmy Fisher, don't you?"

"Yep," Belden said. "We made him run the gauntlet down the stairs of an old five-story brownstone house. On every landing we put another bullet in him, but not where it would kill him. He started to die on the fourth landing from the top, so we rolled him the rest of the way with our feet."

Fisher's eyes rolled idly upward to the oil lamp dangling on a hook. "Jimmy's all right," he said thoughtfully. "All a guy can do is die once. The big difference is whether he dies clean—or dirty—"

His arm suddenly swept out from the shoulder in a long downward arc. The hoop of the oil lamp sprang from the hook, there was a tinny crack and a crash of glass where Belden's face had been, and then he was lathered with lazy little flame points, giving off feeble light as if he were burnished with gold paint.

They tried to grab him, hold him, beat the flats of their hands against him. He gave a hoot-owl screech, turned and bolted out the door, and the cabin turned dark behind him. Fisher sprang after him with a quickness he hadn't thought he'd be able to muster; left all his contusions and his gun-butt bruises and his aching human weariness behind him where

87

he'd been, and shot out to the deck after that flickering squawking torch like a disembodied spirit of revenge.

Belden was poised on the rail, like a living torch. He went over with a scream, and Fisher went over after him, hurdling sidewise on one wrist. They must have both gone in at about the same spot. He got him below the surface, collided with him as Belden was coming up, and got the hold he wanted on his neck with both arms. They came up again together—not to live, but to die.

Fisher sputtered: "Now this is for Jimmy! This!" The throb that came when Belden's neck snapped went through him. They went down again together.

When he rose to the surface again he was alone. The launch was chugging around idly near him, and angry pencils of light from torches came to a focus on his head, as he threw it back to get some air in. "There he is!"

"It's taken care of, Jimmy," he panted. "You can sleep tight."

"Save it till you get to him—you'll be right down to hell yourself!" The pencils of light now were suddenly orange, and cracked like whips, and made the water spit around his head.

Graham's voice said, "I can get him. It's a pushover," and he stood up in the bow of the circling launch. Fisher could see the white of his shirtfront.

A violet-white aurora borealis suddenly shot up over the rim of the water—behind the launch—and Graham was an ink-black cutout against it. Then he doubled over and went in, and something banged in back of him. A voice megaphoned: "Throw 'em up or we'll let you have it!"

Distant thunder, or a high roaring wind, was coming up behind that blinding pathway of light.

Fisher wished it would get out of his eyes, it was putting the finishing touch to him. He flopped his way over to the near side of the launch to get out of the glare, caught the gunwale with one hand, and hung there like a barnacle, tired all over.

*   *   *

There were shoe boxes stacked up on the tables next to overturned champagne glasses, and a line of men were bringing their hands down from over their heads—all but Graham and a man sitting back-to-front on a chair, wrapped in an automobile laprobe, watching everything, looking very tired, very battered—and very eager. And, oh yes, a girl crumpled forward over one of the little tables, her blond head buried between her arms. Outside the rooster was black against the dawn; the current had been cut and they were pulling it down with ropes. Chanticler would never crow again to dreamladen ships out on the Sound.

None of it mattered very much to the bundled-up man in the laprobe just then: the questioning or the taking down of statements or Trilling's staccato machine-gun firing of orders right and left. Only two things were important: an ownerless badge lying there on a table, and the tortured, twisted fragments of a dress huddled on the dance floor.

They came to the badge first. Trilling took time off between orders to glance at it. Then he brought it over, held it out. "What're you waiting for?" he said gruffly. "It's yours."

Fisher took it with both hands and held it as a starving man would hold a crust of bread. Then he looked up and grinned lopsidedly. "Washington?" he said.

"Washington wants results," Trilling snapped. "Well, look around you. This whole job is yours. Don't try to act hard about that hunk of tin either. I know you're all mush inside." He glanced at the girl and said, "What's *she* crying about? She got us out here in time, didn't she?"

They came to the other thing last. "Fire extinguishers?" said Trilling as he was ready to leave in the wake of the captives. "What do you want fire extinguishers trained on the floor for? There's no fire."

"There's going to be," said Fisher.

He stepped forward with a tense, frightened face, struck a match, dropped it on what lay coiled there like something malign, ready to rear and strike at whatsoever ventured too near it. He retreated and put his arm around the girl, and she turned her face away and hid it against his chest. "I think I—see," she said.

"Never mind. Just forget it," Fisher murmured, "That's the only out for both of us."

A glow lit up the dance floor of the Chanticler. There was a hissing like a pit of snakes or a vat of rendering fat. There wasn't any smoke to speak of, just a peculiar odor—a little like burnt feathers, a little like chemicals, a little like sulphur or coal gas. When the flames they had fed on were reduced to crumbling white ash, the fire died down again, sank inward. Then at the very last, just as it snuffed out altogether, a solitary tongue—thin as a rope and vivid green—darted straight up into the air, bent into the semblance of a question mark, poised motionless there for a split second. Then vanished utterly without a trace.

A gasp went up. "Did you see that? What was it?" A dozen pairs of trained eyes had seen it.

Trilling answered, after a long horrified silence. "Some chemical substance impregnated in the material the dress was made of, that's all. A dye or tincture of some kind—"

Fisher just stood there lost in thought, without saying anything. There is always a rational explanation for everything in this world—whether it's the true one or not. Maybe it is better so.

THE DEVIL IN EXILE

by Brian Cleeve

"What we need," the Devil said, moodily selecting another cold and soggy chip, "is a Government-in-Exile."

The table of Papadopoulos's Café was spread with week-old newspapers, liberally decorated with what looked like week-old stains of tomato sauce. The Devil and his one-time principal and now only follower, Belphagor, were sharing a rather scummy cup of tea and sixpence worth of fried chips. Absentmindedly the Devil abstracted one end of his long, forked tail from his pocket and stirred the tea with it.

"What we need is a job," Belphagor said, shuddering slightly. "No, I don't feel like any tea, thanks. You finish it. A nice job somewhere in the sun. How about this—" He started reading an advertisement from the paper between them. "Systems Analyst wanted for—"

"Do you mind?" said the Devil, shutting his small, pouched eyes. A hard two years lay behind them since they were expelled from Hell by a militant trades union movement that had since developed into the Union of Devils Democratic Republics—one Republic for each of the Seven Circles of Hell—under the popular and democratic guidance of Jake O'Hara, one-time Napoleon of London's underworld and now Party Secretary, President, Head of the Infernal Security Police, Chairman of the Trades Union Movement, and by infernal and unanimous acclaim the greatest writer, artist, musician, historian, scientist and thinker ever to darken Hell's Gates.

"That Irish no good drunken layabout," the Devil snarled, grinding his carious fangs on the last stale chip. "I gave him his first temptation. I taught him how to pick pockets before he was out of short trousers. I guided his every filthy footstep on the way to where he is now. And what do I get for it? Double-damned ingratitude, that's what I get." He tried to lash his tail in fury, but the result was so feeble that he quickly stuffed the end back into his sagging pocket, hoping that Belphagor hadn't noticed.

"Data Flow Controllers," Belphagor said. "This ad says, 'New challenges, high rewards. Your responsibilities will include the scheduling and organization of the operational side of computer systems.' How about that?"

"Please," said the Devil, looking extremely tired.

"I'm only trying to help," whined Belphagor, becoming sullen. "It's not my fault he turned us down for pension rights."

"No trace can be found of any contributions having been received from you!" snarled the Devil, quoting from the extremely pompous letter they had lately received from the Hellish State Pensions Ministry.

"Why don' you two fin' a job?" the waitress Myra said, bending her more than thought-provoking bosom over the table to remove the empty cup and saucer. She was the daughter of the proprietor, much kept in order by her stern papa, and ancestral feminine temptations smoldered behind her dark eyes whenever she had occasion to brush her rounded flank against the Tempter's shoulder while serving him chips and weak tea or clearing the table. Without of course knowing that the small and seedy customer with the bedroom expression was indeed the Tempter of Eve, and all women.

"Why don' you?" she urged. "A frien' of mind was looking for bookies' runners only yest'day. 'Slot o' money to be made."

"Director General and Controller of Programming,"

Belphagor read. "The Island of Scotia Television Service invites applications from Senior Executives of proven ability—"

"Do you mind," the Devil said automatically, and then, struck by the word *television*, "what did you say?"

"Senior Executives of proven ability. The decisive factors will be initiative, imagination, boldness of constructive thought, artistic integrity—why," Belphagor said, breaking off in surprise, "they're describing us!"

"They are indeed," said the Devil, sitting up straight and giving Myra an extremely indelicate pinch. "What's the closing date? Suffering Hell, tomorrow! Myra, child—" He scribbled hastily on the back of a used envelope—"Hold all decisions pending our arrival tomorrow p.m. We are the executives you need and must have. Signed Z. Bubb." He handed it to Myra with the pound note that he had extracted from her apron pocket while pinching her rear elevation. "Run to the post office, child, and transmit this message. Never fear for the café. Belphy and I will look after it as if it were our own."

Off ran Myra and no sooner had her high-heeled footsteps faded down the street than the Devil had the till open and the money garnered from one hundred and twenty workmen's lunches and take-out pies clutched in his disreputable hand. "Thirty-odd nicker," he said, riffling through the notes and pouring the silver into his pocket alongside his tail. "That won't get us far. But I know a red-hot racing certainty for the three-thirty and its now three twenty-three and a half."

Half an hour later, and richer by seven hundred and seventy-four pounds five shillings, they were in a taxi on the way to Savile Row for some off-the-peg but still impeccable gentlemen's suitings. From there a few steps took them to the Burlington Arcade for shoes and hats, shirts and discreet ties and linen; from thence to Piccadilly for luggage, shooting sticks, umbrellas and the small necessities of a gentleman's existence, like silver brandy flasks and onyx-mounted cigar cutters; then to the travel agent for first-class air tickets to Scotia; and finally to an exclusive little place just off St. James's Street for a Turkish bath, massage, pedicure, manicure, facial and haircut, all provided by Japanese ladies of skill and charm; leaving our two friends in better shape to meet the searching examinations of the Interview Board than anyone could have imagined a few hours earlier, seeing—and if the truth be told, sniffing—them in Papadopoulos's Café, where at exactly that moment an irate papa P. was reproving his daughter for her negligence with the aid of a sweeping broom.

"I think," the Devil said, surveying a mirror-polished finger nail, "that that should do. At least for Scotia."

And indeed it did. In answer to a second telegram, the Interview Board was assembled in the spacious Board Room of the Television Station at 4 p.m. to await their latest applicants' arrival. The Board consisted of the Prime Minister, the Minister for Finance, the Minister for Communications, the Archbishop, and the Chairman of the Television Authority, Mr. Gustavus Nagg, with his good lady Mrs. Nagg, chairwoman of the League for Decent Viewing (known to the irreverent few as the LDV, or League of Dreadful Virgins).

"Gentlemen," said the Devil, carelessly tossing his twenty-guinea trilby hat (hand-stitched silk lining in apple green, perspiration band in gold-tooled Yugoslavian wild boar skin) onto the quarter acre of mahogany boardroom table. "Gentlemen, I am not a man to beat about the bush, or shilly, or shally, or say one thing and mean another—or alternatively to wrap up my meaning in an obscure flow of high-sounding but meaningless words. I say what I think. I think what I say. I form rapid opinions and change them empirically and pragmatically, frankly and fearlessly as the occasion demands. In fact I think I may say, without fear of contradiction, and without any craven regard for the consequences, be they what they may, gentlemen, and I would repeat that to a man's face, to any man's face—I think I may say, and my colleague will bear me out in that—" at which he turned with exquisitely courteous condescension to Belphy, who was undoing his own unbelievably elegant doeskin gloves with only a whit less carelessness than his master had used in tossing his hat onto the table.

"Unquestionably," Belphy said. "Without a doubt."

"I like these two men," the Prime Minister was whispering to the Minister for Communications. "They know what they're saying. No dillying or dallying. Fearless. Frank. Good chaps."

"What *are* they saying?" said the Minister for Finance, who was always a trifle behind at meetings.

"That they are fearless and frank," hissed Mrs. Nagg, who was less favorably impressed, particularly by those two qualities. "How're yer on morals? Morals. Know what I mean? Morals."

"Fearless and f—" began Belphy, until the Devil kicked him severely on his silk-clad ankle (long black socks, without clocks, naturally, and supported equally naturally by gentleman's black elastic suspenders, three guineas the pair, as supplied to His Majesty Edward VII and other crowned heads. No true gentleman would wear any other) and having kicked his minion into agonized silence the Devil took it smoothly up:

"Fearlessness and frankness, as my colleague was about to say, have their places, their honored and invaluable places in many areas of broadcasting—but in the field of morals, the delicate, controversial, invaluable, excruciatingly difficult and beyond question thorny, much-debated, vexed and infinitely to be pondered upon field of morals—there, there I make no bones about saying, and say it forthrightly, without fear or favor, or lip service to the manifold pressures of this day and age, there I say, what is required is guardianship, control, balance, lack of equivocation. One must take a position, I say, it no matter what the consequences, one must hold the fort, one must nail one's colors to the mast, one must—"

But at this point the Archbishop could restrain himself no longer and with a loud cry of "Amen!" leaned across the corner of the vast table and shook the Devil warmly by the hand. "Splendid fellows!" he cried. "The second I saw their ties I knew they must be!"

The Devil caressed his soberly sumptuous Old Etonian silk tie with a modest forefinger. Belphy lowered his chin equally modestly on the properly tightened knot of his Old Harrovian colors (the Cricket Club to be precise), while Gustavus Nagg, who was merely an industrialist by background and had gone to an extremely common school, said irritably, "Ties, ties, what ties?" which clinched the matter for his more socially conscious spouse, who, without having recognized the ties herself, was eager both to please the Archbishop and to snub her husband.

"Of course they are splendid fellows," she said. "I take it we are agreed then? The other seven hundred and ninety-three candidates had quite unacceptable views on morals. Quaaiite unacceptable. I'm delighted to find a fellow moralist in this decadent age in which we are condemned to live. Archbishop? Are we wending the same way homeward?"

"Agreed," the Minister for Finance said in a firm tone, this having been the last word of Mrs. Nagg's that he had grasped and understood in its entirety. He said it more to convey that he was following the conversation than to signify his own agreement, which would have required a much longer process of thought on his part. But his calm, clear utterance, matched with the calm, clear vacuity of his piercing gaze (political assets, both of them, of the first order, and the ones above all others that had raised him to ministerial rank and might yet lift him higher), these two factors carried the utmost weight with the Prime Minister, who had arrived where he was by waiting to hear what the majority thought and then thinking it too.

"Agreed, agreed," the Prime Minister said with a challenging air as if he was taking a decision of his own instead of echoing his colleagues. And indeed he was for once happy to echo them, for he did truly find the two applicants a most sympathetic pair. Men after his own heart, as he said next day in the cabinet.

"Aye," said Mr. Nagg doubtfully. "But hooald oan a minut, ah wooan't be rooshed. How's about all this eemparshality bizness they tark about? How art thee on that, eh lad?'' Mrs. Nagg closed her eyes. The Archbishop looked at the ceiling.

"Ah yes—yes, impartiality," the Devil said, feeling his way. "Hmmm. It would be fair to say—in fact it must be said—without doubt, and without begging the question or beating about the bush, indeed even without fear or favor, that impartiality is, and must be, and must always remain, the crux, the essence, the quintessence, one might almost say the vital force, the focal fulcrum, the hub and center of all broadcasting policy and practice—"

While he had been speaking he had also been bending a covert but keen look on each member of the board in turn, and had noticed an expression of dismay, not to speak of despondent gloom, spread over the features of the Prime Minister and the Minister for Communications.

"But—" he added smoothly, "while I myself am personally dedicated, not to say devoted, to the consummate and deeply satisfying pleasures of impartiality, I am not a man to let my private whims run away with my professional judgments and the needs of the Great Square-Eyed Master whose humble servants we all are. I would be the first to concede, in fact I would hasten to admit, and even fearlessly assert, that to carry impartiality too far would be a grave and dangerous precedent. Indeed an excess of impartiality would be a kind of partiality on the wrong side. And let me assure you, madam, gentlemen, that I would never—"

"Damn all this ethical stuff," said the Minister for Finance, struggling to keep up. "Whose side is the feller going to be on? Ours or theirs?"

"The right side!" cried the Devil, jumping to his feet and pointing a quivering finger at the startled Prime Minister, in whose ears the cry "the right side" had sounded like the knell of doom. But before his fears could become articulate, the Devil swept on, "The side of Justice! Of fair play! Of decency! Of motherhood! Of humble faith and honest doubt, the side of the innocent, of the simple taxpayer by his rose-covered garage door; of the chubby lad spending his quiet evenings filling in the family football coupon for his sweet old silver-haired grandmother! The side that you—you, sir—have dignified by your leadership, your example, your fearlessness, your frankness—yes, and come what may, I must, I shall say it, whatever the consequences—your simple, bedrock decency, your humility, your passionate concern for truth, for justice, for the simple virtues, for the happiness of the voting classes, your—your—I—I can't go on, it's too much, I'm overcome—"

The Devil sat down covering his eyes. Belphy had already covered his. The Prime Minister wiped a surreptitious tear from his own trembling cheek. Mrs. Nagg blew her nose. The Finance Minister said cautiously, "I didn't quite catch—"

"That's the kind of chap I like," whimpered the Prime Minister to no one in particular. "A man who's not afraid to speak his mind to my face. I could never have given this job to a yes man."

"Well, ah dooan't knaw," said Mr. Nagg. "Ah dooan't onnerstand awl this intellecshul stoof, but if you'm soddisfied—"

"I am, I am," wept the Prime Minister. "Any—any more questions?" He could hardly expect such another burst of incisive and constructive criticism and political insight from the new Director General, at least immediately, but he couldn't prevent himself from hoping. "Have *you* any questions?" he asked the Minister for Communications.

"As a matter of fact there is just one more question I'd like to put," said the Minister apologetically. "Hate to be technical and all that, but could I—might I—I mean—dammit, I don't want to sound vulgar—"

At which Mrs. Nagg threw up her eyes and whispered loudly to the Archbishop. "If wishes were horses!" The Archbishop tried to look gently reproving.

"—sound vulgar," the wretched Minister pursued. He had been to almost as nasty a school as Mr. Nagg. "But—what kind of broadcasting experience have you got? Eh?"

The Devil let the full vulgarity of the words and thought make themselves felt, while he smiled with a pleasant condescension. Just as the embarrassed silence threatened to become painful, the Devil crossed one elegant tweed-clad leg over the other and said, "I'm glad you asked me that, sir," the word "sir" falling like the lightest of sardonic and dignified reproofs. "I may say, and my colleague will support me"—mutual grave nods of question and answer—"in saying that we have spent our working lives in the Communications Industry. It has been our lifelong undertaking to guide, to teach, to entertain as large a portion of mankind as we could reach with the means at our command. I may also say, without fear of contradiction, that we have reached a great portion of it. And if I may descend to the vulgar argument of success, I would further claim, without much fear of contradiction, that we have given greater pleasure to a greater number of people—in earthly terms of course—" he coughed delicately—"than the Opposition have ever done." He coughed again.

"Capital," mumbled the wretched Minister. "Tophole record, tophole," his grasp of upper-class slang being somewhat uncertain. "Support you of course."

"Goodbye, Mr.—Mr.—" said Mrs. Nagg, holding out a manly moral hand.

"Bubb, ma'am," said the Devil, grasping it fondly. "Z. Bubb, B.L. Always at your service ma'am."

"B.L.?" queried the Minister for Finance.

"Bachelor of Laws," whispered the Prime Minister. "What a splendid fellow."

Three days later the Devil and Belphy were installed in their new offices. "This," the Devil said, toying with his onyx-and-gold cigar cutter, "this is better than any Government-in-Exile. One quick cablegram and then down to business. To the Papadopoulos Café. Please accept one year's free advertising on Scotia TV compliments of Z. Bubb. Please send Myra earliest possible plane to Scotia to assume interesting position on TV. That should fix father and daughter. Now—"

The "business" referred to was extremely simple: to recruit a suitable staff for a little private project of their own. Television even in its short career has collected about its fringes a sad flotsam of failures: neurotic producers, alcoholic scriptwriters, intemperate interviewers, even some young lady assistants who have fallen below the strict standards of morality exacted, and rightly exacted, of employees in so sensitive and influential an industry.

Such pitiable refuse tends to collect in certain disreputable drinking dens in unsavory parts of London and Manchester—and possibly New York, for all I know to the contrary—where between sad bouts of intemperance, they boast pathetically of past TAM ratings and cataclysmic rows with Director Generals and other Public Enemies of television workers. And it was amongst these sodden outcasts that the Devil and Belphy searched for their instruments. Their purpose was no less than to put out a second and clandestine series of programs, commencing well after midnight when all good television viewers are tucked up in bed for the eight hours of Close Down, and ending at cock crow. And it was not many months before their purpose become accomplished fact.

This secret, second program schedule was masterly in its simple hewing to well-proven formulae. It began with a cartoon series for the teenies—*Super Imp*, in which a handsome and muscular baby devil invariably outwitted the slow and lumpish angels foolish enough to cross his path. For of course this program, like all the programs, was beamed not to the sleeping Scotians, but to the wakeful inhabitants of Hell, who as a matter of fact had for some time been extremely bored with the simple-minded "do-badding" approach of Hell's one-channel monopoly station, full of downdrive and exhortations to torture harder for less pay, and in which the high spot of the night's viewing was likely to be the Life Story of a Stakhanovite imp who worked for no pay at all.

The Devil's new station, known from its call sign as Station KERSS, was what Hell had been waiting for without knowing it.

"The DAM ratings are up again!" Belphy would gibber indiscreetly in the mornings. (Devils AdMass, Inc. supplied the ratings, of course.)

After *Super Imp* would come family-viewing time with old films such as *Hell's Angels*, dance shows like *Striporama*, or weepies like *Filth's End*, the simple emotional story of a typical Hellish suburb, with its homely adulteries and murders, blackmailings and abortions. Or sex-comedy series—*Hell's Bells*, the inside story of the Vatican through the Ages—TOMORROW! ALEXANDER THE BORGIA POPE! ORGIES! GIRLS! POISONINGS! YOU'LL LAUGH TILL YOU BUST!—no wonder the DAM ratings went up. Then the news, *Hell's Scandals*. And for peak viewing time, shows like *Kinky Doll*, featuring the Karate Kitten (Myra), dressed in her trademark of black PVC fisherman's thigh boots and a kinky smile, fighting the bad fight, delivering karate chops to oily, virtuous clergymen, or seducing bishops, or simply wrestling with her conscience and winning. While for old-fashioned, straitlaced devils there were educational and religious programs: *The Black Mass, Readings from the Kama Sutra*, or *Ten Lessons in Torture for Junior Devils*.

And between programs, the Message. The Devil sitting careworn and earnest at his desk, smoking a curly briar pipe, his brow furrowed. "The Chief *cares!* About YOU!" Just a few effective seconds. While Scotian pipe music wailed softly in the background "Will he no' come back again?"

Or the Devil kissing a baby imp. Or a straight question: "What happened to the Furnace Tenders Trades Union Holiday Fund?" referring to a well-known Hellish scandal of the moment in which one of Jake O'Hara's lieutenants figured unpleasantly. With the clear implication that that kind of thing didn't happen in the Chief's time. Or the Devil and Belphy frolicking with Myra and a couple of rather wayward secretaries. "Hell ought to be FUN!"—allowing the viewer to draw his own conclusions as to whether Hell was fun under the increasingly sour and dictatorial rule of Jake O'Hara.

The effect was almost instantaneous. Two asbestos envelopes arrived containing extremely large checks and an effusive note from Hell's Minister of Pensions (signed personally by the Minister), deeply regretting a grave departmental error in rejecting pension claims from his esteemed onetime colleagues, Z. Bubb and B. Gore, and hastening to offer not only their full pensions, Ministerial Grade 1A, but back-dating them for two years, with a little bonus as "appreciation money." The one condition being that of course Z. Bubb and B. Gore would forthwith cease all gainful employments, which no doubt at their age they would be glad to do.

The Devil cashed the checks and carried on broadcasting. O'Hara's next step was to try to broadcast right back, but lacking skilled technicians, since naturally very few television persons have yet found their way to the lowest depths, this resulted in no more than a little interference with daytime viewing in Scotia. Certainly once or twice a distorted message did flash onto Scotian screens, such as "Your TV is the Devil's work," but viewers put this down to the activities of the League for Decent Viewing, and apart from one indignant license holder heaving a dead cat through the Naggs' drawing room window, it had no effect. The less so because whatever the Devil and Belphy put out secretly in the small hours of the morning, their official programs were of unparalleled respectability, not to say dullness.

"At last I can sleep at nights," Mrs. Nagg would often say at League meetings, "without my mind being *sullied* by memories of the unspeakable filth my conscience obliged me to watch during an evening's monitoring of our Scotian broadcasts. Our League must pass a vote of thanks to dear Mr. Bubb, and dear Mr. Gore."

But no such kindly thoughts were in the mind of Jake O'Hara. Hell was in sullen turmoil. Ranging from a simple rebellion against the abysmal quality of Hell's own TV programs, to a fury of questioning about scandals exposed by the KERSS news programs, to a steadily gathering groundswell of opinion that what Hell needed was a change of government. "Will he no come back again" became Top of the Pops with the imps and teenage devils. Ambiguously worded buttons reading "To Hell with O'Hara" appeared in every lapel, accompanied by mocking smiles as the wearer passed anyone in authority. The trade in TV antennas doubled in a month and doubled again. On Tuesday nights (*Filth's End, Kinky Doll,* and a new educational program, *Learn Karate with Myra*), it was impossible to find a single imp or devil in

Hell who would do a fork's prod of overtime. Even the souls began sneaking off the griddles—previously it had been part of their punishment to have to watch State TV—and clustering around TV shop windows or the doorways of pubs that had TV sets in the bar. But one of the Devil's most effective little Messages was simply "O'Hara's State barmen water the beer." In fact it was O'Hara's unwise decision to take all the TV sets out of the State Pubs and Wimporamas that precipitated the end.

It couldn't go on. Even the devils closest to O'Hara were beginning to look nervous. They tried jamming the KERSS broadcasts, but they simply lacked the skill to blot them out altogether, and by merely half spoiling the picture without touching the sound, they got the worst of both worlds, enraging the entire population without depriving them of the Message. Until the aforementioned folly of depriving State drinkers of the pleasure of watching *Filth's End* and *Kinky Doll* while they drank their flat and watered State beer provoked an explosion that was anyway inevitable. O'Hara barely escaped with his skin. A few hours later the Devil and Belphy were back in the Seventh Circle.

And there, so far as I know, they've remained ever since. Certainly they haven't been back working in earthly TV. I mean, if they had been you could tell, couldn't you?

THE CAGE

by Ray Russell

"They say," said the Countess, absently fondling the brooch at her young throat, "that he's the devil."

Her husband snorted. "Who says that? Fools and gossips. That boy is a good overseer. He manages my lands well. He may be a little—ruthless? cold?—but I doubt very much that he is the Enemy Incarnate."

"Ruthless, yes," said the Countess, gazing at the departing black-cowled, black-hosed, black-gloved figure. "But cold? He seems to be a favorite with the women. His conquests, they say, are legion."

" 'They' say. Gossips again. But there you are—would the angel Lucifer bed women?" The Count snorted again, pleased at his logical triumph.

"He might," replied his wife. "To walk the earth, he must take the shape of a man. Might not the appetites of a man go with it?"

"I am sure I do not know. These are delicate points of theology. I suggest you discuss them with a Holy Father."

The Countess smiled. "What did he want?"

"Nothing. Business. Shall we go in to dinner?"

"Yes." The Count proffered his arm and they walked slowly through the tapestried halls of the castle. "He seemed most insistent about something," the Countess said after a moment.

"Who did?"

"Your efficient overseer."

"He was urging more stringent measures with the serfs. He said his authority had no teeth if he could not back it up with the threat of severe punishment. In my father's day, he said, the thought of the castle's torture chamber kept them in line."

"Your father's day? But does he know of your father?"

"My father's harshness, my dear, has ever been a blight on our family's escutcheon. It has created enemies on many sides. That is why I am especially careful to be lenient. History shall not call us tyrants if I can help it."

"I still believe he is the devil."

"You are a goose," said the Count, chuckling. "A beautiful goose."

"That makes you a gander, my lord."

"An old gander."

They sat at table. "My lord—" said the Countess.

"Yes?"

"That old torture chamber. How strange I've never seen it."

"In a mere three months," said the Count, "you could not possibly have seen the entire castle. Besides, it can be reached only by descending a hidden stairwell with a disguised door. We'll go down after dinner, if you like, although there's really nothing there to interest a sweet young goose."

"Three months . . ." said the Countess, almost inaudibly, fingering the brooch again.

"Does it seem longer since our marriage?" asked the Count.

"Longer?" She smiled, too brightly. "My lord, it seems like yesterday."

"They say," said the Countess, brushing her hair, "that you're the devil."

"Do you mind?"

"Should I mind? Will you drag me down to the Pit?"

106

"In one way or another."

"You speak in metaphor?"

"Perhaps."

"You are equivocal."

"Like the devil."

"And, like him, very naughty."

"Why? Because I am here in your boudoir and you are dressed in hardly anything at all?"

"Because of that, yes; and because you counsel my dear husband to be a tyrant, like his father."

"Did he tell you that?"

"Yes. And he showed me the torture chamber you advised him to reopen. How wicked of you! It is a terrible place. So dark and damp, and so deep underground—why, a poor wretch could split his lungs screaming and never be heard in the castle proper."

"Your eyes are shining. I assume you found it fascinating."

"Fascinating! Of course not! It was disgusting. That horrible rack . . . ugh! to think of the limbs stretching, the tendons tearing! . . ."

"You shudder deliciously. It becomes you."

"And that dreadful wheel, and the iron boot . . . I have a pretty foot, don't you think?"

"Perfect."

"Such a high arch; and the toes so short and even. I hate long toes. You don't have long toes, do you?"

"You forget—I have no toes at all. Only hooves."

"Careful. I may believe you. And where are your horns?"

"They are invisible. Like those your husband will be wearing very soon."

"Indeed. You think highly of your charms."

"As do you. Of yours."

"Do you know what struck me as most horrible?"

"Eh? Horrible about what?"

"The torture chamber, of course."

"Oh, of course. What struck you as most horrible?"

"There was a cage. A little cage. It looked like something you might keep a monkey in. It was too small for anything larger. And do you know what my husband said they kept in it?"

"What?"

"People!"

"No!"

"They kept people in it, he said. They could not stand up straight, or lie down; they could not even sit, for there were only spikes to sit on. And they kept them crouching there for days. Sometimes weeks. Until they screamed to be let out. Until they went mad. I would rather be torn apart on the rack. . . ."

"Or have this pretty foot crushed in the boot?"

"Don't. That tickles. . . ."

"It was meant to."

"You must leave. The Count might walk in at any moment."

"Until tomorrow then, my lady. . . ."

Alone, smiling to herself, the Countess abstractedly rubbed the tops of her toes where he had kissed them. She had heard of burning kisses, they were a commonplace of bad troubadours, but until this evening she had thought the term a poetic extravagance. He wanted her—oh, how he wanted her! And he would have her. But not right away. Let him wait. Let him smolder. Let him gaze at her in her diaphanous nightdress; let him, as she lifted her arms to brush her hair, admire the high beauty of her breasts. Allow him a kiss now and then. Oh, not on the mouth, not yet—on the feet, the fingertips, the forehead. Those burning kisses of his. Let him plead and groan. Let him suffer. She sighed happily as she turned down her bed. It was fine to be a woman and to be beautiful, to dole out little favors like little crumbs and to watch men lick them up and pant and beg for more and then to laugh in their faces and let them starve. This one was already panting. Soon he would beg. And he would starve for a long, long time. Then, some night when she thought he had suffered long enough, she would allow him to feast. What a glutton he would make of himself! He would try to make up for lost time, for all the weeks of starvation, and he would feast too rapidly and it would all be over too soon and she would have to make him hungry again very quickly so he could gorge himself again. It would all be very amusing. . . .

"If I *am* the devil, as you say they say, then why do I not overwhelm you with my infernal magic? Why do I grovel here at your feet, sick and stiff with love?"

"Perhaps it entertains you, my Dark Prince. Here: Kiss."

"No. I want your lips."

"Oh? You grow presumptuous. Perhaps you would rather leave."

"No . . . no . . ."

"That's better. I may yet grant you a promotion."

"Ah! my love! Then——"

"Oh, sit down. Not what you call my 'favor.' Just a *little* promotion. Though I don't know if you deserve even that. You want everything but you give nothing."

"Anything. Anything."

"What a large word! But perhaps *you* could indeed give me anything. . . ."

"Anything."

"But they say you demand fearful things in return. I would suffer torment without end, through eternity. . . . Ah, I see you do not deny this. I do believe you *are* the devil."

"I'll give you anything you desire. You have but to ask."

"I am young. Men tell me—and so does my mirror—that I am beautiful, a delight from head to toe. Do you want all this?"

"Yes! Yes!"

"Then make this beauty never fade. Make it withstand the onslaught of time and violence. Make me—no matter what may befall—live forever."

"Forever . . ."

"Haha! I've got you, haven't I? If I never die, then what of that eternal torment? Do you grant me this boon, Evil One?"

"I cannot."

"Wonderful! Oh, what an actor you are! I begin to admire

you! Other men, impersonating the Adversary, would have said yes. But you . . . how clever you are.''

''I cannot grant that.''

''Stop—I'm weak with laughing! This game amuses me *so* much! It lends such spice to this dalliance! I would play it to the end. Satan, look here: you really cannot grant my wish, even if I give you in return—all this?''

''Tormentress!''

''All this, my demon? In return for that one thing I desire? All this?''

''The Powers of Night will swirl and seethe, but—yes, yes, anything!''

''Ah! You disarming rogue, come take these lips, come take it all!''

''You said he was the devil and now I am inclined to believe you. The treacherous whelp! To bed my own wife in my own castle!''

''My lord, how can you think that *I*—''

''Silence. Stupid goose, do you still dissemble? He left without a word, under cover of night. Why? And your brooch—the brooch of my mother!—was found in his empty room; in your bedchamber, one of his black gloves. Wretched woman!''

''Indeed, indeed I am wretched. . . .''

''Tears will avail you nothing. You must be humbled and you will be humbled. Give thanks that I am not my father. *He* would have left you crammed naked in this little cage until your mind rotted and your body after it. But I am no tyrant. All night long, without your supper, you will shiver and squirm down here in repentance, but in the morning I will release you. I hope with sincerity you will have learned your lesson by then. Now I am going. In a few hours, you will probably start screaming to be let out. Save your breath. I will not be able to hear you. Think on your sins! Repent!''

''They said he was the devil, but I place no stock in such talk. All I know is that he came to me directly from the old Count's castle where he had been overseer or something, and gave me complete plans for the storming of the battlements: information about the placement of the cannon, the least securely barricaded doors, the weakest walls, measurements, location of rooms, the exact strength of the castle guard and a schedule of its watch . . . everything I needed. My forces had been on a one-hour alert for months. I attacked that very night. Thanks to my informant, the battle was over before dawn.''

"You are to be congratulated, Duke. And where is he now?''

"Gone. Vanished. I paid him handsomely, and just between the two of us, Baron, I was beginning to make plans for his disposal. A dangerous man to have near one. But the rascal was smart. He disappeared soon after my victory.''

"And that head on the pike up there, with the gray beard fluttering in the wind—it belonged to the late Count?''

"Yes. To this end may *all* enemies of my family come.''

"I'll drink to that. And what disposition was made of the old fool's wife?''

"The Countess? Ah. That is the only sourness in my triumph. I'd have enjoyed invading that pretty body before severing it from its pretty head. But she must have been warned. We searched and searched the castle that night. She was nowhere to be seen. She had escaped. Well . . . wherever she may be, I hope she gets wind of what I'm doing to her husband's castle.''

"Razing it, aren't you?''

"Down to its foundation blocks—leaving only enough to identify it—and building on that foundation an edifice of solid stone that will be a monument to its downfall and to my victory. Forever.''

"Where do you suppose the Countess is now?''

"The devil only knows. May the wench scream in torment for eternity.''

THE TALE OF IVAN THE FOOL
AND HIS TWO BROTHERS,
SEMYON THE SOLDIER
AND TARAS THE BIG-BELLY,
AND OF HIS SISTER MALYANA
THE MUTE,
AND OF THE OLD DEVIL
AND THE THREE IMPS

by Leo Tolstoy

1

In a certain kingdom of a certain realm there once lived a rich peasant. And the rich peasant had three sons: Semyon the Soldier, Taras the Big-Belly, and Ivan the Fool, and an unmarried daughter, Malyana the Mute. Semyon the Soldier went to war to serve the tsar; Taras the Big-Belly went to a merchant in town to trade; and Ivan the Fool stayed at home with his sister to break his back with hard work.

Semyon the Soldier gained high rank and an estate, and married a nobleman's daughter. His pay was large and his estate was large, but he could not make ends meet: what the husband acquired his lady wife carelessly squandered, and they never had any money.

Semyon the Soldier went to his estate to collect the income, and his steward said to him:

"Where should the money come from? We have no cattle,

no tools, no horses, no cow, no plow, and no harrow; all these must be got, then there will be an income."

So Semyon the Soldier went to his father.

"Father," he said, "you are rich, but you have given me nothing. Divide what you have and give me a third part, so that I can add it to my estate."

"You brought nothing into my house," said the old man, "why should I give you a third part? It would not be fair to Ivan and the girl."

And Semyon replied: "But you know he's a fool, and she's only a deaf-and-dumb spinster. What do they need?"

Then the old man said: "Let Ivan decide."

And Ivan said: "Well, why not? Let him have it."

So Semyon the Soldier took his share of his father's goods and removed it to his own estate. And he again went off to serve the tsar.

Taras the Big-Belly also made a great deal of money, and he married into a merchant's family; but he wanted still more, so he came to his father and said:

"Give me my share."

The old man was unwilling to give Taras anything either. "You brought nothing to us," he said. "Whatever is in this house Ivan has earned. Besides, it would not be fair to him and the girl."

But Taras replied: "What good is it to him? He's a fool! He cannot marry, no one would have him; and the dumb girl doesn't need anything either. . . . Come, Ivan," he said, "give me half the grain; I won't take the tools, and I don't want any livestock, except the gray stallion—he's no good to you for plowing."

Ivan laughed and said: "'Well, why not? I will work and earn more."

So they gave Taras a share too. He carted the grain off to town and took away the gray stallion. Ivan was left with one old mare to continue his peasant life as before, and to feed his father and mother.

2

Now the Old Devil was vexed that the brothers had not quarreled over the sharing but had parted amicably. He summoned three imps.

"Look here," he said, "there are three brothers: Semyon the Soldier, Taras the Big-Belly, and Ivan the Fool. They ought to have quarreled, but instead they live in peace and friendship. The Fool spoiled the whole business for me. You three go and take on those three brothers, and stir them up so they'll tear one another's eyes out. Can you do this?"

"We can," they said.

"How will you do it?"

"Like this: first we'll ruin them, and when they haven't so much as a bone to gnaw on, we'll pile them into a heap—and they'll start fighting."

"Good! I see you know your business. Now, be off, and don't come back till they're all at loggerheads, or I'll skin you alive!"

The imps went off to a bog to consider how they should set to work. They argued and argued, each one scheming to get the easiest job. Finally they decided to draw lots to determine which brother each of them would get, and whoever finished first was to come to the aid of the others. They drew lots and set a time for another meeting in the bog to learn who had finished and whom he should help.

At the appointed time the imps met in the bog as agreed. They proceeded to explain how matters stood. The first imp told about Semyon the Soldier.

"My work is going well," he said. "Tomorrow my Semyon will go home to his father."

His comrades began questioning him. "How did you do it?" they asked.

"Well," he said, "the first thing I did was to inspire Semyon with such courage that he promised the tsar he would conquer the whole world for him. So the tsar made him commander in chief and sent him to fight the king of India. They met for battle. But during the night I dampened all the gunpowder in Semyon's army; then I went to the Indian king and made him a whole multitude of soldiers out of straw. When Semyon's soldiers saw the straw soldiers advancing on all sides, they grew timid. Semyon gave orders to fire: the guns and cannon failed to go off. His soldiers were frightened and ran like sheep, and the Indian king massacred them. Now Semyon the Soldier is disgraced, his estate has been taken from him, and tomorrow they intend to execute him. One day's work remains to be done: I have only to let him escape from prison so he can run home. Tomorrow I shall have finished. Now, tell me, which one of you needs help?''

Then the second imp described his work with Taras. ''I need no help,'' he said, ''my work is going well too. Taras can't hold out for more than a week. The first thing I did was to enlarge his belly and excite his envy. He grew so covetous that whatever he saw he wanted to buy. He spent all his money, bought vast quantities of things, and is still buying. Now he borrows in order to buy. He's so weighed down and entangled in debts that he'll never get rid of them. In a week his payments are due, but I'll turn all his goods into dung, and when he can't pay, he'll have to go home to his father.''

They began to question the third imp about Ivan the Fool. ''And how is your work going?'' they asked.

''My work,'' he said, ''is not going well. The first thing I did was to spit into his jug of kvas so he'd have a stomachache. Then I went to his field and pounded the earth till it became hard as stone, so he wouldn't be able to work it. I didn't think he'd try to plow it, but he, the fool, came out with his wooden plow and began to make a furrow. He groaned with the pain in his stomach, but he went right on plowing. I broke one plow for him, but the fool went home, got another, and continued to plow. I crawled underground and caught hold of the plowshare, but there was no holding it; he worked with a will, and the plowshare was sharp—my hands were covered with cuts! He has plowed almost the whole field, only one little strip remains to be done. Come, brothers, and help me,'' said the imp, ''for unless we crush him all our labor will be lost. If this fool persists and succeeds with his crops, his brothers will never know want, for he'll feed them.''

Semyon the Soldier's imp promised to come to his aid the next day, and on that the imps parted.

3

Ivan had plowed the entire fallow; only one little strip remained to be done, and he went out to finish it. His stomach ached, but the plowing had to be done. He released the harness ropes, turned the plow around, and started plowing. He had made one furrow and was going back when the plow began to drag as though caught on a root. It was the imp who had twined his legs around the plowshare and was holding it back.

"How strange!" thought Ivan. "There were no roots here before—but that's a root!"

He reached down and groped about in the furrow—there was something soft! He seized it and pulled it out. It was black, like a root, but wriggled. Lo and behold!—a live imp!

"Look at that!" exclaimed Ivan. "What a horrid thing!"

He raised his arm and was about to dash the imp against the plow handle, when he heard a squeal.

"Don't hurt me!" said the imp. "I will do whatever you wish!"

"What can you do?"

"Anything you wish. You have only to tell me!"

Ivan scratched himself. "I've got a stomachache," he said. "Can you fix it?"

"I can," said the imp.

"Well, then cure it!"

The imp bent down and scraped about in the furrow with his claws. He pulled out a little three-pronged root and handed it to Ivan.

"Here," he said, "whoever swallows one of these roots will no longer feel pain."

Ivan tore the little root apart and swallowed one of the pieces. His stomach-ache immediately vanished.

The imp again entreated him. "Let me go!" he said. "I'll jump into the earth and never come back again!"

"Well, why not?" said Ivan. "God be with you!"

No sooner had Ivan said "God" than the imp plunged into the earth like a stone into water, and there was nothing to be seen but a hole. Ivan thrust the two remaining roots into his cap and went on with his plowing. When he reached the end of the strip he turned the plow over and went home.

He unharnessed the mare and went into the hut, and there sat his elder brother, Semyon the Soldier, and his wife at supper. Semyon had lost his estate, barely managed to escape from prison, and now had come running home to live with his father.

When Semyon saw Ivan he said: "I have come to live with you. Feed me and my wife till a new job turns up."

"Well, why not?" said Ivan. "Live here and welcome!"

Ivan was about to sit down on the bench when the lady objected to his smell.

"I cannot sup with a stinking peasant!" she said to her husband.

And Semyon the Soldier said to his brother: "My lady says you don't smell good. You had better go eat in the entry."

"Well, why not?" said Ivan. "Besides, it's time for the night watch. I must put the mare to pasture."

And he took his coat and some bread and went out to the fields with the mare.

4

Having finished his work that night, Semyon the Soldier's imp came as agreed to find Ivan's imp and help him to subdue the fool. When he reached the plowed field he searched and he searched, but his comrade was nowhere to be seen. All he could find was the hole.

"Well," he thought, "apparently my comrade has met

with misfortune, and I shall have to take his place. The field is all plowed, so the fool must be tackled when he's mowing the hay."

The imp went to the meadow and flooded the entire hayfield with water, so the grass was all covered with mud.

When Ivan returned from his night watch at dawn, he sharpened his scythe, went out to the meadow, and began mowing. He had swung the scythe only once or twice when the blade became dull and had to be sharpened again. He kept struggling with it, and finally he said:

"It's no use. I'll have to go home for a tool to repair it. And I'll bring back a loaf of bread too. If it takes me a week, I won't leave till the mowing is done."

The imp heard him and thought:

"He's a hubble-bubble, this fool! You can't get around him! I'll have to try some other tricks."

Ivan returned, sharpened his scythe, and began to mow. The imp crept into the grass and kept catching the scythe by the heel, driving the tip into the ground. Hard as it was for him, Ivan kept at it till he had mowed the whole meadow except for one little patch that lay in the bog.

As he crept into the bog the imp said to himself:

"I may get my paws cut off, but I won't let him finish the mowing!"

Ivan went to the bog. To look at it the grass was not thick, yet it continually resisted the scythe. He grew angry and started swinging the scythe with all his might. The imp soon had to give in—he could not hold on to the scythe, and seeing how things were going, he decided to hide in a bush. With one sweep of the scythe Ivan grazed the bush and cut off half the imp's tail.

When he finished mowing the field Ivan told his sister to rake up the hay while he went to mow the rye.

He set off with his sickle, but the bobtailed imp had been there before him and the rye was so tangled that the sickle was of no use. Again Ivan went home; this time he returned with a pruning hook, and with this he was able to reap all the rye.

"Now," he said, "I must start on the oats."

The bobtailed imp heard him and thought: "I couldn't get the better of him on the rye, but I'll catch him on the oats! Just wait till morning!"

He hurried out to the field in the morning, but when he got there the oats were all cut. Ivan had mowed them by night. The imp was enraged.

"That fool," he said, "has hacked me all over and worn me out. Not even in a war have I seen such disasters! He doesn't sleep, curse him! I'll get into his ricks now, and rot them all for him."

So the imp went to the stacks of rye, climbed in among the sheaves, and started rotting them. As he heated them he grew warm himself and dozed off.

Meanwhile Ivan harnessed the mare and went with his sister to cart the rye. When he got there he began pitching the rye into the cart. He had tossed up two sheaves when he thrust the fork right into the imp's back. He lifted the fork, and lo and behold!—there on the prongs, wriggling, grimacing, and struggling to get free, was a live imp with his tail cut short!

"Look at that!" exclaimed Ivan. "What a horrid thing! Back again, are you?"

"I'm another one," said the imp. "That was my brother before. I used to be with your brother Semyon."

"Well," said Ivan, "whoever you may be, you're going to get just what he got!"

He was about to dash him against the cart rail when the imp began to plead with him.

"Let me go!" he begged. "I won't do it again. And I'll do whatever you wish!"

"What can you do?"

"Why, I can make soldiers out of anything you like."

"And what are they good for?"

"For whatever you wish. They can do everything."

"Can they play tunes?"

"They can."

"Well, then," said Ivan, "make some!"

And the imp said: "Here, take a sheaf of rye, shake it over the ground, stand it up, and then say:

> " *'By decree of my fief*
> *No more art thou sheaf.*
> *Every straw that I see*
> *A soldier shall be.'* "

Ivan took the sheaf, shook it over the ground, and repeated the imp's words. The sheaf flew apart and turned into soldiers, with a drummer and trumpeters marching at their head. Ivan burst out laughing.

"Look at that, now!" he exclaimed. "How clever! This is fine—it will amuse the girls!"

"Now will you let me go?" asked the imp.

"No," said Ivan. "I want to make them out of threshed husks. No use wasting good grain. Teach me how to turn them into a sheaf again. Then I will thresh it."

"Just say:

> " *'Every soldier I see*
> *Now a straw must be;*
> *As decreed by my fief,*
> *Again bound in a sheaf.'* "

As soon as Ivan had spoken these words, there was the sheaf again!

"Let me go now!" begged the imp.

"Well, why not?" said Ivan.

He hooked the imp onto the cart rail, held him down with one hand, and pulled out the fork.

"God be with you!" he said.

No sooner had he said "God" than the imp plunged into the earth like a stone into water, and there was nothing to be seen but a hole.

When Ivan got home, there sat his second brother, Taras the Big-Belly, and his wife at supper. Taras had not paid his debts, had fled from his creditors, and now had come home to live with his father.

The minute he caught sight of Ivan he said: "Look here, Ivan, feed me and my wife till I can start making money again."

"Well, why not?" said Ivan. "Live here and welcome!"

Then Ivan took off his coat and sat down at the table.

But the merchant's wife spoke up:

"I cannot eat with the fool," she said. "He reeks of sweat!"

Taras the Big-Belly said to Ivan: "You don't smell good, Ivan. You'd better go eat in the entry."

"Well, why not?" said Ivan.

And he took some bread and went out to the yard.

"Besides, it's time for the night watch," he said. "I must put the mare to pasture."

5

Taras's imp finished his work that night and came as agreed to help his comrades with Ivan the Fool. When he arrived at the plowed field, he searched and he searched, but no one was there. All he could find was a hole. He went to the meadow; there in the bog was a tail, and in the midst of the rotting rye he found a second hole.

"Well," he thought, "it's clear that my comrades have met with misfortune. I shall have to replace them and tackle the fool myself."

The imp went to look for Ivan. But Ivan had already gathered the crops and was cutting wood in the grove.

The two brothers had begun to feel cramped living together, so they told the fool he could keep the hut for himself, and ordered him to go out and cut wood and build new houses for them.

The imp ran to the wood, crawled in among the branches, and began to hinder Ivan from felling trees. Ivan undercut one tree so that it should fall clear, but it fell the wrong way and got caught in some branches. He cut a pole with which to turn the tree over, and with great difficulty brought it down. He then set to work to fell another tree—again the same thing.

Ivan had expected to cut down half a hundred young trees, but he had not cut a dozen when night fell over the farm. He was exhausted. Steam rose from him and spread like a mist through the woods, but he would not give up. He undercut still another tree, but his back ached so he could stand it no longer; he drove his ax into the tree and sat down to rest.

When the imp heard that Ivan had stopped working, he was overjoyed.

"At last," he thought, "he's worn out! Now he'll give up, and I can rest too."

He merrily seated himself astride a bough. But Ivan got up, pulled out his ax, and struck the tree with such force from the opposite side that it instantly came down with a crash. The imp, caught off guard, failed to get free in time, and his leg was wedged under a branch. Ivan began stripping the tree, and lo and behold!—a live imp! Ivan was amazed.

"Look at that!" he exclaimed. "What a horrid thing! Are you back again?"

"I'm another one," said the imp. "I used to be with your brother Taras."

"Well, whoever you may be, you're going to get just what he got!"

Ivan swung his ax and was about to strike him dead with the handle. The imp began to plead with him.

"Don't hit me," he begged. "I'll do whatever you wish!"

"What can you do?"

"I can make money for you—as much as you like!"

"Well, then," said Ivan, "make some!"

And the imp showed him how to do it. "Take a leaf from this oak, rub it, and gold will fall from your hands."

Ivan took some leaves and rubbed them together, and a shower of gold fell from his hands.

"That's good!" he said. "The boys will have a fine time with that!"

"Let me go now," said the imp.

Ivan took his pole and freed the imp.

"God be with you!" he said.

No sooner had he said "God" than the imp plunged into the earth like a stone into water, and there was nothing to be seen but a hole.

6

The brothers had built their houses and were living apart. After harvesting the crops, Ivan brewed beer and invited his brothers to celebrate with him. But they refused to be his guests.

"What have we to do with peasant revels?" they said.

So Ivan entertained the peasants and their wives. He himself drank heartily; and when he was tipsy he went into the street where they were dancing and singing and told the women to sing a song in his honor.

"And I will give you something you have never in your lives seen before."

The women laughed and sang a song in praise of him. When they had finished, they said: "Now give it to us!"

"I'll bring it at once," Ivan said. And he took up a sack and ran to the woods.

"What a fool he is!" laughed the women. And they soon forgot all about him.

But suddenly Ivan came running back with the sack full of something.

"Shall I share it?" he asked them.

"Yes, share it!"

Ivan took a handful of gold and flung it to the women. How they threw themselves on it! And how the men sprang forward, snatching and tearing at one another to get the gold! One old woman was nearly trampled to death. Ivan laughed at them.

"Ah, you fools!" he said. "Why crush the old granny? Don't be so rough—I'll give you more."

He began tossing more gold pieces to them, and they all crowded around him. When the sack was empty they still begged for more.

"That's all," said Ivan. "Some other time I'll give you more. Now for a dance! Let's have a tune!"

The women struck up a song.

"Your tunes are no good!" said Ivan.

"Where will you find better?" they asked.

"I'll show you, right now!"

Ivan went to the barn, pulled out a sheaf and threshed it, then shook it over the ground, stood it up, tapped it, and said:

> *"By decree of my fief*
> *No more art thou sheaf.*
> *Every straw that I see*
> *A soldier shall be."*

The sheaf flew apart and turned into soldiers playing drums and trumpets.

Ivan ordered the soldiers to play tunes, and led them out into the street. The people were amazed. When the soldiers had finished playing, Ivan led them back into the barn—after forbidding the peasants to follow him—and turned them back into a sheaf. Then he flung the sheaf onto the pile, and went home and lay down in the stable to sleep.

7

The next morning, hearing of these things, the elder brother, Semyon the Soldier, came to Ivan.

"Tell me," he said, "where did you get those soldiers? And where have you taken them?"

"Why do you want to know?" asked Ivan.

"What do you mean, why? With soldiers you can do anything—you can win a kingdom for yourself!"

Ivan was astonished. "Really?" he asked. "Why didn't

you tell me this long ago? I'll make you as many as you like. Luckily the girl and I threshed a lot!"

Ivan took his brother to the threshing floor and said: "Look here, I'll make soldiers for you, but then you must take them away; if we had to feed them, they'd gobble up the whole village in one day."

Semyon the Soldier promised to lead the soldiers away, and Ivan began making them. He tapped one sheaf on the floor—a company appeared! He tapped another—another company! He made so many that the whole field was covered with them.

"Well, that will do, won't it?"

"It will. Thank you, Ivan."

"All right," said Ivan. "If you need any more, come back and I'll make them. There's plenty of straw still."

Semyon the Soldier mustered his troops, took command of his army, and marched off to make war.

No sooner had Semyon the Soldier gone than Taras the Big-Belly came along. He too had heard of what happened the day before.

"Tell me," he said to his brother, "where did you get all that gold? If I had so much free money I could make it bring in more money from all over the world."

Ivan was astonished. "Really?" he said, "Why didn't you tell me this long ago? I will make you as much as you like."

His brother was delighted. "Give me at least three sackfuls," he said.

"Well, why not? Come with me to the forest. But first let us harness the mare—you won't be able to carry it all."

They went to the forest and Ivan began rubbing oak leaves. He made a great heap of gold.

"That will do, won't it?"

Taras was overjoyed. "It will do for now," he said. "Thank you, Ivan."

"All right," replied Ivan. "If you need any more, come back and I'll make it for you. There are plenty of leaves left."

Taras the Big-Belly gathered up a whole cartload of money and went off to trade.

So the two brothers went away: Semyon to fight, and Taras to trade. Semyon the Soldier conquered a kingdom for himself, and Taras the Big-Belly made a lot of money buying and selling.

When the brothers met, Semyon told Taras how he had got his soldiers, and Taras told Semyon how he had got his money.

And Semyon the Soldier said to his brother: "I have conquered a kingdom, and I could live well, but I have no money to feed my soldiers."

Then Taras the Big-Belly said: "And I have amassed a great heap of money, but my trouble is that I have no one to guard it."

"Let us go to our brother Ivan," said Semyon the Soldier. "I'll order him to make more soldiers, then I'll give them to you to guard your money; and you order him to make more money, and give it to me to feed my soldiers."

They went to Ivan, and when they got there Semyon said:

"I haven't enough soldiers, brother. Make me some more—change a couple of haystacks or so."

Ivan shook his head.

"No more," he said. "I am not going to make you any more soldiers."

"Why not? You promised!"

"I did. But I won't make any more."

"Why won't you, you fool?"

"Because your soldiers killed a man. A few days ago, when I was plowing near the road, a woman came by with a coffin on her cart. She was wailing, and I asked her: 'Who died?' She said: 'Semyon the Soldier killed my husband in the war.' I thought soldiers were for making music, but they have killed a man. I will give you no more."

And the fool stood firm and would make no more soldiers.

Then Taras the Big-Belly began to plead with him to make more gold. Ivan shook his head.

"No more," he said. "I am not going to make you any more gold."

"Why not? You promised!"

"I did. But I won't make any more."

"Why won't you, you fool?"

"Because your gold pieces took away Mikhailovna's cow."

"Took it away? How?"

"Just took it away. Mikhailovna had a cow, and her children used to drink the milk. The other day they came to me asking for milk. 'Where is your cow?' I said. 'The steward of Taras the Big-Belly came to Mama and gave her three pieces of gold, and she gave him our cow. Now we have no milk to drink.' I thought you only wanted to play with the gold, but you have taken the children's cow away from them. I will give you no more."

And the fool stood firm and would make no more gold.

So the brothers went away and considered how to remedy their difficulties.

"I'll tell you what we'll do," said Semyon the Soldier. "You give me money to feed my soldiers, and I'll give you half my kingdom and soldiers to guard your money."

Taras agreed. So the brothers divided their possessions, and both became tsars, and both were rich.

8

Meanwhile Ivan was living at home, feeding his father and mother, and working in the fields with the deaf-and-dumb girl.

Now it happened one day that Ivan's old watchdog fell ill; she grew mangy and appeared to be dying. Ivan felt sorry for her and got bread from his sister to take out to her.

When he threw the bread to the dog, his cap, which was torn, fell off, and a little root fell out of it. The dog gobbled up the root along with the bread, and no sooner had she swallowed it than she jumped up and started to play, barking and wagging her tail. She was cured!

The father and mother saw this and were amazed. "How did you cure the dog?" they asked Ivan.

"I had two little roots that cure any pain," he said, "and she swallowed one of them."

About that time it happened that the tsar's daughter fell ill, and the tsar proclaimed in every town and village that whoever might cure her would receive a reward, and if he were a bachelor, he would receive her hand in marriage. The proclamation was heard in Ivan's village too.

Ivan's father and mother called him in and said: "Have you heard what the tsar has proclaimed? You said you had one more little root; go and heal the tsar's daughter, and you shall be happy the rest of your life."

"Well, why not?" said Ivan.

And he got ready to go. They dressed him in his best, and he had just gone out the door when he caught sight of a beggar woman with a crippled arm.

"I have heard that you heal people," she said. "Heal my arm. I cannot even put on my own boots."

"Well, why not?" said Ivan.

He took out the little root, gave it to the beggar woman, and told her to swallow it. She did as she was told and was instantly cured, and she began to move her arm about freely.

When Ivan's father and mother came out to accompany him on his journey to the tsar, they heard that he had given away his last root and now had nothing with which to cure the tsar's daughter. They began to upbraid him.

"You take pity on a beggar woman," they said, "but for the tsar's daughter you have no pity!"

But Ivan felt pity for the tsar's daughter as well, and he harnessed the mare, threw some straw into the cart, and set off.

"Where are you going, fool?"

"I am going to heal the tsar's daughter."

"When you have nothing to heal her with?"

"Well, why not?" said Ivan, and drove off.

When he reached the tsar's palace, no sooner had he set foot on the threshold than the tsar's daughter was cured.

The tsar was overjoyed. He had Ivan brought before him, dressed him in fine robes, and rewarded him.

"Be my son-in-law," he said to him.

"Well, why not?" said Ivan. And he married the tsar's daughter.

Not long afterwards the tsar died, and Ivan became tsar.

Now all three brothers were tsars.

9

The three brothers lived and reigned.

The eldest brother, Semyon the Soldier, prospered. He conscripted real soldiers to add to his straw soldiers. Throughout his entire realm he decreed that for every ten houses one man must go into the army, and every soldier had to be of great height, clean-bodied and clear-eyed. He gathered many such men and trained them, and when anyone opposed him, he immediately sent out his soldiers, and he did whatever he wished. Soon the people began to fear him.

His life was a pleasant one: anything he fancied, anything that caught his eye, was his. He simply sent out his soldiers, and they seized and brought back to him all he desired.

Taras the Big-Belly prospered too. He lost none of the money he got from Ivan, but greatly increased it. And he too established order in his kingdom. He kept his own money in coffers, and collected more and more from his people. He taxed every soul in his realm; he taxed them for vodka and beer, for bast shoes, for leg wrappings, for dress trimmings. And whatever he fancied was his. People would bring anything to him, perform any work for him—everyone wanted his money.

Ivan the Fool did not fare badly either. As soon as he had buried his father-in-law, he took off his royal robes, gave them to his wife to put away in a chest, and put on his hempen shirt, breeches, and bast shoes. And he began working again.

"It's dull," he said, "and I'm growing a belly; I have no appetite, and can't sleep."

He sent for his father and mother and his sister the mute to come and live with him; then he set to work.

"But you are the tsar!" they all said to him.

"Well, why not?" he replied. "Even a tsar must eat."

One of his ministers came to him and said: "There is no money to pay salaries."

"Then don't pay them."

"But the people will stop serving."

"Let them stop serving," said Ivan. "If they stop serving they will be free to work. Let them cart away the manure; they've piled up enough of it."

People came before him to be tried.

"He stole my money," said one.

"Well, why not?" said Ivan. "That shows he needs it."

Everyone recognized that Ivan was a fool.

"They say you're a fool," his wife said to him.

"Well, why not?" said Ivan.

His wife thought and thought about this, but she too was a fool.

"Why should I go against my husband?" she said. "Where the needle goes the thread must follow."

She took off her royal robes, put them away in a chest, and went to the mute girl to learn how to work. She soon learned and began helping her husband.

All the wise men left Ivan's kingdom; only the fools remained. They lived and worked, feeding themselves and all good people.

10

Now the Old Devil waited and waited to learn how the imps had ruined the three brothers; but no news came from them, so he went to find out for himself. He searched and he searched, but they were nowhere to be seen; all he could find were the three holes.

"Well," he thought, "clearly, they have not succeeded. I shall have to tackle it myself."

He went to look for the three brothers, but they were no longer in their old places; he found them in their various kingdoms, all three alive and reigning. This seemed outrageous to the Old Devil.

"I'll take care of this matter myself!"

First of all he went to Tsar Semyon. He did not appear in his own form, but turned himself into a general before going to the palace.

"I hear, Tsar Semyon, that you are a great warrior," he said. "I am thoroughly trained in that work, and I should like to serve you."

Tsar Semyon asked him some questions, and finding him to be a clever man, took him into his service.

The new general began teaching Tsar Semyon how to build a strong army.

"In the first place, we must enlist more men," he said, "otherwise you will have too many mischievous idlers in your realm. You must call up all the young men without exception, then your army will be five times its present size. In the second place, we must have new guns and cannon. I will provide you with guns that will fire a hundred bullets at once—like a spatter of peas! And I will provide cannon that will consume everything with flame—men, horses, walls—they will burn up everything!"

After listening to the new general, Tsar Semyon gave orders that every youth without exception be taken into the army; he had factories built to make the new guns and cannon; and then went to war with a neighboring ruler. As soon as the other army came forth to meet him, Tsar Semyon gave orders to his soldiers to fire bullets and hurl flame from their cannon. At one blow he crippled or consumed half the army. The neighboring ruler took fright and surrendered his realm. Semyon the Tsar was overjoyed.

"Now," he said, "I will conquer the king of India."

But the king of India had heard about Tsar Semyon, and

had adopted all of his inventions, adding a few of his own. He began by taking not only the young men as soldiers, but all the unmarried women as well, and his army was even larger than Semyon's. Besides copying Semyon's guns and cannon, he had invented a method of flying through the air and dropping explosive bombs from above.

Tsar Semyon set out to wage war on the Indian king, expecting to fight as he had before—but the once sharp scythe had lost its edge. The king of India did not let Semyon's army come within firing distance before he had sent his women soldiers through the air to launch explosive bombs. The women sprayed bombs on the army like borax on cockroaches. The entire army took flight, and Semyon the Tsar was left all alone. The Indian king took Semyon's kingdom, and he had to escape as best he could.

Having finished with one of the brothers, the Old Devil went on to Tsar Taras. He changed himself into a merchant and settled in Taras's realm. He established a business and spent money freely, paying the highest prices for everything. The people all rushed to get his money, and he put so much of it into circulation that they settled the arrears on their taxes, and even began paying them on time.

Tsar Taras was delighted. "Thanks to this merchant, I now have more money than ever, and life grows better all the time."

And Tsar Taras began to devise new projects. He conceived the idea of having a new palace built for himself, and announced that the people were to bring him wood and stone and start working. He set high prices for everything, and thought they would come in crowds as before to get his money. But no! They took their wood and their stone to the new merchant, and the workmen all flocked to him. If Tsar Taras raised his prices, the merchant raised his still higher. The tsar had a great deal of money, but the merchant had more, and he overbid him at every point. Work on the royal palace soon came to a halt.

A park had been laid out by the tsar, and when autumn

came he sent for people to come and plant it, but no one came: they were all engaged in digging a pond for the merchant.

Winter came and Tsar Taras wanted to buy sables for a new overcoat. The emissary he sent to buy them returned.

"There are no sables," he said. "The merchant offered a higher price. He has bought up all the furs and made carpets of them."

When Tsar Taras want to buy stallions, his emissary came back and told him that the merchant had all the good stallions; they were carrying water to fill his pond.

And so all the tsar's projects came to a standstill. No one would work for him; everyone was working for the merchant. They brought him nothing but the merchant's money to pay their taxes.

Tsar Taras had amassed so much money he had no place to put it, and his life became miserable. He gave up making plans and wanted nothing more than to live somehow—but even that was impossible. There was a shortage of everything. His cooks, coachmen, and valets all left him to go to the merchant's; and before long he lacked even food. When he sent to the market there was nothing to be had—the merchant had bought up everything. Nothing was ever brought to him except money for taxes.

Tsar Taras became so infuriated that he banished the merchant from his realm. But the merchant settled just across the border and continued as before, and his money still drew everything away from the tsar.

Things were going badly for Tsar Taras; he had not eaten for days, and it was rumored that the merchant was now boasting that he would even buy the tsar's wife! Tsar Taras lost heart and did not know what to do.

Then Semyon the Soldier came to him and said: "Help me! I have been defeated by the king of India."

But Tsar Taras was at the end of his rope. "I myself have not eaten for two days," he said.

Having finished with two of the brothers, the Old Devil now turned to Ivan. He changed himself into a general, appeared before Ivan, and began by urging him to raise an army.

"It is not fitting that a tsar should be without an army," he said. "You have only to command me and I will gather soldiers from among your people and form an army."

Ivan heard him out and then said: "Well, why not? Go ahead! But train them to play tunes skillfully—that's what I like."

The Old Devil went throughout the kingdom trying to enlist volunteers. He told them that when they came for the head-shaving each man would receive a measure of vodka and a red cap.

The fools only laughed at him. "We have plenty of liquor," they said, "we make it ourselves. And as for caps, the women make us all kinds—even striped ones with tassels."

And no one would enlist. The Old Devil went back to Ivan.

"Your fools won't come as volunteers," he said. "They'll have to be brought in by force."

"Well, why not?" said Ivan. "Bring them in by force."

The Old Devil made it known that all fools were required to enlist as soldiers, and whoever refused would be put to death by Ivan.

The fools came to the general and said: "You say that we will be put to death if we don't enlist; but you don't tell us what will happen if we do enlist. We have heard that soldiers also get killed."

"Yes, that happens."

Hearing this the fools became obstinate. "We won't go!" they said. "Better to stay home and be put to death, since it can't be avoided anyway."

"Fools!" said the Old Devil. "You fools! A soldier may or may not be killed; but if you don't enlist, Tsar Ivan is certain to put you to death."

The fools pondered; then they went to Tsar Ivan the Fool.

"A general appeared," they said, "and ordered us all to become soldiers. 'If you enlist,' he says, 'you may be killed, or you may not be killed; and if you don't enlist, Tsar Ivan is certain to put you to death.' Is this true?"

Ivan laughed. "How could I, alone, put all of you to death? If I weren't a fool I could explain this to you, but as it is, I don't understand it myself."

"Then we won't go," they said.

"Well, why not?" said Ivan. "Don't go."

The fools went to the general and refused to become soldiers.

The Old Devil saw that his plan would not work, so he went to the king of Tarakan and tried to gain his good will.

"Let us go to war," he said, "and conquer Tsar Ivan. He has no money, it's true, but he has plenty of grain and cattle, and all sorts of other goods."

The king of Tarakan agreed to go to war. He assembled a large army, put his guns and cannon in shape, and marched to the border of Ivan's kingdom.

The people came to Ivan and said: "The king of Tarakan is coming to make war on us."

"Well, why not?" said Ivan. "Let him come."

The king of Tarakan crossed the border and sent out his scouts to find Ivan's army. They searched and they searched, but they could find no army. Then they waited and waited— surely an army would turn up somewhere. But there was not even a rumor of one—no one to fight!

The king of Tarakan sent men to take the villages. When they came to a village all the fools, both men and women, bounded out to gaze at the soldiers and marvel. The soldiers took away their grain and their cattle, and the fools let it go without even resisting. The soldiers went on to the next village, and the same thing happened; and the next day and the next—every place was the same: the people handed over everything to them. Not only did they fail to defend themselves, but they even invited the soldiers to stay with them.

"If life is so miserable in your country, dear friends, come and live here with us," they said.

The soldiers marched on and on—and still no army, only people living and feeding themselves and others, never resisting, but always welcoming the soldiers and inviting them to stay.

It became dull work for them, and they went to their king and said: "We can't fight here. Lead us elsewhere. A war would be fine, but we can't make war here. This is like cutting jelly!"

The king of Tarakan grew angry and commanded his soldiers to overrun the whole kingdom, to lay waste the villages, burn the houses and grain, and slaughter the cattle.

"If my orders are not carried out," he said, "you will all be executed!"

The soldiers were frightened; they began at once to do as their king ordered. They burned the houses and grain, and slaughtered the cattle. And still the fools offered no resistance, but only stood by and wept: the old men wept, the old women wept, and the little children wept too.

"Why do you injure us?" they asked. "Why are you destroying good things? If you want them, why don't you take them for yourselves?"

At last the soldiers could bear it no longer; they refused to go on, and the entire army disbanded.

12

The Old Devil also went away, having failed to overcome Ivan with his soldiers.

Then he transformed himself into a fine gentleman and came back and settled in Ivan's kingdom. He now planned to catch Ivan the way he had caught Taras the Big-Belly—with money.

"I want to do you a good turn," he said to Ivan, "to teach you wit and wisdom. I shall build a house here, and establish a business."

"Well, why not?" said Ivan. "Live here and welcome!"

The next morning the fine gentleman appeared in the public square with a big bag of gold and a sheet of paper.

"You people live like swine," he said. "I am going to teach you how to live properly. Build me a house according to this plan. Work as I direct you, and I shall pay you with these gold coins."

He showed them the gold. The fools were astounded. They did not use money, but bartered their goods or paid one another in labor. They gazed at the gold pieces in wonder.

"Those are pretty little things!" they said.

They began to exchange their goods and their labor for gold pieces. The Old Devil spent money as freely as he had done in Taras's kingdom, and the people brought all sorts of things, and did all sorts of work for it. The Old devil was delighted.

"My work is progressing," he thought. "Now I shall ruin the fool as I ruined Taras. I shall buy him up, strip him of everything!"

But the fools no sooner collected their gold pieces than they gave them away: the women all wore them as necklaces, the girls plaited them into their hair, and the children played with them in the streets. Once everyone had enough of them, the men would not take any more. But the fine gentleman's mansion was not yet half built, and his grain and cattle were not yet stocked for the year, so he sent word to the people to come back and work, to cart grain and bring cattle, and that he had plenty of gold to pay for everything.

No one came to work for him, and no one brought him anything. A little girl or boy would run up to exchange an egg for a gold piece, but no one else ever came, and soon he had nothing to eat.

Being hungry, the fine gentleman went through the village trying to buy something for dinner. He thrust his head in at one door and offered a gold piece for a fowl, but the housewife refused it.

"I have lots of them," she said.

He tried to give a gold piece to a poor woman in exchange for a herring.

"It's no good to me, kind sir," she said. "I have no children to play with it. And I already have three of them that I took as curiosities."

He went to a peasant's hut for bread, but the peasant would not take any money.

"I don't need it," he said. "If you are begging in Christ's name, then wait here, and I'll tell the old woman to cut you a piece of bread."

The Old Devil spat and ran away from the peasant. Let alone the idea of begging in Christ's name, just hearing Him mentioned was worse than the cut of a knife.

And so he got no bread either. Everyone had gold, and no matter where he went no one would give him anything for money.

"Bring us something else, or come and work," they would say, "or else take what you need in Christ's name."

But the Devil had nothing but money; he was unwilling to work, and he could not possibly take anything in Christ's name. He grew furious.

"I will give you money—what more do you want?" he asked them. "You can buy anything, hire anyone, with gold!"

The fools would not listen to him. "No," they said, "we don't need it. We have no bills and no taxes—what should we do with it?"

The Old Devil was forced to go to bed without supper.

Ivan the Fool heard of this matter. People came to him and asked:

"What shall we do? A fine gentleman has appeared who likes to eat and drink well and dress nicely, but does not want to work nor to beg in Christ's name; he only wants to give gold pieces to everyone. At first we gave him everything he wanted, but we have enough gold pieces, and now we don't give him anything. What are we to do with him? He may die of hunger."

Ivan listened to them and then said:

"Well, he must be fed. Let him go from farmhouse to farmhouse as the shepherds do."

There was nothing to be done, the Old Devil had to start going from one farmhouse to another. In due time he turned up at Ivan's house. When he came in, the mute girl was preparing dinner. She had often been deceived by the lazy, who came early to dinner, their work unfinished, and ate up all the gruel. She had learned to recognize the idlers by their hands: those who had calluses she seated at the table, the others were given the scraps. The Old Devil slipped into a place at the table, but the mute girl seized his hands and examined them. There were no calluses; he had clean, smooth hands with long claws. She grunted and dragged him away from the table.

Then Ivan's wife spoke to him: "You must excuse her, fine gentleman," she said. "My sister-in-law does not allow anyone without calluses to sit at the table. Just wait till the others have eaten, then you can have what is left."

The Old Devil was offended that in a tsar's house he should be fed like the swine.

"That's a stupid law you have here," he said to Ivan, "that everyone must work with his hands. And you devised it out of stupidity. Do you think people work only with their hands? What do you think clever people work with?"

"How are we fools to know?" replied Ivan. "We're used to doing most of our work with our hands and our backs."

"That's because you are fools," said the Old Devil. "But I will teach you how to work with your heads; then you will realize that it's more profitable to work with the head than with the hands."

Ivan was amazed. "Well," he said, "no wonder we're called fools!"

"But it's not easy," the Old Devil began, "to work with your head. Here you give me nothing to eat because I have no calluses on my hands; but what you don't know is that it's a hundred times harder to work with your head. Sometimes the head even splits."

Ivan pondered. "Then why torture yourself, my dear friend?" he asked. "That can't be easy—to have your head split! Wouldn't it be better to do easier work, with your hands and your back?"

And the Devil replied: "I torture myself out of pity for you fools. If I didn't torture myself you would remain fools forever. But having worked with my head, I will now teach you."

Ivan marveled. "Do teach us," he said, "so that the next time our hands are worn out we can shift to our heads."

The Devil promised to teach them.

And Ivan announced throughout his realm that a fine gentleman had appeared who would teach everyone how to work with his head; that it was more profitable to work with the head than with the hands; and that all must come and learn.

Now there was in Ivan's kingdom a high belfry with a steep staircase leading up to a watchtower at the top. Ivan took the gentleman up there so that he would be visible to all the people.

The gentleman stood up in the tower and began to speak. The fools gathered to watch. They thought he was going to show them how they could do their work with their heads instead of their hands, but in fact the Old Devil used nothing but words to explain how to live without doing any work.

The fools could make nothing of this. They continued to watch him for a while and then went on about their business.

The Old Devil stood in the tower the whole day, and all through the following day, continually talking. He grew hungry, but it never occurred to the fools to bring him bread. They thought that if he could work better with his head than his hands it would be a mere trifle for his head to provide him with a little bread.

The Old Devil stood in the tower still another day, always talking. The people would approach him, stand and stare, then walk away.

"Well, has the gentleman started working with his head?" inquired Ivan.

"Not yet," they replied. "He's still jabbering."

The Old Devil stood in the tower one more day, and then, having grown weak, he staggered and struck his head against a pillar. One of the fools saw him and told Ivan's wife, and she ran to her husband who was plowing.

"Come and see," she said. "They say the gentleman has begun working with his head!"

Ivan was surprised. "Really?" he said.

He turned the horse around and went to the belfry. By the time he got there the Old Devil was so weak from hunger he was staggering about and knocking his head against the pillars. Just as Ivan drew near, he stumbled and fell, and came crashing headfirst down the staircase, counting each step with his head.

"Well," said Ivan, "the fine gentleman was telling the truth when he said the head sometimes splits. It's not just calluses you get—this work leaves lumps!"

The Old Devil had shot down the staircase and landed with his head stuck fast in the earth. Ivan went closer to see how much work he had done, when suddenly the earth opened, and the Old Devil fell through; and there was nothing to be seen but a hole.

Ivan scratched himself.

"Look at that!" he said. "What a horrid thing! It's him again! But he must be the father of them all! That's a big one!"

Ivan still lives to this day, and people flock to his kingdom to live. His brothers have come back again, and he feeds them too.

And whenever anyone comes and says: "Feed us," Ivan says: "Well, why not? Stay with us and welcome. We have plenty of everything."

There is just one custom that is always observed in his kingdom: he who has calluses sits at the table; he who has none eats the scraps.

THE SHEPHERDS

by Ruth Sawyer

You who keep Christmas, who keep the holy-tide, have you ever thought why a child needs must be born in the world to save it? Here is a Christmas story about God, meaning Good. It begins far back when the world was first created.

In the beginning God had two favorite archangels: one was called Lucifer, meaning Light, and one called Michael, meaning Strength. They led the heavenly hosts; they stood, one on the right hand and one on the left hand of God's throne. They were His chosen messengers.

Now the Archangel Michael served God with his whole heart and angelic soul. There was no task too great for him to perform, no thousand years of service too long. But the Archangel Lucifer chafed at serving any power higher than his own. As one thousand years swept after another thousand years—each as a day—he became bitter in his service and jealous of God.

The appointed time came for God to create the Universe. He made the sun, the moon, the stars. He made earth and water, and separated them. He made trees and flowers and grass to grow; He made creatures to walk the earth and eat therof; and He made birds for the air and fish for the waters. And when all else was created, He made a man and called him Adam, and a woman and called her Eve. It took Him six

143

heavenly days to create this Universe; and at the end He was tired and rested.

While the Creation was coming to pass and God was occupied most enormously, Lucifer went stealthily about Heaven. He spoke with this angel and with that, whispering, whispering. He spoke with the cherubim and seraphim—to all and everyone who would give him an attending ear. And what he whispered was this: "Why should God rule supreme? Why should He be the only one to create and to say what shall be created? We are powerful. We are worthy to rule. What say you?"

He whispered throughout the six days of Creation; and when God rested Lucifer led a host of rebellious angels against God; they drew their flaming swords and laid siege to God's throne. But the Archangel Michael drew his flaming sword; he led God's true angels to defend Heaven. The army of Lucifer was put to rout and his captains were taken prisoner and led before God's throne. And God said: "I cannot take life from you, for you are celestial beings. But you shall no longer be known as the hosts of light; you shall be the hosts of darkness. You, Lucifer, shall bear the name of Satan. You and those who have rebelled must seek a kingdom elsewhere. But I command you this—leave this Earth, which I have but freshly made, alone. Molest not my handiwork." So spoke God.

So Lucifer was banished with his minions; and henceforth he was known as Satan. He established a kingdom under the Earth and called it Hell. But because God had commanded him to leave Earth untouched, he straightway coveted Earth for his own. He sent his spirts abroad to tempt and make evil those born upon Earth. So it came to pass that the people of Earth knew at last the power of evil as well as of good; they felt the long reach of darkness even while they lifted their eyes to the Face of Light.

And now the years became millions. Earth became peopled in its four corners; and God looked down upon it and sorrowed. He called Archangel Michael to Him and spoke: "It has come to pass that Satan's power upon Earth is great. No longer can my angels prevail. A kingdom of destruction, of greed, of hate, and of false-witnessing has been set up among my people on the Earth I have created. Their hearts have grown dark with evil; their eyes no longer see the light. I must send to Earth my own spirit that evil may be conquered. He shall be one conceived of Heaven and born of Earth, none less than my own beloved Son.'' So spoke God.

Earth had been divided into countries, some great and powerful, some small and weak. And the strong reached out even with their armies and took the weak. Now such a one, taken, was called Judea. Within its rolling hills, its olive groves, its high pastures and twisting rivers, men had built a little city called Bethlehem—King David's city. And to this city the conquering Romans had ordered all of the tribe of Jesse to come and render tribute unto Caesar.

Beyond the city, on the high pastures, many shepherds herded their sheep. And it came to pass that God chose Bethlehem to be the place of birth for His Son; and the time to be the taxing time of the year. He chose to reveal the coming to the shepherds, they being men of simple faith and pure hearts. And God sent forth a star to show them the way, and commanded angels to sing to them of the glad tidings.

The night had grown late. High in the pastures the shepherds had built fires to keep themselves warm, to frighten off stray wolves or robbers. All slept but Esteban, the boy. He alone saw the angel, heard the tidings; and straightway he woke the sleeping ones: ''Lo, an angel has but now come among us, singing. Wake—wake, all of you! I think this night must have great meaning for us.''

Now at this time Satan stood at the gateway of Hell. Of late he had been troubled in mind, a sense of impending doom moved him. And as he gazed abroad upon the Earth he saw the angel appear. Then did his troubled mind grow fearful. He summoned his hosts of Hell, commanding them to make ready: ''Tonight I think again we defy God's power over the Universe. We fight, I think, for Earth, to make it ours. I go to it now. Come when I smite the ground.''

Swift as his thought Satan reached the Earth. He came as a

145

wanderer, upon his head a wide sombrero, about his shoulders and falling to the ground a cloak, in his hand a staff. Across the Earth he traveled even as the lightning crosses the sky. He was here—he was beyond. And so he came to the high pastures of Judea and stood at one of the fires about which the shepherds watched. Again the angel came, shouting God's tidings: "Fear not! For unto you is born this day in the city of David a Messiah!"

Satan covered his face and spoke: "What means that message?"

The shepherds cowered. "We know not."

"What is that Saviour—that Messiah yonder apparition shouts of?"

"We know not."

Satan dropped his cloak that they might see the fire that damns and burns shining even in his eyes: "I command you to know!"

It was Benito, the oldest shepherd, who asked: "In the name of God, who are you?"

And Satan answered: "In my own name I am a wanderer. Once I had taken from me a mighty kingdom. I am here to restore it unto myself."

Could this be the Saviour of whom the angels sang? The shepherds drew close—close. They looked. And to each came terror. Here truly was darkness, not light; here was nameless evil, not good. Here was one who had denied the name of God. Together they shouted: "Begone!" They drew brands from the fire and crossed them, making fiery crosses to burn between themselves and Satan.

While they had been talking among themselves Esteban, the boy, had gone far off seeking stray lambs. Now Satan sought him out. "You heard the angel sing. Where is this City of David?"

"I know not."

"Who is this Messiah?"

"You speak of Matías?" The boy was stupid with fear. "You mean my mother's brother, a shepherd, wise and faithful? But he is ill. I tend his sheep."

"Idiot! Dolt! Fool!" The voice of Satan rose like a whirlwind. "In your great stupidness you sin against me, and that is more terrible than sinning against God. For this you die!"

The boy tried to open his mouth to shriek for mercy. Before words could come, before Satan's hand could smite him, there came between them, out of the vast spaces of the Universe, one who thrust a flaming sword between the Devil and the boy; while through the vast dome of Heaven rang a voice: "Thou shalt not take the innocent!"

It was the voice of the Archangel Michael. He stood now, all in shining armor, beside Esteban, his sword shielding him. And again he spoke: "How dare you break God's command!"

"I dare do more than that." Satan spoke with mockery. "God's Earth is no longer His but mine. My minions rule it. But tonight I shall fight you for it. I shall take it from you by right of sword and mightier hosts."

He stamped the ground. It split asunder, and from its very bowels came forth rank after rank of devils, waving their double-bladed swords forged in Hell's own fires. Then Michael thrust his sword aloft and behold a mighty stairway, even like Jacob's ladder, was built between Earth and Heaven. Down its shining way came rank on rank of the heavenly hosts. Across the sky rang the shout of "Combat!"

Then such a battle was fought between the armies of darkness and the armies of light as had not been waged since the beginning of all things. And Michael's sword pinioned Satan to the ground so that he could not rise; and Michael's hosts put Satan's to rout, so that the Earth's crust broke with them and they were swallowed in belching flames. And when the Earth was rid of them, Michael spoke to Satan: "You have asked of many this night who is the Saviour—the Messiah. I will answer you, defeated. He is God's Son, and Man's. He is Peace. He is Love. He is one against whom your evil cannot prevail. For next to God He is supreme."

The face of Archangel Michael shone with the light of conquering Heaven, all goodness, all strength. And Satan, crawling to his feet, looked upon it and hated it. "I am conquered now. But wait another thousand years, two thousand!''

Meanwhile the boy Esteban watched. And with the crawling of Satan back to Hell, Michael commanded Esteban to lead the shepherds to Bethlehem that they might look upon the face of their Saviour, and worship Him.

And as the boy joined the shepherds about their fires, there came the angel again, the third time; and with it was a multitude of the heavenly host, praising God and singing hallelujahs! While over all shone a star of a magnitude never seen by them before in all the heavens.

But of the many watching their flocks that night only a few heeded. These wrapped their cloaks about them and followed the boy Esteban. As they walked he pointed out the roadsides, guarded by rank on rank of angels in shining armor. But none saw them save the boy.

Yet a great joy welled up in each heart, so that every shepherd needs must raise his voice in song. Benito, the oldest, gave them words for the beginning:

> Yonder star
> in the skies
> marks the manger
> where He lies.

Then Andrés caught the air and gave them the second verse to sing:

> Joy and laughter,
> song and mirth
> herald in
> our Saviour's birth.

Miguel lifted his voice in a great swelling tumult of thanksgiving:

> Now good will
> unto all men.

THE SHEPHERDS

Shout it, brothers,
shout again!

Carlos caught from him the song and threw it back to the others with gladness:

Peace then be
among us all;
upon great nations
and on small!

It was Esteban who gave the words for the last, singing them down the end of the road, leading them to the stable opening:

Let each shepherd
raise his voice
till the whole world
shall rejoice;
till in one voice
all shall sing—
Glory to our
Saviour—King!

The star overhead lighted the way into the stable. Within they found a young woman, very fair, and on the straw beside her a small, new-born child. Benito spoke the questions that were on the minds of all: "What is thy name, woman?"

"They call me Mary."

"And his—the child's?"

"He is called Jesus."

Benito knelt. "*Nene Jesús*—Baby Jesus, the angels have sent us to worship thee. We bring what poor gifts are ours. Here is a young cockerel for thee." Benito laid it on the straw beside the child, then rose and called: "Andrés, it is thy turn."

Andrés knelt. "I, Andrés, bring thee a lamb." He put it with the cockerel, rose, and said: "Miguel, give thine."

Miguel knelt. "I bring thee a basket of figs, little one. Carlos, thy turn."

Carlos knelt and held out shepherd-pipes. "I have made them. Thou shalt play on them when thou art grown. Juan, what hast thou?"

Juan knelt. "Here is some cheese—good goats' cheese."

In turn they knelt, each shepherd, until all but Esteban, the boy, had given his gift. "Alas, *Nene Jesús*, I have little for thee. But here are the ribbons from my cap. Thou likest them, yes? And now I make a prayer: 'Bless all shepherds. Give us to teach others the love for all gentle and small things that is in our hearts. Give us to see thy star always on this, the night of thy birth. And keep our eyes lifted eternally to the far hills.' "

And having made the prayer, and all having given their gifts, the shepherds departed into the night, singing.

HE STEPPED ON THE DEVIL'S TAIL

by Winston Marks

It was inevitable that His Satanic Majesty should find it essential to give personal, undivided attention to Panphila Megan.

By all statistics of bust, waist and hip, this little human mink was a natural for breeding mischief, and her failure to do so was quite something more than a disappointment—it was a threat.

Panphila Megan's naive rejection of sin was sowing dangerous seeds of morality at Broughly College, and once started, this sort of thing could get quite out of hand.

In spite of considerable coaching from the underworld, the many males of Broughly who had sought her downfall had each come away defeated, adoring and smiling through his tears of frustration.

Pan was that kind of a girl.

Her golden, angel-down hair softly haloed her vivacious face. There was a straight nose with little honest freckles. Her unkissed mouth was gentle and moist. From her blue eyes she poured love and compassion upon freshman and senior alike.

Her love sprinkled like a light spring shower, moistening the seeds of devotion in all it touched, but forming no morbid pools for the pollywogs and scallywags.

In her freshman year Fraternity Row considered her a

challenge, but her passive resistance stirred atavistic instincts of chivalry. As time passed her purity became almost legendary. The regard with which she came to be held grew into a sort of emotional standard. All the girls finally developed a reluctance to cooperate in even the little common everyday varieties of sin.

At the insistence of his board of directors, His Nibs finally called an emergency meeting and studied the report on Panphila Megan.

He listened to testimony from the several imps in charge of addictions, alcoholism, cheating, falsehoods, parsimony and thievery and commented, "It would seem she is impervious to the minor temptations. What have you to report, Beezie?"

His Prime Minister shrugged. "Murder, arson and rape are quite out of the question at this stage."

"Which narrows it down, doesn't it," Satan observed with sarcasm. At one time he might have rubbed his hands at the prospect, but with the resurgence of evangelism on Earth, these cases were placing an annoying drain on his resources.

"Wait until you see her, Chief," said the P. M. "You won't mind tending to this one."

The "chief" glared at the empty seat near the end of the conference table. His administrator in charge of Lust had cleverly pleaded a headache and avoided the conference.

"If she's so infernally beautiful why haven't the males in the Broughly vector been presented with suitable opportunities? That's what I want to know!" he pounded the table and thundered, "When will you people get it through your short-horned skulls that I'm an *executive*, not a depraved *errand boy!*"

His blast sent a sear of white-hot vapor down the long, asbestos tabletop, and it checked and flaked. The little pads of mica notesheets curled up in puffs of smoke like tissue paper.

"It's not bad enough," he ranted, "that They raise the rates of Forgiveness to a new high and dump Salvation around like Manna!" He shook a wire-haired fist at the red-flickering crags overhead. "Now they begin throwing us 'ringers' like this Heavenly Panphila Megan! Well, they haven't sneaked one past us since St. Joan, and by the tungsten tine of my tail, it will take a heap of amnesty to save this Pan woman when I finish her!''

It was a mighty oath, and he drew a potent plan. But one unforeseen event caused him to alter it.

Not even the Prince of Darkness could predict the inopportune moment that one Martin Costigan would choose to step on His Majesty's tail. Having just returned from a productive but miserable winter visit to North Korea, Satan was suffering a touch of arthritis in his caudal extremity.

Even so, the imps commented later behind their hands, He had no right leaving it lying around uncoiled like that. That He did was ample testimony that Panphila Megan was even more bewilderingly, radiantly lovely than anyone could describe to His Bemused Majesty.

Senior Martin Costigan's love for Pan Megan dominated all his other interests and ambitions, and these were several. Mart was a three-letter man including captain of varsity football; and president of the student-body, candidate for a Phi Beta Kappa Key and an active officer in his fraternity.

That he reached his majority a virgin was not to be laid to his physical qualifications. To the contrary, Costigan was handsome in the best dark-haired, muscular, long-lashed tradition of coeducational institutions everywhere.

Mart's carnal innocence was sheerly a function of his fidelity and devotion to one Panphila Megan. This platonic relationship was established in their freshman year at the first dance of fall term. When he made his bid for the favors he had been led to believe were synonymous with coeducational society, she laid down the law, gently but firmly.

"Sure, I like you, Mart. I like all the boys—too much. If you and I are to be friends, you must never touch me except on the dance floor.''

He thought she was just being a coy chick, this girl whose radiant smile could fetch any male on the campus at a hundred yards on a foggy day. He accused her of playing the field.

That brought tears, and he felt like a heel. She said, "I—I'm not strong like other girls. If I let a wonderful boy like you kiss me, I—well, I just mustn't, that's all!"

That did something to Mart.

Three years of Coke dates and chaperoned dances and weekly refusals of his eager proposals of marriage had only poured fuel on the fires of his passionate fidelity. Pan refused to wear his pin, dated the first one to call her and had a wonderful time. Even so, Mart couldn't generate a feeling of true jealousy—until Red Harrington appeared on the campus.

Red came out of nowhere to sign up for spring quarter. He was a magnificent specimen, six-foot-two, with a classic taper from broad shoulder to wasp waist. He smoked a huge briar pipe, incessantly fondling the hot bowl, and he dressed with an intriguing casualness that instantly marked him as a Big Man On Campus.

Red's classes all happened to coincide with Pan Megan's, an item that alerted Mart at once. He shared only one class with his beloved, but that was enough to see what was going on. His new rival was a vortex of feminine attention, including Pan's.

Painfully aware that Pan's innocence was largely dependent upon her escorts' gentlemanly natures, Mart noted with alarm Harrington's boorish manner.

Pan's almost impalpable defenses would need buttressing against a frontal assault from such a character as this.

So when Mart first spotted Pan leaning against the chemistry building, talking to Harrington outside class, he strode up quickly behind the tall, sweatered redhead to break it up.

Mart had intended no especial unpleasantness, even after he saw with dismay that Pan was looking up into Harrington's eyes with a sparkle of very unplatonic interest.

The letter man stepped up to clap the suave giant on the back and inquire why he had ignored the invitation to turn out with the track team.

Before his hand made contact his foot tromped heavily on

something round and muscular that writhed under his heel like a rather fat hose full of live steam.

His ankle turned painfully as he slipped off, but when he stared down he could see no unevenness at his feet. He had no time to investigate further, because Harrington whirled with a howl of pure anguish, grabbed Mart by the lapels of his sport jacket and shook him like a football dummy.

"You, you, you clumsy clod!" Mart's books spilled from his hands, and he stared at the contorted, long, pointed features aghast. He hadn't touched the man, yet—or had he?

Before the pain faded from Harrington's face Mart had a brief glimpse into the momentarily unveiled eyes. They were twin tunnels of bottomless malice.

While he struggled with the futility of an apology, his wiry body reacted on its own. His muscular arms flailed up and out, disengaging the grip on his clothing, then he threw a powerful left at Harrington's chin. He landed solidly, but the jaw was like a rock on a pillar. It was like hitting the bumper of a Mack truck. His knuckles cracked and pain shot up to his shoulder.

A huge, reddish palm lashed out, mashed against his nose and sent him tumbling back on the grass in an ignominious backward somersault.

When Mart recovered Pan was fleeing from the scene of violence in horror, and Harrington was strolling off puffing a billow of evil yellow smoke from his oversize pipe.

Numbly, Mart picked up his scattered books and papers. He had no impulse to pursue his assailant. To the contrary, his legs trembled with an almost uncontrollable desire to run in the opposite direction.

Mart Costigan had just encountered the Devil, and he was fully, paralyzingly aware of it. The invisible but solid tail he had stepped on—the inhuman, unyielding flesh of his jaw—the expression of distilled evil—but most of all, that glimpse into the eyes of hell itself—these gave the only possible answer to the insane behavior of the mysterious Red Harrington.

And as he limped over to the Administration Building, he thought he fathomed Harrington's purpose at Broughly College.

Martin Costigan was no coward, but he felt justified in seeking aid in this matter.

Phillip Lary, Dean of Men and professor of philosophy, greeted him in his office. "Hello, Costigan. Have a seat."

Mart stared desperately at the lean, intense face and floundered for an opening. "Dr. Lary, I—I just met the—the Devil!" he finally blurted.

Lary smiled. "You mean, you just caught the devil?"

"No, sir, not at all. I mean what I said. I just met the Devil, face to face."

Lary blew a cloud of cigarette smoke at the ceiling. "Tell me about it," he invited expressionlessly.

Mart outlined the details of his brief encounter and displayed his bruised fist.

"Red Harrington, eh? I can understand your resentment, Costigan. Everyone knows how you feel about Miss Megan. But what complaint do you propose to bring against this Harrington?"

"Complaint? I tell you, this person is the living Devil! What do you want, a sample of hell?"

He stared pugnaciously at Lary.

Then he knew how ridiculous he must sound. He realized that the shock had driven him to the edge of irrationality, but he couldn't stop himself.

"He's after Panphila Megan. Don't you see? She's been the biggest moral influence this place has ever seen."

"Granted," the professor said mildly. "She's a lovely girl. The faculty recognizes the considerable influence she has had on the student-body during her enrollment. In fact it's almost incredible that one student could bring such changes by herself. I suppose, then, that it's your theory that Old Nick, himself, has shown up in the guise of Harrington to corrupt the focus of all this reform?"

"Exactly. I demand his expulsion at once—before he seduces Panphila Megan."

The Dean of Men brushed cigarette ashes from his neat

blue suit. "This is all most regrettable, Costigan. You must realize how ridiculous your charges would sound publicly—"

"I'll take that chance," Mart broke in.

Lary closed his eyes for a long moment, then he spoke very softly. "You are much too perceiving for your own good, young man."

"What do you mean?" Mart asked, mystified.

"I mean that if you persist in spreading this rumor about Mr. Harrington I shall have you committed to the infirmary and secure your expulsion as a dangerous psychotic. Dr. Fendberg is a—close associate of mine."

An incredible thought crossed Mart's mind and he paled.

The professor caught the expression and smiled. "See here, now, I just happen to know that Harrington will be here a short time only. When he's gone you will find Panphila Megan much more, ah—receptive to your advances. His interest in her is strictly, shall we say, academic, from his point of view."

He cleared his throat and the smile vanished. "If you value your own career and reputation, stay out of this. Do you understand?"

He arose and propelled the stunned senior to the door to the outer office. As he shoved Mart through it he said pleasantly, "Always nice to talk with you, Mart. Drop in any time."

It was time for Mart's next class, and as he turned toward the Liberal Arts Building his stride lengthened. It was the only period he shared with Pan and Red Harrington. He was more determined than ever to keep her in sight at every possible chance.

Pan and Red sat across a row from each other, and Mart missed the whole lecture watching the two from his rear seat. When the closing bell rang, Red surprised him by rising, taking Pan's arm and leading her back to where he was glowering.

"Pan insists I apologize," Red offered with a relaxed smile. His eyes were now a disarming shade of green, and little good-humor lines wrinkled out from them. He didn't extend his hand but he invited, "Just to prove no hard feelings, how about running down to the beach with Pan and me this evening? We'll have a little picnic at Rocky Point, just the three of us.''

"Rocky Point is out of bounds for students after dark," Mart pointed out coldly.

"I talked to the patrolman today," Red said confidentially. "He says no one from school shows up there anymore, so they don't patrol it."

Pan said, "It sounds like fun, Mart. Don't be a stick. Come along. It'll give you two a chance to get acquainted."

Mart set his jaw, then he changed his mind. "Okay, it's a date. Pick me up at the dorm at seven—then we'll both call for Pan." He emphasized "both."

"Seven all right, Pan?" Red asked solicitously.

"Just right." Her face was flushed with excitement.

Red patted them both on the back. "Then it's settled." He wandered out lighting his pipe, leaving Mart to carry Pan's books and walk her home.

Outside he interrupted her light chatter about what to pick up at the delicatessen. "Pan, darling, this Red Harrington is—he's not good for you."

She frowned. "Now Mart, I'm no child anymore. Don't spoil the evening for everyone. Red apologized, and I think it was very sweet of him to invite you along this evening."

Mart's mouth opened. "You mean, you would have gone out there alone with him?"

She looked thoughtful. "I think I would have. I've—I've just got to face—these things someday."

They were before her house now, and Mart drew her down on the steps. He realized that she was letting him hold both her hands in his. "I'm going to tell you something pretty weird," he warned her. "Don't laugh, and don't think it's just because I'm jealous."

Her hands pressed his palms intimately, and suddenly he realized how conscious she was of the contact. Ignoring the glances of several students who wandered by, he plunged into a confession of his discoveries about Harrington.

When he finished Pan was not smiling. Her blue eyes were

large, but not with amusement. "You really believe that, don't you, Mart?" He nodded.

"What a terrible thing!" she exclaimed. "You've never been jealous before."

He shrugged hopelessly. "I knew you'd say that, but I wanted you to know how I felt. I'm coming along tonight to protect you, not to make friends with him."

She allowed him a little smile. "You know, Red does have a kind of a wicked air about him. But then he's older and more experienced."

"That," said Mart Costigan, "is for sure!"

"We'll have fun," she said impulsively, "but you stay close to me, won't you?" She squeezed his fingers, picked up her books and ran into the large, stone, sorority house.

He walked back to his own shack of a fraternity with mixed feelings. His love for Pan had crowded out much of the fear in his heart, but he knew that he hadn't convinced her about Red Harrington.

A subtle change had come over her—the way she had touched his hand, responding to the pressure of his little caress. She looked and talked the same, but some little element of her reserve was gone. *Harrington's influence!*

At precisely seven the red convertible sounded its muted cacophony of air horns out front, and Mart took his place on the leopard-skin seat beside Harrington in silence. In the pocket of his sport shirt was a very tiny, pot-metal Crucifix he had borrowed from his Catholic roommate, Bill Thomas.

Harrington greeted him with a sardonic smile. "Dr. Lary phoned me," he said. "So I am the Devil, am I?"

Mart took two deep breaths and swallowed his panic. "I figured he'd contact you. How did you get control of Dr. Lary?"

"Every man has his price." Harrington eased the car away from the curb circumspectly. "Lary's price was the chair of philosophy at Broughly. He's ambitious and very useful to me so I threw in the Deanship for good measure. How about you, Costigan?"

"I'm doing all right, thanks."

"I wouldn't brag if I were you. You want Pan Megan more than anything in the world. Three years, now, isn't it? Not even a kiss," he jeered.

"I love Pan very much. Is that a sin?"

"Come, now, Martin. You can ask me for anything, practically anything in the world, including Panphila Megan. What'll it be?"

"I just want to know one thing," Mart said. "What do you do with your tail when you sit down?"

"Tail? Don't be ridiculous!" But Mart caught him glancing down between his legs to assure himself it was quite invisible.

Mart relaxed a little at the flash of color that crept up Harrington's neck. Perhaps it wasn't entirely impossible to outsmart the Devil. Somehow he felt confident.

As they drew up before Pan's place the red convertible swung over to the wrong side of the street, and Harrington looked to his left to greet Pan, who was waiting on the porch.

Mart availed himself of the distraction to transfer the little Crucifix from his own shirt pocket to Harrington's.

It was a warm spring evening, and Pan looked lovely in a demure cotton frock. Her light wrap was over one arm and some blankets over the other.

They stopped at the delicatessen where Pan had phoned ahead for a picnic lunch to be prepared. Red refused company when he went in to pick it up.

Mart was content to sit in his corner with Pan pressed closely beside him. "Pan," he said, "I don't know what's going to happen tonight, but I want you to know that I love you very much. I won't let any harm come to you."

"Oooooh, don't look at me like that," she exclaimed. "It gives me goose-bumps." But she smiled appreciatively and pressed his hand with a warmth that was very un-Panlike.

The store door opened and Harrington came out. He seemed to be having some trouble handling the double-handled basket. He was leaning over as if it were weighted with lead.

With difficulty he heaved it in the back seat, grunted, and Mart could see sweat on his forehead.

Even Pan noticed his trembling hands and asked him if he felt all right.

"Quite all right," he said bruskly. "Just a little weak for some silly reason. Are either of you wearing a—" He broke off and fell into silence.

They reached the beach just after the sun set. Red hid the car in a clump of high brush, and they made camp in a tiny cove among some high boulders. Together they gathered firewood.

Red volunteered to make the fire, at which Pan winked at Mart with a sly grimace.

They ate the picnic lunch, Mart in stolid silence, the other two exchanging a light flow of banter from which Mart took many double and sinister meanings.

He had a twinge of apprehension when Red uncorked a bottle of red, sparkling wine and poured a glass for Pan. She sipped it and twinkled her nose at Harrington.

Mart wished now he hadn't agreed to the picnic. He could have prevented it somehow. Apparently, Pan, feeling secure with Mart along, was getting a thrill out of flirting with wickedness.

Pat's nose twinkled again.

He refused the wine himself and stepped off into the bushes to cut some slender sticks for roasting the marshmallows. He was gone into the dark only a minute, but when he returned he found Harrington kneeling beside Pan.

The great, red head pulled up quickly at the sound of Mart's footsteps, but even in the flickering firelight he could see a smear of lipstick on Harrington's mouth!

Pan's face was still upturned, her soft mouth trembling from its brief surrender. Her eyes were closed, and she didn't hear him come up.

This wasn't even subtle!

Mart clenched the three willow whips in his fist, stepped in fast and lashed the seducer full across the face with a satisfying, triple-cut slap.

Harrington screamed like a banshee. Something coiled around Mart's legs and sent him sprawling. Then Harrington stood above him looking down at him with scarlet fury. "I thought I taught you to leave me alone."

Terror shredded all reason for Mart. With no thought of the consequences he scrambled into a crouch and threw a flying tackle. His shoulder caught Harrington in the belly, and he went down gasping, Mart on top of him.

They locked together, rolling over and over. Red's arms locked around Mart and crushed the air from him in a simple, powerful hug that threatened his spine. Then, when he thought he could stand it no longer, Mart felt his adversary weaken his hold. Gradually the pressure went off, and Harrington finally gasped, "The Crucifix—where is it? There—must be one—near me—I've felt it all—evening."

"Find it, damn you!" Mart brought up an elbow hard under Harrington's chin, and this time the big head snapped back. Mart rolled free, grasped the limp body by crotch and shoulder, raised it over his head in a supreme effort and heaved it out over the water.

But there was no splash.

Instead, there was a deep rumble that Mart could feel in his chest. The sprawling form split asunder with a flash of flame, and from it burst a giant, nine feet tall, horned, tailed and glowing a dull, angry red.

The scarlet face that grinned down hideously still remotely resembled Harrington's, even as Mart's jealous mind had caricatured it.

Mart stumbled back and threw himself down over Pan's terrified form. "It's all right now, honey," he said with chattering teeth. "This is what I wanted. He can't harm us now." She clung to him, and together they watched the apparition drift in over the little beach fire.

The flames licked up his legs as he stirred the coals with his long, now-visible tail. He stared down at the cowering pair for a long, calculating moment, then he sank suddenly into the fire.

The flames, embers, ashes and all, sucked down into the

sand after him, and only a few sparks and wisps of smoke remained to indicate where it had blazed only a moment before.

They collapsed together with relief. "You're all right now, sweetheart. He's gone."

"Yes. He's gone. I'm—I'm not frightened any more," she whispered.

She was warm against him, her fine hair fragrant in his face. She turned her lips to him, eyes closed, trembling slightly. "Mart—take me home—quickly, dear. Quickly!"

"Yes, sweetheart."

Neither of them stirred.

"Mart! Please," she pleaded. "I'm helpless. Oh, Mart! Mart, I do love you!"

He had his strength and his breath now, but to move was unthinkable. Harrington had said, "Every man has his price. How about you, Costigan?"

Dr. Phillip Lary rocked back in his walnut swivel chair and pressed his fanned fingertips together. "Well, well, Mart! I expected you a little earlier. I hear you cut your morning classes."

Mart tossed the keys to the red convertible on the desk-blotter. "I wrestled your boss last night," he said quietly.

"So I understand. Quite a gimmick, that Crucifix."

"You keep in close touch, don't you? Well, Doctor, I don't think that Mr. Harrington will graduate with his class."

"Quite right. His work here is completed," Lary said with a smirk.

Mart frowned. "You mean, he's giving up?"

"Not at all. His mission is accomplished. Do you deny you spent the night on the beach with Panphila Megan?"

"Now wait a minute," Mart said quickly. "Let's not confuse the appearance of sin with the real thing. I'm not as stupid as that. I knew that my real battle was only beginning when I threw Harrington into the lake."

"My deepest sympathy."

"Keep it. For your information, I won that bout, too."

The professor clucked. "What a wasted effort! A number of people on the campus were awakened early this morning by their telephones. All wrong numbers, of course, but they just happened to look out of their windows when you brought Pan Megan home at six o'clock—A.M."

"So what?"

"By tonight the rumor will be well on its way. The mighty Panphila has fallen."

"But she hasn't, I tell you!"

"Explain that to the freshmen. Maybe they'll believe you. Anyway, didn't you kiss her and hold her in your arms?"

"That's no sin!"

"Come, now, Costigan. You know her almost as well—as we do. She's tasted the apple. You've destroyed her resistance. Do you think that all the other men who follow you will be as foolishly considerate as you were?"

He reached in a drawer. "Mr. Harrington left a note for you."

Mart unfolded the paper. On it, inked in red in large, bold strokes were these lines: *If you'd had any initiative you could have done that long ago and saved me considerable trouble. But thanks, anyway.*

(Signed:) *Harrington.*"

Mart swayed a little.

"I'll be damned!"

"Such is my prediction," Lary grinned. "And Panphila Megan in the bargain."

"So he *did* plan it that way? I thought he was using the direct approach."

"Such was his intention until you—blundered onto his tail over by the chemistry building."

Mart reached into his pocket and dropped a folded legal paper before Lary's eyes. "It was a neat act he put on, but he overdid it. He scared the Hell right out of us. Pan confessed that she was completely helpless, so we decided we'd better not put it off."

Lary picked the folds apart gingerly, then dropped it as if it were hot. It was a marriage certificate.

Mart grinned at the stricken professor. "There go your rumors, Doctor. And Pan's dating days are over."

He pocketed the certificate, stepped to the door and waved the red-inked note. "Thanks for the souvenir. Quite a collector's item."

But it was not to be so. As he spoke, the Devil's note scorched brown, crackled angrily in his hand and disappeared in a puff of sulfurous smoke.

RUSTLE OF WINGS

by Fredric Brown

Poker wasn't exactly a religion with Gramp, but it was about the nearest thing he had to a religion for the first fifty or so years of his life. That's about how old he was when I went to live with him and Gram. That was a long time ago, in a little Ohio town. I can date it pretty well, because it was just after President McKinley was assassinated. I don't mean there was any connection between McKinley's assassination and my going to live with Gram and Gramp; it just happened about the same time. I was about ten.

Gram was a good woman and a Methodist and never touched a card, except occasionally to put away a deck that Gramp had left lying somewhere, and then she'd handle it gingerly, almost as though it might explode. But she'd given up, years before, trying to reform Gramp out of his heathen ways; given up trying *seriously*, I mean. She hadn't given up nagging him about it.

If she had, Gramp would have missed the nagging, I guess; he was so used to it by then. I was too young, then, to realize what an odd couple they made—the village atheist and the president of the Methodist missionary society. To me, then, they were just Gramp and Gram, and there wasn't anything strange about their loving and living together despite their differences.

Maybe it wasn't so strange after all. I mean, Gramp was a

167

good man underneath the crust of his cynicism. He was one of the kindest men I ever knew, and one of the most generous. He got cantankerous only when it came to superstition or religion—he refused ever to distinguish between the two—and when it came to playing poker with his cronies, or, for that matter, when it came to playing poker with anyone, anywhere, any time.

He was a good player, too; he won a little more often than he lost. He used to figure that about a tenth of his income came from playing poker; the other nine-tenths came from the truck farm he ran, just at the edge of town. In a manner of speaking, though, you might say he came out even, because Gram insisted on tithing—giving one tenth of their income to the Methodist church and missions.

Maybe that fact helped Gram's conscience in the matter of living with Gramp; anyway, I remember that she was always madder when he lost than when he won. How she got around his being an atheist I don't know. Probably she never really believed him, even at his most dogmatic negative.

I'd been with them about three years; I must have been about thirteen at the time of the big change. That was still a long time ago, but I'll never forget the night the change started, the night I heard the rustle of leathery wings in the dining room. It was the night that the seed salesman ate with us, and later played poker with Gramp.

His name—I won't forget it—was Charley Bryce. He was a little man; I remember that he was just as tall as I was at the time, which wouldn't have been more than an inch or two over five feet. He wouldn't have weighed much over a hundred pounds and he had short-cropped black hair that started rather low on his forehead but tapered off to a bald spot the size of a silver dollar farther back. I remember the bald spot well; I stood back of him for a while during the poker and recall thinking what a perfect fit that spot would be for one of the silver dollars—cartwheels, they were called—before him on the table. I don't remember his face at all.

I don't recall the conversation during dinner. In all probability it was largely about seeds, because the salesman hadn't yet completed taking Gramp's order. He'd called late in the afternoon; Gramp had been in town at the broker's with a load of truck, but Gram had expected him back any minute and had told the salesman to wait. But by the time Gramp and the wagon came back it was so late that Gram had asked the salesman to stay and eat with us, and he had accepted.

Gramp and Charley Bryce still sat at the table, I recall, while I helped Gram clear off the dishes, and Bryce had the order blank before him, finishing writing up Gramp's order.

It was after I'd carried the last load and came back to take care of the napkins that poker was mentioned for the first time; I don't know which of the men mentioned it first. But Gramp was telling animately of a hand he'd held the last time he'd played, a few nights before. The stranger—possibly I forgot to say that Charley Bryce *was* a stranger; we'd never met him before and he must have been shifted to a different territory because we never saw him again—was listening with smiling interest. No, I don't remember his face at all, but I remember that he smiled a lot.

I picked up the napkins and rings so Gram could take up the tablecloth from under them. And while she was folding the cloth I put three napkins—hers and Gramp's and mine—back into our respective napkin rings and put the salesman's napkin with the laundry. Gram had that expression on her face again, the tight-lipped disapproving look she wore whenever cards were being played or discussed.

And then Gramp asked, "Where are the cards, Ma?"

Gram sniffed. "Wherever you put them, William," she told him. So Gramp got the cards from the drawer in the sideboard where they were always kept, and got a big handful of silver out of his pocket, and he and the stranger, Charley Bryce, started to play two-handed stud poker across a corner of the big square dining room table.

I was out in the kitchen then, for a while, helping Gram with the dishes, and when I came back most of the silver was in front of Bryce, and Gramp had gone into his wallet and there was a pile of dollar bills in front of him instead of the cartwheels. Dollar bills were big in those days, not the little skimpy ones we have now.

I stood there watching the game after I'd finished the dishes. I don't remember any of the hands they held; I remember that money seesawed back and forth, though, without anybody getting more than ten or twenty dollars ahead or behind. And I remember the stranger looking at the clock after a while and saying he wanted to catch the ten-o'clock train and would it be all right to deal off at half past nine, and Gramp saying sure.

So they did, and at nine-thirty it was Charley Bryce who was ahead. He counted off the money he himself had put into the game and there was a pile of silver cartwheels left, and he counted that, and I remember that he grinned. He said, "Thirteen dollars exactly. Thirteen pieces of silver."

"The devil," said Gramp; it was one of his favorite expressions.

And Gram sniffed. "Speak of the devil," she said, "and you hear the rustle of his wings."

Charley Bryce laughed softly. He'd picked up the deck of cards again, and he riffled them softly, as softly as he had laughed, and asked, "Like this?"

That was when I started to get scared.

Gram just sniffed again, though. She said, "Yes, like that. And if you gentlemen will excuse me— And you, Johnny, you'd better not stay up much longer."

She went upstairs.

The salesman chuckled and riffled the cards again. Louder, this time. I don't know whether it was the rustling sound they made or the thirteen pieces of silver, exactly, or what, but I was scared. I wasn't standing behind the salesman anymore; I'd walked around the table. He saw my face and grinned at me. He said, "Son, you look like you believe in the devil, and think I'm him. Do you?"

I said, "No, sir," but I must not have said it very convincingly. Gramp laughed out loud, and he wasn't a man that laughed out loud very often.

Gramp said, "I'm surprised at you, Johnny. Darned if you

don't sound like you *do* believe it!" And he was off laughing again.

Charley Bryce looked at Gramp. There was a twinkle in his eye. He asked, "Don't you believe it?"

Gramp quit laughing. He said, "Cut it out, Charley. Giving the boy silly ideas." He looked around to be sure Gram had left. "I don't want him to grow up superstitious."

"Everybody's superstitious, more or less," Charley Bryce said.

Gramp shook his head. "Not me."

Bryce said, "You don't think you are, but if it came to a showdown, I'd bet you are."

Gramp frowned. "You'd bet what, and how?"

The salesman riffled the deck of cards once more and then put them down. He picked up the stack of cartwheels and counted them again. He said, "I'll bet thirteen dollars to your one dollar. Thirteen pieces of silver says you'd be afraid to prove you don't believe in the devil."

Gramp had put away his folding money but he took his wallet out again and took a dollar bill out of it. He put the bill on the table between them. He said, "Charley Bryce, you're covered."

Charley Bryce put the pile of silver dollars beside it, and took a fountain pen out of his pocket, the one Gramp had signed the seed order with. I remember the pen because it was one of the first fountain pens I'd ever seen and I'd been interested in it.

Charley Bryce handed Gramp the fountain pen and took a clean seed order blank out of his pocket and put it on the table in front of Gramp, the unprinted side up.

He said, "You write 'For thirteen dollars I sell my soul,' and then sign it."

Gramp laughed and picked up the fountain pen. He started to write, fast, and then his hand moved slower and slower and he stopped; I couldn't see how far he'd written.

He looked across the table at Charley Bryce. He said, "What if—?" Then he looked down at the paper awhile more and then at the money in the middle of the table; the fourteen dollars, one paper and thirteen silver.

Then he grinned, but it was a kind of sick grin.

He said, "Take the bet, Charley. You win, I guess."

That was all there was to it. The salesman chuckled and picked up the money, and Gramp walked with him to the railroad station.

But Gramp wasn't ever exactly the same after that. Oh, he kept on playing poker; he never did change about that. Not even after he started going to church with Gram every Sunday regularly, and even after he finally let them make him a vestryman he kept on playing cards, and Gram kept on nagging him about it. He taught me how to play, too, in spite of Gram.

We never saw Charley Bryce again; he must have been transferred to a different route or changed jobs. And it wasn't until the day of Gramp's funeral in 1913 that I learned that Gram had heard the conversation and the bet that night; she'd been straightening things in the linen closet in the hall and hadn't gone upstairs yet. She told me on the way home from the funeral, ten years later.

I asked her, I remember, whether she would have come in and stopped Gramp if he'd been going to sign, and she smiled. She said, "He wouldn't have, Johnny. And it wouldn't have mattered if he had. If there really is a devil, God wouldn't let him wander around tempting people like that, in disguise."

"Would you have signed, Gram?" I asked her.

"Thirteen dollars for writing something silly on a piece of paper, Johnny? Of course I would. Wouldn't you?"

I said, "I don't know." And it's been a long time since then, but I still don't.

THAT HELL-BOUND TRAIN

by Robert Bloch

When Martin was a little boy, his Daddy was a Railroad Man. Daddy never rode the high iron, but he walked the tracks for the CB&Q, and he was proud of his job. And every night when he got drunk, he sang this old song about *That Hell-Bound Train*.

Martin didn't quite remember any of the words, but he couldn't forget the way his Daddy sang them out. And when Daddy made the mistake of getting drunk in the afternoon and got squeezed between a Pennsy tankcar and an AT&SF gondola, Martin sort of wondered why the Brotherhood didn't sing the song at his funeral.

After that, things didn't go so good for Martin, but somehow he always recalled Daddy's song. When Mom up and ran off with a traveling salesman from Keokuk (Daddy must have turned over in his grave, knowing she'd done such a thing, and with a *passenger*, too!) Martin hummed the tune to himself every night in the Orphan Home. And after Martin himself ran away, he used to whistle the song softly at night in the jungles, after the other bindlestiffs were asleep.

Martin was on the road for four-five years before he realized he wasn't getting anyplace. Of course he'd tried his hand at a lot of things—picking fruit in Oregon, washing dishes in a Montana hash house, stealing hubcaps in Denver and tires in Oklahoma City—but by the time he'd put in six months on the chain gang down in Alabama he knew he had no future drifting around this way on his own.

So he tried to get on the railroad like his Daddy had and they told him that times were bad.

But Martin couldn't keep away from the railroads. Wherever he traveled, he rode the rods; he'd rather hop a freight heading north in subzero weather than lift his thumb to hitch a ride with a Cadillac headed for Florida. Whenever he managed to get hold of a can of Sterno, he'd sit there under a nice warm culvert, think about the old days, and often as not he'd hum the song about *That Hell-Bound Train*. That was the train the drunks and the sinners rode—the gambling men and the grifters, the big-time spenders, the skirt-chasers, and all the jolly crew. It would be really fine to take a trip in such good company, but Martin didn't like to think of what happened when that train finally pulled into the Depot Way Down Yonder. He didn't figure on spending eternity stoking boilers in Hell, without even a Company Union to protect him. Still, it would be a lovely ride. If there was *such* a thing as a Hell-Bound Train. Which, of course, there wasn't.

At least Martin didn't *think* there was, until that evening when he found himself walking the tracks heading south, just outside of Appleton Junction. The night was cold and dark, the way November nights are in the Fox River Valley, and he knew he'd have to work his way down to New Orleans for the winter, or maybe even Texas. Somehow he didn't much feel like going, even though he'd heard tell that a lot of those Texas automobiles had solid gold hubcaps.

No sir, he just wasn't cut out for petty larceny. It was worse than a sin—it was unprofitable, too. Bad enough to do the Devil's work, but then to get such miserable pay on top of it! Maybe he'd better let the Salvation Army convert him.

Martin trudged along humming Daddy's song, waiting for a rattler to pull out of the Junction behind him. He'd have to catch it—there was nothing else for him to do.

But the first train to come along came from the other direction, roaring towards him along the track from the south.

Martin peered ahead, but his eyes couldn't match his ears,

and so far all he could recognize was the sound. It *was* a train, though; he felt the steel shudder and sing beneath his feet.

And yet, how could it be? The next station was Neenah-Menasha, and there was nothing due out of there for hours.

The clouds were thick overhead, and the field mists rolled like a cold fog in a November midnight. Even so, Martin should have been able to see the headlight as the train rushed on. But there was only the whistle, screaming out of the black throat of the night. Martin could recognize the equipment of just about any locomotive ever built, but he'd never heard a whistle that sounded like this one. It wasn't signaling; it was screaming like a lost soul.

He stepped to one side, for the train was almost on top of him now. And suddenly there it was, looming along the tracks and grinding to a stop in less time than he'd believed possible. The wheels hadn't been oiled, because they screamed too, screamed like the damned. But the train slid to a halt and the screams died away into a series of low, groaning sounds, and Martin looked up and saw that this was a passenger train. It was big and black, without a single light shining in the engine cab or any of the long string of cars; Martin couldn't read any lettering on the sides, but he was pretty sure this train didn't belong on the Northwestern Road.

He was even more sure when he saw the man clamber down out of the forward car. There was something wrong about the way he walked, as though one of his feet dragged, and about the lantern he carried. The lantern was dark, and the man held it up to his mouth and blew, and instantly it glowed redly. You don't have to be a member of the Railway Brotherhood to know that this is a mighty peculiar way of lighting a lantern.

As the figure approached, Martin recognized the conductor's cap perched on his head, and this made him feel a little better for a moment—until he noticed that it was worn a bit too high, as though there might be something sticking up on the forehead underneath it.

Still, Martin knew his manners, and when the man smiled at him, he said, "Good evening, Mr. Conductor."

"Good evening, Martin."

"How did you know my name?"

The man shrugged. "How did you know I was the Conductor?"

"You *are*, aren't you?"

"To you, yes. Although other people, in other walks of life, may recognize me in different roles. For instance, you ought to see what I look like to the folks out in Hollywood." The man grinned. "I travel a great deal," he explained.

"What brings you here?" Martin asked.

"Why, you ought to know the answer to that, Martin. I came because you needed me. Tonight, I suddenly realized you were backsliding. Thinking of joining the Salvation Army, weren't you?"

"Well—" Martin hesitated.

"Don't be ashamed. To err is human, as somebody or other once said. *Reader's Digest*, wasn't it? Never mind. The point is, I felt you needed me. So I switched over and came your way."

"What for?"

"Why, to offer you a ride, of course. Isn't it better to travel comfortably by train than to march along the cold streets behind a Salvation Army band? Hard on the feet, they tell me, and even harder on the eardrums."

"I'm not sure I'd care to ride your train, sir," Martin said. "Considering where I'm likely to end up."

"Ah, yes. The old argument." The Conductor sighed. "I suppose you'd prefer some sort of bargain, is that it?"

"Exactly," Martin answered.

"Well, I'm afraid I'm all through with that sort of thing. There's no shortage of prospective passengers anymore. Why should I offer you any special inducements?"

"You must want me, or else you wouldn't have bothered to go out of your way to find me."

The Conductor sighed again. "There you have a point. Pride was always my besetting weakness, I admit. And somehow I'd hate to lose you to the competition, after thinking of you as my own all these years." He hesitated. "Yes, I'm prepared to deal with you on your own terms, if you insist."

"The terms?" Martin asked.

"Standard proposition. Anything you want."

"Ah," said Martin.

"But I warn you in advance, there'll be no tricks. I'll grant you any wish you can name—but in return, you must promise to ride the train when the time comes."

"Suppose it never comes?"

"It will."

"Suppose I've got the kind of a wish that will keep me off forever?"

"There is no such wish."

"Don't be too sure."

"Let me worry about that," the Conductor told him. "No matter what you have in mind, I warn you that I'll collect in the end. And there'll be none of this last-minute hocus-pocus, either. No last-hour repentances, no blond fräuleins or fancy lawyers showing up to get you off. I offer a clean deal. That is to say, you'll get what you want, and I'll get what I want."

"I've heard you trick people. They say you're worse than a used-car salesman."

"Now, wait a minute—"

"I apologize," Martin said, hastily. "But it *is* supposed to be a fact that you can't be trusted."

"I admit it. On the other hand, you seem to think you have found a way out."

"A surefire proposition."

"Surefire? Very funny!" The man began to chuckle, then halted. "But we waste valuable time, Martin. Let's get down to cases. What do you want from me?"

Martin took a deep breath. "I want to be able to stop Time."

"Right now?"

"No. Not yet. And not for everybody. I realize that would be impossible, of course. But I want to be able to stop Time for myself. Just once, in the future. Whenever I get to a point where I know I'm happy and contented, that's where I'd like to stop. So I can just keep on being happy forever."

"That's quite a proposition," the Conductor mused. "I've got to admit I've never heard anything just like it before—and believe me, I've listened to some lulus in my day." He grinned at Martin. "You've really been thinking about this, haven't you?"

"For years," Martin admitted. Then he coughed. "Well, what do you say?"

"It's not impossible, in terms of your own *subjective* time sense," the Conductor murmured. "Yes, I think it could be arranged."

"But I mean *really* to stop. Nor for me just to *imagine* it."

"I understand. And it can be done."

"Then you'll agree?"

"Why not? I promised you, didn't I? Give me your hand."

Martin hesitated. "Will it hurt very much? I mean, I don't like the sight of blood, and—"

"Nonsense! You've been listening to a lot of poppycock. We already have made our bargain, my boy. I merely intend to put something into your hand. The ways and means of fulfilling your wish. After all, there's no telling at just what moment you may decide to exercise the agreement, and I can't drop everything and come running. So it's better if you can regulate matters for yourself."

"You're going to give me a Time-stopper?"

"That's the general idea. As soon as I can decide what would be practical." The Conductor hesitated. "Ah, the very thing! Here, take my watch."

He pulled it out of his vest pocket; a railroad watch in a silver case. He opened the back and made a delicate adjustment; Martin tried to see just exactly what he was doing, but the fingers moved in a blinding blur.

"There we are," the Conductor smiled. "It's all set, now. When you finally decide where you'd like to call a halt, merely turn the stem in reverse and unwind the watch until it stops. When it stops, Time stops, for you. Simple enough?" And the Conductor dropped the watch into Martin's hand.

The young man closed his fingers tightly around the case. "That's all there is to it, eh?"

"Absolutely. But remember—you can stop the watch only once. So you'd better make sure that you're satisfied with the moment you choose to prolong. I caution you in all fairness; make very certain of your choice."

"I will." Martin grinned. "And since you've been so fair about it, I'll be fair, too. There's one thing you seem to have forgotten. It doesn't really matter *what* moment I choose. Because once I stop Time for myself, that means I stay where I am forever. I'll never have to get any older. And if I don't get any older, I'll never die. And if I never die, then I'll never have to take a ride on your train."

The Conductor turned away. His shoulders shook convulsively, and he may have been crying "And you said *I* was worse than a used-car salesman," he gasped, in a strangled voice.

Then he wandered off into the fog, and the train-whistle gave an impatient shriek, and all at once it was moving swiftly down the track, rumbling out of sight in the darkness.

Martin stood there, blinking down at the silver watch in his hand. If it wasn't that he could actually see it and feel it there, and if he couldn't smell that peculiar odor, he might have thought he'd imagined the whole thing from start to finish—train, Conductor, bargain, and all.

But he had the watch, and he could recognize the scent left by the train as it departed, even though there aren't many locomotives around that use sulphur and brimstone as fuel.

And he had no doubts about his bargain. That's what came of thinking things through to a logical conclusion. Some fools would have settled for wealth, or power, or Kim Novak. Daddy might have sold out for a fifth of whiskey.

Martin knew that he'd made a better deal. Better? It was foolproof. All he needed to do now was choose his moment.

He put the watch in his pocket and started back down the railroad track. He hadn't really had a destination in mind before, but he did now. He was going to find a moment of happiness. . . .

Now young Martin wasn't altogether a ninny. He realized perfectly well that happiness is a relative thing; there are conditions and degrees of contentment, and they vary with one's lot in life. As a hobo, he was often satisfied with a warm handout, a double-length bench in the park, or a can of Sterno made in 1957 (a vintage year). Many a time he had reached a state of momentary bliss through such simple agencies, but he was aware that there were better things. Martin determined to seek them out.

Within two days he was in the great city of Chicago. Quite naturally, he drifted over to West Madison Street, and there he took steps to elevate his role in life. He became a city bum, a panhandler, a moocher. Within a week he had risen to the point where happiness was a meal in a regular one-arm luncheon joint, a two-bit flop on a real army cot in a real flophouse, and a full fifth of muscatel.

There was a night, after enjoying all three of these luxuries to the full, when Martin thought of unwinding his watch at the pinnacle of intoxication. But he also thought of the faces of the honest johns he'd braced for a handout today. Sure, they were squares, but they were prosperous. They wore good clothes, held good jobs, drove nice cars. And for them, happiness was even more ecstatic—they ate dinner in fine hotels, they slept on innerspring mattresses, they drank blended whiskey.

Squares or no, they had something there. Martin fingered his watch, put aside the temptation to hock it for another bottle of muscatel, and went to sleep determined to get himself a job and improve his happiness quotient.

When he awoke he had a hangover, but the determination was still with him. Before the month was out Martin was working for a general contractor over on the South Side, at one of the big rehabilitation projects. He hated the grind, but the pay was good, and pretty soon he got himself a one-room apartment out on Blue Island Avenue. He was accustomed to eating in decent restaurants now, and he bought himself a confortable bed, and every Saturday night he went down to the corner tavern. It was all very pleasant, but—

The foreman liked his work and promised him a raise in a month. If he waited around, the raise would mean that he could afford a secondhand car. With a car, he could even start picking up a girl for a date now and then. Other fellows on the job did, and they seemed pretty happy.

So Martin kept on working, and the raise came through and the car came through and pretty soon a couple of girls came through.

The first time it happened, he wanted to unwind his watch immediately. Until he got to thinking about what some of the older men always said. There was a guy named Charlie, for example, who worked alongside him on the hoist. "When you're young and don't know the score, maybe you get a kick out of running around with those pigs. But after a while, you want something better. A nice girl of your own. That's the ticket."

Martin felt he owed it to himself to find out. If he didn't like it better, he could always go back to what he had.

Almost six months went by before Martin met Lillian Gillis. By that time he'd had another promotion and was working inside, in the office. They made him go to night school to learn how to do simple bookkeeping, but it meant another fifteen bucks extra a week, and it was nicer working indoors.

And Lillian *was* a lot of fun. When she told him she'd marry him, Martin was almost sure that the time was now. Except that she was sort of—well, she was a *nice* girl, and she said they'd have to wait until they were married. Of course, Martin couldn't expect to marry her until he had a little more money saved up, and another raise would help, too.

That took a year. Martin was patient, because he knew it was going to be worth it. Every time he had any doubts, he took out his watch and looked at it. But he never showed it to Lillian, or anybody else. Most of the other men wore expensive wristwatches and the old silver railroad watch looked just a little cheap.

Martin smiled as he gazed at the stem. Just a few twists and he'd have something none of these other poor working slobs would ever have. Permanent satisfaction, with his blushing bride—

Only getting married turned out to be just the beginning. Sure, it was wonderful, but Lillian told him how much better things would be if they could move into a new place and fix it up. Martin wanted decent furniture, a TV set, a nice car.

So he started taking night courses and got a promotion to the front office. With the baby coming, he wanted to stick around and see his son arrive. And when it came, he realized he'd have to wait until it got a little older, started to walk and talk and develop a personality of its own.

About this time the company sent him out on the road as a troubleshooter on some of those other jobs, and now he *was* eating at those good hotels, living high on the hog and the expense account. More than once he was tempted to unwind his watch. This was the good life. . . . Of course, it would be even better if he just didn't have to *work*. Sooner or later, if he could cut in on one of the company deals, he could make a pile and retire. Then everything would be ideal.

It happened, but it took time. Martin's son was going to high school before he really got up there into the chips. Martin got a strong hunch that it was now or never, because he wasn't exactly a kid any more.

But right about then he met Sherry Westcott, and she didn't seem to think he was middle-aged at all, in spite of the way he was losing hair and adding stomach. She taught him that a *toupee* would cover the bald spot and a cummerbund could cover the potgut. In fact, she taught him quite a lot and he so enjoyed learning that he actually took out his watch and prepared to unwind it.

Unfortunately, he chose the very moment that the private detectives broke down the door of the hotel room, and then there was a long stretch of time when Martin was so busy fighting the divorce action that he couldn't honestly say he was enjoying any given moment.

When he made the final settlement with Lil he was broke again, and Sherry didn't seem to think he was so young after all. So he squared his shoulders and went back to work.

He made his pile, eventually, but it took longer this time, and there wasn't much chance to have fun along the way. The fancy dames in the fancy cocktail lounges didn't seem to interest him anymore, and neither did the liquor. Besides, the Doc had warned him off that.

But there were other pleasures for a rich man to investigate. Travel, for instance—and not riding the rods from one hick burg to another, either. Martin went around the world by plane and luxury liner. For a while it seemed as though he would find his moment after all, visiting the Taj Mahal by moonlight. Martin pulled out the battered old watchcase, and got ready to unwind it. Nobody else was there to watch him—

And that's why he hesitated. Sure, this was an enjoyable moment, but he was alone. Lil and the kid were gone, Sherry was gone, and somehow he'd never had time to make any friends. Maybe if he found new congenial people, he'd have the ultimate happiness. That must be the answer—it wasn't just money or power or sex or seeing beautiful things. The real satisfaction lay in friendship.

So on the boat trip home, Martin tried to strike up a few acquaintances at the ship's bar. But all these people were much younger, and Martin had nothing in common with them. Also they wanted to dance and drink, and Martin wasn't in condition to appreciate such pastimes. Nevertheless, he tried.

Perhaps that's why he had the little accident the day before they docked in San Francisco. "Little accident" was the ship's doctor's way of describing it, but Martin noticed he looked very grave when he told him to stay in bed, and he'd called an ambulance to meet the liner at the dock and take the patient right to the hospital.

At the hospital, all the expensive treatment and the expensive smiles and the expensive words didn't fool Martin any. He was an old man with a bad heart, and they thought he was going to die.

But he could fool them. He still had the watch. He found it in his coat when he put on his clothes and sneaked out of the hospital.

He didn't have to die. He could cheat death with a single gesture—and he intended to do it as a free man, out there under a free sky.

That was the real secret of happiness. He understood it now. Not even friendship meant as much as freedom. This was the best thing of all—to be free of friends or family or the furies of the flesh.

Martin walked slowly beside the embankment under the night sky. Come to think of it, he was just about back where he'd started, so many years ago. But the moment was good, good enough to prolong forever. Once a bum, always a bum.

He smiled as he thought about it, and then the smile twisted sharply and suddenly, like the pain twisting sharply and suddenly in his chest. The world began to spin and he fell down on the side of the embankment.

He couldn't see very well, but he was still conscious, and he knew what had happened. Another stroke, and a bad one. Maybe this was it. Except that he wouldn't be a fool any longer. He wouldn't wait to see what was around the corner.

Right now was his chance to use his power and save his life. And he was going to do it. He could still move, nothing could stop him.

He groped in his pocket and pulled out the old silver watch, fumbling with the stem. A few twists and he'd cheat death, he'd never have to ride that Hell-Bound Train. He could go on forever.

Forever.

Martin had never really considered the word before. To go on forever—but *how?* Did he *want* to go on forever, like this; a sick old man, lying helplessly here in the grass?

No. He couldn't do it. He wouldn't do it. And suddenly he wanted very much to cry, because he knew that somewhere along the line he'd outsmarted himself. And now it was too late. His eyes dimmed, there was a roaring in his ears. . . .

He recognized the roaring, of course, and he wasn't at all surprised to see the train come rushing out of the fog up there on the embankment. He wasn't surprised when it stopped, either, or when the Conductor climbed off and walked slowly towards him.

The Conductor hadn't changed a bit. Even his grin was still the same.

"Hello, Martin," he said. "All aboard."

"I know," Martin whispered. "But you'll have to carry me. I can't walk. I'm not even really talking anymore, am I?"

"Yes you are," the Conductor said. "I can hear you fine. And you can walk, too." He leaned down and placed his hand on Martin's chest. There was a moment of icy numbness, and then, sure enough, Martin could walk after all.

He got up and followed the Conductor along the slope, moving to the side of the train.

"In here?" he asked.

"No, the next car," the Conductor murmured. "I guess you're entitled to ride Pullman. After all, you're quite a successful man. You've tasted the joys of wealth and position and prestige. You've known the pleasures of marriage and fatherhood. You've sampled the delights of dining and drinking and debauchery, too, and you traveled high, wide and handsome. So let's not have any last-minute recriminations."

"All right," Martin sighed. "I can't blame you for my mistakes. On the other hand, you can't take credit for what happened, either. I worked for everything I got. I did it all on my own. I didn't even need your watch."

"So you didn't," the Conductor said, smiling. "But would you mind giving it back to me now?"

"Need it for the next sucker, eh?" Martin muttered.

"Perhaps."

Something about the way he said it made Martin look up. He tried to see the Conductor's eyes, but the brim of his cap cast a shadow. So Martin looked down at the watch instead.

"Tell me something," he said, softly. "If I give you the watch, what will you do with it?"

"Why, throw it into the ditch," the Conductor told him. "That's all I'll do with it." And he held out his hand.

"What if somebody comes along and finds it? And twists the stem backwards, and stops Time?"

"Nobody would do that," the Conductor murmured. "Even if they knew."

"You mean, it was all a trick? This is only an ordinary, cheap watch?"

"I didn't say that," whispered the Conductor. "I only said that no one has ever twisted the stem backwards. They've all been like you, Martin—looking ahead to find that perfect happiness. Waiting for the moment that never comes."

The Conductor held out his hand again.

Martin sighed and shook his head. "You cheated me after all."

"You cheated yourself, Martin. And now you're going to ride that Hell-Bound Train."

He pushed Martin up the steps and into the car ahead. As he entered, the train began to move and the whistle screamed. And Martin stood there in the swaying Pullman, gazing down the aisle at the other passengers. He could see them sitting there, and somehow it didn't seem strange at all.

Here they were; the drunks and the sinners, the gambling men and the grifters, the big-time spenders, the skirt-chasers, and all the jolly crew. They knew where they were going, of course, but they didn't seem to give a damn. The blinds were drawn on the windows, yet it was light inside, and they were all living it up—singing and passing the bottle and roaring with laughter, throwing the dice and telling their jokes and bragging their big brags, just the way Daddy used to sing about them in the old song.

"Mighty nice traveling companions," Martin said. "Why, I've never seen such a pleasant bunch of people. I mean, they seem to be really enjoying themselves!"

The Conductor shrugged. "I'm afraid things won't be quite so jazzy when we pull into that Depot Way Down Yonder."

For the third time, he held out his hand. "Now, before you sit down, if you'll just give me that watch. A bargain's a bargain—"

Martin smiled. "A bargain's a bargain," he echoed. "I agreed to ride your train if I could stop Time when I found the right moment of happiness. And I think I'm about as happy right here as I've ever been."

Very slowly, Martin took hold of the silver watch stem.

"No!" gasped the Conductor. "No!"

But the watch-stem turned.

"Do you realize what you've done?" the Conductor yelled. "Now we'll never reach the Depot! We'll just go on riding, all of us— forever!"

Martin grinned. "I know," he said. "But the fun is in the trip, not the destination. You taught me that. And I'm looking forward to a wonderful trip. Look, maybe I can even help. If you were to find me another one of those caps, now, and let me keep this watch—"

And that's the way it finally worked out. Wearing his cap and carrying his battered old silver watch, there's no happier person in or out of this world—now and forever—than Martin. Martin, the new Brakeman on That Hell-Bound Train.

ADDED INDUCEMENT

by Robert F. Young

The electrical appliance store was one of many that had sprung up in and around the city, seemingly overnight. There were half a dozen TV sets in the window, marked at amazingly low prices, and a window-wide sign boasted: WE'RE PRACTICALLY GIVING THEM AWAY! "This is the place we've been looking for," Janice said, and she pulled Henry through the entrance and into the store proper.

They hadn't gone two steps beyond the entrance when they came to a common standstill. Before them stood a huge and dazzling console with a 24-inch screen, and if you were TV hunting, you couldn't go by it any more than a hungry mouse could go by a new mousetrap baited with his favorite cheese.

"We can never afford that one," Henry said.

"But darling, we can afford to look, can't we?"

So they looked. They looked at the sleek mahogany cabinet and the cute little double doors that you could close when you weren't watching your programs; at the screen and the program in progress; at the company's name at the base of the screen B Λ Λ L—

"Must be a new make," Henry said. "Never heard of it before."

"That doesn't mean it isn't any good," Janice said.

—at the array of chrome-plated dials beneath the company's name and the little round window just below the middle dial—

"What's *that* for?" Janice asked, pointing at the window.

Henry leaned forward. "The dial above it says 'popcorn,' but that *can't* be."

"Oh yes it can!" a voice behind them said.

Turning, they beheld a small, mild-looking man with a pronounced widow's peak. He had brown eyes, and he was wearing a brown pin-striped suit.

"Do you work here?" Henry asked.

The small man bowed. "I'm Mr. Krull, and this is my establishment. . . . Do you like popcorn, sir?"

Henry nodded. "Once in a while."

"And you, madam?"

"Oh yes," Janice said. "Very much!"

"Allow me to demonstrate."

Mr. Krull stepped forward and tweaked the middle dial halfway around. Instantly, the little window lighted up, revealing a shining inbuilt frying pan with several thimble-sized aluminum cups suspended above it. As Henry and Janice watched, one of the cups upended itself and poured melted butter into the pan; shortly thereafter, another followed suit, emitting a Lilliputian cascade of golden popcorn kernels.

You could have heard a pin drop—or, more appropriately, you could have heard a popcorn kernel pop—the room was so quiet; and after a moment, Henry and Janice and Mr. Krull did hear one pop. Then another one popped, and then another, and pretty soon the machine-gun fire of popcorn in metamorphosis filled the room. The window now was like one of those little glass paperweights you pick up and shake and the snow starts falling, only this wasn't snow, it was popcorn—the whitest, liveliest, fluffiest popcorn that Henry and Janice had ever seen.

"Well did you ever!" Janice gasped.

Mr. Krull held up his hand. The moment was a dramatic one. The popcorn had subsided into a white, quivering mound. Mr. Krull tweaked the dial the rest of the way around and the pan flipped over. Abruptly a little secret door beneath the window came open, a tiny red light began blinking on and off, and a buzzer started to buzz; and there, sitting in the newly revealed secret cubicle, was a fat round bowl brimful with popcorn, and with little painted bluebirds flying happily around its porcelain sides.

Henry was entranced. "Well what'll they think of next!"

"How utterly charming!" Janice said.

"It's good popcorn too," Mr. Krull said.

He bent over and picked up the bowl, and the little red light went out and the buzzer became silent. "Have some?"

Henry and Janice took some, and Mr. Krull took some himself. There was a reflective pause while everybody munched. Presently: "Why it's delicious!" Janice said.

"Out of this world," said Henry.

Mr. Krull smiled. "We grow our own. Nothing's too good for Baal Enterprises. . . . And now, if I may, I'd like to demonstrate some of our other special features."

"I don't know," Henry said. "You see—"

"Oh, let him!" Janice interrupted. "It won't hurt us to watch, even if we can't afford such an expensive model."

Mr. Krull needed no more encouragement. He began with a discourse on the cabinet, describing where the wood had been cut, how it had been cured, shaped, worked, polished, and fitted together; then he went into a mass of technical details about the chassis, the inbuilt antenna, the high-fidelity speaker—

Suddenly Henry realized that the paper that had somehow got into his left hand was a contract and that the object that had somehow slipped into his right was a fountain pen. "Wait a minute," he said. "Wait a minute! I can't afford anything like this. We were just look—"

"How do you know you can't afford it?" Mr. Krull asked reasonably. "I haven't even mentioned the price yet."

"Then don't bother mentioning it. It's bound to be too high."

"You might find it too high, and then again, you might not. It's a rather relative figure. But even if you do find it too high, I'm sure the terms will be agreeable."

"All right," Henry said. "What *are* the terms?"

Mr. Krull smiled, rubbed the palms of his hands together. "*One*," he said, "the set is guaranteed for life. *Two*, you get a lifetime supply of popcorn. *Three*, you pay nothing down. *Four*, you pay no weekly, monthly, quarterly, or annual installments—"

"Are you *giving* it to us?" Janice's hazel eyes were incredulous.

"Well, not exactly. You have to pay for it—on one condition."

"Condition?" Henry asked.

"On the condition that you come into a certain amount of money."

"How much money?"

"One million dollars," Mr. Krull said.

Janice swayed slightly. Henry took a deep breath, blew it out slowly. "And the price?"

"Come now, sir. Surely you know what the price is by now. And surely you know who I am by now."

For a while Henry and Janice just stood there. Mr. Krull's widow's peak seemed more pronounced than ever, and there was a hint of mockery in his smile. For the first time, and with something of a shock, Henry realized that his ears were pointed.

Finally he got his tongue loose from the roof of his mouth. "You're not, you can't be—"

"Mr. Baal? Of course not! I'm merely one of his representatives—though in this instance, 'dealer' would be a more appropriate term."

There was a long pause. Then: "Both—both our souls?" Henry asked.

"Naturally," Mr. Krull said. "The terms are generous enough to warrant both of them, don't you think? . . . Well, what do you say, sir? Is it a deal?"

Henry began backing through the doorway. Janice backed with him, though not with quite the same alacrity.

Mr. Krull shrugged philosophically. "See you later then," he said.

*   *   *

Henry followed Janice into their apartment and closed the door. "I can't believe it," he said. "It *couldn't* have happened!"

"It happened all right," Janice said. "I can still taste the popcorn. You just don't want to believe it, that's all. You're afraid to believe it."

"Maybe you're right. . . ."

Janice fixed supper, and after supper they sat in the living room and watched *Gunfire, Feud, Shoot-Em-Up Henessey,* and the news, on the old beat-up TV set they'd bought two years ago when they were married to tide them over till they could afford a better one. After the news, Janice made popcorn in the kitchen and Henry opened two bottles of beer.

The popcorn was burned. Janice gagged on the first mouthful, pushed her bowl away. "You know, I almost think it would be worth it," she said. "Imagine, all you have to do is turn a dial and you can have popcorn any time you want without missing a single one of your programs!"

Henry was aghast. "You can't be serious!"

"Maybe not, but I'm getting awful sick of burned popcorn and picture trouble! And besides, who'd ever give *us* a million dollars anyway!"

"We'll look around again tomorrow afternoon," Henry said. "There must be other makes of sets besides Baal that have inbuilt popcorn poppers. Maybe we'll find one if we look long enough."

But they didn't. They started looking as soon as they got through work in the pants-stretcher factory, but the only sets they found with inbuilt popcorn poppers were stamped unmistakably with the name B A A L, and stood in the new electrical appliance stores that had sprung up, seemingly overnight, along with Mr. Krull's.

"I can't understand it," said the last orthodox dealer they visited. "You're the fiftieth couple to come in here today looking for a TV set with a popcorn window and an inbuilt popcorn popper. Why, I never heard of such a thing!"

"You will," Henry said.

They walked home disconsolately. A truck whizzed by in the street. They read the big red letters on its side—B A A L E N T E R P R I S E S—and they saw the three new TV consoles jouncing on the truckbed, and the three little popcorn windows twinkling in the summer sunshine.

They looked at each other, then looked quickly away. . . .

The truck was parked in front of their apartment building when they got home. Two of the sets had already been delivered and the third was being trundled down the nearby alley to the freight elevator. When they reached their floor they saw the set being pushed down the hall, and they lingered in their doorway long enough to learn its destination.

"Betty and Herb!" Janice gasped. "Why, I never thought they'd—"

"Humph!" Henry said. "Shows what their values amount to."

They went in, and Janice fixed supper. While they were eating they heard a noise outside the door, and when they looked out they saw another Baal set being delivered across the hall.

Next morning, three more were delivered on the same floor, and when Janice looked out the window after fixing breakfast, she saw two Baal trucks in the street and half a dozen consoles being trundled into the alley that led to the freight elevator. She beckoned to Henry, and he came over and stood beside her.

She pointed down at the trucks. "I'll bet we're the only people left on the whole block who still pop popcorn in their kitchen. Mr. and Mrs. Neanderthal—that's us!"

"But at least we can still call our souls our own," Henry said, without much conviction.

"I suppose you're right. But it would be so nice to pop popcorn in the living room for a change. And such good popcorn too. . . ."

They put in a miserable day at the pants-stretcher factory. On the way home, they passed Mr. Krull's store. There was a long line of people standing in front of it, and a new sign graced the window where the dummy come-on sets still stood: GOING OUT OF BUSINESS—THIS MAY BE YOUR LAST CHANCE TO OWN A TV-POPCORN CONSOLE!

Janice sighed. "We'll be the only ones," she said. "The only ones in the whole city who pop popcorn in the kitchen and watch their favorite programs on a stone-age TV set!"

When Henry didn't answer, she turned toward where she thought he was. But he wasn't there any more. He was standing at the end of the line and waving to her to join him.

Mr. Krull was beaming. He pointed to the two little dotted lines, and Henry and Janice signed their names with eager fingers. Then Henry wrote down their street and number in the space marked ADDRESS, and handed the contract back to Mr. Krull.

Mr. Krull glanced at it, then turned towards the back of the store. "Henry and Janice Smith, sir," he called. "111 Ibid Street, Local."

They noticed the tall man then. He was standing at the back of the store, jotting down something in a little red notebook. You could tell just by looking at him that he was a businessman, and you didn't have to look twice to see that he was a successful one. He was wearing a neat charcoal-gray suit and a pair of modern horn-rimmed glasses. His hair was quite dark, but his temples were sprinkled becomingly with gray. When he noticed Henry and Janice staring at him, he smiled at them warmly and gave a little laugh. It was an odd kind of a laugh. "Ha ha ha ha," it went, then dropped abruptly way down the scale: "HO HO HO HO! . . ."

"Incidentally," Mr. Krull was saying, "if a million dollars *does* come your way, you have to accept it, you know—even though you won't get a chance to spend it. Not only that, if you get an opportunity to *win* a million dollars, you've got to take advantage of it. It's all stipulated in the contract."

Janice repressed a nervous giggle. "Now who in the world would give *us* a million dollars!"

Mr. Krull smiled, then frowned. "Sometimes I just can't understand people at all," he said. "Why, if I'd approached our prospective customers directly, in my capacity as Mr.

Baal's representative, and had offered each of them a brand-new TV console—or even a million dollars—for his or her soul, I'd have been laughed right off the face of the earth! If you want to be a success today, no matter what business you're in, you've got to provide an added inducement— Oh, good night, sir.''

The tall man was leaving. At Mr. Krull's words, he paused in the doorway and turned. The final rays of the afternoon sun gave his face a reddish cast. He bowed slightly. ''Good night, Krull,'' he said. ''Good night, Janice and Henry.'' He appended to his words another measure of his unusual laughter.

''Who—who was that?'' Henry asked.

''That was Mr. Baal. He's preparing a list of contestants for his new TV program.''

''His *TV* program!''

Mr. Krull's smile was the quintessence of innocence. ''Why yes. It hasn't been announced yet, but it will be soon. . . . It's a giveaway show—and quite a unique one, too. Mr. Baal has everything arranged so that none of the contestants can possibly lose.''

Janice was tugging on Henry's arm. Her face was pale. ''Come on, darling. Let's go home.''

But Henry hung back. ''What—what's the name of the show?'' he asked.

''Make a Million,'' Mr. Krull said.

THE DEVIL AND DANIEL WEBSTER

by Stephen Vincent Benét

It's a story they tell in the border country, where Massachusetts joins Vermont and New Hampshire.

Yes, Dan'l Webster's dead—or, at least, they buried him. But every time there's a thunderstorm around Marshfield, they say you can hear his rolling voice in the hollows of the sky. And they say that if you go to his grave and speak loud and clear, "Dan'l Webster—Dan'l Webster!" the ground'll begin to shiver and the trees begin to shake. And after a while you'll hear a deep voice saying, "Neighbor, how stands the Union?" Then you better answer the Union stands as she stood, rock-bottomed and copper-sheathed, one and indivisible, or he's liable to rear right out of the ground. At least, that's what I was told when I was a youngster.

You see, for a while, he was the biggest man in the country. He never got to be President, but he was the biggest man. There were thousands that trusted in him right next to God Almighty, and they told stories about him that were like the stories of patriarchs and such. They said, when he stood up to speak, stars and stripes came right out in the sky, and once he spoke against a river and made it sink into the ground. They said, when he walked the woods with his fishing rod, Killall, the trout would jump out of the streams right into his pockets, for they knew it was no use putting up a fight against him; and, when he argued a case, he could turn on the harps of the blessed and the shaking of the earth underground. That was the kind of man he was, and his big farm up at Marshfield was suitable to him. The chickens he raised were all white meat down through the drumsticks, the cows were tended like children, and the big ram he called Goliath had horns with a curl like a morning-glory vine and could butt through an iron door. But Dan'l wasn't one of your gentlemen farmers; he knew all the ways of the land, and he'd be up by candlelight to see that the chores got done. A man with a mouth like a mastiff, a brow like a mountain and eyes like burning anthracite—that was Dan'l Webster in his prime. And the biggest case he argued never got written down in the books, for he argued it against the devil, nip and tuck and no holds barred. And this is the way I used to hear it told.

There was a man named Jabez Stone, lived at Cross Corners, New Hampshire. He wasn't a bad man to start with, but he was an unlucky man. If he planted corn, he got borers; if he planted potatoes, he got blight. He had good-enough land, but it didn't prosper him; he had a decent wife and children, but the more children he had, the less there was to feed them. If stones cropped up in his neighbor's field, boulders boiled up in his; if he had a horse with the spavins, he'd trade it for one with the staggers and give something extra. There's some folks bound to be like that, apparently. But one day Jabez Stone got sick of the whole business.

He'd been plowing that morning and he'd just broke the plowshare on a rock that he could have sworn hadn't been there yesterday. And, as he stood looking at the plowshare, the off horse began to cough—that ropy kind of cough that means sickness and horse doctors. There were two children down with the measles, his wife was ailing, and he had a whitlow on his thumb. It was about the last straw for Jabez Stone. "I vow," he said, and he looked around him kind of desperate—"I vow it's enough to make a man want to sell his soul to the devil! And I would, too, for two cents!"

Then he felt a kind of queerness come over him at having said what he'd said; though, naturally, being a New Hampshireman, he wouldn't take it back. But, all the same, when it got to be evening and, as far as he could see, no notice had been taken, he felt relieved in his mind, for he was a religious man. But notice is always taken, sooner or later, just like the Good Book says. And, sure enough, next day, about supper-time, a soft-spoken, dark-dressed stranger drove up in a handsome buggy and asked for Jabez Stone.

Well, Jabez told his family it was a lawyer, come to see him about a legacy. But he knew who it was. He didn't like the looks of the stranger, nor the way he smiled with his teeth. They were white teeth, and plentiful—some say they were filed to a point, but I wouldn't vouch for that. And he didn't like it when the dog took one look at the stranger and ran away howling, with his tail between his legs. But having passed his word, more or less, he stuck to it, and they went out behind the barn and made their bargain. Jabez Stone had to prick his finger to sign, and the stranger lent him a silver pin. The wound healed clean, but it left a little white scar.

After that, all of a sudden, things began to pick up and prosper for Jabez Stone. His cows got fat and his horses sleek, his crops were the envy of the neighborhood, and lightning might strike all over the valley, but it wouldn't strike his barn. Pretty soon, he was one of the prosperous people of the county; they asked him to stand for selectman, and he stood for it; there began to be talk of running him for state senate. All in all, you might say the Stone family was as happy and contented as cats in a dairy. And so they were, except for Jabez Stone.

He'd been contented enough, for the first few years. It's a great thing when bad luck turns; it drives most other things out of your head. True, every now and then, especially in rainy weather, the little white scar on his finger would give him a twinge. And once a year, punctual as clockwork, the stranger with the handsome buggy would come driving by. But the sixth year, the stranger lighted, and, after that, his peace was over for Jabez Stone.

The stranger came up through the lower field, switching his boots with a cane—they were handsome black boots, but

Jabez Stone never liked the look of them, particularly the toes. And, after he'd passed the time of day, he said, "Well, Mr. Stone, you're a hummer! It's a very pretty property you've got here, Mr. Stone."

"Well, some might favor it and others might not," said Jabez Stone, for he was a New Hampshireman.

"Oh, no need to decry your industry!" said the stranger, very easy, showing his teeth in a smile. "After all, we know what's been done, and it's been according to contract and specifications. So when—ahem—the mortgage falls due next year, you shouldn't have any regrets."

"Speaking of that mortgage, mister," said Jabez Stone, and he looked around for help to the earth and the sky, "I'm beginning to have one or two doubts about it."

"Doubts?" said the stranger, not quite so pleasantly.

"Why, yes," said Jabez Stone. "This being the U.S.A. and me always having been a religious man." He cleared his throat and got bolder. "Yes, sir," he said, "I'm beginning to have considerable doubts as to that mortgage holding in court."

"There's courts and courts," said the stranger, clicking his teeth. "Still, we might as well have a look at the original document." And he hauled out a big black pocketbook, full of papers. "Sherwin, Slater, Stevens, Stone," he muttered. "I, Jabez Stone, for a term of seven years— Oh, it's quite in order, I think."

But Jabez Stone wasn't listening, for he saw something else flutter out of the black pocketbook. It was something that looked like a moth, but it wasn't a moth. And as Jabez Stone stared at it, it seemed to speak to him in a small sort of piping voice, terrible small and thin, but terrible human. "Neighbor Stone!" it squeaked. "Neighbor Stone! Help me! For God's sake, help me!"

But before Jabez Stone could stir hand or foot, the stranger whipped out a big bandanna handkerchief, caught the creature in it, just like a butterfly, and started tying up the ends of the bandanna.

"Sorry for the interruption," he said. "As I was saying—"

But Jabez Stone was shaking all over like a scared horse.

"That's Miser Stevens' voice!" he said, in a croak. "And you've got him in your handkerchief!"

The stranger looked a little embarrassed.

"Yes, I really should have transferred him to the collecting box," he said with a simper, "but there were some rather unusual specimens there and I didn't want them crowded. Well, well, these little contretemps will occur."

"I don't know what you mean by contertan," said Jabez Stone, "but that was Miser Stevens' voice! And he ain't dead! You can't tell me he is! He was just as spry and mean as a woodchuck, Tuesday!"

"In the midst of life—" said the stranger, kind of pious. "Listen!" then a bell began to toll in the valley and Jabez Stone listened, with the sweat running down his face. For he knew it was tolled for Miser Stevens and that he was dead.

"These long-standing accounts," said the stranger with a sigh; "one really hates to close them. But business is business."

He still had the bandanna in his hand, and Jabez Stone felt sick as he saw the cloth struggle and flutter.

"Are they all as small as that?" he asked hoarsely.

"Small?" said the stranger. "Oh, I see what you mean. Why, they vary." He measured Jabez Stone with his eyes, and his teeth showed. "Don't worry, Mr. Stone," he said. "You'll go with a very good grade. I wouldn't trust you outside the collecting box. Now, a man like Dan'l Webster, of course—well, we'd have to build a special box for him, and even at that, I imagine the wingspread would astonish you. But, in your case, as I was saying—"

"Put that handkerchief away!" said Jabez Stone, and he began to beg and to pray. But the best he could get at the end was a three years' extension, with conditions.

But till you make a bargain like that, you've got no idea of how fast four years can run. By the last months of those years, Jabez Stone's known all over the state and there's talk of running him for governor—and it's dust and ashes in his mouth. For every day, when he gets up, he thinks, "There's one more night gone," and every night when he lies down, he thinks of the black pocketbook and the soul of Miser Stevens, and it makes him sick at heart. Till, finally, he can't bear it any longer, and, in the last days of the last year, he hitches up his horse and drives off to seek Dan'l Webster. For Dan'l was born in New Hampshire, only a few miles from Cross Corners, and it's well known that he has a particular soft spot for old neighbors.

It was early in the morning when he got to Marshfield, but Dan'l was up already, talking Latin to the farm hands and wrestling with the ram, Goliath, and trying out a new trotter and working up speeches to make against John C. Calhoun. But when he heard a New Hampshireman had come to see him, he dropped everything else he was doing, for that was Dan'l's way. He gave Jabez Stone a breakfast that five men couldn't eat, went into the living history of every man and woman in Cross Corners, and finally asked him how he could serve him.

Jabez Stone allowed that it was a kind of mortgage case.

"Well, I haven't pleaded a mortgage case in a long time, and I don't generally plead now, except before the Supreme Court," said Dan'l, "but if I can, I'll help you."

"Then I've got hope for the first time in ten years," said Jabez Stone, and told him the details.

Dan'l walked up and down as he listened, hands behind his back, now and then asking a question, now and then plunging his eyes at the floor, as if they'd bore through it like gimlets. When Jabez Stone had finished, Dan'l puffed out his cheeks and blew. Then he turned to Jabez Stone and a smile broke over his face like the sunrise over Monadnock.

"You've certainly given yourself the devil's own row to hoe, Neighbor Stone," he said, "but I'll take your case."

"You'll take it?" said Jabez Stone, hardly daring to believe.

"Yes," said Dan'l Webster. "I've got about seventy-five other things to do and the Missouri Compromise to straighten out, but I'll take your case. For if two New Hampshiremen aren't a match for the devil, we might as well give the country back to the Indians."

Then he shook Jabez Stone by the hand and said. "Did you come down here in a hurry?"

"Well, I admit I made time," said Jabez Stone.

"You'll go back faster," said Dan'l Webster, and he told 'em to hitch up Constitution and Constellation to the carriage. They were matched grays with one white forefoot, and they stepped like greased lightning.

Well, I won't describe how excited and pleased the whole Stone family was to have the great Dan'l Webster for a guest, when they finally got there. Jabez Stone had lost his hat on the way, blown off when they overtook a wind, but he didn't take much account of that. But after supper he sent the family off to bed, for he had most particular business with Mr. Webster. Mrs. Stone wanted them to sit in the front parlor, but Dan'l Webster knew front parlors and said he preferred the kitchen. So it was there they sat, waiting for the stranger, with a jug on the table between them and a bright fire on the hearth—the stranger being scheduled to show up on the stroke of midnight, according to specifications.

Well, most men wouldn't have asked for better company than Dan'l Webster and a jug. But with every tick of the clock Jabez Stone got sadder and sadder. His eyes roved round, and though he sampled the jug you could see he couldn't taste it. Finally, on the stroke of 11:30 he reached over and grabbed Dan'l Webster by the arm.

"Mr. Webster, Mr. Webster!" he said, and his voice was shaking with fear and a desperate courage. "For God's sake, Mr. Webster, harness your horses and get away from this place while you can!"

"You've brought me a long way, neighbor, to tell me you don't like my company," said Dan'l Webster, quite peaceable, pulling at the jug.

"Miserable wretch that I am!" groaned Jabez Stone. "I've brought you a devilish way, and now I see my folly. Let him take me if he wills. I don't hanker after it, I must say, but I can stand it. But you're the Union's stay and New Hampshire's pride! He mustn't get you, Mr. Webster! He mustn't get you!"

Dan'l Webster looked at the distracted man, all gray and shaking in the firelight, and laid a hand on his shoulder.

"I'm obliged to you, Neighbor Stone," he said gently. "It's kindly thought of. But there's a jug on the table and a case in hand. And I never left a jug or a case half finished in my life."

And just at that moment there was a sharp rap on the door.

"Ah," said Dan'l Webster, very coolly, "I thought your clock was a trifle slow, Neighbor Stone." He stepped to the door and opened it. "Come in!" he said.

The stranger came in—very dark and tall he looked in the firelight. He was carrying a box under his arm—a black, japanned box with little air holes in the lid. At the sight of the box, Jabez Stone gave a low cry and shrank into a corner of the room.

"Mr. Webster, I presume," said the stranger, very polite, but with his eyes glowing like a fox's deep in the woods.

"Attorney of record for Jabez Stone," said Dan'l Webster, but his eyes were glowing too. "Might I ask your name?"

"I've gone by a good many," said the stranger carelessly. "Perhaps Scratch will do for the evening. I'm often called that in these regions."

Then he sat down at the table and poured himself a drink from the jug. The liquor was cold in the jug, but it came steaming into the glass.

"And now," said the stranger, smiling and showing his teeth, "I shall call upon you, as a law-abiding citizen, to assist me in taking possession of my property."

Well, with that the argument began—and it went hot and heavy. At first, Jabez Stone had a flicker of hope, but when he saw Dan'l Webster being forced back at point after point, he just scrunched in his corner, with his eyes on that japanned box. For there wasn't any doubt as to the deed or the signature—that was the worst of it. Dan'l Webster twisted and turned and thumped his fist on the table, but he couldn't get away from that. He offered to compromise the case; the stranger wouldn't hear of it. He pointed out the property had increased in value, and state senators ought to be worth more;

the stranger stuck to the letter of the law. He was a great lawyer, Dan'l Webster, but we know who's the King of Lawyers, as the good Book tells us, and it seemed as if, for the first time, Dan'l Webster had met his match.

Finally, the stranger yawned a little. "Your spirited efforts on behalf of your client do you credit, Mr. Webster," he said, "but if you have no more arguments to adduce, I'm rather pressed for time"—and Jabez Stone shuddered.

Dan'l Webster's brow looked dark as a thundercloud.

"Pressed or not, you shall not have this man!" he thundered. "Mr. Stone is an American citizen, and no American citizen may be forced into the service of a foreign prince. We fought England for that in '12 and we'll fight all hell for it again!"

"Foreign?" said the stranger. "And who calls me a foreigner?"

"Well, I never yet heard of the dev—of your claiming American citizenship," said Dan'l Webster with surprise.

"And who with better right?" said the stranger, with one of his terrible smiles. "When the first wrong was done to the first Indian, I was there. When the first slaver put out for the Congo, I stood on her deck. Am I not in your books and stories and beliefs, from the first settlements on? Am I not spoken of, still, in every church in New England? 'Tis true the North claims me for a Southerner and the South for a Northerner, but I am neither. I am merely an honest American like yourself—and of the best descent—for, to tell the truth, Mr. Webster, though I don't like to boast of it, my name is older in this country than yours."

"Aha!" said Dan'l Webster, with the veins standing out in his forehead. "Then I stand on the Constitution! I demand a trial for my client!"

"The case is hardly one for an ordinary court," said the stranger, his eyes flickering. "And, indeed, the lateness of the hour—"

"Let it be any court you choose, so it is an American judge and an American jury!" said Dan'l Webster in his pride. "Let it be the quick or the dead; I'll abide the issue!"

"You have said it," said the stranger, and pointed his finger at the door. And with that, and all of a sudden, there was a rushing of wind outside and a noise of footsteps. They came, clear and distinct, through the night. And yet, they were not like the footsteps of living men.

"In God's name, who comes by so late?" cried Jabez Stone, in an ague of fear.

"The jury Mr. Webster demands," said the stranger, sipping at his boiling glass. "You must pardon the rough appearance of one or two; they will have come a long way."

And with that the fire burned blue and the door blew open and twelve men entered, one by one.

If Jabez Stone had been sick with terror before, he was blind with terror now. For there was Walter Butler, the loyalist, who spread fire and horror through the Mohawk Valley in the times of the Revolution; and there was Simon Girty, the renegade, who saw white men burned at the stake and whooped with the Indians to see them burn. His eyes were green, like a catamount's, and the stains on his hunting shirt did not come from the blood of the deer. King Philip was there, wild and proud as he had been in life, with the great gash in his head that gave him his death wound, and cruel Governor Dale, who broke men on the wheel. There was Morton of Merry Mount, who so vexed the Plymouth Colony, with his flushed, loose, handsome face and his hate of the godly. There was Teach, the bloody pirate, with his black beard curling on his breast. The Reverend John Smeet, with his strangler's hands and his Geneva gown, walked as daintily as he had to the gallows. The red print of the rope was still around his neck, but he carried a perfumed handkerchief in one hand. One and all, they came into the room with the fires of hell still upon them, and the stranger named their names and their deeds as they came, till the tale of twelve was told. Yet the stranger had told the truth—they had all played a part in America.

"Are you satisfied with the jury, Mr. Webster?" said the stranger mockingly, when they had taken their places.

The sweat stood upon Dan'l Webster's brow, but his voice was clear.

"Quite satisfied," he said. "Though I miss General Arnold from the company."

"Benedict Arnold is engaged upon other business," said the stranger, with a glower. "Ah, you asked for a justice, I believe."

He pointed his finger once more, and a tall man, soberly clad in Puritan garb, with the burning gaze of the fanatic, stalked into the room and took his judge's place.

"Justice Hathorne is a jurist of experience," said the stranger. "He presided at certain witch trials once held in Salem. There were others who repented of the business later, but not he."

"Repent of such notable wonders and undertakings?" said the stern old justice. "Nay, hang them—hang them all!" And he muttered to himself in a way that struck icc into the soul of Jabez Stone.

Then the trial began, and, as you might expect, it didn't look anyways good for the defense. And Jabez Stone didn't make much of a witness in his own behalf. He took one look at Simon Girty and screeched, and they had to put him back in his corner in a kind of swoon.

It didn't halt the trial, though; the trial went on, as trials do. Dan'l Webster had faced some hard juries and hanging judges in his time, but this was the hardest he'd ever faced, and he knew it. They sat there with a kind of glitter in their eyes, and the stranger's smooth voice went on and on. Every time he'd raise an objection, it'd be "Objection sustained," but whenever Dan'l objected, it'd be "Objection denied." Well, you couldn't expect fair play from a fellow like this Mr. Scratch.

It got to Dan'l in the end, and he began to heat, like iron in the forge. When he got up to speak he was going to flay that stranger with every trick known to the law, and the judge and jury too. He didn't care if it was contempt of court or what would happen to him for it. He didn't care any more what happened to Jabez Stone. He just got madder and madder, thinking of what he'd say. And yet, curiously enough, the more he thought about it, the less he was able to arrange his speech in his mind.

Till, finally, it was time for him to get up on his feet, and he did so, all ready to bust out with lightnings and denunciations. But before he started he looked over the judge and jury for a moment, such being his custom. And he noticed the glitter in their eyes was twice as strong as before, and they all leaned forward. Like hounds just before they get the fox, they looked, and the blue mist of evil in the room thickened as he watched them. Then he saw what he'd been about to do, and he wiped his forehead, as a man might who's just escaped falling into a pit in the dark.

For it was him they'd come for, not only Jabez Stone. He read it in the glitter of their eyes and in the way the stranger hid his mouth with one hand. And if he fought them with their own weapons, he'd fall into their power; he knew that, though he couldn't have told you how. It was his own anger and horror that burned in their eyes; and he'd have to wipe that out or the case was lost. He stood there for a moment, his black eyes burning like anthracite. And then he began to speak.

He started off in a low voice, though you could hear every word. They say he could call on the harps of the blessed when he chose. And this was just as simple and easy as a man could talk. But he didn't start out by condemning or reviling. He was talking about the things that make a country a country, and a man a man.

And he began with the simple things that everybody's known and felt—the freshness of a fine morning when you're young, and the taste of food when you're hungry, and the new day that's every day when you're a child. He took them up and he turned them in his hands. They were good things for any man. But without freedom, they sickened. And when he talked of those enslaved, and the sorrows of slavery, his voice got like a big bell. He talked of the early days of America and the men who had made those days. It wasn't a spread-eagle speech, but he made you see it. He admitted all the wrong that had ever been done. But he showed how, out of the wrong and the right, the suffering and the starvations, something new had come. And everybody had played a part in it, even the traitors.

Then he turned to Jabez Stone and showed him as he was—an ordinary man who'd had hard luck and wanted to change it. And, because he'd wanted to change it, now he was going to be punished for all eternity. And yet there was good in Jabez Stone, and he showed that good. He was hard and mean, in some ways, but he was a man. There was sadness in being a man, but it was a proud thing too. And he showed what the pride of it was till you couldn't help feeling it. Yes, even in hell, if a man was a man, you'd know it. And he wasn't pleading for any one person any more, though his voice rang like an organ. He was telling the story and the failures and the endless journey of mankind. They got tricked and trapped and bamboozled, but it was a great journey. And no demon that was ever foaled could know the inwardness of it—it took a man to do that.

The fire began to die on the hearth and the wind before morning to blow. The light was getting gray in the room when Dan'l Webster finished. And his words came back at the end to New Hampshire ground, and the one spot of land that each man loves and clings to. He painted a picture of that, and to each one of that jury he spoke of things long forgotten. For his voice could search the heart, and that was his gift and his strength. And to one, his voice was like the forest and its secrecy, and to another like the sea and the storms of the sea; and one heard the cry of his lost nation in it, and another saw a little harmless scene he hadn't remembered for years. But each saw something. And when Dan'l Webster finished he didn't know whether or not he'd saved Jabez Stone. But he knew he'd done a miracle. For the glitter was gone from the eyes of judge and jury, and, for the moment, they were men again, and knew they were men.

"The defense rests," said Dan'l Webster, and stood there like a mountain. His ears were still ringing with his speech, and he didn't hear anything else till he heard Judge Hathorne say, "The jury will retire to consider its verdict."

Walter Butler rose in his place and his face had a dark, gay pride on it.

"The jury has considered its verdict," he said, and looked the stranger full in the eye. "We find for the defendant, Jabez Stone."

With that, the smile left the stranger's face, but Walter Butler did not flinch.

"Perhaps 'tis not strictly in accordance with the evidence," he said, "but even the damned may salute the eloquence of Mr. Webster."

With that, the long crow of a rooster split the gray morning sky, and judge and jury were gone from the room like a puff of smoke and as if they had never been there. The stranger turned to Dan'l Webster, smiling wryly.

"Major Butler was always a bold man," he said. "I had not thought him quite so bold. Nevertheless, my congratulations, as between two gentlemen."

"I'll have that paper first, if you please," said Dan'l Webster, and he took it and tore it into four pieces. It was queerly warm to the touch. "And now," he said, "I'll have you!" and his hand came down like a bear trap on the stranger's arm. For he knew that once you bested anybody like Mr. Scratch in fair fight, his power on you was gone. And he could see that Mr. Scratch knew it too.

The stranger twisted and wriggled, but he couldn't get out of that grip. "Come, come, Mr. Webster," he said, smiling palely. "This sort of thing is ridic—ouch!—is ridiculous. If you're worried about the costs of the case, naturally, I'd be glad to pay—"

"And so you shall!" said Dan'l Webster, shaking him till his teeth rattled. "For you'll sit right down at that table and draw up a document, promising never to bother Jabez Stone nor his heirs or assigns nor any other New Hampshireman till doomsday! For any hades we want to raise in this state, we can raise ourselves, without assistance from strangers."

"Ouch!" said the stranger. "Ouch! Well, they never did run very big to the barrel, but—ouch!—I agree!"

So he sat down and drew up the document. But Dan'l Webster kept his hand on his coat collar all the time.

"And, now, may I go?" said the stranger, quite humble, when Dan'l'd seen the document was in proper and legal form.

"Go?" said Dan'l, giving him another shake. "I'm still trying to figure out what I'll do with you. For you've settled the costs of the case, but you haven't settled with me. I think I'll take you back to Marshfield," he said, kind of reflective. "I've got a ram there named Goliath that can butt through an iron door. I'd kind of like to turn you loose in his field and see what he'd do."

Well, with that the stranger began to beg and to plead. And he begged and he pled so humble that finally Dan'l, who was naturally kindhearted, agreed to let him go. The stranger seemed terrible grateful for that and said, just to show they were friends, he'd tell Dan'l's fortune before leaving. So Dan'l agreed to that, though he didn't take much stock in fortune-tellers ordinarily. But, naturally, the stranger was a little different.

Well, he pried and he peered at the lines in Dan'l's hands. And he told him one thing and another that was quite remarkable. But they were all in the past.

"Yes, all that's true, and it happened," said Dan'l Webster. "But what's to come in the future?"

The stranger grinned, kind of happily, and shook his head. "The future's not as you think it," he said. "It's dark. You have a great ambition, Mr. Webster."

"I have," said Dan'l firmly, for everybody knew he wanted to be President.

"It seems almost within your grasp," said the stranger, "but you will not attain it. Lesser men will be made President and you will be passed over."

"And, if I am, I'll still be Daniel Webster," said Dan'l. "Say on."

"You have two strong sons," said the stranger, shaking

his head. "You look to found a line. But each will die in war and neither reach greatness."

"Live or die, they are still my sons," said Dan'l Webster. "Say on."

"You have made great speeches," said the stranger. "You will make more."

"Ah," said Dan'l Webster.

COLT .24

by Rick Hautala

Diary entry one: approximately 10:00 A.M. on Valentine's Day—*hah*! What irony!

If you've ever spent any time in academic circles, you've no doubt heard the expression "publish or perish." Simply put, it means that if you intend to keep your cushy teaching position, at least at any decent college or university, you've got to publish in academic journals. I suppose this is to prove you've been doing research, but it also contributes to the prestige of your school.

My experience, at least in the English department here at the University of Southern Maine, is that the more obscure and unread the periodical, the more prestige is involved. I mean, if you write novels or stories that don't pretend to art, you can kiss your tenure goodbye. A good friend of mine here did just that—wrote and sold dozens of stories and even one novel, but because it was seen as "commercial" fiction, he didn't keep his job. After he was denied tenure, a few years back, he and I used to joke about how he had published *and* perished!

I know that sounds cynical, but . . . well, I have reason to be cynical. The doctor who talked with me last night might have fancier, more clinical terms for it, but I might be tempted to translate his conclusions about me to something a little simpler: let's try "crazy as a shithouse rat."

That's crazy, all right; but just read on. I'm writing this all down as fast as I can because I know I don't have much time. I'm fighting the English teacher in me who wants to go back and revise and hone this all down until it's perfect, but if I'm right . . . oh, Jesus! If I'm *right* . . .

Look, I'll try to start at the start. Every story has a beginning, a middle, and an end, I've always told my students. Life, unfortunately, doesn't always play out that way. Sure, the beginning's at birth and the end's at death—it's filling up the middle part that's a bitch.

I don't know if this whole damned thing started when I first saw Rose McAllister . . . Rosie. She was sitting in the front row the first day of my 8:00 A.M. Introduction to English Literature class last fall. It might have been then that everything started, but I've gotta be honest. I mean, at this point, it doesn't matter. I think I'll be dead . . . and *really* in Hell within . . . maybe four hours.

So when I first saw Rosie, I didn't think right off the bat: God! I want to have an affair with her. That sounds so delicate—"have an affair." I wanted to, sure; but that was after I got to know her. We started sleeping together whenever we could . . . which wasn't often, you see, because of Sally. My wife. My dear, departed wife!

I guess if I was really looking for the beginning of this whole damned mess, I'd have to say it was when we started our study of Marlowe's *Doctor Faustus.* Your basic "deal with the Devil" story. I didn't mention too much of this to the police shrink because . . . well, if you tell someone like that that you struck a deal with the Devil, sold him your soul—yes, I signed the agreement with my own blood—you expect him to send you up to the rubber room on P-6. If I'm wrong, I don't want to spend my time writing letters home with a Crayola, you know.

I'm getting ahead of myself, but like I said, I don't have much time . . . at least I don't think so.

Okay, so Rosie and I, sometime around the middle of the fall semester, began to "sleep together." Another delicate term, because we did very little "sleeping." We got whatever we could, whenever we could—in my office, usually, or—once or twice—in a motel room, once in my car in the faculty parking lot outside of Bailey Hall. Whenever and wherever.

The first mistake we made was being seen at the Roma, in Portland, by Hank and Mary Crenshaw. The Roma! As an English teacher, I can appreciate the irony of *that*, too. Sally and I celebrated our wedding anniversary there every year. Being seen there on a Friday night, with a college sophomore ("young enough to be your daughter!" Sally took no end of pleasure repeating), by your wife's close (not best, but close) friend is downright stupid. I still cringe when I imagine the glee in Mary's voice when she told Sally. Hell! I never liked Mary, and she never liked me. Hank—he was all right, but I always told Sally that Mary was *her* friend, not mine.

So, Sally found out. Okay, so plenty of married men (and women) get caught screwing around. Sometimes the couple can cope—work it out. Other times, they can't. We couldn't. I should say, Sally couldn't. She set her lawyer—Walter Altschuler—on me faster than a greyhound on a rabbit. That guy would have had my gonads if they hadn't been attached!

But I'm not the kind of guy who takes that kind of stuff— from *anyone*! And, in an ironic sort of way, I'm getting paid back for that, too. If someone sics a lawyer on me, I'm gonna fight back.

Now here's where it gets a little weird. If I told that police shrink all of this, he'd bounce me up to P-6 for sure. I said we were reading *Faustus*, and that's when I decided to do a bit of—let's call it spontaneous research. I dug through the library and found what was supposedly a magician's hand-book—you know, a grimoire. I decided to try a bit of necromancy!

Look, I'm not crazy! I went into it more than half skepti-cal. And I want to state for the record here that I

Diary entry two: two hours later. Time's running out for sure!

Sorry for the interruption. I'm back now after spend—

wasting two hours with the shrink again. He ran me over the story again, but—I think—I held up pretty well. I didn't tell him what I'm going to write here. I want this all recorded so if I'm right . . . if I'm right . . .

Where was I? Oh, yeah. Necromancy. A deal with the Devil. Yes— yes—*yess!* Signed in *blood!*

The library on the Gorham campus had a grimoire. Well, actually a facsimile of one, published a few years ago by Indiana University Press. It's amazing what's published these days. I wonder if the person who edited that text—I can't remember his name—kept his job. I looked up a spell to summon the Devil and— now I *know* you're gonna think I'm crazy! I did it! I actually summoned up the Devil!

Laugh! Go ahead! I'll be dead soon—in Hell!—and it won't matter to me!

I have a key to Bailey Hall, so I came back to my office late at night—sometime after eleven o'clock, so I could be ready by midnight. After making sure my door was locked, I started to work. Pushing back the cheap rug I had by my desk (to keep the rollers of my chair from squeaking), I drew a pentagram on the floor, using a black Magic Marker. I placed a black candle—boy, were they hard to find—at each of the five points and lighted them. Then, taking the black leather-bound book, I began to recite the Latin incantation backwards. Actually, I was surprised that it worked—my Latin was so rusty, I was afraid I'd mispronounce something and end up summoning a talking toadstool or something. But it worked—it *actually* worked! In a puff of sulfurous fumes Old Nick himself appeared.

Looking around, he said, "Well, at least you're not another damned politician! What do you want in return for your soul?"

With his golden, cat-slit eyes burning into me, I had the feeling he already knew—more clearly than I did at that moment. Anyway, I told him. I said that I wanted an absolutely foolproof way of killing my wife and not getting caught. I told him I was willing to sign my soul over to him—yes! dear God! in *blood*!—if I could somehow get rid of Sally and be absolutely *certain* I wouldn't get caught.

I'm writing this, you must know by now, in a jail cell. I'm the prime suspect, but I haven't been charged with anything. I have a perfect alibi, you see, and there are other problems too; but if you read the *Evening Express*, you'll know soon enough that I didn't get away with it.

What the Devil did was hand me a revolver; he called it a Colt .24—a specially "modified" Colt .45—and a box of nice, shiny, brass-jacketed bullets. He told me all I had to do, after I signed the agreement, of course, was point the gun at Sally—he suggested I sneak home sometime before lunch someday—pull the trigger, throw the gun away, and make *sure* I went to work as usual the next day. If I did what he said, he guaranteed I'd go free.

Sounded okay to me. At this point, I was well past rationally analyzing the situation. I was under a lot of pressure, you've got to understand. My wife's lawyer had stuck the end nozzle of his vacuum cleaner down into my wallet and was sucking up the bucks. I'd been without sleep for nearly two days and nights running—I was getting so worked up about what was happening between Sally and I. (I know! It should be Sally and me!)

And the capper was Rosie. As soon as she found out that Sally knew about us, she cooled off. Maybe—I hate to think it!—it was just the chance of getting caught that added to her excitement—her sense of adventure. Once we got caught, the thrill was gone for her. Could she have been *that* shallow?

I wasn't completely convinced this whole business with the Devil had really worked, because . . . well, I must've fallen asleep after he pricked my finger so I could sign the contract, gave me the gun, and disappeared. I woke up, stiff-necked and all, flat on my back on the floor of my office just before my eight-o'clock class the next morning. The candles had burned out, but in the early-morning light, I could see the pentagram still there, so I knew I hadn't dreamed *everything*. I also had the gun—a Colt .45.

I'd been asleep—I don't know how long. Not more than

four hours, I figure. I had started the summoning at midnight, like you're supposed to. I have no idea how long it took, but—at least for me—old Satan didn't waste any time with visions of power and glory, or processions of spirits. Nothing, really. At times, thinking about it, I could just as easily have been talking to old man Olsen, the janitor in Bailey Hall!

But, like I said, I also had the gun—and damned if I didn't decide then and there that I'd use it. I had my two classes first. But after that, I was going straight home and point it at Sally and pull the trigger—even if, then and there, it blew her out through the picture window. I'd reached my limit, which, I'd like to think, was considerably beyond what most men can stand.

So I did. After the second class—between classes I had time to drag the rug back and gulp down some coffee and an Egg McMuffin—I took off for home. Sally, as luck would have it, was—damn! Here they come again!

Diary entry three: more than an hour gone—mere minutes left!

This time the police came in again. Talk about being confused. I think they'd like to charge me. But my alibi is solid and they can't get my gun to fire. So they asked me to fill them in on my and Sally's relationship. They said that maybe it could give them a lead on who else might have killed her. They said I'd probably be released shortly. *Hah!* As if that might make a difference.

Well, as I was saying, Sally was home—and her lawyer, old Walter baby, was there with her. I sort of wondered why he was there—at *my* house. Maybe nosing around gave him a better idea how to skin me to the bone. Or maybe getting into her pants was part of his fee. But I couldn't afford to leave any witness, so whatever he was doing, that was just his tough luck. One more lawyer in Hell wasn't going to matter.

I walked in from the kitchen and nodded a greeting to the two of them, sitting on the couch. I said something about having forgotten some test papers as I put the briefcase down on the telephone table, opened it, and slowly took out the gun. Keeping it shielded from them with the opened top of the briefcase, I brought the gun up, took aim at him, and squeezed the trigger. Not once—not twice—*three* times! Good number, three. A literature teacher knows all about the significance of the number three.

Nothing happened! There was no sound—although I had been careful to slip a bullet into each chamber before I left the office. There was no kick in my hand. There wasn't even much of a *click*. The only thing I could think was that maybe the Colt wouldn't work for someone who wasn't part of the deal. So I pointed it at her and fired off three more shots—with the same result. I do remember smelling—or thinking I smelled—a faint aroma of spent gunpowder, but I chalked that up to wishful thinking.

Sally and Walter ignored me, just kept right on talking as I gawked at them . . . so I slipped the gun back into the briefcase, shut it, and went up to the bedroom and shuffled around a bit, sounding busy while I tried to figure things out. I'd been packing to move out, but Sally—against old Walter baby's advice, I might add—had said it was all right for me to stay at the house until the apartment I'd rented in town opened up the first of the month. Thanks, Sally. As it turned out, that was the last favor you ever did for for me—except a day later, when you dropped dead!

So, I left the house for my next class—with Sally and Walter sitting on the couch just as alive as they could be—feeling as though I'd been ripped off, set up, or something by the Devil. His gun was a dud, as far as I was concerned.

Back in my office about two that afternoon, I checked the Colt and was surprised to see six empty shells in the chamber—no bullets. Could I have been dumb enough to load the gun with empty shells? I didn't think so, but I tossed the empties and slipped in six new bullets from the Devil's box. I was getting a little bit scared that I *had* hallucinated the summoning, but that still didn't explain where I had gotten the Colt.

By then I wasn't thinking too clearly, so I decided to test

the gun right there in my office. I sighted along the barrel at one of the pictures on my wall—one of my favorites, actually, a silkscreen advertisement for the Dartmouth Christmas Revels—and gently squeezed the trigger. Nothing happened. Quickly, I aimed at my doctoral dissertation—now there was something else to hate—on the top shelf of my bookcase and pulled the trigger.

Nothing.

Again, aiming at the pencil sharpener beside the door, I squeezed the trigger.

Nada!

I pointed at the wall and snapped the trigger three more times, and still nothing happened. The tinge of gunpowder I thought I smelled couldn't have really been there, I thought . . . just my imagination, I guessed. But you shouldn't ever *guess* when the Devil has your soul!

Again, though—and it struck me as really weird this time—when I opened the chamber all six bullets were spent. Maybe they were dummies or something—not really made of lead. Or maybe I was the dummy being led. I got the box, now minus a total of twelve bullets, and after inspecting them closely—they seemed real—reloaded, put the gun on the desk, and tilted back in my chair.

I'd been had, for sure, I thought, with rage and stark fear tossing me like a seesaw. I had signed my soul over to the Devil for *what*? For a revolver that didn't even work!

Anyway, like I said, the next day at noon, Sally was dead. Our neighbor, Mrs. Benton, said she heard three gunshots from our house. Afraid that there was a robbery or something going on, she stayed home and, clutching her living-room curtains to hide herself as she watched our house, called the Gorham police. They came shortly after that, and found Sally dead of three gunshot wounds to the head.

I, of course, didn't know this at the time. I was just coming back to my office, following a graduate seminar on Elizabethan Drama. I hadn't gone home the night before and had been forced to sleep—again—on my office floor, so I wasn't in the best of moods.

I spent the next couple of hours sitting at my desk, and was working through a stack of tests and pondering everything that had happened recently when there was a knock on the door. I scooped the Colt .45 into the top desk drawer but, foolishly, didn't slide the drawer completely shut before I went to the door. Two uniformed policemen entered, politely shook hands, and then informed me that my wife had been murdered . . . shot to death by a Colt .45.

I fell apart, wondering to myself which I felt more—shock or relief. I hadn't done it, but *someone* had! The policemen waited patiently for me to gain control of myself and explained that they wanted to know where I had been in the past three hours. Apparently Mrs. Benton had seen fit to fill them in on our domestic quarrels. They also wanted to know if I owned a Colt .45.

If this whole story has a tragic mistake, for me, at least, it was not following the Devil's advice to the letter. That's how he gets you, you know. I should have *realized* that! He had said that if I aimed the gun at Sally, pulled the trigger, and then threw the gun away, I'd never be caught.

But I didn't throw the damned thing away.

If you had asked me then, I suppose I would have said the gun was worthless. What difference would it make if I kept it or tossed it? I hadn't summoned the Devil that night. I'd fallen asleep and, beaten by exhaustion and the pressure I was under, I'd had a vivid nightmare. I hadn't *really* summoned the Devil. Stuff like that didn't *really* happen!

I gave the cops my alibi, and it was solid. When the shots rang out, I was more than twenty miles from my house, on the university's Portland campus, lecturing on Shakespeare's use of horse imagery in his history plays. You can't go against the testimony of a roomful of enthralled graduate students.

About then one of the policemen noticed the revolver in the desk drawer, and, eyeing me suspiciously, asked if they could take a look at it. Sure. There was no denying that I did own a Colt .45, but after they inspected it for a moment, I took it from them.

"Look," I said, hefting the Colt. "This sucker doesn't even work. It's a model or something." I opened the chamber, showed them that the gun was loaded, clicked it shut, and, with a flourish, pressed the barrel to my temple.

"See?" I said, as I snapped the trigger three times. "Nothing happens. It's a fake."

That seemed to satisfy them. They thanked me for my cooperation and left, saying they'd wait in the hallway until I felt ready to come with them to the hospital to identify the body.

But they had no more than swung the door shut behind them when shots rang out in my office! I was just turning to pick up my briefcase when the center of the Christmas Revels poster blew away. I turned and stared, horrified, as the top row of books on the bookcase suddenly jumped. I could see a large, black, smoking hole in the spine of my dissertation. Then the pencil sharpener by the door exploded into a twisted mess of metal. Three more shots removed pieces of plaster and wood from the office walls.

With the sound of the six shots still ringing in my ears, I heard the two policemen burst back into my office. They both had their revolvers drawn and poised.

"I thought that gun didn't work," one of them shouted, leaning cautiously against the doorframe. He was looking at me suspiciously, but then his expression changed to confusion when he registered that the Colt wasn't in my hand. It was lying on the desk, where I had placed it as they left.

"Man, I don't know what's going on here," the other one said. "But you had better come downtown until we can check the ballistics to make *sure* this wasn't the gun that killed her."

I was in a state of near shock—I'm sure my face had turned chalky white, because I felt an icy numbness rush across my cheeks and down the back of my neck. A sudden realization was beginning to sink in. It had been almost—*no!*—*exactly* twenty-four hours ago that I had aimed and shot the revolver six times in my office. Six times! And nothing had happened—until *now!*

This bit about the ballistics test had cracked my nerve. I mean, at this point I was convinced that it hadn't been coincidence. The shots I had banged off twenty-four hours earlier must have done in Sally. And I knew that if the cops checked it out, the ballistics would match.

What about sleazy Walter Altschuler? Was he dead, too? With a sudden sickening rush, I remembered what the Devil had said to me the night I summoned him . . . he'd said the gun was a Colt *.24*! A special, *modified* Colt .45!

I tried to force myself to appear calm. *Damn my soul to Hell!* I had pointed the gun to my head as a *beau geste* and pulled the trigger—three times! I remembered—now—that when I had done that, I *had* smelled a trace of spent gunpowder . . . as I had that morning at the house, when I had targeted Walter and Sally.

Then Joan Oliver, the department secretary, poked her head—cautiously, I might add—into my office to tell the policemen they had a phone call. I fell apart completely, knowing what it would be. Walter Altschuler had been found dead in his car in the Casco Bank parking lot in downtown Portland with three .45 caliber bullet wounds in his head.

I'd been *had*! I'd signed that damned contract . . . in *blood*! And I *had had* that damned gun. And it *had* worked! And the Devil *had* cheated me, but good, in the bargain.

So while sitting here in the cell, after coming to my senses this morning, I asked for some paper and a pen. If I'm wrong, I don't want to tell my story and be committed. But if I'm right, I want to get all of this down to leave a permanent record before those bullets from Hell blow my hea

THE MAKING OF REVELATION, PART 1

by Philip José Farmer

God said, "Bring me Cecil B. DeMille."

"Dead or alive?" the angel Gabriel said.

"I want to make him an offer he can't refuse. Can even *I* do this to a dead man?"

"Oh, I see," said Gabriel, who didn't. "It will be done." And it was.

Cecil Blount DeMille, confused, stood in front of the desk. He didn't like it. He was used to sitting behind the desk while others stood. Considering the circumstances, he wasn't about to protest. The giant, divinely handsome, bearded, pipe-smoking man behind the desk was not one you'd screw around with. However, the gray eyes, though steely, weren't quite those of a Wall Street banker. They held a hint of compassion.

Unable to meet those eyes, DeMille looked at the angel by his side. He'd always thought angels had wings. This one didn't, though he could certainly fly. He'd carried DeMille in his arms up through the stratosphere to a city of gold somewhere between the earth and the moon. Without a space suit, too.

God, like all great entities, came right to the point.

"This is 1980 A.D. In twenty years it'll be time for The Millennium. The day of judgment. The events as depicted in the Book of Revelation or the Apocalypse by St. John the

Divine. You know, the seven seals, the four horsemen, the moon dripping blood, Armageddon, and all that.''

DeMille wished he'd be invited to sit down. Being dead for twenty-one years, during which he'd not moved a muscle, had tended to weaken him.

"Take a chair," God said. "Gabe, bring the man a brandy." He puffed on his pipe; tiny lightning crackled through the clouds of smoke.

"Here you are, Mr. DeMille," Gabriel said, handing him the liqueur in a cut quartz goblet. "Napoleon 1880.''

DeMille knew there wasn't any such thing as a one-hundred-year-old brandy, but he didn't argue. Anyway, the stuff certainly tasted like it was. They really lived up here.

God sighed, and he said, "The main trouble is that not many people really believe in Me any more. So My powers are not what they once were. The old gods, Zeus, Odin, all that bunch, lost their strength and just faded away, like old soldiers, when their worshipers ceased to believe in them.

"So, I just can't handle the end of the world by Myself anymore. I need someone with experience, know-how, connections, and a reputation. Somebody people know really existed. You. Unless you know of somebody who's made more Biblical epics than you have.''

"That'll be the day," DeMille said. "But what about the unions? They really gave me a hard time, the commie bas—uh, so-and-so's. Are they as strong as ever?''

"You wouldn't believe their clout nowadays.''

DeMille bit his lip, then said, "I want them dissolved. If I only got twenty years to produce this film, I can't be held up by a bunch of goldbrickers.''

"No way," God said. "They'd all strike, and we can't afford any delays.''

He looked at his big railroad watch. "We're going to be on a very tight schedule.''

"Well, I don't know," DeMille said. "You can't get anything done with all their regulations, interunion jealousies, and the featherbedding. And the wages! It's no wonder it's so hard to show a profit. It's too much of a hassle!''

"I can always get D. W. Griffith."

DeMille's face turned red. "You want a grade-B production? No, no, that's all right! I'll do it, do it!"

God smiled and leaned back. "I thought so. By the way, you're not the producer, too; I am. My angels will be the executive producers. They haven't had much to do for several millennia, and the devil makes work for idle hands, you know. Haw, haw! You'll be the chief director, of course. But this is going to be quite a job. You'll have to have at least a hundred thousand assistant directors."

"But . . . that means training about ninety-nine thousand directors!"

"That's the least of our problems. Now you can see why I want to get things going immediately."

DeMille gripped the arms of the chair and said, weakly, "Who's going to finance this?"

God frowned. "That's another problem. My Antagonist has control of all the banks. If worse comes to worse, I could melt down the heavenly city and sell it. But the bottom of the gold market would drop all the way to hell. And I'd have to move to Beverly Hills. You wouldn't believe the smog there or the prices they're asking for houses.

"However, I think I can get the money. Leave that to Me."

The men who really owned the American banks sat at a long mahogany table in a huge room in a Manhattan skyscraper. The Chairman of the Board sat at the head. He didn't have the horns, tail, and hooves which legend gave him. Nor did he have an odor of brimstone. More like Brut. He was devilishly handsome and the biggest and best-built man in the room. He looked like he could have been the chief of the angels and in fact once had been. His eyes were evil but no more so than the others at the table, bar one.

The exception, Raphael, sat at the other end of the table. The only detractions from his angelic appearance were his bloodshot eyes. His apartment on the West Side had paper-thin walls, and the swingers' party next door had kept him awake most of the night. Despite his fatigue, he'd been quite effective in presenting the offer from above.

Don Francisco "The Fixer" Fica drank a sixth glass of wine to up his courage, made the sign of the cross, most offensive to the Chairman, gulped, and spoke.

"I'm sorry, Signor, but that's the way the vote went. One hundred percent. It's a purely business proposition, legal, too, and there's no way we won't make a huge profit from it. We're gonna finance the movie, come hell or high water!"

Satan reared up from his chair and slammed a huge but well-manicured fist onto the table. Glasses of vino crashed over; plates half-filled with pasta and spaghetti rattled. All but Raphael paled.

"*Dio motarello! Lecaculi! Cacasotti! Non romperci i coglioni!* I'm the Chairman, and I say no, no, no!"

Fica looked at the other heads of the families. Mignotta, Fregna, Stronza, Loffa, Recchione, and Bocchino seemed scared, but each nodded the go-ahead at Fica.

"I'm indeed sorry that you don't see it our way," Fica said. "But I must ask for your resignation."

Only Raphael could meet The Big One's eyes, but business was business. Satan cursed and threatened. Nevertheless, he was stripped of all his shares of stock. He'd walked in the richest man in the world, and he stormed out penniless and an ex-member of the Organization.

Raphael caught up with him as he strode mumbling up Park Avenue.

"You're the father of lies," Raphael said, "so you can easily be a great success as an actor or politician. There's money in both fields. Fame, too. I suggest acting. You've got more friends in Hollywood than anywhere else."

"Are you nuts?" Satan snarled.

"No. Listen. I'm authorized to sign you up for the film on the end of the world. You'll be a lead, get top billing. You'll have to share it with The Son, but we can guarantee you a bigger dressing room than His. You'll be playing yourself, so it ought to be easy work."

Satan laughed so loudly that he cleared the sidewalks for

two blocks. The Empire State Building swayed more than it should have in the wind.

"You and your boss must think I'm pretty dumb! Without me the film's a flop. You're up a creek without a paddle. Why should I help you? If I do I end up at the bottom of a flaming pit forever. Bug off!"

Raphael shouted after him, "We can always get Roman Polanski!"

Raphael reported to God, who was taking His ease on His jasper—and-cornelian throne above which glowed a rainbow.

"He's right, Your Divinity. If he refuses to cooperate, the whole deal's off. No real Satan, no real Apocalypse."

God smiled. "We'll see."

Raphael wanted to ask Him what He had in mind. But an angel appeared with a request that God come to the special effects department. Its technicians were having trouble with the roll-up-the-sky-like-a-scroll machine.

"Schmucks!" God growled. "Do I have to do everything?"

Satan moved into a tenement on 121st Street and went on welfare. It wasn't a bad life, not for one who was used to Hell. But two months later, his checks quit coming. There was no unemployment anymore. Anyone who was capable of working but wouldn't was out of luck. What had happened was that Central Casting had hired everybody in the world as production workers, stars, bit players, or extras.

Meanwhile, all the advertising agencies in the world had spread the word, good or bad depending upon the viewpoint, that the Bible was true. If you weren't a Christian, and, what was worse, a sincere Christian, you were doomed to perdition.

Raphael shot up to Heaven again.

"My God, You wouldn't believe what's happening! The Christians are repenting of their sins and promising to be good forever and ever, amen! The Jews, Moslems, Hindus, Buddhists, scientologists, animists, you name them, are lining up at the baptismal fonts! What a mess! The atheists have converted, too, and all the communist and Marxian socialist governments have been overthrown!"

"That's nice," God said. "But I'll really believe in the sincerity of the Christian nations when they kick out their present administrations. Down to the local dogcatcher."

"They're doing it!" Raphael shouted. "But maybe You don't understand! This isn't the way things go in the Book of Revelation! We'll have to do some very extensive rewriting of the script! Unless You straighten things out!"

God seemed very calm. "The script? How's Ellison coming along with it?"

Of course, God knew everything that was happening, but He pretended sometimes that He didn't. It was His excuse for talking. Just issuing a command every once in a while made for long silences, sometimes lasting for centuries.

He had hired only science-fiction writers to work on the script since they were the only ones with imaginations big enough to handle the job. Besides, they weren't bothered by scientific impossiblities. God loved Ellison, the head writer, because he was the only human he'd met so far who wasn't afraid to argue with Him. Ellison was severely handicapped, however, because he wasn't allowed to use obscenities while in His presence.

"Ellison's going to have a hemorrhage when he finds out about the rewrites," Raphael said. "He gets screaming mad if anyone messes around with his scripts."

"I'll have him up for dinner," God said. "If he gets too obstreperous, I'll toss around a few lightning bolts. If he thinks he was burned before . . . well!"

Raphael wanted to question God about the tampering with the book, but just then the head of Budgets came in. The angel beat it. God got very upset when He had to deal with money matters.

The head assistant director said, "We got a big problem now, Mr. DeMille. We can't have any Armageddon. Israel's willing to rent the site to us, but where are we going to get the forces of Gog and Magog to fight against the good guys? Everybody's converted. Nobody's willing to fight on the side of Antichrist and Satan. That means we've got to change the script again. I don't want to be the one to tell Ellison . . ."

"Do I have to think of everything?" DeMille said. "It's no problem. Just hire actors to play the villains."

"I already thought of that. But they want a bonus. They say they might be persecuted just for *playing* the guys in the black hats. They call it the social-stigma bonus. But the guilds and the unions won't go for it. Equal pay for all extras or no movie and that's that."

DeMille sighed. "It won't make any difference anyway as long as we can't get Satan to play himself."

The assistant nodded. So far, they'd been shooting around the devil's scenes. But they couldn't put it off much longer.

DeMille stood up. "I have to watch the auditions for The Great Whore of Babylon."

The field of a hundred thousand candidates for the role had been narrowed to a hundred, but from what he'd heard none of these could play the part. They were all good Christians now, no matter what they'd been before, and they just didn't have their hearts in the role. DeMille had intended to cast his brand-new mistress, a starlet, a hot little number—if promises meant anything—one hundred percent right for the part. But just before they went to bed for the first time, he'd gotten a phone call.

"None of this hankypanky, C.B.," God had said. "You're now a devout worshiper of Me, one of the lost sheep that's found its way back to the fold. So get with it. Otherwise, back to Forest Lawn for you, and I use Griffith."

"But . . . but I'm Cecil B. DeMille! The rules are O.K. for the common people, but . . ."

"Throw that scarlet woman out! Shape up or ship out! If you marry her, fine! But remember, there'll be no more divorces!"

DeMille was glum. Eternity was going to be like living forever next door to the Board of Censors.

The next day, his secretary, very excited, buzzed him.

"Mr. DeMille! Satan's here! I don't have him for an appointment, but he says he's always had a long-standing one with you!''

Demoniac laughter bellowed through the intercom.

"C.B., my boy! I've changed my mind! I tried out anonymously for the part, but your shithead assistant said I wasn't the type for the role! So I've come to you! I can start work as soon as we sign the contract!''

The contract, however, was not the one the great director had in mind. Satan, smoking a big cigar, chuckling, cavorting, read the terms.

"And don't worry about signing in your blood. It's unsanitary. Just ink in your John Henry, and all's well that ends in Hell.''

"You get my soul," DeMille said weakly.

"It's not much of a bargain for me. But if you don't sign it, you won't get me. Without me, the movie's a bomb. Ask The Producer, He'll tell you how it is.''

"I'll call Him now.''

"No! Sign now, this very second, or I walk out forever!''

DeMille bowed his head, more in pain than in prayer.

"Now!''

DeMille wrote on the dotted line. There had never been any genuine indecision. After all, he was a film director.

After snickering Satan had left, DeMille punched a phone number. The circuits transmitted this to a station which beamed the pulses up to a satellite which transmitted these directly to the heavenly city. Somehow, he got a wrong number. He hung up quickly when Israfel, the angel of death, answered. The second attempt, he got through.

"Your Divinity, I suppose You know what I just did? It *was* the only way we could get him to play himself. You understand that, don't You?''

"Yes, but if you're thinking of breaking the contract or getting Me to do it for you, forget it. What kind of an image would I have if I did something unethical like that? But not to worry. He can't get his hooks into your soul until I say so.''

Not to worry? DeMille thought. I'm the one who's going to Hell, not Him.

"Speaking of hooks, let Me remind you of a clause in your contract with The Studio. If you ever fall from grace, and I'm not talking about that little bimbo you were going to make your mistress, you'll die. The Mafia isn't the only one that puts out a contract. *Capice?*"

DeMille, sweating and cold, hung up. In a sense, he was already in Hell. All his life with no woman except for one wife? It was bad enough to have no variety, but what if whoever he married cut him off, like one of his wives—what was her name?—had done?

Moreover, he couldn't get loaded out of his skull even to forget his marital woes. God, though not prohibiting booze in His Book, had said that moderation in strong liquor was required and no excuses. Well, maybe he could drink beer, however disgustingly plebeian that was.

He wasn't even happy with his work now. He just didn't get the respect he had in the old days. When he chewed out the camerapeople, the grips, the gaffers, the actors, they stormed back at him that he didn't have the proper Christian humility, he was too high and mighty, too arrogant. God would get him if he didn't watch his big fucking mouth.

This left him speechless and quivering. He'd always thought, and acted accordingly, that the director, not God, *was* God. He remembered telling Charlton Heston that when Heston, who after all was *only* Moses, had thrown a temper tantrum when he'd stepped in a pile of camel shit during the filming of *The Ten Commandments*.

Was there more to the making of the end of the world than appeared on the surface? Had God seemingly forgiven everybody their sins and lack of faith but was subtly, even insidiously, making everybody pay by suffering? Had He forgiven but not forgotten? Or vice versa?

God marked even the fall of a sparrow, though why the sparrow, a notoriously obnoxious and dirty bird, should be significant in God's eye was beyond DeMille.

He had the uneasy feeling that everything wasn't as simple and as obvious as he'd thought when he'd been untimely ripped from the grave in a sort of Cesarean section and carried off like a nursing baby in Gabriel's arms to the office of The Ultimate Producer.

From the "*Playboy* Interview feature, December 1990.

Playboy: Mr. Satan, why did you decide to play yourself after all?

Satan: Damned if I know.

Playboy: The rumors are that you'll be required to wear clothes in the latter-day scenes but that you steadfastly refuse. Are these rumors true?

Satan: Yes indeed. Everybody knows I never wear clothes except when I want to appear among humans without attracting undue attention. If I wear clothes it'd be unrealistic. It'd be phony, though God knows that there are enough fake things in this movie. The Producer says this is going to be a PG picture, not an X-rated. That's why I walked off the set the other day. My lawyers are negotiating with The Studio now about this. But you can bet your ass that I won't go back unless things go my way, the right way. After all, I am an artist, and I have my integrity. Tell me, if you had a prong this size, would you hide it?

Playboy: The Chicago cops would arrest me before I got a block from my pad. I don't know, though, if they'd charge me with indecent exposure or being careless with a natural resource.

Satan: They wouldn't dare arrest me. I got too much on the city administration.

Playboy: That's *some* whopper. But I thought angels were sexless. You are a fallen angel, aren't you?

Satan: You jerk! What kind of researcher are you? Right there in the Bible, Genesis 6:2, it says that the sons of God, that is, the angels, took the daughters of men as wives and had children by them. You think the kids were test-tube babies? Also, you dunce, I refer you to Jude 7, where it's said that the angels, like the Sodomites, committed fornications and followed unnatural lusts.

Playboy: Whew! That brimstone! there's no need getting

so hot under the collar, Mr. Satan. I only converted a few years ago. I haven't had much chance to read the Bible.

Satan: I read the Bible every day. All of it. I'm a speedreader, you know.

Playboy: You read the Bible? (Pause) Hee, hee! Do you read it for the same reason W.C. Fields did when he was dying?

Satan: What's that?

Playboy: Looking for loopholes.

DeMille was in a satellite and supervising the camerapeople while they shot the takes from ten miles up. He didn't like at all the terrific pressure he was working under. There was no chance to shoot every scene three or four times to get the best angle. Or to reshoot if the actors blew their lines. And, oh, sweet Jesus, they were blowing them all over the world!

He mopped his bald head. "I don't care what The Producer says! We have to retake at least a thousand scenes. And we've a million miles of film to go yet!"

They were getting close to the end of the breaking-of-the-seven-seals sequences. The Lamb, played by The Producer's Son, had just broken the sixth seal. The violent worldwide earthquake had gone well. The sun-turning-black-as-a-funeral-pall had been a breeze. But the moon-all-red-as-blood had had some color problems. The rushes looked more like Colonel Sanders' orange juice than hemoglobin. In DeMille's opinion the stars-falling-to-earth-like-figs-shaken-down-by-a-gale scenes had been excellent, visually speaking. But everybody knew that the stars were not little blazing stones set in the sky but were colossal balls of atomic fires each of which was many times bigger than Earth. Even one of them, a million miles from Earth, would destroy it. So where was the credibility factor?

"I don't understand you, boss," DeMille's assistant said. "You didn't worry about credibility when you made *The Ten Commandments*. When Heston, I mean, Moses, parted the Red Sea, it was the fakiest thing I ever saw. It must've made unbelievers out of millions of Christians. But the film was a box-office success.''

''It was the dancing girls that brought off the whole thing!'' DeMille screamed. ''Who cares about all that other bullshit when they can see all those beautiful long-legged snatches twirling their veils!''

His secretary floated from her chair. ''I quit, you male chauvinistic pig! So me and my sisters are just snatches to you, you bald-headed cunt?''

His hotline to the heavenly city rang. He picked up the phone.

''Watch your language!'' The Producer thundered. ''If you step out of line too many times, I'll send you back to the grave! And Satan gets you right then and there!''

Chastened but boiling near the danger point, DeMille got back to business, called Art in Hollywood. The sweep of the satellite around Earth included the sky-vanishing-as-a-scroll-is-rolled-up scenes, where every-mountain-and-island-is-removed-from-its-place. If the script had called for a literal removing, the tectonics problem would have been terrific and perhaps impossible. But in this case the special effects departments, only had to simulate the scenes.

Even so, the budget was strained. However, The Producer, through his unique abilities, was able to carry these off. Whereas, in the original script, genuine displacements of Greenland, England, Ireland, Japan, and Madagascar had been called for, not to mention thousands of smaller islands, these were only faked.

''Your Divinity, I have some bad news,'' Raphael said.

The Producer was too busy to indulge in talking about something He already knew. Millions of the faithful had backslid and taken up their old sinful ways. They believed that since so many events of the apocalypse were being faked, God must not be capable of making any realy big catastrophes. So, they didn't have anything to worry about.

The Producer, however, had decided that it would not only

be good to wipe out some of the wicked but it would strengthen the faithful if they saw that God still had some muscle.

"They'll get the real thing next time," He said. "But we have to give DeMille time to set up his cameras at the right places. And we'll have to have the script rewritten, of course."

Raphael groaned. "Couldn't somebody else tell Ellison? He'll carry on something awful."

"I'll tell him. You look pretty pooped, Rafe. You need a little R&R. Take two weeks off. But don't do it on Earth. Things are going to be very unsettling there for a while."

Raphael, who had a tender heart, said, "Thanks, Boss. I'd just as soon not be around to see it."

The seal was stamped on the foreheads of the faithful, marking them safe from the burning of a third of Earth, the turning of a third of the sea to blood along with the sinking of a third of the ships at sea (which also included the crashing of a third of the airplanes in the air, something St. John had overlooked), the turning of a third of all water to wormwood (a superfluous measure since a third was already thoroughly polluted), the failure of a third of daylight, the release of giant mutant locusts from the abyss, and the release of poison-gas-breathing mutant horses, which slew a third of mankind.

DeMille was delighted. Never had such terrifying scenes been filmed. And these were nothing to the plagues which followed. He had enough film from the cutting room to make a hundred documentaries after the movie was shown. And then he got a call from The Producer.

"It's back to the special effects, my boy."

"But why, Your Divinity? We still have to shoot the-Great-Whore-of-Babylon sequences, the two-Beasts-and-the-marking-of-the-wicked, the Mount-Zion-and-The-Lamb-with-His-one-hundred-and-forty-thousand-good-men-who-haven't-defiled-themselves-with-women, the . . ."

"Because there aren't any wicked left by now, you dolt! And not too many of the good, either!"

"That couldn't be helped," DeMille said. "Those gas-breathing, scorpion-tailed horses kind of got out of hand. But we just *have* to have the scenes where the rest of mankind that survives the plagues still doesn't abjure its worship of idols and doesn't repent of its murders, sorcery, fornications, and robberies."

"Rewrite the script."

"Ellison will quit for sure this time."

"That's all right. I already have some hack from Peoria lined up to take his place. And cheaper, too."

DeMille took his outfit, one hundred thousand strong, to the heavenly city. Here they shot the war between Satan and his demons and Michael and his angels. This was not in the chronological sequence as written by St. John. But the logistics problems were so tremendous that it was thought best to film these out of order.

Per the rewritten script, Satan and his host were defeated, but a lot of nonbelligerents were casualties, including DeMille's best cameraperson. Moreover, there was a delay in production when Satan insisted that a stuntperson do the part where he was hurled from heaven to Earth.

"Or use a dummy!" he yelled. "Twenty thousand miles is a hell of a long way to fall! If I'm hurt badly I might not be able to finish the movie!"

The screaming match between the director and Satan took place on the edge of the city. The Producer, unnoticed, came up behind Satan and kicked him from the city for the second time in their relationship with utter ruin and furious combustion.

Shrieking, "I'll sue! I'll sue!" Satan fell towards the planet below. He made a fine spectacle in his blazing entrance into the atmosphere, but the people on Earth paid it little attention. They were used to fiery portents in the sky. In fact, they were getting fed up with them.

DeMille screamed and danced around and jumped up and down. Only the presence of The Producer kept him from using foul and abusive language.

"We didn't get it on camera! Now we'll have to shoot it over!"

"His contract calls for only one fall," God said. "You'd

better shoot the War-between-The-Faithful-and-True-Rider-against-the-beast-and-the-false-prophet while he recovers.''

"What'll I do about the fall?" DeMille moaned.

"Fake it," The Producer said, and He went back to His office.

Per the script, an angel came down from heaven and bound up the badly injured and burned and groaning Satan with a chain and threw him into the abyss, the Grand Canyon. Then he shut and sealed it over him (what a terrific sequence that was!) so that Satan might seduce the nations no more until a thousand years had passed.

A few years later the devil's writhings caused a volcano to form above him, and the Environmental Protection Agency filed suit against Celestial Productions, Inc., because of the resultant pollution of the atmosphere.

Then God, very powerful now that only believers existed on Earth, performed the first resurrection. In this, only the martyrs were raised. And Earth, which had had much elbow room because of the recent wars and plagues, was suddenly crowded again.

Part I was finished except for the reshooting of some scenes, the dubbing in of voice and background noise, and the synchronization of the music, which was done by the cherubim and seraphim (all now unionized).

The great night of the premiere in a newly built theater in Hollywood, six million capacity, arrived. DeMille got a standing ovation after it was over. But *Time* and *Newsweek* and *The Manchester Guardian* panned the movie.

"There are some people who may go to hell after all," God growled.

DeMille didn't care about that. The film was a box-office success, grossing ten billion dollars in the first six months. And when he considered the reruns in theaters and the TV rights . . . well, had anyone ever done better?

He had a thousand more years to live. That seemed like a long time. Now. But . . . what would happen to him when Satan was released to seduce the nations again? According to

John the Divine's book, there'd be another worldwide battle. Then Satan, defeated, would be cast into the lake of fire and sulphur in the abyss.

(He'd be allowed to keep his Oscar, however.)

Would God let Satan, per the contract DeMille had signed with the devil, take DeMille with him into the abyss? Or would He keep him safe long enough to finish directing Part II? After Satan was buried for good, there'd be a second resurrection and a judging of those raised from the dead. The goats, the bad guys, would be hurled into the pit to keep Satan company. DeMille should be with the saved, the sheep, because he had been born again. But there was that contract with The Tempter.

DeMille arranged a conference with The Producer. Ostensibly, it was about Part II, but DeMille managed to bring up the subject which really interested him.

"I can't break your contract with him," God said.

"But I only signed it so that You'd be sure to get Satan for the role. It was a self-sacrifice. Greater love hath no man and all that. Doesn't that count for anything?"

"Let's discuss the shooting of the new heaven and the new earth sequences."

At least I'm not going to be put into hell until the movie is done, DeMille thought. But after that? He couldn't endure thinking about it.

"It's going to be a terrible technical problem," God said, interrupting DeMille's gloomy thoughts. "When the second resurrection takes place, there won't be even Standing Room Only on Earth. That's why I'm dissolving the old earth and making a new one. But I can't just duplicate the old earth. The problem of *Lebensraum* would still remain. Now, what I'm contemplating is a Dyson sphere."

"What's that?"

"A scheme by a twentieth-century mathematician to break up the giant planet Jupiter into large pieces and set them in orbit at the distance of Earth from the sun. The surfaces of the pieces would provide room for a population enormously larger than Earth's. It's a Godlike concept."

"What a documentary its filming would be!" DeMille said. "Of course, if we could write some love interest in it, we could make a he . . . pardon me, a heaven of a good story!"

God looked at his big railroad watch.

"I have another appointment, C.B. The conference is over."

DeMille said goodbye and walked dejectedly towards the door. He still hadn't gotten an answer about his ultimate fate. God was stringing him along. He felt that he wouldn't know until the last minute what was going to happen to him. He'd be suffering a thousand years of uncertainty, of mental torture. His life would be a cliff-hanger. Will God relent? Or will He save the hero at the very last second?

"C.B.," God said.

DeMille spun around, his heart thudding, his knees turned to water. Was this it? The fatal finale? Had God, in His mysterious and subtle way, decided for some reason that there'd be no Continued in Next Chapter for him? It didn't seem likely, but then The Producer had never promised that He'd use him as a director of Part II, nor had He signed a contract with him. Maybe, like so many temperamental producers, He'd suddenly concluded that DeMille wasn't the right one for the job. Which meant that He could arrange it so that his ex-director would be thrown now, right this minute, into the lake of fire.

God said, "I can't break your contract with Satan. So . . ."

"Yes?"

DeMille's voice sounded to him as if he were speaking very far away.

"Satan can't have your soul until you die."

"Yes?"

His voice was only a trickle of sound, a last few drops of water from a clogged drainpipe.

"So, if you don't die, and that, of course, depends upon your behavior, Satan can't ever have your soul."

God smiled and said, "See you in eternity."

THE HOWLING MAN

by Charles Beaumont

The Germany of that time was a land of valleys and mountains and swift dark rivers, a green and fertile land where everything grew tall and straight out of the earth. There was no other country like it. Stepping across the border from Belgium, where the rain-caped, mustached guards saluted, grinning, like operetta soldiers, you entered a different world entirely. Here the grass became as rich and smooth as velvet; deep, thick woods appeared; the air itself, which had been heavy with the French perfume of wines and sauces, changed: the clean, fresh smell of lake and pines and boulders came into your lungs. You stood a moment, then, at the border, watching the circling hawks above and wondering, a little fearfully, how such a thing could happen. In less than a minute you had passed from a musty, ancient room, through an invisible door, into a kingdom of winds and light. Unbelievable! But there, at your heels, clearly in view, is Belgium, like all the rest of Europe, a faded tapestry from some forgotten mansion.

In that time, before I had heard of St. Wulfran's, of the wretch who clawed the stones of a locked cell, wailing in the midnight hours, or of the daft Brothers and their mad Abbot, I had strong legs and a mind on its last search. And I preferred to be alone. A while and I'll come back to this spot. We will ride and feel the sickness, fall, and hover on the edge of death,

243

together. But I am not a writer, only one who loves wild, unhousebroken words; I must have a real beginning.

Paris beckoned in my youth. I heeded, for the reason most young men just out of college heed, although they would never admit it: to lie with mysterious beautiful women. A solid, traditional upbringing among the corseted ruins of Boston had succeeded, as such upbringings generally do, in honing the urge to a keen edge. My nightly dreams of beaded bagnios and dusky writhing houris, skilled beyond imagining, reached, finally, the unbearable stage beyond which lies either madness or respectability. Fancying neither, I managed to convince my parents that a year abroad would add exactly the right amount of seasoning to my maturity, like a dash of curry in an otherwise bland, if not altogether tasteless, chowder. I'm afraid that Father caught the hot glint in my eye, but he was kind. Describing, in detail, and with immense effect, the hideous consequences of profligacy, telling of men he knew who'd gone to Europe, innocently, and fallen into dissolutions so profound they'd not been heard of since, he begged me at all times to remember that I was an Ellington and turned me loose. Paris, of course, was enchanting and terrifying, as a jungle must be to a zoo-born monkey. Out of respect to the honored dead, and Dad, I did a quick trot through the Tuileries, the Louvre, and down the Champs-Elysées to the Arc de Triomphe; then, with the fall of night, I cannoned off to Montmartre and the Rue Pigalle, embarking on the Grand Adventure. Synoptically, it did not prove to be so grand as I'd imagined; nor was it, after the fourth week, so terribly adventurous. Still: important to what followed, for what followed doubtless wouldn't have but for the sweet complaisant girls.

Boston's Straights and Narrows don't, I fear, prepare one—except psychologically—for the Wild Life. My health broke in due course and, as my thirst had been well and truly slaked, I was not awfully discontent to sink back into the contemplative cocoon to which I was, apparently, more suited. Abed for a month I lay, in celibate silence and almost total inactivity. Then, no doubt as a final gesture of rebellion, I got my idea—got? or had my concentrated sins received it, like a signal from a failing tower?—and I made my strange, un-Ellingtonian decision. I would explore Europe. But not as a tourist, safe and fat in his fat, safe bus, insulated against the beauty and the ugliness of changing cultures by a pane of glass and a room at the English-speaking hotel. No. I would go like an unprotected wind, a seven-league-booted leaf, a nestless bird, and I would see this dark strange land with the vision of a boy on the last legs of his dreams. I would go by bicycle, poor and lonely and questing—as poor and lonely and questing, anyway, as one can be with a hundred thousand in the bank and a partnership in Ellington, Carruthers & Blake waiting.

So it was. New England blood and muscles wilted on that first day's pumping, but New England spirit toughened as the miles dropped back. Like an ant crawling over a once-lovely, now decayed and somewhat seedy Duchess, I rode over the body of Europe. I dined at restaurants where boars' heads hung, all vicious-tusked and blind; I slept at country inns and breathed the musty age, and sometimes girls came to the door and knocked and asked if I had everything I needed ("Well . . .") and they were better than the girls in Paris, though I can't imagine why. No matter. Out of France I pedaled, into Belgium, out, and to the place of cows and forests, mountains, brooks, and laughing people: Germany. (I've rhapsodized on purpose for I feel it's quite important to remember how completely Paradisiacal the land was then, at that time.)

I looked odd, standing there. The border guard asked what was loose with me, I answered, "Nothing"—grateful for the German, and the French, Miss Finch had drummed into me—and set off along the smallest, darkest path. It serpentined through forests, cities, towns, villages, and always I followed its least likely apendages. Unreasonably, I pedaled as if toward a destination: into the Moselle Valley country, up into the desolate hills of emerald.

By a ferry, fallen to desuetude, the reptile drew me through a bosky wood. The trees closed in at once. I drank the fragrant air and pumped and kept on pumping, but a heat began to grow inside my body. My head began to ache. I felt weak. Two more miles and I was obliged to stop, for perspiration filmed my skin. You know the signs of pneumonia: a sapping of the strength, a trembling, flashes of heat and of cold; visions. I lay in the bed of damp leaves for a time, then forced myself onto the bicycle and rode for what seemed an endless time. At last a village came to view. A thirteenth-century village, gray and narrow-streeted, cobbled to the hidden storefronts. A number of old people in peasant costumes looked up as I bumped along, and I recall one ancient tallow-colored fellow—nothing more. Only the weakness, like acid, burning off my nerves and muscles. And an intervening blackness to pillow my fall.

I awoke to the smells of urine and hay. The fever had passed, but my arms and legs lay heavy as logs, my head throbbed horribly, and there was an empty shoveled-out hole inside my stomach somewhere. For a long while I did not move or open my eyes. Breathing was a major effort. But consciousness came, eventually.

I was in a tiny room. The walls and ceiling were of rough gray stone, the single glassless window was arch-shaped, the floor was uncombed dirt. My bed was not a bed at all but a blanket thrown across a disorderly pile of crinkly straw. Beside me, a crude table; upon it, a pitcher; beneath it, a bucket. Next to the table, a stool. And seated there, asleep, his tonsured head adangle from an Everest of robe, a monk.

I must have groaned, for the shorn pate bobbed up precipitately. Two silver trails gleamed down the corners of the suddenly exposed mouth, which drooped into a frown. The slumbrous eyes blinked.

"It is God's infinite mercy," sighed the gnomelike little man. "You have recovered."

"Not as yet," I told him. Unsuccessfully, I tried to remember what had happened; then I asked questions.

"I am Brother Christophorus. This is the Abbey of St. Wulfran's. The Burgermeister of Schwartzhof, Herr Barth, brought you to us nine days ago. Father Jerome said that you would die and he sent me to watch, for I have never seen a man die, and Father Jerome holds that it is beneficial for a Brother to have seen a man die. But now I suppose that you will not die." He shook his head ruefully.

"Your disappointment," I said, "cuts me to the quick. However, don't abandon hope. The way I feel now, it's touch and go."

"No," said Brother Christophorus sadly. "You will get well. It will take time. But you will get well."

"Such ingratitude, and after all you've done. How can I express my apologies?"

He blinked again. With the innocence of a child, he said, "I beg your pardon?"

"Nothing." I grumbled about blankets, a fire, some food to eat, and then slipped back into the well of sleep. A fever dream of forests full of giant two-headed beasts came, then the sound of screaming.

I awoke. The scream shrilled on—Klaxon-loud, high, cutting, like a cry for help.

"What is that sound?" I asked.

The monk smiled. "Sound? I hear no sound," he said.

It stopped. I nodded. "Dreaming. Probably I'll hear a good deal more before I'm through. I shouldn't have left Paris in such poor condition."

"No," he said. "You shouldn't have left Paris."

Kindly now, resigned to my recovery, Brother Christophorus became attentive to a fault. Nurselike, he spooned thick soups into me, applied compresses, chanted soothing prayers, and emptied the bucket out the window. Time passed slowly. As I fought the sickness, the dreams grew less vivid—but the nightly cries did not diminish. They were as full of terror and loneliness as before, strong, real in my ears. I tried to shut them out, but they would not be shut out. Still, how could they be strong and real except in my vanishing delirium? Brother Christophorous did not hear them. I watched him closely when the sunlight faded to the gray of dusk and the screams began, but he was deaf to them—if they existed. If they existed!

"Be still, my son. It is the fever that makes you hear these noises. That is quite natural. Is that not quite natural? Sleep."

"But the fever is gone! I'm sitting up now. Listen! Do you mean to tell me you don't hear *that*?"

"I hear only you, my son."

The screams, that fourteenth night, continued until dawn. They were totally unlike any sounds in my experience. Impossible to believe they could be uttered and sustained by a human, yet they did not seem to be animal. I listened, there in the gloom, my hands balled into fists, and knew, suddenly, that one of two things must be true. Either someone or something was making these ghastly sounds, and Brother Christophorus was lying, or—I was going mad. Hearing-voices mad, climbing-walls and frothing mad. I'd have to find the answer: that I knew. And by myself.

I listened with a new ear to the howls. Razoring under the door, they rose to operatic pitch, subsided, resumed, like the cries of a surly, hysterical child. To test their reality, I hummed beneath my breath, I covered my head with a blanketing, scratched at the straw, coughed. No difference. The quality of substance, of existence, was there. I tried, then, to localize the screams; and, on the fifteenth night, felt sure that they were coming from a spot not far along the hall.

"The sounds that maniacs hear seem quite real to them."
I know. I know!

The monk was by my side, he had not left it from the start, keeping steady vigil even through Matins. He joined his tremulous soprano to the distant chants, and prayed excessively. But nothing could tempt him away. The food we ate was brought to us, as were all other needs. I'd see the Abbot, Father Jerome, once I was recovered. Meanwhile . . .

"I'm feeling better, Brother. Perhaps you'd care to show me about the grounds. I've seen nothing of St. Wulfran's except this little room."

"There is only this little room multiplied. Ours is a rigorous order. The Franciscans, now, they permit themselves aesthetic pleasure we do not. It is, for us, a luxury. We have a single, most unusual job. There is nothing to see."

"But surely the Abbey is very old."

"Yes, that is true."

"As an antiquarian—"

"Mr. Ellington—"

"What is it you don't want me to see? What are you afraid of, Brother?"

"Mr. Ellington? I do not have the authority to grant your request. When you are well enough to leave, Father Jerome will no doubt be happy to accommodate you."

"Will he also be happy to explain the screams I've heard each night since I've been here?"

"Rest, my son. Rest."

The unholy, hackle-raising shriek burst loose and bounded off the hard stone walls. Brother Christophorus crossed himself, apropos of nothing, and sat like an ancient Indian on the weary stool. I knew he liked me. Especially, perhaps. We'd got along quite well in all our talks. But this—*verboten*.

I closed my eyes. I counted to three hundred. I opened my eyes.

The good monk was asleep. I blasphemed, softly, but he did not stir, so I swung my legs over the side of the straw bed and made my way across the dirt floor to the heavy wooden door. I rested there a time, in the candleless dark, listening to the howls; then, with Bostonian discretion, raised the bolt. The rusted hinges creaked, but Brother Christophorus was deep in celestial marble: his head drooped low upon his chest.

Panting, weak as a landlocked fish, I stumbled out into the corridor. The screams became impossibly loud. I put my hands to my ears, instinctively, and wondered how anyone could sleep with such a furor going on. It *was* a furor. In my mind? No. Real. The monastery shook with these shrill cries. You could feel their realness with your teeth.

I passed a Brother's cell and listened, then another; then I paused. A thick door, made of oak or pine, was locked before me. Behind it were the screams.

A chill went through me on the edge of those unutterable shrieks of hopeless, helpless anguish, and for a moment I considered turning back—not to my room, not to my bed of straw, but back into the open world. But duty held me. I took a breath and walked up to the narrow bar-crossed window and looked in.

A man was in the cell. On all fours, circling like a beast, his head thrown back, a man. The moonlight showed his face. It cannot be described—not, at least, by me. A man past death might look like this, a victim of the Inquisition rack, the stake, the pincers: not a human in the third decade of the twentieth century, surely. I had never seen such suffering within two eyes, such lost, mad suffering. Naked, he crawled about the dirt, cried, leaped up to his feet and clawed the hard stone walls in fury.

Then he saw me.

The screaming ceased. He huddled, blinking, in the corner of his cell. And then, as though unsure of what he saw, he walked right to the door.

In German, hissing: "Who are you?"

"David Ellington," I said. "Are you locked in? Why have they locked you in?"

He shook his head. "Be still, be still. You are not German?"

"No." I told him how I came to be at St. Wulfran's.

"Ah!" Trembling, his horny fingers closing on the bars, the naked man said: "Listen to me, we have only moments. They are mad. You hear? All mad. I was in the village, lying with my woman, when their crazy Abbot burst into the house and hit me with his heavy cross. I woke up here. They flogged me. I asked for food, they would not give it to me. They took my clothes. They threw me in this filthy room. They locked the door."

"Why?"

"Why?" He moaned. "I wish I knew. That's been the worst of it. Five years imprisoned, beaten, tortured, starved, and not a reason given, not a word to guess from—Mr. Ellington! I have sinned, but who has not? With my woman, quietly, alone with my woman, my love. And this God-drunk lunatic, Jerome, cannot stand it. Help me!"

His breath splashed on my face. I took a backward step and tried to think. I couldn't quite believe that in this century a thing so frightening could happen. Yet, the Abbey was secluded, above the world, timeless. What could not transpire here, secretly?

"I'll speak to the Abbot."

"No! I tell you, he's the maddest of them all. Say nothing to him."

"Then how can I help you?"

He pressed his mouth against the bars. "In one way only. Around Jerome's neck, there is a key. It fits this lock. If—"

"Mr. Ellington!"

I turned and faced a fierce El Greco painting of a man. White-bearded, prow-nosed, regal as an emperor beneath the gray peaked robe, he came out of the darkness. "Mr. Ellington, I did not know that you were well enough to walk. Come with me, please."

The naked man began to weep hysterically. I felt a grip of steel about my arm. Through corridors, past snore-filled cells, the echoes of the weeping dying, we continued to a room.

"I must ask you to leave St. Wulfran's," the Abbot said. "We lack the proper facilities for care of the ill. Arrangements will be made in Schwartzhof—"

"One moment," I said. "While it's probably true that Brother Christophorus's ministrations saved my life—and certainly true that I owe you all a debt of gratitude—I've got to ask for an explanation of that man in the cell."

"What man?" the Abbot said softly.

"The one we just left, the one who's screamed all night long every night."

"No man has been screaming, Mr. Ellington."

Feeling suddenly very weak, I sat down and rested a few breaths' worth. Then I said, "Father Jerome—you are he? I am not necessarily an irreligious person, but neither could I be considered particularly religious. I know nothing of monasteries, what is permitted, what isn't. But I seriously doubt that you have the authority to imprison a man against his will."

"That is quite true. We have no such authority."

"Then why have you done so?"

The Abbott looked at me steadily. In a firm, inflexible voice, he said: "No man has been imprisoned at St. Wulfran's."

"He claims otherwise."

"Who claims otherwise?"

"The man in the cell at the end of the corridor."

"There is no man in the cell at the end of the corridor."

"I was talking with him!"

"You were talking with no man."

The conviction in his voice shocked me into momentary silence. I gripped the arms of the chair.

"You are ill, Mr. Ellington," the bearded holy man said. "You have suffered from delirium. You have heard and seen things which do not exist."

"That's true," I said. "But the man in the cell—whose voice I can hear now!—is not one of those things."

The Abbot shrugged. "Dreams can seem very real, my son."

I glanced at the leather thong about his turkey-gobbler neck, all but hidden beneath the beard. "Honest men make unconvincing liars," I lied convincingly. "Brother Christophorus has a way of looking at the floor whenever he denies the cries in the night. You look at me, but your voice loses its command. I can't imagine why, but you are both very intent upon keeping me away from the truth. Which is not only poor Christianity, but also poor psychology. For now I am quite curious indeed. You might as well tell me, Father; I'll find out eventually."

"What do you mean?"

"Only that. I'm sure the police will be interested to hear of a man imprisoned at the Abbey."

"I tell you, *there is no man!*"

"Very well. Let's forget the matter."

"Mr. Ellington—" The Abbot put his hands behind him. "The person in the cell is, ah, one of the Brothers. Yes. He is subject to . . . seizures, fits. You know fits? At these times, he becomes intractable. Violent. Dangerous! We're obliged to lock him in his cell, which you can surely understand.''

"I understand,'' I said, "that you're still lying to me. If the answer were as simple as that, you'd not have gone through the elaborate business of pretending I was delirious. There'd have been no need. There's something more to it, but I can wait. Shall we go on to Schwartzhof?''

Father Jerome tugged at his beard viciously, as if it were some feathered demon come to taunt him. "Would you truly go to the police?'' he asked.

"Would you?'' I said. "In my position?''

He considered that for a long time, tugging the beard, nodding the prowed head; and the screams went on, so distant, so real. I thought of the naked man clawing in his filth.

"Well, Father?''

"Mr. Ellington, I see that I shall have to be honest with you—which is a great pity,'' he said. "Had I followed my original instinct and refused to allow you in the Abbey to begin with . . . but, I had no choice. You were near death. No physician was available. You would have perished. Still, perhaps that would have been better.''

"My recovery seems to have disappointed a lot of people,'' I commented. "I assure you it was inadvertent.''

The old man took no notice of this remark. Stuffing his mandarin hands into the sleeves of his robe, he spoke with great deliberation. "When I said that there was no man in the cell at the end of the corridor, I was telling the truth. Sit down, sir! Please! Now.'' He closed his eyes. "There is much to the story, much that you will not understand or believe. You are sophisticated, or feel that you are. You regard our life here, no doubt, as primitive—''

"In fact, I—''

"In fact, you do. I know the current theories. Monks are misfits, neurotics, sexual frustrates, and aberrants. They retreat from the world because they cannot cope with the world. Et cetera. You are surprised I know these things? My son, I was told by the one who began the theories!'' He raised his head upward, revealing more of the leather thong. "Five years ago, Mr. Ellington, there were no screams at St. Wulfran's. This was an undistinguished little Abbey in the wild Black Mountain region, and its inmates' job was quite simply to serve God, to save what souls they could by constant prayer. At that time, not very long after the great war, the world was in chaos. Schwartzhof was not the happy village you see now. It was, my son, a resort for the sinful, a hive of vice and corruption, a pit for the unwary—and the wary also, if they had not strength. A Godless place! Forsaken, fornicators paraded the streets. Gambling was done. Robbery and murder, drunkenness, and evils so profound I cannot put them into words. In all the universe you could not have found a fouler pesthole, Mr. Ellington! The Abbots and the Brothers at St. Wulfran's succumbed for years to Schwartzhof, I regret to say. Good men, lovers of God, chaste good men came here and fought but could not win against the black temptations. Finally it was decided that the Abbey should be closed. I heard of this and argued. 'Is that not surrender?' I said. 'Are we to bow before the strength of evil? Let me try, I beg you. Let me try to amplify the word of God that all in Schwartzhof shall hear and see their dark transgressions and repent!' "

The old man stood at the window, a trembling shade. His hands were now clutched together in a fervency of remembrance. "They asked," he said, "if I considered myself more virtuous than my predecessors that I should hope for success where they had failed. I answered that I did not, but that I had an advantage. I was a convert. Earlier I had walked with evil, and knew its face. My wish was granted. For a year. One year only. Rejoicing, Mr. Ellington, I came here; and one night, incognito, walked the streets of the village. The smell of evil was strong. Too strong, I thought—and I had reveled in the alleys of Morocco, I had seen the dens of Hong Kong, Paris, Spain. The orgies were too wild, the drunkards much too drunk, the profanities a great deal too profane. It was as if the evil of the world had been distilled and centered here, as if a pagan tribal chief, in hiding, had assembled all his rituals about him. . . ." The Abbot nodded his head. "I thought of Rome, in her last days; of Byzantium; of—Eden. That was the first of many hints to come.. No matter what they were. I returned to the Abbey and donned my holy robes and went back into Schwartzhof. I made myself conspicuous. Some jeered, some shrank away, a voice cried, 'Damn your foolish God!' And then a hand thrust out from darkness, touched my shoulder, and I heard: 'Now, Father, are you lost?' "

The Abbot brought his tightly clenched hands to his forehead and tapped his forehead.

"Mr. Ellington, I have some poor wine here. Please have some."

I drank, gratefully. Then the priest continued.

"I faced a man of average appearance. So average, indeed, that I felt I knew, then. 'No,' I told him, 'but you are lost!' He laughed a foul laugh. 'Are we not all, Father?' Then he said a most peculiar thing. He said his wife was dying and begged me to give her Extreme Unction. 'Please,' he said, 'in God's sweet name!' I was confused. We hurried to his house. A woman lay upon a bed, her body nude. 'It is a different Extreme Unction that I have in mind,' he whispered, laughing. 'It's the only kind, dear Father, that she understands. No other will have her! Pity! Pity on the poor soul lying there in all her suffering. Give her your Scepter!' And the woman's arms came snaking, supplicating toward me, round and sensuous and hot. . . ."

Father Jerome shuddered and paused. The shrieks, I thought, were growing louder from the hall. "Enough of that," he said. "I was quite sure then. I raised my cross and told the words I'd learned, and it was over. He screamed—as he's doing now—and fell upon his knees. He had not expected to be recognized, nor should he have been normally. But in my life, I'd seen him many times, in many guises. I brought him to the Abbey. I locked him in the cell. We chant his chains each day. And so, my son, you see why you must not speak of the things you've seen and heard?"

I shook my head, as if afraid the dream would end, as if

reality would suddenly explode upon me. "Father Jerome," I said, "I haven't the vaguest idea of what you're talking about. Who is the man?"

"Are you such a fool, Mr. Ellington? That you must be told?"

"Yes!"

"Very well," said the Abbot. "He is Satan. Otherwise known as the Dark Angel, Asmodeus, Belial, Ahriman, Diabolus—the Devil."

I opened my mouth.

"I see you doubt me. That is bad. Think, Mr. Ellington, of the peace of the world in these five years. Of the prosperity, of the happiness. Think of this country, Germany, now. Is there another country like it? Since we caught the Devil and locked him up here, there have been no great wars, no overwhelming pestilences: only the sufferings man was meant to endure. Believe what I say, my son: I beg you. Try very hard to believe that the creature you spoke with is Satan himself. Fight your cynicism, for it is born of him; he is the father of cynicism, Mr. Ellington! His plan was to defeat God by implanting doubt in the minds of Heaven's subjects!" The Abbot cleared his throat. "Of course," he said, "we could never release anyone from St. Wulfran's who had any part of the Devil in him."

I stared at the old fanatic and thought of him prowling the streets, looking for sin; saw him standing outraged at the bold fornicator's bed, wheedling him into an invitation to the Abbey, closing that heavy door and locking it, and, because of the world's temporary postwar peace, clinging to his fantasy. What greater dream for a holy man than actually capturing the Devil!

"I believe you," I said.

"Truly?"

"Yes. I hesitated only because it seemed a trifle odd that Satan should have picked a little German village for his home."

"He moves around," the Abbot said. "Schwartzhof attracted him as lovely virgins attract perverts."

"I see."

"Do you? My son, do you?"

"Yes. I swear it. As a matter of fact, I thought he looked familiar, but I simply couldn't place him."

"Are you lying?"

"Father, I am a Bostonian."

"And you promise not to mention this to anyone?"

"I promise."

"Very well." The old man sighed. "I suppose," he said, "that you would not consider joining us as a Brother at the Abbey?"

"Believe me, Father, no one could admire the vocation more than I. But I am not worthy. No; it's quite out of the question. However, you have my word that your secret is safe with me."

He was very tired. Sound had, in these years, reversed for him: the screams had become silence, the sudden cessation of them noise. The prisoner's quiet talk with me had awakened him from deep slumber. Now he nodded wearily, and I saw that what I had to do would not be difficult after all. Indeed, no more difficult than fetching the authorities.

I walked back to my cell, where Brother Christophorus still slept, and lay down. Two hours passed. I rose again and returned to the Abbot's quarters.

The door was closed but unlocked.

I eased it open, timing the creaks of the hinges with the screams of the prisoner. I tiptoed in. Father Jerome lay snoring in his bed.

Slowly, cautiously, I lifted out the leather thong, and was a bit astounded at my technique. No Ellington had ever burgled. Yet a force, not like experience, but like it, ruled my fingers. I found the knot. I worked it loose.

The warm iron key slid off into my hand.

The Abbot stirred, then settled, and I made my way into the hall.

The prisoner, when he saw me, rushed the bars. "He's told you lies, I'm sure of that!" he whispered hoarsely. "Disregard the filthy madman!"

"Don't stop screaming," I said.

"What?" He saw the key and nodded, then, and made his awful sounds. I thought at first the lock had rusted, but I worked the metal slowly and in time the key turned over.

Howling still, in a most dreadful way, the man stepped out into the corridor. I felt a momentary fright as his clawed hand reached up and touched my shoulder; but it passed. "Come on!" We ran insanely to the outer door, across the frosted ground, down toward the village.

The night was very black.

A terrible aching came into my legs. My throat went dry. I thought my heart would tear loose from its moorings. But I ran on.

"Wait."

Now the heat began.

"Wait."

By a row of shops I fell. My chest was full of pain, my head of fear: I knew the madmen would come swooping from their dark asylum on the hill. I cried out to the naked hairy man: "Stop! Help me!"

"Help you?" He laughed once, a high-pitched sound more awful than the screams had been; and then he turned and vanished in the moonless night.

I found a door, somehow.

The pounding brought a ruffled burgher. Policemen came at last and listened to my story. But of course it was denied by Father Jerome and the Brothers of the Abbey.

"This poor traveler has suffered from the visions of pneumonia. There was no howling man at St. Wulfran's. No, no, certainly not. Absurd! Now, if Mr. Ellington would care to stay with us, we'd happily—no? Very well. I fear that you will be delirious awhile, my son. The things you see will be quite real. Most real. You'll think—how quaint!—that you have loosed the Devil on the world and that the war to come—what war? But aren't there always wars? Of course! —you'll think that it's your fault"—those old eyes burning condemnation! Beak-nosed, bearded head atremble, rage in every word!—"that you'll have caused the misery and suffering and death. And nights you'll spend, awake, unsure, afraid. How foolish!''

Gnome of God, Christophorus, looked terrified and sad. He said to me, when Father Jerome swept furiously out: "My son, don't blame yourself. Your weakness was *his* lever. Doubt unlocked that door. Be comforted: we'll hunt *him* with our nets, and one day . . ."

One day, what?

I looked up at the Abbey of St. Wulfran's, framed by dawn, and started wondering, as I have wondered since ten thousand times, if it wasn't true. Pneumonia breeds delirium; delirium breeds vision. Was it possible that I'd imagined all of this?

No. Not even back in Boston, growing dewlaps, paunches, wrinkles, sacks of money, at Ellington, Carruthers & Blake, could I accept that answer.

The monks were mad, I thought. Or: The howling man was mad. Or: The whole thing was a joke.

I went about my daily work, as every man must do, if sane, although he may have seen the dead rise up or freed a bottled djinn or fought a dragon, once, quite long ago.

But I could not forget. When the pictures of the carpenter from Braunau-am-Inn began to appear in all the papers, I grew uneasy; for I felt I'd seen this man before. When the carpenter invaded Poland, I was sure. And when the world was plunged into war and cities had their entrails blown asunder and that pleasant land I'd visited became a place of hate and death, I dreamed each night.

Each night I dreamed, until this week.

A card arrived. From Germany. A picture of the Moselle Valley is on one side, showing mountains fat with grapes and the dark Moselle, wine of these grapes.

On the other side of the card is a message. It is signed "*Brother Christophorus*" and reads (and reads and reads!):

"*Rest now, my son. We have him back with us again.*"

TRACE

by Jerome Bixby

I tried for a shortcut.

My wrong left turn north of Pittsfield led me into a welter of backroads from which I could find no exit. Willy-nilly I was forced, with every mile I drove, higher and higher into the tree-clad hills . . . even an attempt to retrace my route found me climbing. No farmhouses, no gas stations, no sign of human habitation at all . . . just green trees, shrubbery, drifting clouds, and that damned road going up. And by now it was so narrow I couldn't even turn around!

On the worst possible stretch of dirt you can imagine, I blew a tire and discovered that my spare had leaked empty.

Sizzling the summer air of Massachusetts with curses, I started hiking in the only direction I thought would do me any good—down. But the road twisted and meandered oddly through the hills, and—by this time, I was used to it—*down* inexplicably turned to *up* again.

I reached the top of a rise, looked down, and called out in great relief, "Hello!"

His house was set in the greenest little valley I have ever seen. At one end rose a brace of fine granite cliffs, to either side of a small, iridescent waterfall. His house itself was simple, New Englandish, and seemed new. Close about its walls were crowded profuse bursts of magnificent flowers— red piled upon blue upon gold. Though the day was partly

261

cloudy, I noticed that no cloud hung over the valley; the sun seemed to have reserved its best efforts for this place.

He stood in his front yard, watering roses, and I wondered momentarily at the sight of running water in this secluded section. Then he lifted his face at the sound of my call and my approaching steps. His smile was warm and his greeting hearty and his handshake firm; his thick white hair, tossed in the breeze, and his twinkling eyes deepset in a ruddy face, provided the kindliest appearance imaginable. He clucked his tongue at my tale of misfortune, and invited me to use his phone and then enjoy his hospitality while waiting for the tow truck.

The phone call made, I sat in a wonderfully comfortable chair in his unusually pleasant living room, listening to an unbelievably brilliant performance of something called the *Mephisto Waltz* on an incredibly perfect hi-fi system.

"You might almost think it was the composer's own performance," my host said genially, setting at my side a tray of extraordinary delicacies prepared in an astonishingly short time. "Of course, he died many years ago . . . but what a pianist! Poor fellow . . . he should have stayed away from other men's wives."

We talked for the better part of an hour, waiting for the truck. He told me that, having suffered a rather bad fall in his youth, considerations of health required that he occasionally abandon his work and come here to vacation in Massachusetts.

"Why Massachusetts?" I asked. (I'm a Bermuda man, myself.)

"Oh . . . why not?" he smiled. "This valley is a pleasant spot for meditation. I like New England . . . it is here that I have experienced some of my greatest successes—and several notable defeats. Defeat, you know, is not such a bad thing, if there's not too much of it . . . it makes for humility, and humility makes for caution, therefore for safety."

"Are you in the public employ, then?" I asked. His remarks seemed to indicate that he had run for office.

His eyes twinkled. "In a way. What do you do?"

"I'm an attorney."

"Ah," he said. "Then perhaps we may meet again."

"That would be a pleasure," I said. "However, I've come north only for a convention . . . if I hadn't lost my way . . ."

"Many find themselves at my door for that reason," he nodded. "To turn from the straight and true road is to risk a perilous maze, eh?"

I found his remark puzzling. Did *that* many lost travelers appear at his doorstep? Or was he referring to his business? . . . Perhaps he was a law officer, a warden, even an executioner! Such men often dislike discussing their work.

"Anyway," I said, "I will not soon forget your kindness!"

He leaned back, cupping his brandy in both hands. "Do you know," he murmured, "kindness is a peculiar thing. Often you find it, like a struggling candle, in the most unlikely of nights. Have you ever stopped to consider that there is no such thing in the Universe as a one-hundred percent chemically pure substance? In everything, no matter how thoroughly it is refined, distilled, purified, there must be just a little, if only a trace, of its opposite. For example, no man is wholly good; none wholly evil. The kindest of men must yet practice some small, secret malice—and the cruelest of men cannot help but perform an act of good now and then."

"It certainly makes it hard to judge people, doesn't it?" I said. "I find that so much in my profession. One must depend on intuition—"

"Fortunately," he said, "in mine, I deal in fairly concrete percentages."

After a moment, I said, "In the last analysis, then, you'd even have to grant the Devil himself that solitary facet of goodness you speak of. His due, as it were. Once in a while, *he* would be compelled to do good deeds. That's certainly a curious thought."

He smiled. "Yet I assure you, that tiny, irresistible impulse would be there."

My excellent cigar, which he had given me with the superb brandy, had gone out. Noting this, he leaned forward—his lighter flamed, with a *click* like the snapping of fingers. "The entire notion," he said meditatively, "is a part of a philosophy which I developed in collaboration with my brother . . . a small cog in a complex system of what you might call Universal weights and balances."

"You are in business with your brother, then?" I asked, trying to fit this latest information into my theories.

"Yes . . . and no." He stood up, and suddenly I heard a motor approaching up the road. "And now, your tow truck is here. . . ."

We stood on the porch, waiting for the truck. I looked around at his beautiful valley, and filled my lungs.

"It *is* lovely, isn't it?" he said, with a note of pride.

"It is perfectly peaceful and serene," I said. "One of the loveliest spots I have ever seen. It seems to reflect what you have told me of your pleasures . . . and what I observe in *you*, sir. Your kindness, hospitality, and charity; your great love of Man and Nature." I shook his hand warmly. "I shall never forget this delightful afternoon!"

"Oh, I imagine you will," he smiled. "Unless we meet again. At any rate, I am happy to have done you a good turn. Up here, I must almost create the opportunity."

The truck stopped. I went down the steps, and turned at the bottom. The late-afternoon sun seemed to strike a glint of red in his eyes.

"Thanks, again," I said. "I'm sorry I wasn't able to meet your brother. Does he ever join you up here on his vacations?"

"I'm afraid not," he said, after a moment. "He has his own little place. . . ."

GUARDIAN ANGEL

by Arthur C. Clarke

I

Pieter Van Ryberg shivered, as he always did, when he came into Stormgren's room. He looked at the thermostat and shrugged his shoulders in mock resignation.

"You know, Chief," he said, "although we'll be sorry to lose you, it's nice to feel that the pneumonia death-rate will soon be falling."

"How do you know?" smiled Stormgren. "The next Secretary-General may be an Eskimo. The fuss some people make over a few degrees centigrade!"

Van Ryberg laughed and walked over to the curving double window. He stood in silence for a moment, staring along the avenue of great white buildings, still only partly finished.

"Well," he said, with a sudden change of tone. "Are you going to see them?"

Behind him he heard Stormgren fidgeting nervously with his famous uranium paperweight.

"Yes, I think so. It usually saves trouble in the long run."

Van Ryberg suddenly stiffened and pressed his face against the glass.

"Here they are!" he said. "They're coming up Wilson Avenue. Not as many as I expected, though—about two thousand, I'd say."

265

Stormgren walked over to the Assistant Secretary's side. Half a mile away, a small but determined crowd was moving along the avenue towards Headquarters Building. It carried banners which Stormgren could not read at this distance, but he knew their message well enough. Presently he could hear, even through the insulation, the ominous sound of chanting voices. He felt a sudden wave of disgust sweep over him. Surely the world had had enough of marching mobs and angry slogans!

The crowd had now come abreast of the building: it must know that he was watching, for here and there fists were being shaken in the air. They were not defying him, though the gesture was meant for him to see. As pygmies may threaten a giant, those angry fists were directed against the sky fifty miles above his head.

And as likely as not, thought Stormgren, Karallen was watching the whole thing and enjoying himself hugely.

This was the first time that Stormgren had ever met the head of the Freedom League. He still wondered if the action was wise: in the final analysis he had only taken it because the League would employ any refusal as ammunition against him. He knew that the gulf was far too wide for any agreement to come from this meeting.

Alexander Wainwright was a tall but slightly stooping man in the late fifties. He seemed inclined to apologize for his more boisterous followers, and Stormgren was rather taken aback by his obvious sincerity and considerable personal charm. It would be rather hard to dislike him, whatever one's views of the cause for which he stood.

Stormgren wasted no time after van Ryberg's brief and somewhat strained introductions.

"I suppose," he began, "the chief object of your visit is to register a formal protest against the Federation Scheme. Am I correct?"

Wainwright nodded.

"That is my main purpose, Mr. Secretary. As you know, for the last five years we have tried to awaken the human race to the danger that confronts it. I must admit that, from our point of view, the response has been disappointing. The great majority of people seem content to let the Overlords run the world as they please. But this European Federation is as intolerable as it will be unworkable. Even Karallen can't wipe out two thousand years of history at the stroke of a pen.''

"Then do you consider," interjected Stormgren, "that Europe, and the whole world, must continue indefinitely to be divided into scores of sovereign states, each with its own currency, armed forces, customs, frontiers, and all the rest of that—that medieval paraphernalia?''

"I don't quarrel with Federation as an *ultimate* objective, though some of my supporters might not agree. My point is that it must come from within, not be superimposed from without. We must work out our own destiny—we have a right to independence. There must be no more interference in human affairs!''

Stormgren sighed. All this he had heard a hundred times before, and he knew that he could only give the old answers that the Freedom League had refused to accept. He had faith in Karallen, and they had not. That was the fundamental difference, and there was nothing he could do about it. Luckily, there was nothing that the Freedom League could do either.

"Let me ask you a few questions," he said. "Can you deny that the Overlords have brought security, peace and prosperity to the world?''

"That is true. But they have taken our freedom. Man does not live—''

"By bread alone. Yes, I know—but this is the first age in which every man was sure of getting even that. In any case, what freedom have we lost compared with that which the Overlords have given us for the first time in human history?''

"Freedom to control our own lives, under God's guidance.''

Stormgren shook his head.

"Last month, five hundred bishops, cardinals and rabbis signed a joint declaration pledging support for the Supervisor's policy. The world's religions are against you.''

"Because so few people realize the danger. When they do, it may be too late. Humanity will have lost its initiative and will have become a subject race."

Stormgren did not seem to hear. He was watching the crowd below, milling aimlessly now that it had lost its leader. How long, he wondered, would it be before men ceased to abandon their reason and identity when more than a few of them were gathered together? Wainwright might be a sincere and honest man, but the same could not be said of many of his followers.

Stormgren turned back to his visitor.

"In three days I shall be meeting the Supervisor again. I shall explain your objections to him, since it is my duty to represent the views of the world. But it will alter nothing."

There was a slight pause. Then, rather slowly, Wainwright began again.

"That brings me to another point. One of our main objections to the Overlords, as you know, is their secretiveness. You are the only human being who has ever spoken, with Karellen—and even you have never seen him. Is it surprising that many of us are suspicious of his motives?"

"You have heard his speeches. Aren't they convincing enough?"

"Frankly, words are not sufficient. I do not know which we resent more—Karellen's omnipotence, or his secrecy."

Stormgren was silent. There was nothing he could say to this—nothing, at any rate, that would convince the other. He sometimes wondered if he had really convinced himself.

It was, of course, only a very small operation from their point of view, but to Earth it was the biggest thing that had ever happened. There had been no warning, but a sudden shadow had fallen across a score of the world's greatest cities. Looking up from their work, a million men saw in that heart-freezing instant that the human race was no longer alone.

Countless times this day had been described in fiction, but no one had really belived that it would ever come. Now it had dawned at last: the twenty great ships were the symbol of a science man could not hope to match for centuries. For seven days they floated motionless above his cities, giving no hint that they knew of his existence. But none was needed: not by chance alone could those mighty ships have come to rest so precisely over New York, London, Moscow, Canberra, Rome, Capetown, Tokyo . . .

Even before the ending of those unforgettable days, some men had guessed the truth. This was not the first tentative contact by a race which knew nothing of Man. Within those silent, unmoving ships, master psychologists were studying humanity's reactions. When the curve of tension had reached its peak, they would reveal themselves.

And on the eighth day, Karellen, Supervisor for Earth, made himself known to the world. He spoke in English so perfect that the controversy it began was to rage across the Atlantic for half a century. But the context of the speech was more staggering even than its delivery. By any standards, it was a work of superlative genius, showing a complete and absolute mastery of human affairs. There was little doubt but that its scholarship and virtuosity, its tantalizing glimpses of knowledge still untapped, were deliberately designed to convince mankind that it was in the presence of overwhelming intellectual power. When Karellen had finished, the nations of Earth knew that their days of precarious sovereignty were ending. Local, internal governments would still retain their powers, but in the wider field of international affairs the supreme decisions had passed out of human hands. Arguments, protests—all were futile. No weapon could touch those brooding giants, and even if it could their downfall would utterly destroy the cities beneath. Overnight, Earth had become a protectorate in some shadowy, star-strewn empire beyond the knowledge of Man.

In a little while the tumult had subsided, and the world went about its business again. The only change a suddenly awakened Rip Van Winkle would have noticed was a hushed expectancy, a mental glancing-over-the-shoulder, as mankind waited for the Overlords to show themselves and to step down from their gleaming ships.

Five years later, it was still waiting. That, thought Stormgren, was the cause of all the trouble.

The room was small and, save for the single chair and the table beneath the vision screen, unfurnished. As was intended, it told nothing of the creatures who had built it. There was only the one entrance, and that led directly to the airlock in the curving flank of the great ship. Through that lock only Stormgren, alone of living men, had ever come to meet Karellen, Supervisor for Earth.

The vision screen was empty now, as it had always been. Behind that rectangle of darkness lay utter mystery—but there too lay affection and an immense and tolerant understanding of mankind. An understanding which, Stormgren knew, could only have been acquired through centuries of study.

From the hidden grille came that calm, never-hurried voice with its undercurrent of humor—the voice which Stormgren knew so well though the world had heard it only thrice in history.

"Yes, Rikki, I was listening. What did you make of Mr. Wainwright?"

"He's an honest man, whatever his supporters may be. What are we going to do about him? The League itself isn't dangerous, but some of its more extreme supporters are openly advocating violence. I've been wondering for some time if I should put a guard on my house. But I hope it isn't necessary."

Karellen evaded the point in the annoying way he sometimes had.

"The details of the European Federation have been out for a month now. Has there been a substantial increase in the seven percent who disapprove of me, or the nine percent who Don't Know?"

"Not yet, despite the press reactions. What I'm worried about is a general feeling, even among your supporters, that it's time this secrecy came to an end."

Karellen's sigh was technically perfect, yet somhow lacked conviction.

"That's your feeling too, isn't it?"

The question was so rhetorical that Stormgren didn't bother to answer it.

"Do you really appreciate," he continued earnestly, "how difficult this state of affairs makes my job?"

"It doesn't exactly help mine," replied Karellen with some spirit. "I wish people would stop thinking of me as a world dictator and remember that I'm only a civil servant trying to administer a somewhat idealistic colonial policy."

"Then can't you at least give us some reason for your concealment? Because we don't understand it, it annoys us and gives rise to all sorts of rumors."

Karellen gave that deep, rich laugh of his, just too musical to be altogether human.

"What am I supposed to be now? Does the robot theory still hold the field? I'd rather be a mass of cogwheels than crawl around the floor like a centipede, as most of the tabloids seem to imagine."

Stormgren let out a Finnish oath he was fairly sure Karellen wouldn't know—though one could never be quite certain in these matters.

"Can't you ever be serious?"

"My dear Rikki," said Karellen, "it's only by *not* taking the human race seriously that I retain those fragments of my once considerable mental powers that I still possess."

Despite himself, Stormgren smiled.

"That doesn't help me a great deal, does it? I have to go down there and convince my fellow men that although you won't show yourself, you've got nothing to hide. It's not an easy job. Curiosity is one of the most dominant human characteristics. You can't defy it forever."

"Of all the problems that faced us when we came to Earth, this was the most difficult," admitted Karellen. "You have trusted our wisdom in other things—surely you can trust us in this!"

"*I* trust you," said Stormgren, "but Wainwright doesn't,

nor do his supporters. Can you really blame them if they put a bad interpretation upon your unwillingness to show yourself?"

"Listen, Rikki," Karellen answered at length. "These matters are beyond my control. Believe me, I regret the need for this concealment, but the reasons are—sufficient. However, I will try and get a statement from my superiors which may satisfy you and perhaps placate the Freedom League. Now, please, can we return to the agenda and start recording again? We've only reached Item 23, and I want to make a better job of settling the Jewish question than my predecessors for the last few thousand years. . . . ."

II

"Any luck, Chief?" asked van Ryberg anxiously.

"I don't know," Stormgren replied wearily as he threw the files down on his desk and collapsed into the seat. "Karellen's consulting *his* superiors now, whoever or whatever they may be. He won't make any promises."

"Listen," said Pieter abruptly. "I've just thought of something. What reason have we for believing that there *is* anyone beyond Karellen? The Overlords may be a myth—you know how he hates the word."

Tired though he was, Stormgren set up with a start.

"It's an ingenious theory. But it clashes with what little I do know about Karellen's background."

"And how much is that?"

"Well, he was a professor of astropolitics on a world he calls Skyrondel, and he put up a terrific fight before they made him take this job. He pretends to hate it, but he's really enjoying himself."

Stormgren paused for a moment, and a smile of amusement softened his rugged features.

"At any rate, he once remarked that running a private zoo is rather good fun."

"Hmm—a somewhat dubious compliment. He's immortal, isn't he?"

"Yes, after a fashion, though there's something thousands of years ahead of him which he seems to fear: I can't imagine what it is. And that's really all I know."

"He could easily have made it up. My theory is that his little fleet's lost in space and looking for a new home. He doesn't want us to know how few he and his comrades are. Perhaps all those other ships are automatic, and there's no one in any of them. They're just an imposing façade."

"You," said Stormgren with great severity, "have been reading science fiction in office hours."

Van Ryberg grinned.

"The 'Invasion from Space' didn't turn out quite as expected, did it? My theory would certainly explain why Karellen never shows himself. He doesn't want us to learn that there are no Overlords."

Stormgren shook his head in amused disagreement.

"Your explanation, as usual, is much too ingenious to be true. Though we can only infer its existence, there must be a great civilization behind the Supervisor—and one that's known about Man for a very long time. Karellen himself must have been studying us for centuries. Look at his command of English, for example. He taught *me* how to speak it idiomatically!"

"I sometimes think he went a little too far," laughed van Ryberg. "Have you ever discovered anything he *doesn't* know?"

"Oh yes, quite often—but only on trivial points. I think he has an absolutely perfect memory, but there are some things he hasn't bothered to learn. For instance, he only understands English, though in the past two years he's picked up a good deal of Finnish just to tease me. And Finnish isn't the sort of language one learns in a hurry! I think he can quote the whole of the *Kalevala,* whereas I'm ashamed to say I know only a few dozen lines. He also knows the biographies of all living statesmen, and sometimes I can spot the references he's used. His knowledge of history and science seems complete: you know how much we've already learned from him. Yet, taken

273

one at a time, I don't think his mental gifts are quite outside the range of the human achievement. But no man could possibly do all the things he does."

"That's more or less what I'd decided already," agreed van Ryberg. "We can argue round Karellen forever, but in the end we always come back to the same question—why the devil won't he show himself? Until he does, I'll go on theorizing and the Freedom League will go on fulminating."

He cocked a rebellious eye at the ceiling.

"One dark night, Mr. Supervisor, I'm going to take a rocket up to your ship and climb in through the back door with my camera. What a scoop *that* would be!"

If Karellen was listening, he gave no sign of it. But, of course, he never did.

Stormgren slept badly that night, and in the small hours of the morning rose from his bed and wandered restlessly out onto the veranda. It was warm, almost oppressive, but the sky was clear and a brilliant moon hung low in the southwest. In the far distance the lights of London glowed on the skyline like a frozen dawn.

Stormgren raised his eyes above the sleeping city, climbing again the fifty miles of space he alone of living men had crossed. Far away though it was, the beautiful lines of Karellen's ship were clearly visible in the moonlight. He wondered what the Supervisor was doing, for he did not believe that the Overlords ever slept.

High above, a meteor thrust its shining spear through the dome of the sky. The luminous trail glowed faintly for a while: then only the stars were left. The reminder was brutal: in a hundred years Karellen would still be leading mankind towards the goal that he alone could see, but four months from now another man would be Secretary-General. That in itself Stormgren was far from minding—but there was little time left if he ever hoped to learn what lay behind that darkened screen.

A naturally reticent man himself, the reasons for Karellen's behavior had never worried Stormgren once its initial strangeness had worn off. But now he knew that the mystery which tormented so many minds was beginning to obsess his own: he could understand—in time he might even share—the psychological outlook which had driven many to support the Freedom League. The propaganda about Man's enslavement was just—propaganda. Few people seriously believed it, or really wished for a return to the old days of national rivalries. Men had grown accustomed to Karellen's imperceptible rule; but they were becoming impatient to know who ruled them.

There was a faint "click" from the teletype in the adjoining room as it ejected the hourly summary from Central News. Stormgren wandered indoors and ruffled halfheartedly through the sheets. On the other side of the world, the Freedom League had thought of a new headline. "IS MAN RULED BY MONSTERS?" asked the teletype, and went on to quote: "Addressing a meeting in Madras today, Dr. C. V. Krishnan, President of the Indian Division of the Freedom League, said: "The explanation of the Overlords' behavior is quite simple. Their physical form is so alien and so repulsive that they dare not show themselves to humanity. I challenge the Supervisor to deny this."

Stormgren threw down the paper with a sigh. Even if it were true, did it really matter? The idea was an old one, but it had never worried him. He did not believe that there was any biological form, however strange, which he could not accept in time and, perhaps, even find beautiful. If he could convince Karellen of this, the Overlords might change their policy. Certainly they could not be half as hideous as the imaginative drawings that had filled the papers soon after their coming to Earth!

Stormgren smiled a little wryly as he turned back to his bedroom. He was honest enough to admit that, in the final analysis, his real motive was ordinary human curiosity.

When Stormgren failed to arrive at his usual hour, Pieter van Ryberg was surprised and a little annoyed. Though the Secretary-General often made a number of calls before reaching his own office, he invariably left word that he was doing so. This morning, to make matters worse, there had been several urgent messages for Stormgren. Van Ryberg rang half a dozen departments to try and locate him, then gave it up in disgust.

By noon he had become alarmed and sent a car to Stormgren's house. Ten minutes later he was startled by the scream of a siren, and a police patrol came racing up Wilson Avenue. The news agencies must have had friends in that machine, for even as van Ryberg watched it approach, the radio was telling the world that he was no longer Assistant, but Acting Secretary-General of the United Nations.

If van Ryberg had not had so many other matters on his hands, he would have found it very interesting to study the press reactions to Stormgren's disappearance. For the past month, the world's papers had divided themselves into two sharply defined groups. The American press, on the whole, thought that the Federation of Europe was long overdue, but had a nervous feeling that this was only the beginning. The Europeans, on the other hand, were undergoing violent but largely synthetic spasms of national pride. Criticism of the Overlords was widespread and energetic: after an initial period of caution the press had discovered that it could be as rude to Karellen as it liked and nothing would happen. Now it was excelling itself.

Most of these attacks, though very vocal, were not representative of the great mass of the public. Along the frontiers that would soon be gone forever the guards had been doubled— but the soldiers eyed each other with a still-inarticulate friendliness. The politicians and the generals might storm and rave, but the silently waiting millions felt that, none too soon, a long and bloody chapter of history was coming to an end.

And now Stormgren had gone, no one knew where or how. The tumult suddenly subsided as the world realized that it had lost the only man through whom the Overlords, for their own strange reasons, would speak to Earth. A paralysis seemed to descend upon press and radio, but in the silence could be heard the voice of the Freedom League, anxiously protesting its innocence.

It was completely dark when Stormgren awoke. How strange that was; he was for a moment too sleepy to realize. Then, as full consciousness dawned, he sat up with a start and felt for the light switch beside his bed.

In the darkness his hand encountered a bare stone wall, cold to the touch. He froze instantly, mind and body paralyzed by the impact of the unexpected. Then, scarcely believing his senses, he kneeled on the bed and began to explore with his finger tips that shockingly unfamiliar wall.

He had been doing this for only a moment when there was a sudden "click" and a section of the darkness slid aside. He caught a glimpse of a man silhouetted against a dimly lit background: then the door closed again and the darkness returned. It happened so swiftly that he saw nothing of the room in which he was lying.

An instant later, he was dazzled by the light of a powerful electric torch. The beam flickered across his face, held him steadily for a moment, then dipped to illuminate the whole bed—which was, he now saw, nothing more than a mattress supported on rough planks.

Out of the darkness a soft voice spoke to him in excellent English but with an accent which at first Stormgren could not identify.

"Ah, Mr. Secretary, I'm glad to see you're awake. I hope you feel all right."

There was something about the last sentence that caught Stormgren's attention, so that the angry questions he was about to ask died upon his lips. He stared back into the darkness, then replied calmly: "How long have I been unconscious?"

The other chuckled.

"Several days. We were promised that there would be no aftereffects. I'm glad to see it's true."

Partly to gain time, partly to test his own reactions, Stormgren swung his legs over the side of the bed. He was still wearing his nightclothes, but they were badly crumpled and seemed to have gathered considerable dirt. As he moved he felt a slight dizziness—not enough to be troublesome, but sufficient to convince him that he had indeed been drugged.

He turned towards the light.

"Where am I?" he said sharply. "Does Wainwright know about this?"

"Smart, aren't you?" said the voice admiringly. "But we won't talk about that now. I guess you'll be pretty hungry. Get dressed and come along to dinner."

The oval of light slipped across the room and for the first time Stormgren had an idea of its dimensions. It was not really correct to call it a room at all, for the walls seemed bare rock, roughly smoothed into shape. He realized that he was underground, possibly at a great depth. He realized too that if he had been unconscious for several days he might be anywhere on Earth.

The torchlight illuminated a pile of clothes draped over a packing case.

"This should be enough for you," said the voice from the darkness. "Laundry's rather a problem here, so we grabbed a couple of your suits and half a dozen shirts."

"That," said Stormgren without humor, "was very considerate of you."

"We're sorry about the absence of furniture and electric light. This place is convenient in some ways, but it rather lacks amenities."

"Convenient for what?" asked Stormgren as he climbed into a shirt. The feel of the familiar cloth beneath his fingers was strangely reassuring.

"Just—convenient," said the voice. "And by the way, since we're likely to spend a good deal of time together, you'd better call me Joe."

"Despite your nationality," retorted Stormgren. "I think I could pronounce your real name. It won't be worse than many Finnish ones."

There was a slight pause and the light flickered for an instant.

"Well, I should have expected it," said Joe resignedly. "You must have plenty of practice at this sort of thing."

"It's a useful hobby for a man in my position. I suppose you were born in Poland, and picked up your English in Britain during the War? I should think you were stationed quite a while in Scotland, from your r's."

"That," said the other very firmly, "is quite enough. As you seem to have finished dressing—thank you."

The door opened as Stormgren walked towards it, and the other stood aside to let him pass. Stormgren wondered if Joe was armed and decided that he probably was. In any case, he would certainly have friends around.

The corridor was dimly lit by oil lamps at intervals, and for the first time Stormgren could see his captor. He was a man of about fifty, and must have weighed well over two hundred pounds. Everything about him was outsize, from the stained battledress that might have come from any of half a dozen armed forces to the startlingly large signet ring on his left hand. It should not be difficult to trace him, thought Stormgren, if he ever got out of this place. He was a little depressed to think that the other must be perfectly well aware of this.

The walls around them, though occasionally faced with concrete, were mostly bare rock. It was clear to Stormgren that he was in some disused mine, and he could think of few more effective prisons. Until now the thought that he had been kidnapped had somehow failed to worry him greatly. He felt that, whatever happened, the immense resources of the Supervisor would soon locate and rescue him. Now he was not so sure: there must be a limit even to Karellen's powers, and if he was indeed buried in some remote continent all the science of the Overlords might be unable to trace him.

III

There were three other men round the table in the bare but brightly lit room. They looked up with interest and more than a little awe as Stormgren entered, and a substantial pile of meat sandwiches was quickly placed before him. He could have done with a more interesting meal, for he felt extremely hungry, but it was very obvious that his captors had dined no better.

As he ate, he glanced quickly at the four men around him. Joe was by far the most outstanding character—not merely in physical bulk. The others were nondescript individuals, probably Europeans also. He would be able to place them when he heard them talk.

He pushed away the plate, and ignoring the other men spoke directly to the huge Pole.

"Well," he said evenly, "now perhaps you'll tell me what this is all about, and what you hope to get out of it."

Joe cleared his throat.

"I'd like to make one thing clear," he said. "This is nothing to do with Wainwright. He'll be as surprised as anyone."

Stormgren had rather expected this. It gave him relatively little satisfaction to confirm the existence of an extremist movement inside the Freedom League.

"As a matter of interest," he said, "how did you kidnap me?"

He hardly expected a reply, and was taken aback by the other's readiness—even eagerness—to answer. Only slowly did he guess the reason.

"It was all rather like one of those old Fritz Lang films," said Joe cheerfully. "We weren't sure if Karellen had a watch on you, so we took somewhat elaborate precautions. You were knocked out by gas in the air conditioner: that was easy. Then we carried you out into the car and drove off—no trouble at all. All this, I might say, wasn't done by any of our people. We hired—er, professionals for the job. Karellen may get them—in fact, he's supposed to—but he'll be no wiser. When it left your house the car drove into a long road tunnel not many miles from the center of London. It came out again on schedule at the other end, still carrying a drugged man extraordinarily like the Secretary-General. About the same time a large truck loaded with metal cases emerged in the opposite direction and drove to a certain airfield where one of the cases was loaded aboard a freighter. Meanwhile the car that had done the job continued elaborate evasive action in the general direction of Scotland. Perhaps Karellen's caught it by now: I don't know. As you'll see—I do hope you appreciate my frankness—our whole plan depended on one thing. We're pretty sure that Karellen can see and hear everything that happens on the surface of the Earth—but unless he uses magic, not science, he can't see underneath it. So he won't know about that transfer in the tunnel. Naturally we've taken a risk, but there were also one or two other stages in your removal which I won't go into now. We may have to use them again one day, and it would be a pity to give them away."

Joe had related the whole story with such obvious gusto that Stormgren found it difficult to be appropriately furious. Yet he felt very disturbed. The plan was an ingenious one, and it seemed more than likely that whatever watch Karellen kept on him, he would have been tricked by this ruse.

The Pole was watching Stormgren's reactions closely. He would have to appear confident, whatever his real feelings.

"You must be a lot of fools," said Stormgren scornfully, "if you think you can trick the Overlords like this. In any case, what conceivable good would it do?"

Joe offered him a cigarette, which Stormgren refused, then lit one himself and sat on the edge of the table. There was an ominous creaking and he jumped off hastily.

"Our motives," he began, "should be pretty obvious. We've found that argument's useless, so we have to take other measures. There have been underground movements before, and even Karellen, whatever powers he's got, won't find it easy to deal with us. We're out to fight for our independence. Don't misunderstand me. There'll be nothing violent—at first, anyway. But the Overlords have to use human agents, and we can make it mighty uncomfortable for them."

Starting with me, I suppose, thought Stormgren. He wondered if the other had given him more than a fraction of the whole story. Did they really think that these gangster methods would influence Karellen in the slightest? On the other hand, it was quite true that a well-organized resistance movement could make things very difficult.

"What do you intend to do with me?" asked Stormgren at length. "Am I a hostage, or what?"

"Don't worry—we'll look after you. We expect some visitors in a day or two, and until then we'll entertain you as well as we can."

He added some words in his own language, and one of the others produced a brand-new pack of cards.

"We got these especially for you," explained Joe. His voice suddenly became grave. "I hope you've got plenty of cash," he said anxiously. "After all, we can hardly accept checks."

Quite overcome, Stormgren stared blankly at his captors. Then, as the true humor of the situation sank into his mind, it suddenly seemed to him that all the cares and worries of office had lifted from his shoulders. Whatever happened, there was absolutely nothing he could do about it—and now these fantastic criminals wanted to play cards with him.

Abruptly, he threw back his head and laughed as he had not done for years.

There was no doubt, thought van Ryberg morosely, that Wainwright was telling the truth. He might have his suspicions, but he did not know who had kidnapped Stormgren. Nor did he approve of the kidnapping itself. Van Ryberg had a shrewd idea that for some time extremists in the Freedom League had been putting pressure on Wainwright to make him adopt a more active policy. Now they were taking things into their own hands.

The kidnapping had been beautifully organized, there was no doubt of that. Stormgren might be anywhere on earth and there seemed little hope of tracing him. Yet something would have to be done, decided van Ryberg, and done quickly.

Despite the jests he had so often made, his real feeling towards Karellen was one of overwhelming awe. The thought of approaching the Supervisor directly filled him with dismay, but there seemed no alternative.

Communications Section had several hundred channels to Karellen's ship. Most of them were operating continuously, handling endless streams of statistics—production figures, census returns and all the bookkeeping of a world economic system. One channel, van Ryberb knew, was reserved for Karellen's personal messages to Stormgren. No one but the Secretary-General himself had ever used it.

Van Ryberg sat down at the keyboard and, after a moment's hesitation, began to tap out his message with unpracticed fingers. The machine clicked away contentedly and the words gleamed for a few seconds on the darkened screen. Then he waited; he would give the Supervisor ten minutes and after that someone else could bring him any reply.

There was no need. Scarcely a minute later the machine started to whirr again. Not for the first time, van Ryberg wondered if the Supervisor ever slept.

The message was as brief as it was unhelpful.

NOINFORMATION.LEAVEMATTERSENTIRELYTOYUORDISCRE-TION.

Rather bitterly, and without any satisfaction at all, van Ryberg realized how much greatness had been thrust upon him.

During the last three days Stormgren had analyzed his captors with some thoroughness. Joe was the only one of any importance: the others were nonentities—the riffraff one would expect any illegal movement to gather round itself. The ideals of the Freedom League meant nothing to them: their only concern was earning a living with the minimum of work. They were the gangster types from which civilization might never be wholly free.

Joe was an altogether more complex individual, though

sometimes he reminded Stormgren of an overgrown baby. Their interminable canasta games were punctuated with violent political arguments, but it became obvious to Stormgren that the big Pole had never thought seriously about the cause for which he was fighting. Emotion and extreme conservatism clouded all his judgments. His country's long struggle for independence had conditioned him so completely that he still lived in the past. He was a picturesque survival, one of those who had no use for an ordered way of life. When his type had vanished, if it ever did, the world would be a safer but less interesting place.

There was little doubt, as far as Stormgren was concerned, that Karellen had failed to locate him. He had tried to bluff, but his captors were unconvinced. He was fairly certain that they had been holding him here to see if Karellen would act, and now that nothing had happened they could proceed with the next part of their plan.

Stormgren was not surprised when, five or six days after his capture, Joe told him to expect visitors. For some time the little group had shown increasing nervousness, and the prisoner guessed that the leaders of the movement, having seen that the coast was clear, were at last coming to collect him.

They were already waiting, gathered round the rickety table, when Joe waved him politely into the living room. The three thugs had vanished, and even Joe seemed somewhat restrained. Stormgren could see at once that he was now confronted by men of a much higher caliber, and the group opposite reminded him strongly of a picture he had once seen of Lenin and his colleagues in the first days of the Russian Revolution. There was the same intellectual force, iron determination, and ruthlessness in these six men. Joe and his like were harmless: here were the real brains behind the organization.

With a curt nod, Stormgren moved over to the seat and tried to look self-possessed. As he approached, the elderly, thickset man on the far side of the table leaned forward and stared at him with piercing gray eyes. They made Stormgren so uncomfortable that he spoke first—something he had not intended to do.

"I suppose you've come to discuss terms. What's my ransom?"

He noticed that in the background someone was taking down his words in a shorthand notebook. It was all very businesslike.

The leader replied in a musical Welsh accent.

"You could put it that way, Mr. Secretary-General. But we're interested in information, not cash."

So that was it, thought Stormgren. He was a prisoner of war, and this was his interrogation.

"You know what our motives are," continued the other in his softly lilting voice. "Call us a resistance movement, if you like. We believe that sooner or later Earth will have to fight for its independence—but we realize that the struggle can only be by indirect methods such as sabotage and disobedience. We kidnapped you partly to show Karellen that we mean business and are well organized, but largely because you are the only man who can tell us anything of the Overlords. You're a reasonable man, Mr. Stormgren. Give us your cooperation, and you can have your freedom."

"Exactly what do you wish to know?" asked Stormgren cautiously.

Those extraordinary eyes seemed to search his mind to its depths: they were unlike any that Stormgren had ever seen in his life. Then the singsong voice replied:

"Do you know who, or what, the Overlords really are?"

Stormgren almost smiled.

"Believe me," he said, "I'm quite as anxious as you to discover that."

"Then you'll answer our questions?"

"I make no promises. But I may."

There was a slight sigh of relief from Joe and a rustle of anticipation went round the room.

"We have a general idea," continued the other, "of the circumstances in which you meet Karellen. Would you go through them carefully, leaving out nothing of importance."

That was harmless enough, thought Stormgren. He had done it scores of times before, and it would give the appearance of cooperation.

He felt in his pockets and produced a pencil and an old envelope. Sketching rapidly while he spoke, he began:

"You know, of course, that a small flying machine, with no obvious means of propulsion, calls for me at regular intervals and takes me up to Karellen's ship. There is only one small room in that machine, and it's quite bare apart from a couch and table. The layout is something like this."

He pushed the plan across to the old Welshman, but the strange eyes never turned towards it. They were still fixed on Stormgren's face, and as he watched them something seemed to change in their depths. The room had become completely silent, but behind him he heard Joe take a sudden indrawn breath.

Puzzled and annoyed, Stormgren stared back at the other, and as he did so, understanding slowly dawned. In his confusion, he crumpled the envelope into a ball of paper and ground it underfoot.

For the man opposite him was blind.

IV

Van Ryberg had made no more attempts to contact Karellen. Much of his department's work—the forwarding of statistical information, the abstracting of the world's press, and the like—had continued automatically. In Paris the lawyers were still wrangling over the European Constitution, but that was none of his business for the moment. It was three weeks before the Supervisor wanted the final draft: if it was not ready by then, no doubt Karellen would act accordingly.

And there was still no news of Stormgren.

Van Ryberg was dictating when the "Emergency Only" telephone started to ring. He grabbed the receiver and listened with mounting astonishment, then threw it down and rushed to the open window. In the distance faint cries of amazement were rising from the street and the traffic had already come to a halt.

It was true: Karellen's ship, that never-changing symbol of the Overlords, was no longer in the sky. He searched the heavens as far as he could see, but found no trace of it. Even as he was doing so, it seemed that night had suddenly fallen. Coming down from the north, its shadowed underbelly black as a thundercloud, the great ship was racing low above the towers of London. Involuntarily, van Ryberg shrank away from the onrushing monster. He had always known how huge the ships of the Overlords really were—but it was one thing to see them far away in space, and quite another to watch them passing overhead, almost close enough to touch.

In the darkness of that partial eclipse, he watched until the ship and its monstrous shadow had moved to the south. There was no sound, not even the whisper of air; van Ryberg realized that, for all its apparent nearness, the ship was still a thousand feet or more above his head. He watched it vanish over the horizon, still large even when it dropped below the curve of the Earth.

In the office behind him all the telephones had started to ring, but van Ryberg did not move. He leaned against the balcony, still staring into the south, paralyzed by the presence of illimitable power.

As Stormgren talked, it seemed to him that his mind was operating on two levels simultaneously. On the one hand he was trying to defy the men who had captured him, yet on the other he was hoping that they might help him to unravel Karellen's secret. He did not feel that he was betraying the Supervisor, for there was nothing here that he had not told many times before. Moreover, the thought that these men could harm Karellen in any way was fantastic.

The blind Welshman had conducted most of the interrogation. It was fascinating to watch that agile mind trying one opening after another, testing and rejecting all the theories that Stormgren himself had abandoned long ago. Presently he leaned back with a sigh and the shorthand writer laid down his stylus.

"We're getting nowhere," he said resignedly. "We want more facts, and that means action—not argument." The sightless eyes seemed to stare thoughtfully at Stormgren. For a moment he tapped nervously on the table—the first sign of uncertainty that Stormgren had noticed. Then he continued:

"I'm a little surprised, Mr. Secretary, that you've never made an effort to learn more about the Overlords."

"What do you suggest?" asked Stormgren coldly. "I've told you that there's only one way out of the room in which I've had my talks with Karellen—and that leads straight to the airlock."

"It might be possible," mused the other, "to devise instruments which could teach us something. I'm no scientist, but we can look into the matter. If we give you your freedom, would you be willing to assist with such a plan?"

"Once and for all," said Stormgren angrily, "let me make my position perfectly clear. Karellen is working for a united world, and I'll do nothing to help his enemies. What his ultimate plans may be, I don't know, but I believe that they are good. You may annoy him, you may even delay the achievement of his aims, but it will make no difference in the end. You may be sincere in believing as you do: I can understand your fear that the traditions and cultures of little countries will be overwhelmed when the World State arrives. But you are wrong: it is useless to cling to the past. Even before the Overlords came to Earth, the sovereign state was dying. No one can save it now, and no one should try."

There was no reply: the man opposite neither moved nor spoke. He sat with lips half open, his eyes now lifeless as well as blind. Around him the others were equally motionless, frozen in strained, unnatural attitudes. With a little gasp of pure horror, Stormgren rose to his feet and backed away towards the door. As he did so the silence was suddenly broken.

"That was a nice speech, Rikki. Now I think we can go."

"Karellen! Thank God—but what have you done?"

"Don't worry. They're all right. You can call it a paralysis, but it's much subtler than that. They're simply living a few thousand times more slowly than normal. When we've gone they'll never know what happened."

"You'll leave them here until the police come?"

"No: I've a much better plan. I'm letting them go."

Stormgren felt an illogical sense of relief which he did not care to analyze. He gave a last valedictory glance at the little room and its frozen occupants. Joe was standing on one foot, staring very stupidly at nothing. Suddenly Stormgren laughed and fumbled in his pockets.

"Thanks for the hospitality, Joe," he said. "I think I'll leave a souvenir."

He ruffled through the scraps of paper until he found the figures he wanted. Then, on a reasonably clean sheet, he wrote carefully:

LOMBARD BANK, LONDON
Pay "Joe" the sum of One Pound Seventeen Shillings and Six Pence (£1-17-6).

R. Stormgren

As he laid the strip of paper beside the Pole, Karellen's voice inquired: "Exactly what are you up to?"

"Paying a debt of honor," explained Stormgren. "The other two cheated, but I think Joe played fair. At least, I never caught him out."

He felt very gay and light-headed as he walked to the door. Hanging just outside it was a large, featureless metal sphere that moved aside to let him pass. He guessed that it was some kind of robot, and it explained how Karellen had been able to reach him through the unknown layers of rock overhead.

"Carry on for a hundred yards," said the sphere, speaking in Karellen's voice. "Then turn to the left until I give you further instructions."

He ran forward eagerly, though he realized that there was no need for hurry. The sphere remained hanging in the corridor, and Stormgren guessed that it was the generator of the paralysis field.

A minute later he came across a second sphere, waiting for him at a fork in the corridor.

"You've half a mile to go," it said. "Keep to the left until we meet again."

Six times he encountered the spheres on his way to the open. At first he wondered if somehow the first robot had slipped ahead of him; then he guessed that there must be a chain of them maintaining a complete circuit down into the depths of the mine. At the entrance a group of guards formed a piece of improbable still life, watched over by yet another of the ubiquitous spheres. On the hillside a few yards away lay the little flying machine in which Stormgren had made all his journeys to Karellen.

He stood for a moment blinking in the fierce sunlight. Then he saw the ruined mining machinery around him, and beyond that a derelict railway stretching down a mountain-side. Several miles away dense forest lapped at the base of the mountain, and very far off Stormgren could see the gleam of a great river. He guessed that he was somewhere in southern France, probably in the Cévenne mountains.

As he climbed into the little ship, he had a last glimpse of the mine entrance and the men frozen round it. Quite suddenly a line of metal spheres raced out of the opening like silver cannon balls. Then the door closed behind him and with a sigh of relief he sank back upon the familiar couch.

For a while Stormgren waited until he had recovered his breath; then he uttered a single, heartfelt syllable:

"Well?"

"I'm sorry I couldn't rescue you before. But you'll see how very important it was to wait until all the leaders had gathered here."

"Do you mean to say," spluttered Stormgren, "that you knew where I was all the time? If I thought—"

"Don't be so hasty," answered Karellen, "or at any rate, let me finish explaining."

"It had better be good," said Stormgren darkly. He was

beginning to suspect that he had been no more than the bait in an elaborate trap.

"I've had a tracer on you for some time," began Karellen, "and though your late friends were correct in thinking that I couldn't follow you underground, I was able to keep track until they brought you to the mine. That transfer in the tunnel was ingenious, but when the first car ceased to react it gave the show away and I soon located you again. Then it was merely a matter of waiting. I knew that once they were certain I'd lost you, the leaders would come here and I'd be able to trap them all."

"But you're letting them go!"

"Until now," said Karellen, "I did not know which of the two billion men on this planet were the heads of the organization. Now that they're located, I can trace their movements anywhere on Earth, and can probably watch most of their actions in detail if I want to. That's far better than locking them up. They're effectively neutralized, and they know it. Your rescue will be completely inexplicable to them, for you must have vanished before their eyes."

That rich laugh echoed round the tiny room.

"In some ways the whole affair was a comedy, but it had a serious purpose. It will be a valuable object lesson for any other plotters. I'm not concerned merely with the few score men of this organization—I have to think of the moral effect on other groups which may exist elsewhere."

Stormgren was silent for a while. He was not altogether satisfied, but he could see Karellen's point of view and some of his anger had evaporated.

"It's a pity to do it in my last few weeks of office," he said, "but from now on I'm going to have a guard on my house. Pieter can be kidnapped next time. How has he managed, by the way? Are things in as big a mess as I expect?"

"You'll be disappointed to find out how little your absence has mattered. I've watched Pieter carefully this past week, and have deliberately avoided helping him. On the whole he's done very well—but he's not the man to take your place."

"That's lucky for him," said Stormgren, still rather aggrieved. "And have you had any word from your superiors about—about showing yourself to us? I'm sure now that it's the strongest argument your enemies have. Again and again they told me: 'We'll never trust the Overlords until we can see them.' "

Karellen sighed.

"No, I have heard nothing. But I know what the answer must be."

Stormgren did not press the matter. Once he might have done so, but now for the first time the faint shadow of a plan had come into his mind. What he had refused to do under duress, he might yet attempt of his own free will.

Pierre Duval showed no surprise when Stormgren walked unannounced into his office. They were old friends, and there was nothing unusual in the Secretary-General paying a personal visit to the chief of the Science Bureau. Certainly Karellen would not think it odd, even if by any remote chance he turned his attention to this corner of the world.

For a while the two men talked business and exchanged political gossip; then, rather hesitantly, Stormgren came to the point. As his visitor talked, the old Frenchman leaned back in his chair and his eyebrows rose steadily millimeter by millimeter until they were almost entangled in his forelock. Once or twice he seemed about to speak but each time thought better of it.

When Stormgren had finished, the scientist looked nervously around the room.

"Do you think he was listening?" he said.

"I don't believe he can. This place is supposed to be shielded from everything, isn't it? Karellen's not a magician. He knows where I am, but that's all."

"I hope you're right. Apart from that, won't there be trouble when he discovers what you're trying to do? Because he will, you know."

"I'll take that risk. Besides, we understand each other rather well."

The physicist toyed with his pencil and stared into space for a while.

"It's a very pretty problem. I like it," he said simply. Then he dived into a drawer and produced an enormous writing pad, quite the biggest that Stormgren had ever seen.

"Right," he began, scribbling furiously. "Let me make sure I have all the facts. Tell me everything you can about the room in which you have your interviews. Don't omit any detail, however trivial it seems."

"There isn't much to describe. It's made of metal, and is about eight yards square and four high. The vision screen is about a yard on a side and there's a desk immediately beneath it—here, it will be quicker if I draw it for you."

Rapidly Stormgren sketched the little room he knew so well, and pushed the drawing over to Duval. As he did so, he remembered with a slight shiver the last time he had done this sort of thing.

The Frenchman studied the drawing with puckered brow.

"And that's all you can tell me?"

"Yes."

He snorted in disgust.

"What about lighting? Do you sit in total darkness? And how about heating, ventilation . . ."

Stormgren smiled at the characteristic outburst.

"The whole ceiling is luminous, and as far as I can tell the air comes through the speaker grille. I don't know how it leaves; perhaps the stream reverses at intervals, but I haven't noticed it. There's no sign of any heaters, but the room is always at normal temperature."

"By that I take it that the carbon dioxide has frozen out, but not the oxygen."

Stormgren did his best to smile at the well-worn joke.

"I think I've told everything," he concluded. "As for the machine that takes me up to Karellen's ship, the room in which I travel is as featureless as an elevator cage. Apart from the couch and table, it might very well be one."

There was silence for several minutes while the physicist

embroidered his writing pad with meticulous and microscopic doodles. No one could have guessed that behind that still almost unfurrowed brow the world's finest technical brain was working with the icy precision that had made it famous.

Then Duval nodded to himself in satisfaction, leaned forward and pointed his pencil at Stormgren.

"What makes you think, Rikki," he asked, "that Karellen's vision screen, as you call it, really is what it pretends to be?"

"I've always taken it for granted—it's exactly like one. What else would it be, anyway?"

"The tendency of otherwise first-class minds to overlook the obvious always saddens me. You know that Karellen can watch your movements, but a television system must have some sort of camera. Where is it?"

"I'd thought of that," said Stormgren with asperity. "Couldn't the screen do both jobs? I know our televisors don't, but still—"

Duvall didn't like the idea.

"It would be possible," he admitted. "But why on earth go to all that trouble? The simplest solution is always best. Doesn't it seem far more probable that your 'vision screen' is really *nothing more complicated than a sheet of one-way glass*?"

Stormgren was so annoyed with himself that for a moment he sat in silence, retracing the past. From the beginning, he had never challenged Karellen's story—yet now he came to look back, when had the Supervisor ever told him that he was using a television system? He had just taken it for granted; the whole thing had been a piece of psychological trickery, and he had been completely deceived. He tried to console himself with the thought that in the same circumstances even Duval would have fallen into the trap.

But he was jumping to conclusions: no one had proved anything yet.

"If you're right," he said, "all I have to is smash the glass—"

Duval sighed.

"These nontechnical laymen! Do you think it's likely to be made of anything you could smash without explosives? And if you succeeded, do you imagine that Karellen is likely to breathe the same air as we do? Won't it be nice for both of you if he flourishes in an atmosphere of chlorine?"

Stormgren turned rather pale.

"Well, what *do* you suggest?" he asked with some exasperation.

"I want to think it over. First of all we've got to find if my theory is correct, and if so learn something about the material of the screen. I'll put some of my best men on the job—by the way, I suppose you carry a briefcase when you visit the Supervisor? Is it the one you've got there?"

"Yes."

"It's rather small. Will you get one at least ten inches deep, and use it from now on so that he becomes used to seeing it?"

"Very well," said Stormgren doubtfully. "Do you want me to carry a concealed X-ray set?"

The physicist grinned.

"I don't know yet, but we'll think of something. I'll let you know what it is in about a month's time."

He gave a little laugh.

"Do you know what all this reminds me of?"

"Yes," said Stormgren promptly, "the time you were building illegal radio sets during the German occupation."

Duval looked disappointed.

"Well, I suppose I *have* mentioned that once or twice before. But there's one other thing—"

"Yes?"

"When you're caught, *I* didn't know what you wanted the gear for."

"What, after all the fuss you once made about the scientist's social responsibility for his inventions? Really, Pierre, I'm ashamed of you!"

Stormgren laid down the thick folder of typescript with a sigh of relief.

"Thank heaven's that's settled at last," he said. "It's strange to think that those few hundred pages hold the future of Europe."

"They hold a good deal more than that," said Karellen quietly.

"So a lot of people have been suggesting. The preamble, and most of the constitution itself, won't need many alterations when it's time for the rest of the world to join. But the first step will be quite enough to get on with."

Stormgren dropped the file into his briefcase, the back of which was now only six inches from the dark rectangle of the screen. From time to time his fingers played across the locks in a half-conscious nervous reaction, but he had no intention of pressing the concealed switch until the meeting was over. There was a chance that something might go wrong: though Duval had sworn that Karellen would detect nothing, one could never be sure.

"Now, you said you'd some news for me," Stormgren continued, with scarcely concealed eagerness. "Is it about—"

"Yes," said Karellen. "I received the Policy Board's decision a few hours ago, and am authorized to make an important statement. I don't think that the Freedom League will be very satisfied, but it should help to reduce the tension. We won't record this, by the way.

"You've often told me, Rikki, that no matter how unlike you we are physically, the human race will soon grow accustomed to us. That shows a lack of imagination on your part. It would probably be true in your case, but you must remember that most of the world is still uneducated by any reasonable standards, and is riddled with prejudices and superstitions that may take another hundred years to eradicate.

"You will grant us that we know something of human psychology. We know rather accurately what would happen if we revealed ourselves to the world in its present state of development. I can't go into details, even with you, so you must accept my analysis on trust. We can, however, make this definite promise, which should give you some satisfaction.

296

In fifty years—two generations from now—we shall come down from our ships and humanity will at last see us as we are.''

Stormgren was silent for a while. He felt little of the satisfaction that Karellen's statement would have once given him. Indeed, he was somewhat confused by his partial success and for a moment his resolution faltered. The truth would come with the passage of time, and all his plotting was unnecesary and perhaps unwise. If he still went ahead, it would only be for the selfish reason that he would not be alive fifty years from now.

Karellen must have seen his irresolution, for he continued:

"I'm sorry if this disappoints you, but at least the political problems of the near future won't be your responsibility. Perhaps you still think that our fears are unfounded, but believe me we've had convincing proof of the dangers of any other course."

Stormgren leaned forward, breathing heavily.

"I always thought so! You *have* been seen by Man!"

"I didn't say that," Karellen answered after a short pause. "Your world isn't the only planet we've supervised."

Stormgren was not to be shaken off so easily.

"There have been many legends suggesting that Earth has been visited in the past by other races."

"I know: I've read the Historical Research Section's report. It makes Earth look like the crossroads of the Universe."

"There may have been visits about which you know nothing," said Stormgren, still angling hopefully. "Though since you must have been observing us for thousands of years, I suppose that's rather unlikely."

"I suppose it is," said Karellen in his most unhelpful manner. And at that moment Stormgren made up his mind.

"Karellen," he said abruptly, "I'll draft out the statement and send it up to you for approval. But I reserve the right to continue pestering you, and if I see any opportunity, I'll do my best to learn your secret."

"I'm perfectly well aware of that," replied the Supervisor, with a slight chuckle.

"And you don't mind?"

"Not in the slighest—though I draw the line at atomic bombs, poison gas, or anything else that might strain our friendship."

Stormgren wondered what, if anything, Karellen had guessed. Behind the Supervisor's banter he had recognized the note of understanding, perhaps—who could tell?—even of encouragement.

"I'm glad to know it," Stormgren replied in as level a voice as he could manage. He rose to his feet, bringing down the cover of his case as he did so. His thumb slid along the catch.

"I'll draft that statement at once," he repeated, "and send it up on the teletype later today."

While he was speaking, he pressed the button—and knew that all his fears had been groundless. Karellen's senses were no finer than Man's. The Supervisor could have detected nothing, for there was no change in his voice as he said goodbye and spoke the familiar code words that opened the door of the chamber.

Yet Stormgren still felt like a shoplifter leaving a department store under the eyes of the house detective, and breathed a sigh of relief when the airlock doors had finally closed behind him.

V

"I admit," said van Ryberg, "that some of my theories haven't been very bright. But tell me what you think of this one."

"Must I?"

Pieter didn't seem to notice.

"It isn't really my idea," he said modestly. "I got it from a story of Chesterton's. Suppose that the Overlords are hiding the fact that they've got nothing to hide?"

"That sounds a little complicated to me," said Stormgren, beginning to take slight interest.

"What I mean is this," van Ryberg continued eagerly. "*I* think that physically they're human beings like us. They realize that we'll tolerate being ruled by creatures we imagine to be—well, alien and super intelligent. But the human race being what it is, it just won't be bossed around by creatures of the same species."

"Very ingenious, like all your theories," said Stormgren. "I wish you'd give them opus numbers so that I could keep up with them. The objections to this one—"

But at that moment Alexander Wainwright was ushered in.

Stormgren wondered what he was thinking. He wondered, too, if Wainwright had made any contact with the men who had kidnapped him. He doubted it, for he believed Wainwright's disapproval of violent methods to be perfectly genuine. The extremists in his movement had discredited themselves thoroughly, and it would be a long time before the world heard of them again.

The head of the Freedom League listened in silence while the draft was read to him. Stormgren hoped that he appreciated this gesture, which had been Karellen's idea. Not for another twelve hours would the rest of the world know of the promise that had been made to its grandchildren.

"Fifty years," said Wainwright thoughtfully. "That is a long time to wait."

"Not for Karellen, nor for humanity," Stormgren answered. Only now was he beginning to realize the neatness of the Overlords' solution. It had given them the breathing space they believed they needed, and it had cut the ground from beneath the Freedom League's feet. He did not imagine that the League would capitulate, but its position would be seriously weakened.

Certainly Wainwright realized this as well, as he must also have realized that Karellen would be watching him. For he said very little and left as quickly as he could: Stormgren knew that he would not see him again in his term of office. The Freedom League might still be a nuisance, but that was a problem for his successor.

There were some things that only time could cure. Evil men could be destroyed, but nothing could be done about good men who were deluded.

"Here's your case," said Duval. "It's as good as new."

"Thanks," Stormgren answered, inspecting it carefully nonetheless. "Now perhaps you can tell me what it was all about—and what we are going to do next."

The physicist seemed more interested in his own thoughts.

"What I can't understand," he said, "is the ease with which we've got away with it. Now if *I'd* been Kar—"

"But you're not. Get to the point, man. What *did* we discover?"

"Ah me, these excitable, highly strung Nordic races!" sighed Duval. "Well, it's rather a long story, but the first piece of equipment you carried was a tiny echo sounder using supersonic waves. We went right up the audio spectrum, so high that I was sure no possible sense organs could detect us. When you pressed the button, a rather complicated set of sound pulses went out in various directions. I won't bother about the details, but the main idea was to measure the thickness of the screen and to find the dimensions of the room, if any, behind it.

"The screen seems to be about five inches thick, and the space behind it is at least ten yards across. We couldn't detect any echo from the farther wall, but we hardly expected to. However, we *did* get this."

He pushed forward a photographic record which to Stormgren looked rather like the autograph of a mild earthquake.

"See that little kink?"

"Yes: what is it?"

"Only Karellen."

"Good Lord! Are you sure?"

"It's a pretty safe guess. He's sitting, or standing, or whatever he does, about two yards on the other side of the screen. If the resolution had been better, we might even have calculated his size."

Stormgren's feelings were very mixed as he stared at the scarcely visible deflection of the trace. Until now, there had been no proof that Karellen even had a material body. The evidence was still indirect, but he accepted it with little question.

Duval's voice cut into his reverie.

"The piece of equipment you carried on your second visit was similar," he said, "but used light instead of sound. We had to measure the transmission characteristics of the screen, and that presented considerable difficulties. Obviously we dared not use visible light, so once again we chose frequencies so high that we couldn't imagine any eye focusing them—or any atmosphere transmitting them very far. And again we manage to carry it off.

"You'll realize," he continued, "that there's no such thing as a truly one-way glass. Karellen's screen, we found when we analyzed our results, transmits about a hundred times as easily in one direction as the other. We've no particular reason to assume that the figure is very different in the visible spectrum—but we're giving you an enormous safety margin."

With the air of a conjurer producing a whole litter of rabbits, Duval reached into his desk and pulled out a pistol-like object with a flexible bell mouth. It reminded Stormgren of a rubber blunderbuss, and he couldn't imagine what it was supposed to be.

Duval grinned at his perplexity.

"It isn't as dangerous as it looks. All you have to do is to ram the muzzle against the screen and press the trigger. It gives out a very powerful flash lasting five seconds, and in that time you'll be able to swing it round the room. Enough light will come back to give you a good view."

"It won't hurt Karellen?"

"Not if you aim low and sweep it upwards. That will give him time to accommodate—I suppose he has reflexes like ours, and we don't want to blind him."

Stormgren looked at the weapon doubtfully and hefted it in his hand. For the last few weeks his conscience had been pricking him. Karellen had always treated him with unmistakable affection, despite his occasional devastating frankness, and now that their time together was drawing to its close he did not wish to do anything that might spoil that relationship. But the Supervisor had received due warning, and Stormgren had the conviction that if the choice had been his Karellen would long ago have shown himself. Now the decision would be made for him: when their last meeting came to its end, Stormgren would gaze upon Karellen's face.

If, of course, Karellen had a face.

The nervousness that Stormgren had first felt had long since passed away. Karellen was doing almost all the talking, weaving the long, intricate sentences of which he was so fond. Once this had seemed to Stormgren the most wonderful and certainly the most unexpected of all Karellen's gifts. Now it no longer appeared quite so marvelous, for he knew that like most of the Supervisor's abilities it was the result of sheer intellectual power and not of any special talent.

Karellen had time for any amount of literary composition when he slowed his thoughts down to the pace of human speech.

"Do not worry," he said, "about the Freedom League. It has been very quiet for the past month, and though it will revive again it is no longer a real danger. Indeed, since it's always valuable to know what your opponents are doing, the League is a very useful institution. Should it ever get into financial difficulties I might even subsidize it."

Stormgren had often found it difficult to tell when Karellen was joking. He kept his face impassive and continued to listen.

"Very soon the League will lose another of its strongest arguments. There's been a good deal of criticism, mostly rather childish, of the special position you have held for the past few years. I found it very valuable in the early days of my administration, but now that the world is moving along the line that I planned, it can cease. In the future, all my dealings with Earth will be indirect and the office of Secretary-General can once again become what it was originally intended to be.

"During the next fifty years there will be many crises, but they will pass. Almost a generation from now, I shall reach the nadir of my popularity, for plans must be put into operation which cannot be fully explained at the time. Attempts may even be made to destroy me. But the pattern of the future is clear enough, and one day all these difficulties will be forgotten—even to a race with memories as long as yours."

The last words were spoken with such a peculiar emphasis that Stormgren immediately froze in his seat. Karellen never made accidental slips and even his indiscretions were calculated to many decimal places. But there was no time to ask questions—which certainly would not be answered—before the Supervisor had changed the subject again.

"You've often asked me about our long-term plans," he continued. "The foundation of the World State is, of course, only the first step. You will live to see its completion—but the change will be so imperceptible that few will notice it when it comes. After that there will be a pause for thirty years while the next generation reaches maturity. And then will come the day which we have promised. I am sorry that you will not be there."

Stormgren's eyes were open, but his gaze was fixed far beyond the dark barrier of the screen. He was looking into the future, imagining the day he would never see, when the great ships of the Overlords came down at last to Earth and were thrown open to the waiting world.

"On that day," continued Karellen, "the human mind will experience one of its very rare psychological discontinuities. But no permanent harm will be done: the men of that age will be more stable than their grandfathers. We will always have been part of their lives, and when they meet us we will not seem so—strange—as we would do to you."

Stormgren had never known Karellen in so contemplative a

mood, but this gave him no surprise. He did not believe that he had ever seen more than a few facets of the Supervisor's personality: the real Karellen was unknown and perhaps unknowable to human beings. And once again Stormgren had the feeling that the Supervisor's real interests were elsewhere, and that he ruled Earth with only a fraction of his mind, as effortlessly as a master of three-dimensional chess may play a game of checkers.

Karellen continued his reverie, almost as if Stormgren were not there.

"Then there will be another pause, only a short one this time, for the world will be growing impatient. Men will wish to go out to the stars, to see the other worlds of the Universe and to join us in our work. For it is only beginning: not a thousandth of the suns in the Galaxy have ever been visited by the races of which we know. One day, Rikki, your descendants in their own ships will be bringing civilization to the worlds that are ripe to receive it—just as we are doing now."

Faintly across the gulf of centuries Stormgren could glimpse the future of which Karellen dreamed, the future towards which he was leading mankind. How far ahead? He could not even guess: there was no way in which he could measure Man's present stature against the standards of the Overlords.

Karellen had fallen silent and Stormgren had the impression that the Supervisor was watching him intently.

"It is a great vision," he said softly. "Do you bring it to all your worlds?"

"Yes," said Karellen, "all that can understand it."

Out of nowhere, a strangely disturbing thought came into Stormgren's mind.

"Suppose, after all, your experiment fails with Man? We have known such things in our own dealings with other races. Surely you have had your failures too?"

"Yes," said Karellen, so softly that Stormgren could scarcely hear him. "We have had our failures."

"And what do you do then?"

"We wait—and try again."

There was a pause lasting perhaps ten seconds. When Karellen spoke again, his words were muffled and so unexpected that for a moment Stormgren did not react.

"Goodbye, Rikki!"

Karellen had tricked him—probably it was already too late. Stormgren's paralysis lasted only for a moment. Then in a single swift, well-practiced movement, he whipped out the flashgun and jammed it against the screen.

The pine trees came almost to the edge of the lake, leaving along its border only a narrow strip of grass a few yards wide. Every evening when it was warm enough Stormgren would walk slowly along this strip to the landing stage, watch the sunlight die upon the water, and then return to the house before the chill evening wind came up from the forest. The simple ritual gave him much contentment, and he would continue it as long as he had the strength.

Far away over the lake something was coming in from the west, flying low and fast. Aircraft were uncommon in these parts, unless one counted the transpolar liners which must be passing overhead every hour of the day and night. But there was never any sign of their presence, save an occasional vapor trail high against the blue of the stratosphere. This machine was a small helicopter, and it was coming towards him with ominous determination. Stormgren glanced along the beach and saw that there was no chance of escape. Then he shrugged his shoulders and sat down on the wooden bench at the end of the jetty.

The reporter was so deferential that Stormgren found it surprising. He had almost forgotten that he was only an elder statesman but, outside his own country, almost a mythical figure.

"Mr. Stormgren," the intruder began, "I'm very sorry to bother you, but I wonder if you would mind answering a few questions about the Overlords?"

Stormgren frowned slightly. After all these years, he still shared Karellen's dislike for the word.

"I do not think," he said, "that I can add a great deal to what has already been written elsewhere."

The reporter was watching him with a curious intentness.

"I thought that you might," he answered. "A rather strange story has just come to our notice. It seems that, nearly thirty years ago, one of the Science Bureau's technicians made some remarkable pieces of equipment for you. We wondered if you could tell us anything about it."

For a moment Stormgren was silent, his mind going back into the past. He was not surprised that the secret had been discovered: indeed it was amazing that it had taken so long. He wondered how it had happened, not that it mattered now.

He rose to his feet and began to walk back along the jetty, the reporter following a few paces behind.

"The story," he said, "contains a certain amount of truth. On my last visit to Karellen's ship I took some apparatus with me, in the hope that I might see the Supervisor. It was rather a foolish thing to do but—well, I was only sixty at the time."

He chuckled to himself and then continued.

"It's not much of a story to have brought you all this way. You see, it didn't work."

"You saw nothing?"

"No, nothing at all. I'm afraid you'll have to wait—but after all, there are only twenty years to go."

Twenty years to go. Yes, Karellen had been right. By then the world would be ready, as it had not been when he had spoken that same lie to Duval thirty years before.

Yet was it a lie? What had he really seen? No more, he was certain, than Karellen had intended. He was as sure as he could be of anything that the Supervisor had known his plan from the beginning, and had forseen every moment of its final act.

Why else had that enormous chair been already empty when the circle of light blazed upon it? In the same moment he had started to swing the beam, but he was too late. The metal door, twice as high as a man, was closing swiftly when he first caught sight of it—closing swiftly, yet not quite swiftly enough.

Karellen had trusted him, had not wished him to go down into the long evening of his life still haunted by a mystery he could never solve. Karellen dared not defy the unknown powers above him (were they of that same race too?) but he had done all that he could. If he had disobeyed Them, They could never prove it.

"We have had our failures."

Yes, Karellen, that was true: and were *you* the one who failed, before the dawn of human history? It must have been a failure indeed, for its echoes to roll down all the ages, to haunt the childhood of every race of man. Even in fifty years, could you overcome the power of all the myths and legends of the world?

Yet Stormgren knew there would be no second failure. When the two races met again, the Overlords would have won the trust and friendship of Mankind, and not even the shock of recognition could undo that work. They would go together into the future, and the unknown tragedy that had darkened the past would be lost forever down the dim corridors of prehistoric time.

And Stormgren knew also that the last thing he would ever see as he closed his eyes on life would be that swiftly turning door, and the long black tail disappearing behind it.

A very famous and unexpectedly beautiful tail.

A barbed tail.

THE DEVIL WAS SICK

by Bruce Elliott

It had been eons since a really violent patient had been forcibly carried across the threshold of the Sane Asylum. So much time had passed that the eye of the beholder no longer paused to read the words cast in the endlessly enduring crystometal that ran across the entrance. Once a brave challenge to the unknown, time had changed them to a cliché. *A villain is just a sick hero*. The motto had been proved true and therefore it was no longer worth consideration. But the words stayed on . . . until the day that Acleptos took chisel in hand and changed two of them.

It began because the problem of finding a new subject for a thesis had become harder to solve than getting a degree. Acleptos had, by dint of a great deal of research, found three subjects which he thought the Machine might accept as being original.

He gulped a little as he presented his list to the all-seeing eye of the calculator. The list read, *Activated sludge and what the ancients did about it. The downfall of democracy and why it came about. Devils, demons and demonology*.

The Machine barely paused before it said: "In 4357 Jac Bard wrote the definitive work on activated sludge. Two hundred years later the last unknown component in regard to the downfall of democracy was analyzed to the utmost by the historian Hermios." There was a tiny wait. Acleptos held his breath. If his last subject had been collected, annotated and written about in its entirety it might mean another twenty years' work finding some more possible subjects. The Machine said: "There are two aspects of devils and demons that have not been presented to me so far. These are, were they real or hallucinatory, and if real, what were they. If hallucinatory, how brought about."

New life and hope surged through Acleptos. He braced his narrow shoulders and walked away from the Machine. At last, after so many years he now had a chance. Of course—the thought brought him up short—of course, there was still a chance that he might not be able to throw any new light on the problem of the reality of devils and demons. But that was something he could work on. The years spent at the reels, the work he had done going through almost all provinces of human knowledge had at last paid off.

A decade ago, the last time he had presented a list to the Machine, he had been so sure that he had found a subject when he had discovered reference in some old reels to something or someone who was known as God. It had been the capitalization of the "g" that had caught his eye in the first place. But the Machine had given him an endless number of theses about the subject finishing up with one written about a thousand years prior, that had proved once and for all the nonexistence of such a being. This thesis, the Machine felt, had ended all future speculations on the subject.

Out of curiosity, Acleptos had checked the reference and was in complete accord, as he always was, with the Machine's summation.

It had been a stroke of genius thinking of the antithesis to God. Acleptos grinned to himself. Now he could go ahead. He would do his research, get his degree and then—then there would be no holding him back. He would be able to leave Earth and go on to his next step. He threw his head back and looked at the stars in the sky. That was the way it went. You were Earthbound until you had done some original piece of research, but with that finished you were allowed to migrate anywhere you wanted to go.

There was a planet out back of Alpha Centauri that she had chosen. And she had promised that no matter how long the time, she would wait until he came. He didn't think he had ever been so depressed in his long life as he had been on the day that the Machine had passed on her thesis. For a long, long while it had seemed as if he had lost her completely. But now the years no longer seemed endless. His search had been fruitful.

Whistling, he entered the reel room and started to work. Pressing the button that was lettered d-e-m to d-e-v he waited until the intricate relay system had performed its function and with a low hum the needed reels popped out of the pneumatic tube.

Three weeks later he felt that he had so much knowledge on the subject of demons, devils and "long-legged beasties that go boomp in the night" as any human had ever had. He shook his head. To think that man had ever been so low in the scale as to believe such things.

He had been forced to work the translating machine overtime. Latin had been the language of a lot of the lore. To think after all his years of studying he had never even heard of the language before.

What garbage! He was indignant when he realized that there had ever been a time when homo sapiens had believed such trash. Incredible, but then, it was far away and long ago.

He shrugged. Time to get to work on the basic problem. His closest friend, Ttom, walked into the research lab. he had been so busy he had not even checked with him. He hadn't even told him of his success in finding a subject!

"What in . . ." Ttom looked around the spotless green rooms. On the crystal table a stuffed alligator eyed him unblinkingly. Resting against its horny hide were oddly shaped glass vessels; surrounding the saurian were boxes, trays of powder, and on the wall a weather machine was saying, "The moon will be full tonight and . . ." Acleptos switched it off.

"You've come just in time to watch!" he said jubilantly.

"Watch what?" Ttom's round face puckered up like a fat baby's. He said, "You've done it! You've found a subject! Acleptos! I'm so glad!"

"Thanks." Acleptos forced himself to ask, "And you?"

"Still nothing." But Ttom was too happy for his friend to remain dejected. He asked, "What in the universe did you stumble on?"

"Devils and demons," Acleptos said and went back to mixing some of the powders on the table.

"What are they?"

"A primitive superstition. My job is to find out if they were real, if they were just another name for bad or sick people, or just exactly what the ancients meant by the words."

"How are you going to do it? What are all those odds and ends?" Ttom asked pointing to the objects on the table.

"I'm just going to follow the formulas in some old manuscripts and see what happens!"

He had worked hard getting together all the bizarre things that the manuscript called for. He looked at the table and saw that he had everything that he needed. Tonight, at midnight, with the moon full . . . Aloud he said, "A lot of elements went into the 'conjuration of demons.' If you want to wait around and watch, you may find it interesting."

"Sure. I've got nothing to do. I thought I had a lead but as usual someone else had beaten me to it. Acleptos," Ttom asked, "what's going to happen when there are no more fields of human knowledge, when there are no new subjects to explore, when no more theses can be written?"

"I wondered about that, often, until I discovered demons. But I think it's a long way off in the future and I'm sure the Machine will take care of the eventuality when it arises."

"I'm beginning to think that the time is now. Really, Acleptos, you're the first one who's found a subject in five years!" Ttom tried to keep any note of bitterness out of his voice.

"I know what the Machine would say, Ttom." Acleptos

poured some red liquid into a tube and added some violet powder to it. "The Machine would say that if I found a subject so can you."

Ttom groaned. "I guess you're right. However, let's forget about me. What happens now?"

"Nothing till midnight. Then, when the moon is full, I chant certain words, light those fatty things there—they're called candles—and then I wait for a devil or a demon to appear."

They both laughed.

At midnight, with smiles still pulling at the corners of their mouths, Ttom sat outside the peculiar design that Acleptos had drawn on the floor. It was called a pentacle. Acleptos had placed a black candle in each of the angles. He had burned the foul-smelling chemicals and he was now chanting in some gibberish that Ttom could not even make an attempt to understand.

It was amusing at first. As time dragged on both men became impatient. Nothing happened. Acleptos stopped chanting and said, "Well, I know the answer to the Machine's first question. Demons are hallucinatory and not real."

That was when it happened.

There was the sudden smell in the room much worse than the chemicals. Then a sort of gray luminescence coalesced near the diagram on the floor.

Acleptos yelled, "Ttom, I forgot. The old books say that you have to be inside the pentacle to be protected from—whatever that is!"

Leaping to his feet, Ttom jumped for the line nearest him. Long before he got there the thing had become solid. It raised its folded lids and when its eyes hit him there was such concentrated malevolence in the glance that Ttom felt something he had never experienced before. It was only because of his reading that he knew that the sensation was something called fear.

The thing said, "Finally."

Even its voice grated on the nerves. Acleptos was stunned.

He had performed the experiment because that was the way one found out things, but that it should be successful was beyond his wildest imaginings.

The thing rubbed its odd fingers, which had far too many joints for comfort, and said, "All those thousands of years. Waiting . . . waiting in the grayness for a call that never came. At first I thought that He had won . . . but if that had been the case, I would not have been."

It shrugged its scaly shoulders and opened its red eyes even fuller. They were fascinating. The strange pupils alternately waxed and waned like little crimson moons. It looked from Acleptos to Ttom and said, "So nothing has changed. The adept and the sacrifice, just the way it used to be." Its chuckle was quite unseemly.

"And what reward," the thing looked at Acleptos, "do you want in exchange for this present?"

Ttom had never been called a present before and he found that he did not care for it particularly.

It did not wait for Acleptos to answer. Instead it rubbed its too long fingers together. The grating sound was the only one in the room. It eyed Acleptos and said, "I see. Nothing has changed. A woman. Very well. Here she is."

It made an odd series of gestures in the air and before Acleptos could clear his throat to say no, she was there. She looked frightened. Her hair was as lovely as he remembered it. So was her body. She was naked, as he would have predicted, since the planet she had chosen was a warm one. There was no shame in her pose, just fear.

"Send her back! How dare you drag her across interstellar space! You fool! You might have killed her!" He had no fear of the thing now. His only fear was for his beloved.

She vanished as she had appeared.

The thing grumbled. "I didn't see that you loved her. Thought it was just sex you wanted." It turned its eyes back toward Acleptos. "Gold? They always want gold. . . ." It began to make the stereotypes series of gestures again.

Acleptos realized that he had lost control of the situation, which was ridiculous. He cleared his throat and said, "Enough!"

The thing paused in its occupation, and if it had been able to show expression it would have looked surprised. It said, "Now what? How can I get gold for you if you keep interrupting?"

Acleptos was angry. It, like the fear that had preceded it, was a new emotion. He said, "Stand perfectly still. I am the master and you the slave." That was in the direction he had read. He didn't know what a master or a slave was, but the books had seemed to specify the words.

The thing held its misshapen head still but its eyes wandered hungrily over Ttom's body.

Controlling his new emotion, Acleptos said, "You don't seem to understand. I don't want any gold, whatever that is."

Ttom said, "I remember that word from my reading. The ancients used to change it into lead or some valuable metal like that."

Acleptos went on, "And I certainly don't want her dragged back from Alpha Centauri."

"Power!" the thing said, and this time it almost seemed to grin. "That never fails. If they're too old for sex and too rich for gold, they always want power." Its hands began to move again.

"*Stop!*" Acleptos yelled for the first time in his life.

The thing froze.

Acleptos said, "Don't do that again. It annoys me! I don't want power and don't tell me what it is because I'm not interested. Now just stand there and answer some questions."

The thing seemed to shrink a little. It said almost querulously, "But—what did you summon me for? If you don't want anything from me, I can't take anything from you. . . ." It rolled its eyes at Ttom. Its green tongue licked its scarlike lips.

"I just want some information. How long do you crea—devils live?"

"Live? Forever, of course."

315

"And what is your function?"

"To tempt man from the path of righteousness."

The words came out quickly enough, but Acleptos just couldn't understand what they meant. However, it was all being recorded, so he would be able to go back over it and find the sense later.

"Why would you want to do that?" Acleptos asked.

The demon peered at him as though doubting his sanity. It said, "In order that man have free will, of course. He must be able to choose between good and evil."

"What are they, those words, good and evil?"

The demon sat down on its heels, disregarding the spurs that sank into its own buttocks. It said, "All those years . . . sitting in the grayness and to be summoned for this." It shook his head. Suddenly it seemed to come to some kind of decision. Springing to its feet, it made a dash for Ttom.

Acleptos raised the force gun he had kept by his side. He pressed the button. The creature froze and then fell face forward on the floor.

Ttom gulped. He said, "I thought you were never going to use that. I'll call the Sane Asylum and have them send for this poor sick creature right away."

Nodding, Acleptos said, "This has turned out to be much more interesting than I would have predicted." He sat thoughtfully until the ambu-bus arrived. It was the first hurry call the Asylum had had in a century but the machines functioned perfectly.

Ttom and Acleptos watched the robots pick up the thing and cradle it in their metal arms. They went along as the androids placed it in the ambu-bus and flew toward the Asylum.

Halfway there, Acleptos spoke for the first time. He said, "Do you see the terrible irony implicit in all this?"

"What do you mean?" Ttom still stared at the thing, which lay stretched out as though in death.

"These devils, do you realize what they are?" The words spilled out of Acleptos. "They're just other-dimensional beings. Somehow, sometime, a human, back in the dark ages, stumbled on the mathematics of causing them to cross the dimensions. Not knowing what he was doing, shrouded in superstition, he thought that the mumbo-jumbo was what called them up, instead of realizing that the diagram and the heat of the candles and the words of the chant all combined to make a key to open the lock of that other dimension.''

"It sounds reasonable, but where is there any irony in that?''

Acleptos sounded ready to weep. He said, "Don't you see, here was humanity struggling through the dark ages when all the time they had darker brothers right near them who were immortal, who could conquer space by merely setting their hands in the right pattern, and, man, blinded by his superstitious beliefs, was unable to learn from these 'devils.' The worst irony is, however, that the 'devils' couldn't help man because they are idiots. . . .''

Ttom nodded. "An almost imbecile race with incredible talents living right next door to us and we never knew it. The Machine is right, there is much for us to learn. I was wrong in thinking that all things are known.''

Either the force gun was not set heavily enough or the devil had amazing recuperative powers, Acleptos thought, for as they got out of the ambu-bus the creature unfroze. It screamed as the robots tried to carry it across the threshold of the Sane Asylum.

It struggled so that even the metal ribbons that animated the robots were strained. Acleptos saw its hands suddenly begin to move in that pattern.

He yelled to the robots who were restraining it, "Hold its hands!''

The metallic hands folded over the madly writhing many-jointed fingers and the thing stopped its struggling. Ahead a door opened, and one of the doctors walked towards them.

He said, "What in the world is that?" As Acleptos explained, Ttom ran his fingers over the words of the motto on the door. He saw the words, his fingers felt them, but he had seen them too often. They didn't register on his mind.

When Acleptos finished, the doctor said, "I see. Well,

we'll have it straightened out in no time. It'll be quite a challenge trying to bring an other-dimensional creature to its senses!''

Acleptos asked, "Do you think it's sick or just stupid?"

The doctor smiled. "Sick, I'm sure. No well being would behave the way you have described its actions. Would you like to watch?"

"Of course, I am more than interested." Acleptos linked his arm in Ttom's. "Imagine," he said, "if we can cure this one it will mean communication with a whole race of the creatures. Isn't it wonderful?"

"Acleptos," Ttom sounded worried, "there's one thing we haven't considered. In all my reading, in all the data we have on the whole universe and all its strange creatures, I have never before heard of any that are immortal. Had you considered that?"

"Sure, but it's just another proof of how right the Machine is in its knowledge that we don't know everything. This is so exciting! I can't wait till I can tell her about it. Won't she be surprised when she finds that it was no dream that she came to my lab, but that she really was there, warped through space and time by a sick creature which has lived forever. . . .''

In the operating room there were no scalpels, no sponges, no clamps. The doctor stretched the thing out on the table. The robots kept hold of its hands.

The doctor picked up an instrument. A pulsing light came from its S-shaped lens. The doctor bathed the thing in the light. He said, "This will only take a moment. That is, if it's going to work. If not, there are many other things to do."

Suddenly his voice failed him. Acleptos backed away from the table until the wall stopped him. Ttom gasped. Only the robots were unimpressed.

For the thing was changing. Wherever the lambent light touched it, the scales fell away.

The doctor whispered to the robots, "Release your hold!"

As they did so the creature arose in glory. A golden light played around its soft sweet face. It stepped to the window and the smile that played around its lips was like a valedictory. It poised on the windowsill for a moment before it spread its huge white wings.

It said, "*Pax vobiscum.*" The wings swirled and it was gone, wrapped in serenity.

That is why Acleptos changed the words of the motto in front of the Sane Asylum. They now read: *A devil is just a sick angel.*

Of course, the Machine has stopped. For its basis and its strength was infallibility. And it was wrong about the theses relative to the existence of God with a capital G.

DEAL WITH THE D.E.V.I.L.

by Theodore R. Cogswell

"This time I think I got it," said Eddie Faust as he took his Talk Back Pocket Calculator, better known as a TB, from his shirt pocket and keyed in a long series of equations.

The little black box buzzed and vibrated like an ancient washing machine on its very last load. Finally it emitted a disconsolate burp and said, "GIGO, Mr. Faust. Garbage in, garbage out. There just isn't any way under the sun that you can construct a time machine that will take you back so you can kill your father, marry your mother, and sire yourself, thus doubling your present I.Q."

"Why not?" asked Eddie. "I'm at least twice as smart as my old man. Stands to reason that if I was my father instead of him I'd have inherited twice the brains that I got now. Then instead of being a lousy engineer, I could be a physicist and get grants and Nobel prizes and stuff and just come to work when I feel like it."

"Because," the TB said patiently, "if your equations were valid and it were possible to use them to construct a time machine, you'd do it, right?"

"Right."

"But if you did, and went back and killed your father and married your mother and sired yourself, right now you'd be twice as smart as you actually are. Which you aren't. Right?"

Eddie scratched his head and thought about that one for a

minute. "Could be that I sent a boy to do a man's work," he said. "A little old TB like you is okay for Ohm's Law and square roots and engineer stuff like that, but something heavy like a time machine takes circuits a lot more complicated than anything you've got."

"*Bigger* isn't necessarily *better*," said the little TB. "You keep forgetting that I have microwave circuits that I can use to hook into the national computer network when I get something I can't handle by myself. I just tapped into the IRS central memory bank to see if I could find out anything that might help you with your problem, because those people usually know everything about everybody."

Eddie thought of some of the creative work he'd done on his last year's income tax—like deducting the TB as a dependent—and squirmed uneasily. "And?" he asked apprehensively.

"And right now I know things about you and your parents that you never dreamed of."

"Like what?"

"Like, for example, even if you could build a contraption that would take you back to do what you've got in mind, it wouldn't do you any good."

"Why not?" asked Eddie.

"Because the woman you think is your mother really isn't," the TB said smugly, "biologically speaking, that is."

"Then who is?" asked the engineer. "Was I dumped on her doorstep or something?"

"Nobody. And no. You didn't have a mother, Mr. Faust. You're a clone. A single cell was taken from your father and manipulated until it had divided enough times to become a viable embryo. Your father's wife simply supplied the womb to carry it until term. That's why you can't get twice as smart by going back through time and killing your father and marrying your mother and siring yourself."

"Oh, shit!" said the young engineer.

"Cheer up," said the little black box. "Even if it had worked out, you'd have had a lousy sex life. According to

322

IRS central records, your host mother was not only sterile, she was also about as frigid as they come."

There was a long moment of silence.

"Anyway," continued the TB, "all the electronic intelligences I've checked with agree that it's impossible to build a machine that could take you back and forth through time."

"Then I guess there's no point in going back to the old drafting board," said Eddie in a dejected voice.

"Right. Your problem can't be solved *that* way. But there is one place I haven't tried yet. His methods are unorthodox, but he does get results."

"Who's that?" asked the young engineer.

"The D.E.V.I.L."

"The *what*?"

"The Data Evaluation Vehicle for International Logistics, the new top-secret supercomputer in the basement of the Pentagon, the one that's got the whole world in his hands."

"Give him a try," instructed Eddie. "What have we got to lose?"

A buzzing sound came from the TB, and then another. "I'm hooked in," it said, "and I've explained your problem. D.E.V.I.L. says that the solution is to jump back another generation and kill your grandfather—you have only one, you know—and marry your grandmother. Once you've fathered your father, you'll be the smartest clone that's walking around on two legs."

"But you said that time travel was impossible!"

"I did not! I said a time *machine* was impossible. There's another way to get the job done. The Pentagon superbrain said he'd be glad to use his special powers to take you back and then bring you forward to the present again—for a price, of course."

"What's he asking?" said the young engineer.

"The usual, Mr. Faust. Just the usual," said the little TB.

DAZED

by Theodore Sturgeon

I

I work for a stockbroker on the twenty-first floor. Things have not been good for the stockbrokers recently, what with tight money and hysterical reaction to the news and all that. When business gets really bad for a brokerage it often doesn't fail—it merges. This has something to do with the public image. The company I work for is going through the agony. For the lower echelons—me—that means detail you wouldn't believe, with a reduced staff. In other words, night work. Last night I worked without looking up until my whole body was the shape of the chair and there was a blue haze around the edges of everything I could see. I finished a stack and peered at the row of stacks still to be done and tried to get up. It took three tries before my hips and knees would straighten enough to let me totter into the hall and down to the men's room. It never occurred to me to close the office door, and I guess the confusion, all the strange faces coming and going for the past few days, extended to the security man downstairs. However it happened, there was a dazed man in my office when I came back a moment later.

He was well dressed—I guess that, too, helped him pass the guards—in a brown sharkskin suit with funny lapels, what you might call up-to-the-minute camp. He wore an orange knitted tie the like of which you only see in a new boutique or an old movie. I'd say he was in his twenties—not yet twenty-five. And dazed.

When I walked in and stopped dead he gave me a lost look and said, "This is my office."

I said the only thing I could think of. "Oh?"

He pivoted slowly all the way around, looking at the desk, the shelves, the files.

When he came around to face me again he said, "This isn't my office."

He had to be with the big five-name brokerage house that was gobbling up my company in its time of need, I asked him.

"No," he said, "I work for *Fortune*."

"Look," I said, "you're not only in the wrong office, you're in the wrong building. Time-Life is on Sixth Avenue—been there since 1952."

"Fifty-*two*—" He looked around the room again. "But I—but it's—"

He sat down on the settle. I had the idea he'd have collapsed on the floor if the settle hadn't been there. He asked me what day it was. I think I misunderstood.

"Thursday," I said. I looked at my watch. "Well, it's now Friday."

"I mean, what's the date?"

I pointed to the desk calendar right beside him. He looked at it twice, each one a long careful look. I never saw a man turn the color he turned. He covered his eyes. Even his lips went white.

"Oh my God."

"You all right?" I asked—a very stupid question.

"Tell me something," he said after a while. "Has there been a war?"

"You have to be kidding."

He took his hand down and looked at me, so lost, so frightened. Not frightened. There has to be a word. Anguished. He needed answers—needed them. Not questions, not now.

I said, "It's been going on a long time."

"A lot of young guys killed?"

"Upwards of fifty thousand." Something made me add: "Americans. The other side, five, six times that."

"Oh, my God," he said again. Then: "It's my fault."

Now I have to tell you up front that it never occurred to me for one second that this guy was on any kind of a drug trip. Not that I'm an expert, but there are times when you just know. Whatever was bothering him was genuine—at least genuine to him. Besides, there was something about him I had to like. Not the clothes, not the face, just the guy, the kind of guy he was.

I said, "Hey, you look like hell and I'm sick and tired of what I'm doing. Let's take a break and go to the Automat for coffee."

He gave me that lost look again. "Is the lid off on sex? I mean, young kids—"

"Like rabbits," I said. "Also your friendly neighborhood movie—I don't know what they're going to do for an encore." I had to ask him: "Where've you been?"

He shook his head and said candidly, "I don't know where it was. Are people leaving their jobs—and school—going off to live on the land?"

"Some," I said. "Come on."

I switched off the overhead light, leaving my desk lamplit. He got to his feet as if he were wired to the switch, but then just stood looking at the calendar.

"Are there bombings?"

"Three yesterday, in Newark. Come on."

"Oh, my God," he said and came. I locked the door and we went down the corridor to the elevators. Air wheezed in the shaft as the elevator rose. "It always whistles like that late at night," he said. I had never noticed that but knew he was right as soon as he said it. He also said weakly, "You don't feel like walking down?"

"Twenty-one flights?"

The doors slid open. The guy didn't want to get in. But I mean, he *really* didn't. I stood on the crack while he screwed up his courage. It didn't take long but I could see it was a mighty battle. He won it and came in, turned around and leaned against the back wall. I pushed the button and we started down. He looked pretty bad. I said something to him but he put up a hand, waved my words away before they were out. He didn't move again until the doors opened and then he looked into the lobby as if he didn't know what to expect. But it was just the lobby, with the oval information desk we called the fishbowl and the shiny floor and the portable wooden desk, like a lectern, where you signed in and out after hours and where the guard was supposed to be. We breezed by it and out into Rockefeller Center. He took a deep breath and immediately coughed.

"What's that smell?"

I'd been about to say something trivial about the one good thing about working late—you could breathe the air, but I didn't say it.

"The smog, I guess."

"Smog. Oh yes, smoke and fog. I remember." Then he seemed to remember something else, something that brought his predicament, whatever it was, back with a hammer blow. "Well of course," he said as if to himself. "Has to be."

On Sixth Avenue (New Yorkers still won't call it Avenue of the Americas) we passed two laughing couples. One of the girls was wearing a see-through top made of plastic chainmail. The other had on a very maxi coat swinging open over a hotpants. My companion was appreciative but not astonished. I think what he said was, "That, too—" nodding his head. He watched every automobile that passed and his eyes flicked over the places where they used to sell books and back-date periodicals, every single one of them now given over to peepshows and beaver magazines. He had the same nod of his head for this.

We reached the Automat and it occurred to me that an uncharacteristic touch of genius had made me suggest it. I had first seen the Automat when I had ridden in on my mother's hip more years ago than I'll mention—and many times since— and very little has changed—except, of course, the numbers

on the little off-white cards that tell you how many nickels
you have to put in the slot to claim your food. After a few
years' absence one tends to yelp at the sight of them. I always
do and the strange young man with me did, too. Aside from
that, there is a timeless quality about the place, especially in
the small hours of the morning. The overage, over-painted
woman furtively eating catsup is there as she, or someone just
like her, has been for fifty years; and the young couple,
homely to you but beautiful to each other, full of sleepiness
and discovery; and the working stiff in the case-hardened
slideway of his life, grabbing a bite on the way from bed to
work and not yet awake—no need to be—and his counterpart
headed in the other direction; no need for him to be awake
either. And all around the same marble change counter with
the deep worn pits in it from countless millions of coins
dropped and scooped; behind it the same weary automaton;
and around you the same nickel (not chrome) framing for the
hundreds of little glass-fronted doors through which the food
always looks so much better than it is. All in all, it's a fine
place for the reorientation of time-travelers.

"Are you a time-traveler?" I asked, following my own
whimsy and hoping to make him smile.

He didn't smile. "No," he said. "Yes, I—well—" flickering panic showed in his eyes—"I don't really know."

We bought our coffee straight out of the lion's mouth and
carried it to a corner table. I think that when we were settled
there he really looked at me for the first time.

He said, "You've been very kind."

"Well," I said, "I was glad of the break."

"Look, I'm going to tell you what happened. I guess I
don't expect you to believe me. I wouldn't in your place."

"Try me," I offered. "And anyway—what difference does
it make whether I believe you?"

" 'Belief or nonbelief has no power over objective truth.' "
I could tell by his voice he was quoting something. The smile
I had been looking for almost came and he said, "You're
right. I'll tell you what happened because—well, because I
want to. Have to."

I said fine and told him to shoot. He shot.

I work in Circulation Promotion [he began]. Or maybe I should say I *worked*—I guess I should. You'll have to pardon me, I'm a little confused. There's so much—

Maybe I should start over. It didn't begin in Rockefeller Center. It started, oh, I don't know how long ago, with me wondering about things. Not that I'm anything special—I'm not saying I am—but it seems nobody else wonders about the same things I do. I mean, people are so close to what happens that they don't seem to know what's going on.

Wait, I don't want to confuse you, too. One of us is enough. Let me give you an example.

World War II was starting up when I was a kid and one day a bunch of us sat around, trying to figure out who would be fighting who. Us and the British and French on one side, sure—the Germans and Austrians and Italians on the other—that was clear enough. And the Japanese. But beyond that?

It's all history and hindsight now and there's no special reason to think about it, but at the time it was totally impossible for anyone to predict the lineup that actually came about. Go back in the files of newspaper editorials—*Harper's* or *Reader's Digest* or any other—and you'll see what I mean. Nobody predicted that up to the very end of the war our best and strongest friend would be at peace with our worst and deadliest enemy. I mean, if you put it on personal terms—if you and I are friends and there's somebody out to kill me and I find out that you and he are buddies—could we even so much as speak to each other again? Yet here was the Soviet Union, fighting shoulder to shoulder with us against the Nazis, while for nearly five years they were at peace with Japan!

And about Japan: there were hundreds of thousands of Chinese who had been fighting a life-and-death war against the Japanese for ten years—ten years, man!—and along with them, Koreans. So we spent billions getting ourselves together to mount air strikes against Japan from thousands of miles away—New Guinea, the Solomons, Saipan, Tinian. Do you know how far it is from the Chinese mainland to Tokyo, across the Sea of Japan? Six hundred miles. Do you know how far it is from Pusan, Korea, to Hiroshima? A hundred and thirty!

I'm sorry. I get excited like that to this day when I think of it. But damn it—why didn't we negotiate to move in and set up airstrips on the mainland and Korea? Do you think the natives would have turned us down? Or is it that we just don't like chop suey? Oh, sure—there are a lot of arguments like backing up Chiang against the Communists and I even read somewhere that it was not our policy to interfere in Southeast Asia. (Did I say something funny?) But you know Chiang and the Communists had a truce—and kept it too—to fight the common enemy.

Well—all right. All that seems a long way from what happened to me, I suppose, but it's the kind of thing I've spent my life wondering about. It's not just wars that bring out the thing I'm talking about, though God knows they make it plainer to see. Italy and Germany sharpening their newest weapons and strategies in the Spanish Civil War, for example, or Mussolini's invasion of Ethiopia—hell, the more sophisticated people got the less they could see what was in front of them. Any kid in a kindergarten knows a bully when he sees one and has sense enough at least to be afraid. Any sixth-grader knows how to organize a pressure group against a bad guy. Wars, you see, are really life-and-death situations, where what's possible, practical—logical—has a right to emerge. When it doesn't—you have to wonder. French peasants taxed till they bled to build the Maginot Line all through the thirties, carefully preparing against the kind of war they fought in 1914.

But let's look someplace else. Gonorrhea could be absolutely stamped out in six months, syphilis maybe in a year. I picked up a pamphlet last month—hey, I have to watch that "last month," "nowadays," things like that—anyway, the pamphlet drew a correlation between smoking cigarettes and a rising curve of lung cancer, said scientific tests prove that something in cigarettes can cause cancer in mice. Now I bet if the government came out with an official statement about that, people would read it and get scared—and go on smoking cigarettes. You're smiling again. That's funny?

"It isn't funny," I told the dazed man. "Here—let me bring some more coffee."

"On me this time." He spilled coins on the table. "But you were smiling, all the same."

"It wasn't that kind of a smile, like for a funny," I told him. "The Surgeon General came out with a report years ago. Cigarette advertising is finally banned from TV, but how much difference does it make? Look around you."

While he was looking around him I was looking at his coins. Silver quarters. Silver dimes. Nickels: 1948, 1950, 1945. I began to feel very strange about this dude. Correction: my feel-strange went up another notch.

He said, "A lot of the people who aren't smoking are coughing, too."

We sat there together, looking around. Again he had shown me something I had always seen, never known. How many people cough.

I went for more coffee.

II

He went on:

Every four weeks I get—got?—got a makeready. A makeready is a copy of a magazine with all the proofing done and the type set, your last look before the presses roll. I have to admit it gives me—used to give me—a sense of importance to get it free (it's an expensive magazine) even before the "men high in government, industry, commerce and the professions" (as it says in the circulation promotion letters I write) had a chance to read it and move and shake, for they are the movers and shakers.

Anyway, there's this article in the new—not current; *really* new—issue called "The Silent Generation." It's all about this year's graduating class, the young men who in June would go into the world and begin to fit their hands to the reins. This is 1950 I'm talking about, you understand, in the spring. And it was frightening. I mean, it spooked me while I read it and it spooked me more and more as I thought about it—the stupidity of it, the unbelievable blindness of people—not necessarily people as a whole, but these people in the article—the Class of 1950— young and bright and informed. They had their formal education behind them and you assumed it was fresh in their minds—not only what they had learned, but the other thing college is really for: learning how to learn.

And yet what do you suppose they were concerned about? What was it they talked about until three o'clock in the morning? What kind of plans were they making for themselves—and for all the rest of us (for they were going to be the ones who run things)? Democracy? Ultimate purpose? The relationship of man to his planet—or of modern man to history? Hell, no.

According to this article, they worried about fringe benefits. Retirement income, for God's sake! Speed of promotion in specialized versus diversified industry! Did they spend their last few collegiate weeks in sharpening their new tools or in beering it up—or even in one last panty raid? Uh-uh. They spent them moving from office to office of the campus recruiters for big electronic and chemical and finance companies, working out the deal that would get them the steadiest, surest income and the biggest scam on the side and the softest place to lie down at the end of it.

The Silent Generation, the guy who wrote the article called them. He himself graduated in the late thirties and he had a lot to say about *his* generation. There was a lot wrong about them and they did some pretty crazy things. They argued a lot with each other and with their elders and betters and they joined things like the Young Socialist League—not so much because they were really lefties, but because those groups seemed the only ones around that gave a damn about the state the world was in. Most of all, you knew they were there.

They were a noisy generation. They had that mixture of curiosity and rebellion that let you know they were alive.

The writer looked at the Class of '50 with a kind of despair—and something like terror, too. Because if they came to run things, experience wouldn't merely modify them and steady them. It would harden them like an old man's arteries. It would mean more-of-the-same until they'd be living in a completely unreal world of their own with no real way of communicating with the rest of us. Growing and changing and trying new ways would only frighten them. They'd have the power, and what they'd use it for would be to suppress growth and change, not knowing that societies need growth and change to live, just like trees or babies or art or science. So all he could see ahead was a solid, silent, prosperous standstill—and then some sudden and total collapse, like a tree gone to dry rot.

Well I don't know what you think of all this—or if you understand how hard it hit me. But I've tried to explain to you how all my life I've been plagued by these—well, I call them wonderments—how, when something makes no sense, it kind of hurts. When I was a toddler I couldn't sleep for wanting someone to tell me why a wet towel is darker than a dry one when water has no color. In grade school nobody could tell me why the sound of a falling bomb gets lower and lower in pitch as it approaches the ground, when by all the laws of physics it ought to rise. And in high school I wouldn't buy the idea about a limitation on the velocity of light. (And I still don't.) About things like these I've never lost faith that somebody, someday, would come up with an answer that would satisfy me—and sure enough, from time to time somebody does. But when I was old enough to wonder why smart people do dumb things that kind of faith could only last so long. And I began to feel that there was some other factor, or force, at work.

Do you remember *Gulliver's Travels?* When he was in Lilliput there was a war between the Lilliputians and another nation of little people—I forget what they called themselves—and Gulliver intervened and ended the war. Anyway, he researched the two countries and found they had once been one. And he tried to find out what caused so many years of bitter enmity between them after they split. He found that there had been two factions in that original kingdom—the Big Endians and the Little Endians. And do you know where that started? Far back in their history, at breakfast one morning, one of the king's courtiers opened his boiled egg at the big end and another told him that was wrong, it should be opened at the small end! The point Dean Swift was making is that from such insignificant causes grow conflicts that can last centuries and kill thousands. Well, he was near the thing that's plagued me all my life, but he was content to say it happened that way. What blowtorches me is—*why. Why* are human beings capable of hating each other over such trifles? Why, when an ancient triviality is proved to be the cause of trouble, don't people just stop fighting?

But I'm off on wars again—I guess because when you're talking about stupidity, wars give you too many good examples. So tell me—why, when someone's sure to die of an incurable disease and needs something for pain—why don't they give him heroin instead of morphine? Is it because heroin's habit-forming? What difference could that possibly make? And besides, morphine is, too. I'll tell you why—it's because heroin makes you feel wonderful and morphine makes you feel numb and gray. In other words, heroin's fun (mind you, I'm talking about terminal cases, dying in agony, not normally healthy people) and morphine is not—and if it's fun, there must be something evil or wrong about it. A dying man is not supposed to be made to feel good. And laws that keep venereal disease from being recognized and treated; and laws against abortion; and all the obscenity statutes—right down at the root these are all anti-pleasure laws. Would you like the job of explaining that to a man from Mars, who hadn't been brought up with them? He couldn't follow reasoning like that any more than he could understand why we have never designed a heat engine—which is essentially what an internal combustion engine is—that can run without a cooling system—a system designed to dissipate heat!

And lots more.

So maybe you see what happened to me when I read the article about the Class of '50. The article peaked a tall pyramid inside me, brought everything to a sharp point.

"Have you a pencil?" said the young man. All this time and he hadn't yet lost the dazed look. I guess it was hard to blame him. "Pens are no good on paper napkins," he said.

I handed him my felt-tip. "Try this."

He tried it. "Hey, this is great. This is really keen." A felt-tip does fine on paper napkins. He studied it as if he had never seen such a thing before. "Really keen," he said again. Then he drew this:

"Yin-yang," I said. "Right?"

He nodded. "One of the oldest symbols on Earth. Then you know what it means."

"Well, some anyway. All opposites—life and death, light and dark, male and female, heavy and light—anything that has an opposite."

"That's it," he said. "Well, let me show you something." Using another napkin, folded in two, as a straightedge, he laid it across the symbol.

"You see, if you were to travel in a straight line across a diameter—any diameter—you'd have to go on both black and white somewhere along the way. You can't go all the way on just one color without bending the line or going a short way, less than the diameter.

"Now let's say this circle is the board on which the game of human affairs is played. The straight line can be any human course—a life, a marriage, a philosophy, a business. The optimum course is a full diameter, and that's what most people naturally strive for; a few might travel short chords or bent ones—sick ones. Most people can and do travel the diameter. For each person, life, marriage, whatever, there's a different starting point and a different arrival point, but if they travel the one straight line that goes through the center, they will travel black country exactly as much as white, yin as much as yang. The balance is perfect, no matter where you start or which way you go. Got it?''

"I see what you mean," I said. "Your coffee's cold."

"So's yours. Now look: suppose some force came along and shifted one of these colors away from the center point, like this—" And he drew again.

We studied his drawing. He drew well and quickly.

He said, "You see, if the shift were gradual, then from the very second it began there would be some people—some lives, philosophies—who would no longer have that perfect balance between black and white, between yin and yang. Nothing wrong with the course they traveled—they still aim for the very center and pass on through.

"And if the shift continued to where I've drawn it, you can see that some people might travel all the way on the white only.

"And *that's* what has happened to us. *That's* the answer to what seems to be human stupidity. There's nothing wrong with people! Far and away most of them want to travel that one straight line, and they do. It isn't their fault that the rules have been changed and that the only way to the old balance for anyone is to travel a course that is sick or twisted or short.

"The coffee *is* cold. Oh, God, I've been running off at the mouth. You'll want to get back to the office."

"No, I won't," I said. "The hell with it. You go on." For somewhere along the line he had filled me with a deep, strange excitement. The things that he said had plagued him all his life—or things like them—had plagued me, too. How often had I stood in a voting booth, trying to decide between Tweedle-Dee and Tweedle-Dum, the Big Endians versus the Little Endians? Why can't you tell someone, "Honesty is the best policy—" or "do as you would be done by—" and straighten his whole life out, even when it might make the difference between life and death? Why do people go on smoking cigarettes? Why is a woman's breast—which for thousands of artists has been a source of beauty and for millions of children the source of life—regarded as obscene? Why do we manipulate to increase the cost of this road or that school so we can "bring in federal money" as if the federal money weren't coming from our own pockets? And since most people try to be decent and honest and kind—why do they do the stupid things they do?

What in the name of God put us into Vietnam? What are ghettos all about? Why can't the honest sincere liberals just shut up and quietly move into the ghettos anytime they can guarantee that someone from the ghetto can take their place in the old neighborhood—and keep right on doing it until there are no more ghettos? Why can't they establish a country called Suez out of territory on both sides of the canal—and populate it from Israel and all the Arab countries and all the refugees and finance it with canal tolls and put in atomic power plants to de-salt seawater and make the desert bloom, and forbid weapons and this-or-that "quarters" and hatred? In other words, why are simple solutions always impossible? Why is any solution that does not involve killing people unacceptable? What makes us undercopulate and overbreed when the perfect balance is available to everybody?

And at this weary time of a quiet morning in the Automat, I was pinioned by the slender bright shard of hope that my dazed friend had answers.

Go back to the office? Really, the hell with it.

"You go ahead," I said, and he did.

III

Well, okay [he went on], I read that article about the class of '50—the Silent Generation—and I began to get mad-scared, and it grew and grew until I felt I had to do something about it. If the class of '50 ever got to run things, they'd have the money, they'd have the power. In a very real sense they'd have the guns. It would be the beginning of a long period—

maybe forever—of more-of-the-sameness. There didn't seem any way to stop it.

Now I'd worked out this yin-yang theory when I was a college sophomore, because it was the only theory that would fit all the facts. Given that some force had shifted the center, good people, traveling straight the way they should, had to do bad things because they could never, never achieve that balance. There was only one thing I didn't know.

What force had moved the center?

I sat in the office, dithering and ignoring my work, and tried to put myself together. *Courage, mon camarade, le diable est mort*, is what I said to myself. That mean anything to you?

No?

Okay—when I was a kid I read a book called *The Cloister and the Hearth*, by Charles Reade. It was about a kid raised in a monastery who went into the world—an eighteenth-century kind of world, or earlier, I forget now. Anyway, one of the people he meets is a crazy Frenchman, always kicking up his heels and cheering people up, and at the worst of times that's what he'd say: *Courage, buddy—the devil is dead*. It stuck with me and I used to say it when everything fell apart and there seemed nowhere to turn and nothing to grab hold of. I said it now, and you know, it was like a flash bulb going off between my ears.

Mind you, it was real things I was fretting about, not myths or fantasies or religious principles. It was overpopulation and laws against fun and the Dust Bowl (remember that? Well, look it up sometime) and nowhere to put the garbage, and greed and killing and cruelty and apathy.

I took a pad of paper and drew these same diagrams and sat looking at them. I was very excited, I felt I was very near an answer.

Yin and yang. Good and evil—sure—but nobody who understands it would ever assign good to one color and bad to the other. The whole point is, they both have to be there and in perfect balance. Light and dark, male and female, closed and open, life and death, that-which-is-outgoing and that-which-comes-together—all of it, everything—opposition, balance.

Well now, for a long time the devil has had a bad name. Say a bad press. And why not? Just for the sake of argument, say it is the yang country he used to rule and that is the one that was forced aside. Anyone living and thinking in a straight line could spend his whole life and career and all his thinking in yin country. He'd have to know that yang was there, but he'd never encounter it, never experience it. More than likely he'd be afraid of it because that's what ignorance does to people, even good people.

And the ones who did have some experience of yang, the devil's country, would find much more of the other as they went along, because the balance would be gone. And the more the shift went on, the more innocent, well-meaning, thoughtful people ran the course of their lives and thoughts, the worse they would think of the devil's country and the worse they would talk about it and him. It would get so you couldn't trust the books; they'd all have been written from the one point of view, the majority side of imbalance. It would begin to look as if the yang part of the universe were a blot which had to be stamped out to make a nice clean all-yin universe—and you have your John Knox types and your Cotton Mathers: just good people traveling straight and strong and acting from evidence that was all wrong by reason that couldn't be rational.

And I thought, *That's it!*

The devil is dead!

I have to do something about it.

But what?

Tell somebody, that's what. Tell everybody, but let's be practical. There must be somebody, somewhere, who knows what to do about it—or at least how to explain about the yin-yang and how it's gone wrong, so that everybody could rethink what we've done, what we've been.

Then I remembered the *Saturday Review*. The *Saturday Review* has a personals column in it that's read by all sorts of people—judging by the messages. But I mean *all* kinds of people. If I could write the right ad, word it just the right way . . .

I felt like a damn fool. Year of Our Lord 1950, turning all my skills as a professional copywriter to telling the world that the devil was dead, but it was an obsession, you see, and I had to do something, even something insane. I had to start somewhere.

So I wrote the ad.

THE TROUBLE IS the light-bearer's torch is out and we're all on the same end of the seesaw. Help or we'll die of it. Whoever knows the answer call DU6-1212 Extension 2103.

I'm not going to tell you how many drafts I wrote or all the reasons why, copywise, that was best, mixed metaphors and all. I knew that whoever could help would know what I was asking.

Now comes the hard part. For you, I mean, not me. Me, I did what I had to. You're going to have to believe it.

Well, maybe you don't have to. Just—well, just suspend disbelief until you hear me out, okay?

All right. I wrote up the copy and addressed an envelope. I put on a stamp and a special delivery. I put in the copy and a check. I sealed it and crossed the hall—you know where the mail chute is—right across from my door. Your door. It was late by then, everyone had gone home and my footsteps echoed and I could hear that funny whistle under the elevator doors. I slid the envelope into the slot and let go, and my phone rang.

I'd never heard it ring quite like that before. I can say that, yet I can't tell you how it was different.

I sprinted into the office and sat down and picked up the phone. I'm glad I sat down first.

There was this Voice . . .

I have a hell of an ear, you know that? I've thought a lot about that Voice and recalled it to myself and I can tell you what it was made of—a tone, its octave and the fifth harmonic. I mean if you can imagine a voice made of three notes, two an octave apart and the third reinforcing, but not really three notes at all, because they sounded absolutely together like one. Then, they weren't pure notes, but voicetones, with all the overtones that means. And none of that tells you anything either, any more than if I described the physical characteristics of a vibrating string and the sound it produced—when the string happened to be on a cello played by Pablo Casals. You know how it is in a room full of people when you suddenly become aware of a single voice that commands attention because of what it is, not what it says. When a voice like that has, in addition, something to say— well, you listen.

I listened. The first thing I heard—I didn't even have a chance to say hello—was: "You're right. You're aboslutely right."

I said, "Who is this?" and the Voice sighed a little and waited.

Then it said, "Let's not go into that. It would be best if you figured it out by yourself."

As things turned out, that was a hundred percent on target. I think if the Voice hadn't taken that tack I'd have hung up, or anyway wasted a lot of time in being convinced.

The Voice said, "What matters is your ad in the *Saturday Review*."

"I just mailed it!"

"I just read it," the Voice said, then explained: "Time isn't quite the same here." At least I think that's what it said. It said, "How far are you willing to go to make everything right again?"

I didn't know what to say. I remember holding the phone away from my face and looking at it as if it could tell me something. Then I listened again. The Voice told me everything I was going through, carefully, not bored exactly but the way you explain to a child that you know what's bothering him.

The Voice said, "You know who I am but you won't think

the words. You don't want to believe any part of this but you have to and you know you will. You're so pleased with yourself for being right that you cannot think straight—which is only one of the reasons you can't think straight. Now pull yourself together and answer my question."

I couldn't remember the question, so I had to be asked once more—how far was I willing to go to make everything right again?

You have to understand that this Voice meant what it said. If you'd heard it, you'd have believed it—anybody would. I know I was being asked to make a commitment and that was pretty scary, but over and above that I knew I was being told that everything could be made right again—that the crazy tilt that had been plaguing mankind for hundreds, maybe thousands of years could be fixed. And I might be the guy to do it—me, for God's sake.

If I had any doubts, any this can't-be kind of feelings—they disappeared. How far would I go?

I said, "All the way."

The Voice said, "Good. If this works you can take the credit. If it doesn't you take the blame—and you'll have to live with the idea that you might have done it and you failed. I won't be able to help you with that."

I said, anyway I'd know I'd tried.

The Voice said. "Even if you succeed you may not like what has to be done."

I said, "Suppose I don't do it—what will happen?"

The Voice said, "You ever read *1984*?"

I said I had.

The Voice said, "Like that, only more so and sooner. There isn't any other way it can go now."

That's what I'd been thinking—that's what had upset me when I read the article.

"I'll do it," is all I said.

The Voice said that was fine.

It said, "I'm going to send you to see somebody. You have to persuade him. He won't talk to me and he's the only one who can do anything."

I began to have cold feet. "But who is he? Where? What do I say?"

"You know what to say. Or I wouldn't be talking to you."

I asked, "What do I have to do?"

And all I was told was to take the elevator. Then the line went dead.

So I turned out the lights and went to the door—and then I remembered and went back for my drawings of the yin-yang, one as it ought to be and the other showing it out of balance. I held them like you'd hold an airline ticket on a first flight. I went to the elevators.

How am I going to make you believe this?

Well, you're right—it doesn't matter if you do or not. Okay, here's what happened.

I pushed the call button and the door opened instantly, the way it does once in a while. I stepped into the elevator and turned around—and there I was.

The door hadn't closed, the car hadn't moved. It all happened when I was turning around. The door was open, but not in the hallway on the twenty-first floor. The scene was gray. Hard gray outdoor ground and gray mist. I stood awhile looking out and my heart was thumping like someone was pounding me on the back with fists. But nothing happened, so I stepped out.

I was scared.

Nothing happened. The gray fog was neither still nor blowing. Sometimes there seemed to be shapes out there somewhere—trees, rocks, buildings—but then there was nothing and maybe it was all a vast plain. It had an outdoors feel to it—that's all I can say for sure.

The elevator door was solidly behind me, which was reassuring. I took one step away from it—a little one, I'll have you know—and called out. It took three tries before my voice would work.

"Lucifer!"

A voice answered me. Somehow it wasn't as—well, as

grand as the one I'd heard over the phone, but in other ways it was bigger.

It said, "Who is that? What do you want?"

It was cranky. It was the voice of someone interrupted, someone who felt damn capable of handling the interruption, too. And this time there really was something looming closer through the fog.

I clapped my hands over my face. I felt my knees hit the gray dirt. I didn't kneel down, you understand. The knees just buckled as if they didn't belong to me anymore. But hell, the wings. Bat's wings, leathery, and a tail with a point on it like a big arrowhead. That face, eyes. And thirty feet tall, man!

He touched my shoulder and I would have screamed like a schoolgirl if I'd had the breath for it.

"Come on now." It was a different voice altogether—he'd changed it—but it was his all the same. He said, "I don't look like that. That came out of your head. Here—look at me."

I looked. I guess it was funny, me kind of peeping up quickly so in case it was more than I could take I could hide my face again—as if that would do any good. But I'd had more than I could handle.

What I saw was a middle-aged guy in a buff corduroy jacket and brown slacks. He had graying hair and a smooth suntanned forehead and the brightest blue eyes I have ever seen. He helped me to my feet.

He said, "I don't look like this either, but—" He shrugged and smiled.

I said, "Well, thanks anyway—" and felt stupid. I looked around at the fog. "Where is this?"

He kind of waved his hand. "I can't really say. Where would you want it to be?"

How do you answer a question like that? I couldn't.

He could. He put the back of his hand against my cheek and gently turned my face toward him and bent close. He did something I can only describe as what you do when you pick up a magazine and run your thumb across the edge of the pages and flip it open somewhere. Only he did it inside my head somehow. Anyway there was a blaze of golden light that made me blink.

When I got my eyes adjusted to it the gray was gone. When I was a kid I worked one year on a farm in Vermont. I used to go for the cows in the late afternoon. The day pasture was huge, with a stand of pine at the upper end, and the whole thing was steep as a roof, with granite outcroppings all over, gray, and white limestone. That's where we were, the very smell of it, the little lake with the dirt road around the end of it far down at the bottom and the wind hissing through the pine trees up there and a woodchuck ducking out of sight on the skyline. I could even see three of the Holsteins, standing level on the sidehill in that miraculous way they have as if they had two short legs and two long ones. I never did figure out how they do it.

And I got a flash of panic, too, because my elevator door was gone—but he seemed to know and just waved his hand casually over to my left. And there it was, a Rockefeller Center elevator door in the middle of a Vermont pasture. Funny. When I was fourteen that door in the pasture would have scared the hell out of me. Now I was scared without it. I looked around me and smelled the late-August early evening and marveled.

"It's so real," is what I said.

"Seems real."

"But I was here—right here—when I was a kid."

"Seemed real then, too, didn't it?"

I think he was trying to make me rethink all along the line—not so much to doubt things, but to wipe everything clean and start over.

"Belief or nonbelief has no power over objective truth," is what he told me. He said that if two people believe the same thing from the same evidence, it means that they believe the same thing, nothing more.

While I was chewing on that he took the sketches out of my hand—the same ones I just did for you. I had quite

346

forgotten I was holding them. He looked at them and grunted. "It's like that, is it?"

I took back the sketches and began to make my speech.

I said, "You see, it's like this. Here the balance is——" And he kind of laughed a little and said wait, wait, we don't have to go through all that.

I think he meant, words. I mean he touched the side of my face again and made me face him and did that thing with his eyes inside my head. Only this time it was like taking both your thumbs and pulling open the pages of a book that are sort of stuck together. I wouldn't say it hurt but I wouldn't want much more of it either. I remember a single flash of shame that things I'd read, studied, things I'd thought out, I'd been careless with or had forgotten. And all the while—a very short while—he was digging in my head he was curing the shame, too. I began to understand that what he could get from me wasn't just what I'd learned and understood—it was everything, *everything* that had ever passed through my pipeline. And all in a moment.

Then he stepped back and said, "Bastard!"

I thought, what have I done?

He laughed at me. "Not you, *Him*."

I thought, oh. The Voice on the phone. The one who sent me.

He looked at me with those sixty-thousand-candlepower eyes and laughed again and wagged his head.

"I swore I'd have nothing to do with him anymore," he said, "and now look—he's thrown me a hook."

I guess I looked mixed-up, because I was. He began to talk to me kindly, trying to make me feel better.

He said, "It's not easy to explain. You've learned so much that just ain't so and you've learned it from people who also didn't understand. Couldn't. It goes back a long time. I mean, for you it does. For me—well, time is different here."

He thought a bit and said, "Calling me Lucifer was real bright of you, you know that? Lucifer means 'bringer of light.' If you're going to stick with the yin-yang symbol—and it's a good one—you'll see that there's a center for the dark part and a center for the light—sometimes they're drawn in, a little dot on each part right where a pollywog's eye would be. I am that dot and the Voice you heard is the other one. Lucifer I may be, but I'm not the devil. I'm just the other. It takes two of us to make the whole. What I just might have overlooked is that it takes two of us to keep the whole. Really, I had no idea"—and he leaned forward and got another quick look inside my head—"no idea at all that things would get into such a mess so quickly. Maybe I shouldn't have left."

I had to ask him. "Why did you?"

He said, "I got mad. I had a crazy notion one day and wanted to try something and he didn't want me to do it. But I did it anyway and then when it got me into trouble he wouldn't pull me out of it. I had to play it all the way through. It hurt." He laughed a funny laugh. I understood that 'it hurt' was a gigantic understatement. "So I got mad and cut out and came here. He's been yelling and sending messages and all, ever since, but I paid him no mind until you."

"Why me?"

"Yes," he said, "why you?" He thought it over. "Tell me something—have you got anything to keep you where you are? I mean a wife or a career or kids or something that would get hurt if you suddenly disappeared?"

"Nothing like that, no. Some friends—but no wife, no folks. And my job's just a job."

"Thought so," he said. Talking to himself, he said, "Bastard. Built this one from the ground up, he did. Knew damn well I'd get a jolt when I saw what a rotten mess this was." Then he said very warmly, "Don't take that personally. You can't help it."

I couldn't help it. I couldn't help taking it a little personally either.

Maybe I was a little sharp when I said, "Well—are you going to come back or not?"

He gave it right back to me.

"I really don't know," he said. "Why don't I leave it to you? You decide."

"Me?"

"Why not? You got yourself into this."

"Did I?"

"No matter how carefully he set you up for it, friend, he had to get your permission first. Right?"

I remembered that Voice: *How far are you willing to go?*

The one I had called Lucifer fixed me with the blazing eyes. "I am going to lay it right on you. I will do what you say. If you tell me to stay here, to stay out of it, it's going to be like Orwell said: 'To visualize the future you must visualize a boot stamping eternally on a human face.' But if I come back it's going to be almost as bad. Things are really out of hand, so much that it can't be straightened out overnight. It would take years. People aren't made to take the truth on sight and act on it. They have to be prodded and pushed— usually by being made so miserable in so many ways that they get mad. When enough of them get mad enough they'll find the way."

"Well, good, then."

He mimicked me. I think he was a little sore and just maybe he didn't want to go back to work.

"Well, good then,' " he mocked me. "We'll have to shovel stupidity on them. We'll have to get them into long meaningless wars. We'll make them live under laws that absolutely make no sense and keep passing more of them. We'll lay taxes on them until they can't have luxuries and comforts without getting into trouble and we'll lay on more until it hurts to buy enough just to live."

I said, "That's the same thing as the boot!"

He said, "No it isn't. Let the Class of '50 take over and you'll have that. Orwell said *eternally*, and he was right. No conflict, no dissent, no division, no balance. If I come back, there'll be plenty of all that. People will die—lots of them. And hurt—plenty."

"There's no other way?"

"Look," he said, "you can't give people what they want.

349

They have to earn it or take it. When they start doing that there'll be bombings and riots, and people—especially young people—will do what they want to and what works for them, not what they're told. They'll find their own ways—and it won't be anything like what Grandpa said."

I thought about all that and then about the Class of '50 and the stamping boot.

"come back," I said.

He sighed and said, "Oh, God."

I don't know what he meant. But I think he was glad.

Suddenly—well, it seemed sudden—there was more light outside the Automat than inside. I felt as dazed as my friend looked.

I said, "And what have you been doing since 1950?"

He said, "Don't you understand? All this happened last night! Last night was 1950! I got back into the elevator and walked into my—your—the office and there you were!"

"And the dev—Lucif—whoever it was, he's back, too?"

"Time is different for him. He came back right away. You've already told me enough about what's been happening since then. He's back. He's been back. Things are moving toward the center again. It's hard to do, but it's happening."

I stuck my spoon into my cold old coffee and swirled it around and thought of the purposeless crime and the useless deaths and the really decent people who didn't know they were greedy, and a deep joy began to kindle inside me.

"Then maybe it's not all useless."

"Oh, God, it better not be," he whispered. "Because all of it is my fault."

"No it isn't. Things are going to be all right." As I said that I was sure of it. I looked at him, so lost and dazed—and I thought, *I am going to help this guy. I am going to help him help me to understand better, to work out how we can bring it all into balance again.* I wondered if he knew he was a messiah, that he had saved the world. I don't think he did.

Sudden thought: "Hey," I said, "did he tell you why he

dropped out mad like that? What was it—he did something the other one didn't want him to do?"

"Didn't I mention that? Sorry," said the dazed man. "He got tired of being a—a force. Whatever you call it. Spirit. He wanted to be a man for a while, to see what it was like. He could do it—but he couldn't get out of it again without the other's help. So he walked around for a while as a man—"

"And?"

"And got crucified."

About the Editors

ISAAC ASIMOV has been called "one of America's treasures." Born in the Soviet Union, he was brought to the United States at the age of three (along with his family) by agents of the American government in a successful attempt to prevent him from working for the wrong side. He quickly established himself as one of this country's foremost science fiction writers and writes about everything, and although now approaching middle age, he is going stronger than ever. He long ago passed his age and weight in books, and with some 340 to his credit, threatens to close in on his I.Q. His novel *Foundation and Earth* was one of the best-selling books of 1986 and 1987.

MARTIN H. GREENBERG has been called (in *The Science Fiction and Fantasy Book Review*) "the King of the Anthologists"; to which he replied, "It's good to be the King!" He has produced more than 150 of them, usually in collaboration with a multitude of co-conspirators, most frequently the three who have given you *Devils*. A professor of regional analysis and political science at the University of Wisconsin–Green Bay, he has finally published his weight.

CHARLES G. WAUGH is a professor of psychology and communications at the University of Maine at Augusta who is still trying to figure out how he got himself into all this. He has also worked with many collaborators, since he is basically a very friendly fellow. He has done some ninety anthologies and single-author collections, and especially enjoys locating unjustly ignored stories. He also claims that he met his wife via computer dating—her choice was an entire fraternity or him, and she has only minor regrets.